I0661478

Warning Miracle

By John Klee

Published in the United States of America
John Klee Publishing
c/o 1601 W 5th Ave #291
Columbus, Ohio 43212

Cover Designer: William Deeter
www.williamdeeter.com

ISBN: 978-0-615-25489-0

First Printing March 2009
978-0-615-25489-0

Manufactured in the United States of America

This novel is dedicated to all my English
teachers, from grade school to college…
thanks for the timeless wisdom
you imparted.

Much thanks to Jim Flynn and David Szarko for editing and
proofreading this book.

Chapter 1

"Roger that, Cessna Five-oh-one-niner-foxtrot-whiskey…you are number two to land behind the Falcon now turning base."

Dexter had been rummaging through his flight bag, oblivious for the moment to the controller's instructions.

"Cessna five-oh-one-niner-foxtrot-whiskey: do you copy?" said the controller again, a little louder this time.

"Huh? Oh." Dexter keyed the mike and sat upright. "Roger that, OSU Tower. Landing on Runway Niner."

"Do you see traffic?" asked the controller.

Dexter glanced out the right side of his Cessna and saw a Beech King Air turning off the runway.

"Roger, traffic in sight." Dexter flipped the visor down, but was still having trouble seeing the runway because of the sun in his eyes. "That sun is a pain in the butt!" he muttered under his breath. "I might have to land on five."

He was just about to call the tower when out of the corner of his eye he saw a white shape rapidly approaching from the left.

"Cessna on final!" the radio blared. "Immediate right turn--NOW!"

Dexter rammed the control yoke to the right and instinctively pushed in the throttle, his stomach feeling like he had been kicked by a hippopotamus.

The Falcon business jet broke to the left, its left wing pointing at the ground, as its engines also spooled up to maximum power.

"How the heck did *that* happen?!" shouted Dexter to the empty cockpit. "Holy heck, that was close!" He leveled off at a thousand feet and flew due south, awaiting instructions from the tower. His heart felt like the repeated recoil of a shotgun blast in his chest.

"Cessna five-oh-one-niner-foxtrot-whiskey, report to the tower after landing. You have some serious explaining to do. You are cleared for landing runway niner. There is no other traffic in the pattern. The Falcon will land after you."

"GOT THAT RIGHT!" said the captain of the Falcon, breaking into the radio transmission.

"Roger that," said Dexter meekly. "Cleared for landing runway niner." He let out a long sigh, still holding down the mike button. "Sorry," he said.

Ten minutes later, Dexter was sitting in the base of the control tower at the Ohio State University airport. A door marked "Stairs to Tower" opened and a portly middle-aged man entered the lobby. He said nothing as he pulled up a chair in front of Dexter, sat down, and handed him a copy of the FAR/AIM Handbook.

"Why don't you read Section 91.13?" he said tersely to Dexter.

"Out loud?"

"Right."

Dexter fumbled through the pages, then put his finger on the appropriate paragraph. "Okay...uhh...all right, well, it says: *Careless or reckless operation. (a) Aircraft operations for the purpose of air navigation. No person may operate an aircraft in a careless or reckless manner so as to endanger the life or property of another.*"

"Stop right there, Dexter. Did I or did I not--"

"How do you know my name?" asked Dexter.

"I know a heck of a lot more about you than you would care to imagine!" said the controller, his voice rising. "Now, tell me, did I give you permission to--"

The door to the airplane ramp swung open and the Falcon captain rushed in. "Which one of you is the IDIOT?!" he said loudly.

Neither Dexter nor the controller said anything.

"Oh, right!" shouted the pilot. "It's obviously YOU!" he said, pointing at Dexter.

Dexter averted his eyes and shifted in his seat.

"How long you been flyin', boy?"

"Just about four years." Dexter swallowed and cleared his throat. "I've got two hundred hours."

"Two hundred hours!" said the Falcon captain derisively. "You shouldn't be riding a *bicycle*, much less flying an *airplane*!"

The door opened behind the captain and his first officer walked in. The captain turned around to face his crewmate and pointed at Dexter. "Can you believe it, Larry? This kid's got *two hundred hours*! Isn't it amazing?"

"He definitely needs some help, that's for sure," said Larry. "Anyway, we have to move the Falcon, we're blocking the taxiway."

"I'll be out in a minute," said the captain. He turned to face Dexter again. "You just listen and listen *good*, bud. You almost killed us both up there today, and I've got a wife and kids to think about." He shook his index finger. "You never--*never*--come that close to another plane in the pattern again...*got it*? I don't know what distracted you in the cockpit, but you darn well better never let it happen again. You want to kill *yourself*, that's your problem, but you aren't going to take anyone else down with you." The captain glared at Dexter for a few seconds, then swiveled around and walked out the door.

Dexter met the gaze of the controller briefly, then cast his eyes at the floor.

"I don't know if I need to say anything else...that pilot summed it up pretty well," said the controller, standing up and moving his chair back to its original position. He turned to face Dexter, opened his mouth, then stopped, pursing his lips.

Dexter glanced up, but said nothing.

"I think I'm going to have to--" the controller brought his hand up to his chin and thought for a half minute. "All right, Dexter. I'll tell you what I'm going to do. By all rights I should ground you for a few months, but I looked at your record before I came down and it's clean. So, you're going to get off with a warning this time, but--"

"Sweet!" said Dexter, a wide grin spreading across his face.

"Not so fast, my friend. One more violation like this and I'll turn you over to my boss--and he won't be so kind."

"Yes, I understand," said Dexter respectfully. "It was entirely my fault. I should have requested another runway. The sun was in my eyes."

"Consider yourself lucky, Dexter. That'll be all." The controller took the FAR/AIM manual back from Dexter and disappeared through the door to the stairwell.

As soon as he was outside, Dexter pumped his fist in the air.

"Yes!" he said in a loud whisper. "Heck, yes, I'm lucky! Chalk one up for the Dex!" He walked over to the plane, tied it down and sauntered to his car. A note on the dashboard reminded him that he needed to pick up his dry cleaning in Dublin, an up and coming suburb to the northwest of Columbus. Twenty minutes later, the shirts were in the trunk and he was motoring down Riverside Drive. Dexter had a penchant for the scenic route when driving around Central Ohio, and with the trees in their peak fall colors, the road along the Scioto River was worth the extra time it would take. The Maple trees glowed in their reddish hues and the Birch trees added to the festivities with their golden yellow leaves which sometimes happened to outdo themselves and shine forth in a glorious burst of orange. As he passed under Route 161 he was greeted by a phalanx of purplish-red dogwoods that seemed to salute as he drove by in his royal carriage. Dexter opened up the sunroof and looked up at the mix of golden sunlight, blue sky and scarlet leaves that filled the opening in the car's roof. This *is why I don't live in California*, he thought. Who could pass up such natural beauty that presented itself once a year, free of charge? Sure, it could get cold in the Midwest, and hot too, but, as he liked to tell his friends from college it really was bad for only six weeks in the winter and six weeks in the summer. Other than that, Columbus was idyllic when you thought about it. *Heck*, he smiled to himself, *"C-town" had just been rated the number six best place to live in the country. Yeah, I should thank my ancestors for settling here. There were worse places in which to find oneself.* Dexter turned on a CD of Vivaldi, the Four Seasons, and followed the road as it turned with the curves of the river.

Before he changed lanes, Dexter glanced in the rearview mirror to check the blind spot. He caught himself admiring his brownish-blond hair and "California-handsome face" as one girl at Stanford had dubbed it. *I have to admit she had a point there*, Dexter thought to himself. Standing six-foot, two and weighing in at two-hundred pounds, Dexter looked all the world like the typical "All-American Boy." Even in image-conscious California, where he had attended college, Dexter stood out as particularly attractive to the opposing gender. His blue eyes had the intensity of an October sky and his high brow gave him the look of the landed gentry.

He turned off at Fifth Avenue and started thinking about work--if it could truly be called work. The fact was Dexter enjoyed his work so much that he considered it more a hobby than anything coming close to work. His grandfather had left Dexter and his sister a trust fund amounting to about forty million dollars each. The only stipulation Grandfather Helms had written in his will was that the money be used for only two things: education and entrepreneurship. That had suited Dexter perfectly. He had wanted to start his own company since fifth-grade, when he had sold a few small home-made parachutes to his classmates for a quarter apiece. His four years of studying electrical engineering at Stanford University had used up only a tiny fraction of the money, tapping into the interest without even touching the principal. Upon graduation, Dexter had considered going to work for a robotics company, but eventually decided against it. He knew of the whole problem of intellectual property rights, the tangled mess of trying to invent something on your own when in fact it could legally belong to the company for which you were employed when you first had the idea. So, in the end, Dexter finished up his Bachelor's degree and headed back to Ohio to set up shop. He bought a few books on building personal robots and went to work, consulting professors at Ohio State when he had any truly vexing problem. After five years of work, he and his team of engineers were nearing the point of having a saleable product. Originally, he had planned to approach the field incrementally, starting out with simple, single-purpose robots and slowly building more and more complicated models. The result after two years was a painting robot, used for painting the interior walls of office buildings. With a little more effort and investment Dexter could have turned it into a modest profit, but it was something he had read about Bill Lear, of Learjet fame, that caused him to change the direction of his company three years earlier. It seems that Mr. Lear was not without his share of detractors when it came to his vision of building the world's first business jet. Most "experts" in the late 50s and early 60s were of the opinion that it would take ten years and one hundred million dollars to develop such an aircraft as Bill Lear had in mind. Lear did it in three years for a fraction of that cost. That was what Dexter planned to do in the field of robotics. The majority of researchers concentrated on one or two aspects of a robot, such as speech, vision, mobility, dexterity, or decision-making. Dexter simply wanted the complete package. He knew it was a risk, but the reward for making it to market first with a truly human-like robot would be great.

As he pulled into the parking lot of his small office/factory he noticed a brand new car in one of the parking slots. *Must be Jerry's new ride*, mused Dexter. Jerry was the chief engineer of Grobotics. Dexter had been lucky enough to meet Jerry while visiting the office of one of the professors at The Ohio State University. Dexter chuckled to himself as he remembered how Jerry had rushed into Professor Singh's office and promptly knocked over one of the professor's stacks of books on his desk. "Professor," he had said, panting heavily, "here's my final exam! The TA left the room before I could catch him and now I can't find him!" Dexter had been paradoxically impressed by an undergraduate's moxie to test the patience of the TA and then the tolerance of a full professor. After a few more chance meetings, Jerry had begun to work part-time at Dexter's company. He hired on full-time after he graduated with his Master's degree. *My company*, thought Dexter. *Ha!* Presently, it consisted of Dexter, Jerry, five other research engineers and a part-time secretary, Mrs. Downing, the official "mother" of Grobotics. *What a large company.* He often consoled himself with the probability that it would be much bigger if--when--they went into production of their robot.

"Bon Matin!" said Mrs. Downing as Dexter walked past her desk.   It was always a different language everyday--sometimes annoying, but Dexter usually got a kick out of it.

"Good Morning, Marie Antoinette."

"The guy from Woodward just called. He said he can fit you in Friday. I left his name and number on your desk."

"Thanks, Mrs. Downing." Mrs. Downing insisted on a formal title at work. She said it was better protocol. She was also against "dressing down" on Fridays. Dexter usually went along with her ideas since they did seem to make sense when he took the time to think about them.

He was about to call the Woodward company but put the receiver down when he remembered that he had better clear it with Jerry first. It wouldn't be the first time that he had botched a demo. In the first year of Grobotics he had ruined the carpet of one of his customers when his experimental painting robot had decided to disconnect itself from its vision system and begin "painting" the expensive Oriental rug of what Dexter thought was going to be his first paying customer. That had been the time when Jerry had not yet come aboard. The workload was a little lighter now, but Dexter still wanted to be sure everything was ready before calling his next potential customer.

"Nice wheels, Jerry! I assume that is your new car out in the lot?" asked Dexter as he walked into the back of the building.

"You called it, bro," said Jerry with a goofy grin on his face. "I couldn't resist the call of the new car smell."

"What about the call of the high monthly payment?"

"I didn't come out so bad, especially with the good deal I got on my trade-in."

"Glad to hear it. So, look, Jerry, are we good to go with the demo for Woodward on Friday? I have to take a quick trip to California tomorrow, but I'll be back by the end of the week. I was going to setup the appointment now."

"Depends on whether you want me to use the Intel™ or AMD™ chip. It'll work with the AMD™ chip, but it has trouble with the Intel™. Intel™ is a great chip, don't get me wrong, but for this application, I think we should use the AMD™."

"Can we get enough memory with the AMD™? I know the Intel™ was better in that area."

"As long as we don't have to take on the whole Iraqi military. The AMD™ will give us about five live targets."

"That's fine," said Dexter. "Go with the AMD™. I'll set it up for Friday at two. That fine with you?"

"Copasetic, chief."

Dexter returned to his office and punched in the number for Paul Gardos at the Woodward Company. The Woodward Company was a moderate sized firm that served the security industry, most notably the police departments of a dozen or so cities in the Midwest. Dexter had approached them three years ago with a proposal for Rambo, a fully autonomous "urban security asset," as the lingo in the trade papers went. Rambo had started out as basically a handgun on wheels, designed to be used as an aide for a police officer in hunting down a suspect on city streets. Subsequent iterations of the design had led up to its current configuration: a strikingly human-looking biped about five feet tall. If it looked similar to the Honda Asimo robot, seen from time to time on commercials for Honda cars, there was a reason: Dexter had hired two of the Japanese engineers away from the Asimo project and convinced them they could use their talents better on the Rambo project. The name had since changed from

Rambo to Bobby and the gun had been replaced with a pepper spray mechanism.

Dexter settled into his chair and switched the phone to his right hand. "Paul, it's Dexter from Grobotics," he said, leaning back and crossing his legs.

"Dexter, good to hear from you! How's everything?"

"I can't complain, yourself?"

"Still a million dollars short of being a millionaire."

"I think I have just the solution to that problem."

"A heavy briefcase full of unmarked bills?"

"A little man by the name of Bobby the Fifth."

"Oh, so that's what you're naming him now, eh?"

"Well, it's either that or Johnny Five, but I think that was used in a movie once."

"So is Mr. Bobby feeling better?" asked Paul. Dexter's previous demonstration of Bobby to the Woodward Company had been less than perfect. No carpets were sprayed, but neither was anything else.

"Paul," said Dexter, "this time I promise you that Bobby will be on his best behavior. Matter of fact, I'll put a dinner at the Florentine on the line."

"Oh, now you're serious! Far be it from you to joke about the Florentine." The Florentine was, according to Dexter, the best Italian restaurant in Columbus. Rarely a week passed without Dexter patronizing the establishment.

"A deal's a deal! How about I bring Bobby to you Friday around two?"

"Sounds good. Okay if I supply the pepper spray this time?"

"Fine with me; Bobby is a machine of many talents."

"Ciao, Dexter."

"Bye."

****

The next day Dexter was up early to catch a commercial flight to the West Coast where he had a meeting with an aluminum supplier. A five thousand mile round trip was a little too far for his own private plane to make in the short time he had available. After a quick breakfast of cereal and yogurt, he picked up the phone to call a taxi.

"Hello, may I have the address of the location at which you'd like to be picked up?" asked the Orange Cab dispatcher.

"Eleven thirteen Urlin Avenue," said Dexter.

"And your destination?"

"The airport."

"All right, thank you for calling Orange Cab. Bye."

"Bye."

Dexter put the phone back in its cradle and double-checked his baggage. He never knew whether the taxi would take five minutes or twenty-five minutes to arrive, although he suspected an airport trip from Grandview, costing about twenty-five dollars, would bring an eager cabbie to his door rather quickly. He wasn't to be disappointed, as he heard the taxi's horn no more than ten minutes later. After ensuring the burners were off on his stove, he went out the front door and locked it behind him.

"Greetings, sir," said the taxi driver as he opened the trunk.

"How ya doin?" asked Dexter.

"Just fine, yourself?"

"Can't complain."

"We're headed to the airport, right?"

"That's correct--is traffic bad?"

"No more than usual; we shouldn't run into much on our way there."

Dexter settled in for the ride, surprised to see how clean the cab was, both inside and out.

"You keep your cab in good condition, if I may say so."

"I own it, so I've been able to keep it up. Most drivers drive shift cabs, and they rarely put much effort into the appearance of the cab they happen to be driving on any given day."

"I see." Dexter picked up the copy of *The Columbus Dispatch* that was lying on the seat. He was about to leaf through the Sports section to catch up on his beloved Buckeye football team when he noticed a brochure that had been lying under the newspaper. *An Explanation of the Warning* was printed in bold letters across the front of the brochure. *Huh?* He thought. *Is this about pro football? The two minute warning?* He opened the tri-folded page and glanced at the opening paragraph: *What will soon happen to all of us has been predicted for years. Wait a minute,* Dexter thought, *are they talking*

*about some psychological awakening or something? The "Warning."
Mmmph. "Predicted for years?" Huuuhhh?*

    "Excuse me, could I take this with me?" Dexter asked the driver.

    "What's that? Oh--the brochure? Sure! I've been handing them out to people for the past couple of weeks. Be my guest."

    "Thanks. What is this about being predicted for years?"

    "Oh, you see it all started with some visionary mystics back in the 60s."

    "Who exactly?" asked Dexter,

    "Some people who lived in Spain," said the driver.
"Oh."

    "They said there would be a worldwide awakening of consciences in which everyone would see their souls as God sees them."

    "I saw something about that on TV a couple of weeks ago. This psychologist said something like that happened in the 18th Century with the 'Great Awakening.' Back then a lot of people in North America went through a religious revival."

    "But this will be world wide," pointed out the driver. "And it will be all at once."

    "You really believe this stuff?" asked Dexter, peering more intently at the brochure. "This thing--it says 'apparition'-- happened in Spain, I guess? How do you say this name?"

    "It's Garabandal. 'Gair-a-ban-DULL' is the correct pronunciation."

    Dexter spent the next few minutes reading the brochure. He put it in his shirt pocket and resumed reading the sports section. He made a mental note to look up that place in Spain on the internet. The traffic was unusually light and they made it to the airport a short while later. Dexter thanked the driver and rolled his bags to the skycap.

Chapter 2

A couple of days later, after he had returned from his trip to California, Dexter was driving home from picking up an ink cartridge at an office supply store. He had just gotten on Route 315, heading south toward Grandview. Of all the freeways in Columbus, 315 was Dexter's favorite. He had unofficially dubbed it "The Woody," in honor of Woody Hayes, the legendary Ohio State football coach. Dexter thought it only reasonable to give the freeway that name, since it ran through the Ohio State University campus, passing no more than a quarter-mile from Ohio Stadium itself. Dexter's mind began to wander as he began to weigh Ohio State's chances at another national championship this year. *If only that quarterback can learn to scramble outside the pocket a little better and if only---wait a second*, thought Dexter. *What's that smell? I know I've smelled that before. Is that smoke coming from under the hood?*

"Awww, nooo!" said Dexter aloud. "Not now! C'mon!" He slowed the car and pulled to the side of the highway, just as the dashboard warning lights began to come on. He wasted no time in shutting off the engine and raising the hood.

"Dog-gone-it! I hope it's not the radiator! Man, I just had the hoses replaced on this!"

He was shuffling around the front of the car, trying to look at the engine through the smoke when he realized he ought to call a tow truck on his cell phone. He reached into his pocket, only to remember he had left it at home to recharge.

"What else can go wrong?" he rhetorically asked the car. He looked past the car and saw a taxi coming down the freeway. Without a moment's hesitation, he stepped to the edge of the road and frantically waved his arms.

"Yo! Taxi! Hey!"

......

Thad Rankin slowed as he saw the man gesturing to him by the side of the road. *Must be late for an appointment,* he thought. He stopped his taxi on the side of the freeway and carefully began to back up. At five-foot ten and one-hundred eighty pounds, Thad was beginning to look like the typical taxi-driver. Over the past year he had added a small potbelly to his profile, which he disdainfully referred to as "the Stum." Blessed with thick black hair and JFK looks, he was often questioned by his passengers as to his "other job." Somehow Thad didn't seem to fit the image most riders expected of a cabbie. The fact was that, although Thad thoroughly enjoyed the cabbie life, he didn't plan on making it a career. He had developed an acute case of insomnia a few years ago and was forced to put his real career on hold. His doctors had told him that he should avoid the high-pressure engineering jobs he had held and pursue something a little more "bucolic," to use their expression. Consequently Thad had drifted from job to job until he "discovered" the job of taxi driver. He immediately liked the work and had been doing it for over a year now. He knew someday he would return to aerospace engineering, his "first love," but until then, he was quite satisfied to live the cabbie lifestyle.

Thad stopped the cab and climbed out.

"Man, am I glad to see you!" Dexter said as Thad walked toward his car.

"No problem," said Thad. "I'm not on a call right now, so I'm available. What seems to be the problem? Radiator burst?"

"I'm not really sure...I just had the hoses replaced a couple months ago..." Dexter stopped and tilted his head back slightly. "Hey, you're that guy that gave me a ride to the airport a few days ago."

Thad looked puzzled for a moment and pressed his lips together. "Uhh, let's see...you were in Arlington, was it?"

"Grandview."

"Oh, yeah, Grandview! Now I remember--hey, did you read that pamphlet I gave you--the one about Garabandal?"

A sheepish look crossed Dexter's face. "Not really, I've been sort of busy lately."

"My name's Thad Rankin, by the way," said Thad, holding out his hand.

"Nice to meet you...I'm Dexter Griffith." They shook hands.

"About that brochure--you seemed so interested in it then," said Thad.

"Yeah, maybe I was...uhh, look, I really need to get going." He turned toward his car and abruptly stopped. "What am I thinking?" he said. He walked over to Thad. "Why don't I just use your cell phone? I can call a tow-truck and ride with him. My mechanic's place is a few blocks from my house."

"Oh," said Thad, showing a hint of disappointment. "I suppose you're right. Here you are." He handed his phone to Dexter.

Dexter arranged for a wrecker to come, handed the phone back to Thad and thanked him for his time. "Here," he said, reaching for his wallet, "let me give you something for your trouble."

"N-n-n-no," replied Thad, brightening somewhat as a mischievous grin spread across his face. "I know just how you can repay me." He reached back for his wallet and pulled out a business card. "Here. Take this." He placed the card in Dexter's hand. "Talk to this man--call him up. He's my brother."

"Huuhhh?" asked Dexter, reading the card. "'Father Matt Rankin.'" Why would I want to talk to him? Is he a preacher or something?"

"He can explain that brochure I gave you, all that stuff that happened in Spain."

"Hey, I appreciate it, but you've got the wrong guy." Dexter held out the card for Thad to take. "I'm really not interested, but I appreciate your help."

"A deal's a deal," said Thad, backing away from Dexter's outstretched hand. "At least think about it. Keep the card for now. And, while I'm at it..." He pulled a different card out of his pocket and also put it in Dexter's hand. "Take my card as well. If you ever need a taxi you can call my cell phone."

"Whatever." Dexter shoved the cards into his pocket and waved goodbye to Thad. "See ya!"

"Okay! Hope your car is okay."

Thad drove away and Dexter only had to wait another ten minutes before the tow-truck arrived.

****

"Parakeet twenty-eight, hike, HIKE!" Kevin Conaway took the snap from under center and ran left. The Ohio State football team had been practicing the option since the beginning of fall camp, but they weren't quite adept at it yet. Kevin looked for Jason Manera and--*where the heck was Jason*!?

The coach's whistle blew and Kevin threw the football into the ground. "Son of a bitch, Jason!" he yelled. "This is the *option*, for Pete's sake! Where *were* you?"

"Sorry, man," said Jason, running up to his quarterback. "I got a little confused."

"That'll be all," said Dan Panaski, OSU's head coach. "Let's try it again...mistakes will be made. Jason, you with the program now?"

"I'm all over it, coach! Sorry about that; I just got distracted."

They ran the play again and this time it went picture perfect. Jason managed to gain fifteen yards, even though he was up against Ohio State's legendary first-team defense, and even though the defense knew what to expect.

"Good deal! Good deal!" said Panaski, clapping his hands along with the rest of the OSU coaching staff. "Take five, guys! Conaway, I want to talk to you for a minute."

Kevin jogged over to get a few pointers from the head coach. He was all of six-foot, four and two hundred and twenty-seven pounds, and he looked exactly like what a college quarterback was supposed to look like. Kevin's close shaven red hair, intelligent-looking green eyes, and chiseled face spoke of a youthful vigor tempered by a mature wisdom which helped him be the leader he was on the field. Affectionately known as the "Red Baron"--for his aerial prowess with the football--Kevin mixed well with his troops and was surprisingly competent in his schoolwork, much to the relief of the coaches.

Head coach Dan Panaski gave Kevin a few pointers on the intricacies of running the option. It had been a first for OSU when Panaski introduced the option at the beginning of this season since Ohio State had long been known for its formidable running game. Granted the quarterback didn't *have* to choose the passing option, but there were signs so far this season that OSU might actually start putting the ball in the air more often. And so far this season things were looking very much *up* in the one statistic that mattered: the win-loss record. The fact was that the Buckeyes were still undefeated and it was the second week in October. Their record of six and oh put them at the number three spot in the national rankings and Columbus was astir with memories of the fabled 2002 National Championship team which went fourteen and oh and set a benchmark for Buckeyes around the country and especially in good ol' "C-town." Not a week went by this fall without some zealous sportswriter proclaiming in *The Columbus Dispatch* that the ghosts of championships past were in town again and ready to visit the dear old village on the banks of the Olentangy and Scioto Rivers with yet another national title. And squarely at the center of the gathering maelstrom was none other than Kevin Conaway, the standout Buckeye quarterback who had come to the spotlight a year earlier when he stepped in for an injured teammate during the Michigan game and engineered a come-from-behind victory over "the people from that state that begins with the letter after 'L'" as his dad was wont to say. Yes, Kevin Conaway seemed destined for this season since his youth. He had been a star player at Lakewood Saint Ed's High School in Cleveland Ohio and had chosen to attend Ohio State over such other high profile places as Miami, Tennessee, and USC. Now in his senior year, he had been backup quarterback for the last three seasons, and was putting all his doubters to shame. It had always been the same story each of the previous seasons: some upperclassman was just a smidgen better. Not enormously better, but just enough to convince the coaches that it wasn't quite Kevin's year yet. But this season, all the keys were tuned in Kevin's piano and he was giving Buckeye Nation the best recital they'd heard in a while.

"So wait for the running back to get outside the pocket before *you* leave the pocket, got it?" Coach Panaski was saying.

"Right," said Kevin. "But what if there's a blitz? I can't just sit there and wait, right?"

"If there's a blitz, roll out of the pocket and look for open receivers. Remember, it's called 'blitz' for a reason. You should always have a way out if everyone else is doing their job the way they're supposed to."

"Got it."

"Another thing," said Ed Rebaugh, the quarterbacks coach,

gesturing to Kevin. "Don't be afraid to run the ball *yourself* on the option. That's the beauty of this play! There are really about three or four options you can choose from, when it comes down to it."

"But, Coach Rebaugh," said Tom Romasco, one of the reserve quarterbacks, "I would think the running back has the best chance at any positive yardage, since the defense is going to know just about immediately what's up."

"That's true," said Coach Rebaugh, "but don't give the defense *too* much credit yet. I'll have to show you some game tape from one of Penn State's games earlier this year. Purdue ran the option against them *four* times, and Penn State only picked up on it *once*." OSU was playing Penn State on Saturday and the Buckeyes weren't really sure what to expect, since the Nittany Lions had a new coach this year. Joe Paterno had retired at the end of the previous season, having set a win record that probably wouldn't be surpassed anytime soon.

"Yeah, I would like to see that sometime," said Tom. "Maybe tomorrow; I've got a midterm to study for tonight."

"Sounds good," said Coach Rebaugh. "You should look at it, too," he said to Kevin.

"Will do, Coach."

The team ran a few more plays before calling it a day. Kevin caught a ride back to his apartment with Chad Walling, one of the tight ends, an old friend from his high school days.

"Did you see that thing in the paper about the prisoner asking the judge to let him stay in the county jail?" Chad asked Kevin as they climbed into Chad's Ford.

"No, I didn't."

"This guy who was convicted of some robbery or something doesn't want to miss our game this Saturday, so he asked the judge who sentenced him to let him stay in the county jail over the weekend because he'll be able to see the game there on TV. I guess if they transfer him Friday to some holding tank, he'd miss the game because the holding tank doesn't have any TVs."

"And...?" asked Kevin as he buckled his seat belt.

"The judge said 'okay'! Wild, huh?"

"If you think that's crazy, did I ever tell you the story, or maybe 'legend,' might be the better word, that my uncle told me?"

"I don't think so."

"Similar situation, but this was about the OSU-Michigan

game...happened in the 60s. That game saved some guy's *life!*"

"Huh?"

"No kidding! My uncle told me this when I was in grade school. There was this convict who was scheduled to be executed on the Friday before the Michigan game. He had protested his innocence all along, but to no avail. He petitions the judge to move the execution to the Monday after the Michigan game. The judge agrees and the execution is rescheduled--I guess it was right down here, near downtown. There used to be a penitentiary there, I think. So the guy gets to see the game on TV, which was rare in those days. He watches the game on TV on Saturday, then, on Sunday, the day after the game, some scuba divers find a car in the Scioto River, a car which turned out to be the supposed murder weapon used by the guy on death row. As the story goes, this guy killed his girlfriend's other boyfriend by running his car into him on a bridge over the Scioto River. The accused man said he slid on some ice and his brakes failed, but witnesses said it looked very much like the guy meant to kill the victim. Anyway, the death row guy's car, after hitting the victim, went off the bridge and into the river. The accused was able to jump clear and landed on the ice on the river. The car, meanwhile, crashed through the ice and disappeared. Police couldn't search for the car because of the ice which completely covered the river. The death row man told the court that his brakes had failed and he accidentally hit the pedestrian. The plaintiff's lawyer, however, had made the point that this guy's brakes had just *happened* to fail just when his 'nemesis' had just *happened* to be walking across the bridge. It was also pointed out in the trial that the accused had a history of arrests for fighting, so in the end the jury convicted him of vehicular homicide. In the following spring, when the ice had melted the police had searched for the car in the river, but to no avail. But then on the Sunday after the Michigan game, police divers were searching the river for the body of a missing girl and they happened upon the death row guy's car. After it was pulled from the river, the authorities examined the brakes and, lo and behold, they found that the brake lines were indeed ruptured and the accused was telling the truth. So, the OSU-Michigan game was responsible for saving someone's life!"

"Cosmic, man!" said Chad. "I'd never heard that; when did it happen?"

"My uncle said it happened in the sixties; I never did get the exact year."

"I'll have to remember that. Speaking of court trials, you still thinking about law school, Kevin?"

"*Thinking* would be the key word there," replied Kevin, looking out the right side window.

"Oh, come on, dude! You and I both know there're things called deadlines! You seriously telling me you haven't put in any applications anywhere?"

"I'm not *seriously* telling you anything right now."

"Huh?"

"I'm a little preoccupied with the team, right now, Chad. I really don't have much time for law school."

"The 'bull detector' is picking up some indications, I think--by the way, you like the style of that Architecture building?" Chad pointed out the passenger window.

"It's decent, I suppose," said Kevin, "although I prefer the style of the Admin building a little better."

"Yeah, anyway, uh, I was saying...oh, yeah! Look, where there's a will there's a way. You should be applying to Harvard, Yale, and all that stuff."

"I know, I know," sighed Kevin.

"Or are you really thinking about the pros? You think you can make it through the combine okay?"

"Uhh...well--I suppose," stammered Kevin. "That's always a possibility. Coach Panaski seems to think--" He broke off in midsentence, remembering something.

"What?" asked Chad.

Kevin said nothing, lost in thought.

"Hellooo?!!"

"Oh, yeah," said Kevin, giving a quick shake of his head. "Yeah, Coach Panaski says I could probably go at least second round. That's--sort of...why I'm not applying to law school right away. And even if I don't go into the pros, I still might--" He glanced over at Chad.

"Go on." Chad pointed to the left. "Hey, can I go east on Northwood? I've been here four years and I still can't get these one-way streets down."

"Yeah, you can. That's the fastest way from here. Turn left on Waldeck."

Chad gave Kevin a knowing look. "Wait a minute...you're not

still thinking of flying jets in the military, are you?"

Kevin quickly shook his head. "No, no, no. That went out about two years ago. But I still think I…" His voice trailed off and he looked out the window again.

"Kevin: we've been friends for ten years. Spit it out, dude! What?"

Kevin hesitated momentarily, then quickly spoke. "I promised Anne that if we win the national championship, I'll marry her right after graduation."

Chad opened his mouth and looked over at Kevin. "You're serious? Huh? I haven't heard you talk about that for over a year now. To be perfectly honest, I thought that went out the last time you broke up with her."

"Right, right," said Kevin, nodding his head. "There are still some technical details to work out."

"*Technical details*?" asked Chad. "You call marrying a beauty like Anne a *technical detail*?"

"Well, I don't know if she took it the right way."

"What did she say?"

"Well, you know how women are. She *acted* like she approved, but there's been little things…"

"Little things?"

"Yeah, like, uh," Kevin scratched his head. "I think she's been taking a little longer than usual to return my phone calls…stuff like that."

"Well, dude, you know, it *is* a tad 'ass-skew.' Women don't take kindly to being treated like trophies."

"'Trophy wife' I believe is the term they use, right?"

"Exactly, Kevin! Maybe you ought to tell Anne you'll marry her regardless of how the team does this season." Chad stopped the car in front of Kevin's apartment building.

"But maybe I'm not sure I want to marry her."

"Then why did--" Chad was interrupted by a car horn behind him. "Oh, man, where can I park? This street is packed!"

"Pull around behind my building into the alley," said Kevin.

"Right." A minute later Chad stopped in the alley and put the car in park.

"You were saying…"

"Yeah, why did you promise her you'd marry her if you're not sure?"

"Basically, she kept bringing up the topic and I thought this would silence her for a little while--I really meant it as a half-joke actually."

"You probably don't think we can win it, do you?" Chad looked at Kevin with at trace of disdain.

"Up yours, buddy!" said Kevin heatedly. "We're going to win it--get that straight right now! This entire city *lives* for OSU football, Chad! You know what I'm talking about. Some people are turned off by the enthusiasm of the typical die-hard Buckeye fan, but those fans are as old as Columbus itself.   Buckeye football is the most widely-loved team in the most widely-loved sport in America."

"That's a little strong, isn't it?" asked Chad, chuckling.

"Not by much...think about it: football is basically the most watched sport of any in the United States, and college football has the most spirit of all levels of football."

"What about the Super Bowl? I thought that was the most watched game?"

"True, it probably is, but, c'mon! Everyone likes the rah-rah atmosphere surrounding college football."

"You've got a point--what about auto racing?"

"Well, yeah, but I'm talking about--I don't know--you know what I'm saying!" said Kevin.

"I understand."

"Columbus and OSU football are one and the same," continued Kevin. "This town lives for it. Anyway, we're going to win the national title...don't worry about Anne and me."

"Well, you sure put yourself into one hell of a bind, bud!"

"I'll work it out, trust me."

"The team needs you one-hundred percent, Kevin. You better put all these woman problems aside for now."

"Understood. Not to worry. And, hey--Chad--not a word of this to anyone, understood?"

"Scouts honor, Kevin. This team has enough on its mind."

"See ya tomorrow," said Kevin. He took his gym bag from the backseat and closed the car door.

"Same time, same place," said Chad as he drove off.

****

Forty more dollars and Thad would beat his all-time record. He was driving an elderly lady home from the mall and trying to figure out how much money he had made so far. One of the fun things about driving a cab was the game of making money. You never made the same amount everyday, and any day could be a record breaker. It was like football, Thad had explained to more than one fare. You needed the "big plays" to win the game. Without the forty and fifty dollar trips from Dublin to the airport, you weren't going to make a whole lot of money. Thad also liked to compare it to the insurance business: the expensive rides subsidized the cheaper ones. Sure, it seemed a tad unfair to be paid fifty dollars for a twenty minute ride to the airport, but was it really fair for a cabbie to drive five miles to pick up an old lady who wanted to go a half mile for a grand total of three-dollars and twenty cents? Yeah, Thad often concluded, it all worked out in the end. And if some days he made two hundred dollars profit? Well, free enterprise was what the USA was all about.

"Thank you, Mrs. Afton," said Thad as the elderly lady left the taxi and shut the door. He pushed the "clear" button on the meter and parked the cab in an empty lot down the street from Mrs. Afton's house. He looked at the computer screen to see if there were any fares waiting nearby. There were two fares waiting in zone ninety-four and one in eighty-five. *Not even worth checking*, Thad reasoned. *The two in ninety-four are probably one mile grocery runs and the one in eighty-five probably some drunk wanting to hit the next bar on his list.*

It really was a big video game that Thad played everyday in his taxi. Orange Cab had devised an interesting method of dispatching its cabs. Long gone were the days of controlling the taxis by voice over the radio. Now the taxis were sent on their various trips by a computer installed in each car. Each computer had a small LCD screen and keypad. Orange Cab had divided the city into about ninety zones, numbered two through ninety-nine, with some numbers in that range being omitted. If a customer called in from north central Columbus, Clintonville, for example, the number eighty-three would appear on all the taxi computer screens. The first driver to "book" into zone eighty-three would "get" that fare. On his screen would appear the address at which the customer wished to be picked up, as well as the address to which the customer wished to go. The cab driver could then accept the fare or reject it. If he rejected it, the fare would go to the cabbie who was in position two, i.e., the driver who had "booked" into zone eighty-three second. In other words, whoever had the fastest fingers got the best fares.

Thad sat hunched over the computer, his left hand on the "send" button, his right on the number "nine button." The difference between getting a fare and winding up in second or third position was often a matter of milliseconds. Suddenly, zone ninety-five appeared on the screen. Thad instantly pushed the nine button, the five button, and the send button. The computer clicked once, twice, then paused, then--"Zone 95, Position 2" appeared on the screen. *Aargh!* thought Thad. *How could anyone have beaten me on that one? Must be some dude closer to the radio base antenna downtown.* Then zone eighty-nine popped up on the screen. *Bingo! This could be a trip from Dublin to the airport!* Thad punched in the numbers and pressed send. With a reassuring buzz, the computer displayed the pickup information. *Hmm, 2475 Sutter Parkway...to...* Thad pushed the "line" button to cycle to the next screen. *To...1253 Third Avenue...not bad...not the airport, but not bad.* Thad wasn't sure he should accept the fare. The computer gave him about twenty seconds to decide. He flipped back to the first screen and looked at the name of the passenger. *Betty-- ahh! Yes, yes...I like that name.* Thad pushed the "accept" button and looked up Sutter Parkway on his map. *Right off of Sawmill Road...at least it's easy to get to.* Thad put the map away and got on Route 315, careful not to speed in his eagerness to pick up "Betty."

It wasn't for therapeutic reasons alone that Thad drove a taxi. After a few weeks on the job, he quickly realized that it was also a very convenient way to "Cherchez Les Femmes," as the French liked to say. Thad had been thinking about marriage for the past few years, but was unsure about the situation because of his health problems. He really didn't want to marry someone if he wasn't well enough to earn a decent living. His doctors had told him he would most probably be able to return to his engineering career when he was sufficiently healed. They were a little hesitant to give him a time frame, but they generally agreed that it shouldn't take more than one or two years. Thad had felt much better in recent months, although his sleep still wasn't perfect. He kept an eye out, though, for Miss Right, figuring he would probably be back on a well-paying job within at most a year. So it was with high hopes that he drove to pickup this "Betty" from Dublin. For some reason, he always pictured that the Betty's of the world were all blonde, maybe because the Betty character in the "Archie" comic books was blonde.

Ten minutes later he arrived at 2475 Sutter Parkway and honked the horn. He never seemed to be able to get the right sounding honk. Two long blasts sounded impatient, while two staccato honks were often not heard by a customer watching TV or the like. Nevertheless, Betty opened her door and walked to Thad's cab.

Rats! thought Thad as he saw her approach. *I was wrong! She's a brunette.*

"Good Morning!" said Thad as she opened the door and sat down.

"How are ya?"

"Good, and you?" Thad turned to face her and smiled.

"Good. Third and Grandview, please," she said coldly.

Aren't we feeling unsociable today, thought Thad.

"I'll just take 270 to 315, if that's OK with you," said Thad.

"Great."

Thad turned onto Sawmill Road and got onto the Outer belt. *What can I ask her? She doesn't seem like the friendliest type right now. Maybe a little humor is in order?*

"Hey, you've heard of that Army recruiting slogan: 'Travel the world. Meet interesting people, then kill them.' She said nothing. "Well, uh," Thad said, then cleared his throat. "I made up one for cab drivers: 'Travel the city. Meet interesting people, then fleece them.'" He turned and smiled at her. "Pretty clever, huh?"

"Yeah, it's nice." Thad could see out of the corner of his eye that she had picked up the newspaper that was lying on the seat and was reading it.

Maybe she doesn't want to talk, he thought. *But she's young and apparently available! And she's not bad looking either! Good point,* he told himself. He let a few minutes pass before trying again. "You see that Buckeye game last Saturday?" He half-turned around to look at her.

"No."

"Oh, so you don't tend to follow OSU football, then?"

"No."

This wasn't going the way Thad liked. He tried yet again. "Did you go to Ohio State?"

"No."

The hell with it, he concluded. *That was what?--three or four strikes, I've lost count. This'll never work, I guess. Was it the job? Does she really think I'm a cab driver? Next time, I'll have to impress one of these chicks with my background.*

Five minutes later, they arrived at the address on Third Avenue.

"Eighteen, eighty," he said.

"Here's twenty. Keep the change." She left the cab before Thad could even thank her.

Lousy one dollar and twenty cent tip, he complained to himself. *She didn't even smile at me.*

He reset the meter, found an empty lot, and waited for his next fare to pop up on the screen.

****

After putting in a few late nights, Jerry had the robot in peak condition and was ready to show off Grobotics' mechanical wonder, now that it was Friday. He and Dexter had arrived at the Woodward Company an hour early, so they were chomping at the bit by two o'clock.

"If you'd be so kind as to don this helmet we can begin the demonstration," said Dexter as he handed a modified welding helmet to Paul Gardos.

"Your robot won't---"

"'Bobby'--" said Dexter. "We like to keep things personal around him. Reminds us what our goal really is--a mechanical humanoid."

"Fine," said Paul. "'Bobby' won't miss like he did last time and spray my clothes with pepper spray, will he?"

"Definitely not," said Jerry with a smile. "But just in case we encounter Murphy's Law Number Eight, you might want to put on this plastic jumpsuit." Jerry handed a wad of bright yellow plastic to Paul.

"In other words, you're not sure," said Paul.

"Oh, we're just protecting ourselves against unforeseen

events."

"Fine," repeated Paul, his voice muffled inside the helmet.

This was the third demonstration that Grobotics had given for the Woodward Company, but Dexter had yet to secure Purchase Order Number One from its president, Paul Gardos. The idea was that Bobby would 'confront' a suspect and spray a pepper fluid into his face, thus disabling him with less-than-deadly force. Eventually, it was hoped that Bobby would be so well armored that he could withstand a hail of bullets and continue to carry out his mission. For the time being, though, Bobby was virtually unprotected, his low battery power forcing him to be lightweight.

Dexter, Jerry, and Paul were outside, in the Woodward Company's loading dock area. They had set up a small table to hold the computer and radio that controlled Bobby. A small group of Woodward employees had gathered as well, though not too close to the robot, as Jerry had warned them of the possible danger of being hit with pepper spray.

"I thought we were using Firewire connectors, Jerry," said Dexter as he examined some of the computer's hardware. "These look like USB to me."

"Yeah, I know…they'll work just fine. I just didn't have the time to replace them."

"Great…just make sure they're in for next time. Are we ready to go?"

"Ready when you are, boss," said Jerry. He sat down behind the computer monitor and punched in the various initialization parameters. Bobby stirred to life from his default position. The crowd of onlookers reacted with assorted oohs and aahs as Bobby went through head, arm, and leg checks. Satisfied that all was set, Jerry gave Dexter the thumbs-up sign.

"Okay. Paul--if you'll just stand over here," said Dexter, motioning to a spot about ten yards from Bobby. "Now," he began, turning to the assembled employees, "what you see before you is a truly autonomous bipedal, self-contained security assistant. Or you might know him better as 'Robocop.'" A few titters arose from the group. "Grobotics is pleased to present the policeman of the future-- one that does not require disability compensation when shot and one that does not accept bribes from corrupt city officials. This robot is able to pursue and disable a suspect as long as his batteries allow him, which currently is somewhere around a mile and a half--well beyond the range of typical urban foot pursuits. Although in the future he may carry a firearm, this robot today is armed only with pepper spray, since his vision systems do not yet ensure the safety of innocent bystanders when he fires a gun."

The crowd murmured and took a step or two back.

"But not to worry, ladies and gentlemen. The only target today is your own Paul Gardos."

At the mention of their beloved CEO, the crowd gave a small round of applause. It wasn't often they got to see their leader in the guise of a hunted criminal.

"So, with no further ado," said Dexter, "I present to you 'Bobby'! Paul, the game is afoot! You are free to move about the parking lot." Dexter turned to Jerry. "Let him go!"

Jerry punched in a few commands on the keyboard and Bobby began to walk toward Paul, who immediately dashed away from the menacing machine. A game of cat and mouse ensued, as Paul used his best basketball moves to avoid Bobby.

"As you can see, ladies and gentlemen," said Dexter, "Bobby is completely on his own. Jerry, if you would?" Jerry stood up and backed away from the computer. "See," said Dexter, "Jerry is doing nothing to control Bobby."

Bobby appeared to be boxing Paul into the far corner of the parking lot, but Paul successfully eluded the robot and came running toward the crowd with both thumbs raised.

"Hey! Stay away from us!" yelled one of the machinists. "We don't have helmets on, like you do."

Bobby, however, became a little confused and stayed in the corner of the parking lot. Evidently a few birds walking on the ground in that area had caused his vision sensors to lock on them. Bobby stood still for a few seconds, until its memory realized that it had lost its original target. Paul waved his arms and yelled a few times until Bobby reacquired him and came running toward him at full speed.

"NA-na-na-NA-na!" Paul said, bobbing and weaving in front of the spectators.

"Hey," said the machinist again, "keep that thing away from us!"

Just then Bobby lunged toward Paul and let out a ten foot long stream of pepper spray. Paul, however, had stepped aside and the pepper spray hit two of the women in the crowd, right in their faces.

"Ahhwww!" they cried out in unison.

"Get me some water!" one of them said, stumbling backwards and almost tripping over a picnic table sitting there.

"Jerry!" yelled Dexter, "get some water from the bathroom! Paul, where is your first aid kit?"

Meanwhile Bobby continued to chase Paul, oblivious to the injuries he had caused.

"Oh, hell, I forgot about the stinkin' robot!" said Dexter as he ran to the computer console. He punched in the shutdown commands and Bobby froze in his tracks. Paul tore off the welder's mask and ran over to the stricken women.

"Dave," he said to one of the employees, "get the first aid kit from Human Resources--get the eye cream!"

"Here's some water!" said Jerry breathlessly, running out of the building with two cups in his hand.

Paul literally threw the water into the face of one of the women, then did the same to the other woman. "Get some more!" he ordered Jerry. A minute later Dave returned with the eye salve, which Paul applied to the first victim, then the other. "Is that better?" he asked in a paternal tone. Both women murmured their assent and began to drink the Cokes which someone had thoughtfully brought out for them.

"You sure you're alright?" asked Dexter, well aware of the repercussions his company might suffer if Bobby continued to malfunction. After getting assurances from both women, he turned to Paul.

"I'm really sorry about this, Paul. It looks like Bobby just can't distinguish between friend and foe. As usual, the culprit is the vision system." Dexter and the rest of the robotics community had been perplexed by the complexities of machine vision for years. It was well known that vision was the lagging member of the movement marching toward the perfect robot.

"Well, you darn well better get it fixed before demo-ing that hunk of metal in front of *my* employees again," said Paul. "It's bad enough having to wear that mask--man, that thing gets hot! And this monkey suit is an oven too."

"I understand, Paul," said Dexter reassuringly. "No more mistakes next time. Maybe we'll get someone else to be the 'criminal' next time. Don't worry, we'll fix Bobby's vision problems. I was reading a white paper from IEEE last week and I think Jerry and I may know exactly what to do to perfect Bobby's eyes."

"Glad to hear it. How long will it take for this pepper spray to wear off?"

"They should be fine in about thirty minutes. We weren't using the really potent stuff, so they shouldn't be very severely affected."

After apologizing to the women, Paul headed back to his office. Dexter and Jerry packed Bobby and the ancillary gear into the company van and drove back down the outer belt to Grobotics.

"You think it will be an easy fix, Jerry?" Dexter asked.

"To be perfectly honest, I can't be sure. Besides the brain, isn't the eye the most complex organ in the human body?"

"I suppose you're right."

"Bobby runs into trouble when he tries to distinguish between more than one moving object. Notice that he had no problem when Paul was running next to the parked cars; it was when Paul ran up to the spectators that he got confused. They were probably moving back and forth, moving their hands around--that's what Bobby can't handle."

"Jerry, as I was just telling Paul, I read a white paper from IEEE last week on machine vision and I think you should study it too. They cover some algorithms in there which might be just what we need."

"Sounds good. Matter of fact," said Jerry, "I'll take it home with me tonight."

Chapter 3

"Welcome to Columbus Custom Cab!" said Thad with a smile as Dexter climbed into the backseat of Thad's taxi. Since it was Saturday, Dexter thought he'd hang out at a friend's house in Bexley, a stately inner suburb of Columbus. Dexter's Charger was going to take a couple of days to be fixed, so he figured he would make use of the personal cell number Thad had given him to get a ride across town.

"Glad to be a customer," replied Dexter with a half-smile. "Is that really the name of your company?"

"Oh, no, I just like to come up with different-sounding names once in a while."

"So you really like driving a cab in Columbus?"

"You know, I really *do* like it," said Thad. "I'm proud of Columbus and like to show off our fair city to people."

"No pun intended."

"Whaaa?"

"You know," said Dexter. "*'Fair* city'-- 'taxi *fare.*'"

"Ahh, touché! I like it! I like it!" Thad put the car in gear and started moving. "Bexley, right?"

"Right. South Columbia Avenue."

"Anyway," said Thad, "yeah, I really like Columbus. I was born and raised here and I wouldn't live anywhere else. I've lived a short time in Houston, LA, and Chicago, and, in my opinion, they don't have anything on Columbus. As a friend of mine likes to say, Columbus is a nice place to live, but you wouldn't want to visit there. There's really a lot of truth to that: I mean apart from Ohio State football games, what do we have? Yeah, we have the Ohio State Fair, and a few museums, but what else? But, you know what I think? I think it's best that way. We're basically an overgrown cow-town, really. We have all the benefits of a large city with few of the drawbacks. We really don't have very bad traffic--that is, compared with huge cities. We don't have much crime. At the same time, we have a thriving downtown, a symphony orchestra--we've got German Village, the Brewery District, the Arena District, Short North--"

"The Blue Jackets!" interjected Dexter. "Don't forget about them!"

"Right, right, that's true, we do have pro hockey. One of the things I like about Columbus is that it has no geographic boundaries--we can grow out in all four directions without running into a lake or ocean or whatever. This might sound a bit odd, but I like to think of it in philosophical terms as well: we can grow as persons without any boundaries or limits."

"Hmm," said Dexter, "I never thought of it that way." *Typical taxi driver*, thought Dexter. *'Colorful' is the adjective that comes to mind.* Dexter recalled the sign he had seen hanging in the local barber shop: "Why is it that the only people who know how to run the world are either cutting hair or driving a taxi?"

"Hey, I just remembered something," said Thad as he pulled onto Dublin Road. "How would you like to ride for free today?"

Oh, no, thought Dexter. "What's the catch?"

"I just need ten minutes of your time. I need to fix a piece of equipment owned by our cab company."

"Well, I suppose I could spare ten minutes...sure!"

The next thing Dexter knew he was standing out in the open on the top of a skyscraper. The Lincoln-Leveque was the first "sky-scraper" in Columbus and one of the few non-New York buildings over thirty stories in the country when it was completed in 1931. Back then it was known as the American Industrial Union Building, but was given its present name when the Leveques bought it. As much a symbol of Columbus as the beloved Ohio Stadium, the Lincoln-Leveque possessed a sublime architectural grace. Cut from the mold of the Art Deco period of the early 20th Century, it was a far cry from some of its sister buildings in downtown Columbus. Its sculpted top and intricate gargoyles were markedly different from the straight "steel and glass"

Huntington and Riffe Tower buildings just around the corner of Broad and High. Dexter had grown up affectionately calling it simply "the finger building," since it did resemble that appendage.

"Can you see if this cable is connected?" asked Thad as he climbed up the antenna and traced the path of a black and white cable. Thad's cab company, "Orange Cab," had an antenna at the top of the Lincoln-Leveque.

"Uhh," began Dexter, "what should it be connected to?"

"Follow it into that gray metal box and look for a plug that's labeled "Orange Feed Seven.""

Dexter moved his hand along the cable, following it as it meandered through a group of a half-dozen other cables of various colors. The Lincoln-Leveque was a popular place for a good number of other companies needing radio broadcasting in central Ohio. Dexter eventually traced the cable to the metal box.

"Yeah, it's in the right place," said Dexter, "Orange Feed Seven."

"Darn, I knew it!" said Thad. "There must be a problem in the junction box down on the twentieth floor."

"You sure it's not in this other wire over here?" Dexter followed a black wire that came out of "Orange Misc." The wire disappeared over the edge of the parapet.

"What's that again?" asked Thad, still checking out the connections up on the antenna. He didn't see Dexter start to crawl out to the edge of the masonry to get a better look at the wire.

Dexter was leaning over the edge of the turret-shaped ledge, trying to catch a glimpse of the wire when one of the stone blocks gave way! Already too far out for his legs to stop his fall, Dexter fell headlong over the edge!

"Dexter, grab the wire!" yelled Thad as he scrambled down the antenna. He reached the metal electrical box just as the "Orange Misc." wire was pulled from its socket. Thad deftly snatched the wire with both hands and braced himself against a metal post. He could tell from the pull on the wire that fortunately Dexter was on the other end. The only problem was that Dexter outweighed him by at least twenty pounds. With uncanny strength he wrapped the wire around the post and tied it off. Only when he was sure it would not slip did he creep to the edge to look down at Dexter.

"Son of a bitch, Thad!" screamed Dexter as he dangled from

the wire. "Do something! This wire is beginning to slip!" Dexter had looked down once, and that was enough. There was nothing but four hundred feet of thin air between the bottom of his shoes and the hard cement sidewalk!

Thad whipped out his cell phone and was just about to dial 911 when he realized it was too late for that. Dexter couldn't possibly hold onto that thin wire for more than a minute or two! Frantically looking around for a rope, Thad's eyes fell upon the cable he had just been inspecting. Perfect! He ripped the cable away from its mountings and, calling on his Boy Scout training, he expertly tied a bowline, a knot that formed a loop that would not slip. He tied the other end around the post.

"Hey, buddy, hang on for just a few more seconds!" he said to Dexter as he inched out to the edge.

"Thad! I'm slipping! Help, please!" begged Dexter.

"Grab this, Dexter! It's a loop that won't slip. It should be easier than that wire."

Dexter desperately lunged for the cable with the bowline. With superhuman effort he was able to work the loop over his head, around his back, and under his arms.

Several people had by now gathered around the edge and helped pull Dexter up to safety. As if gravity would have the last say, just as Dexter came over the top, one of his shoes slipped off and fell to the street below, just missing a policeman directing traffic.

"Holy Hell!" cried Dexter, rolling onto his back, trying to catch his breath. "Thank you, Thad! Thank all of you!"

"Good thing you grabbed that wire, Dexter," said Thad.

"Hey," said Dexter between breaths, "I'm just glad you grabbed the other end!"

"What are friends for, buddy?! Thank God you didn't fall all the way down."

"Well, thank *someone*, I guess."

After Dexter rested a little while longer, the two of them took the elevator to the ground floor, only to be mobbed by a loud contingent of TV newspeople as soon as they stepped onto the sidewalk. After a brief exchange and a few photo ops, Dexter rode home with Thad.

They stopped in front of Dexter's house and Dexter patted Thad on the shoulder. "Hey, guy, thanks again--that was close!"

"You're, uh, quite…welcome," said Thad hesitantly.

"What?" asked Dexter, sensing Thad wanted to say something.

"Well, you thank me--you thanked me for that and, uh, I was just thinking..."

"What, you want a cold beer or something?" asked Dexter laughing.

"How 'bout if you thank me by visiting my brother?"

"Your *brother*! What do you mean?"

"You know," said Thad shyly, "I gave you his card the other day."

"Ohhh, yeah...the priest."

"Right. Whaddya say?"

"Let me sleep on it, okay?"

"Fine."

Dexter thanked Thad again and walked into his house. It was only after he changed clothes and sat down in the living room that Dexter began to reflect on his near-fatal encounter. He turned on the TV to some mindless midday chatter, but just as quickly shut it off and decided he needed to sort a few things out. His conscience wouldn't leave him alone, not after what had just happened. *The headlong plunge off the Lincoln-Leveque...his shoe falling off just as he was saved.* Dexter shook his head and rose from the couch. *I'm just shaken up, that's all,* he thought. He grabbed a beer from the refrigerator and sat back down on the couch. He thought briefly about turning the TV on again, but knew that wouldn't help. *I sure was desperate up there--hanging helpless at the top of the Lincoln-Leveque Tower...the thought of...what?*, he asked himself. *Yeah!* he started to shout internally, *the thought of what!?*

"What's your problem!?" he said aloud to the empty house. *What is my problem?* he asked himself. He checked the label on the beer. The "Born On" date showed it was only a few weeks old. *No, it wasn't the beer.* Something continued to nag at the edges of his conscience. *What's happening to me?* he thought. He hadn't felt this way since, well since...*well? Have I ever felt this way?* Dexter turned on the TV and tuned to a rerun of a Blue Jackets hockey game. Finally, he sighed, *that* problem is solved.

"Maybe you should call that priest like the taxi driver suggested," said a little voice in his head.

"Who asked you?" Dexter said to the empty room.

"And your brush with death today?" continued the little voice.

"*Just shut the hell up!*" he silently told his conscience.

****

Thad decided the best way to get the whole Lincoln-Leveque episode out of his head was to work. Taxi driving was very good in that respect as well. It was therapeutic in that serving others, helping others with their problems, made you quickly forget your own hurts. And he wasn't about to let the strikeout with Betty a few days ago dampen his enthusiasm for "cherchez-ing the femmes."

He drove from Dexter's house to the parking lot of the Grandview library and booked into zone seventy-four, the Grandview area. Zone four, a downtown zone, appeared on the screen, but Thad decided to let it go. A few other distant zones popped up, none of which interested Thad. He was starting to get a little drowsy when zone ninety showed on the screen. *Golden!* he thought. Zone ninety was in Dublin, one of the wealthiest suburbs of Columbus. He rapidly booked into zone ninety and was rewarded a few seconds later by the buzzer sounding and the fare appearing on his screen. *An airport run! Bingo! And the name? "Ginger Evans!" Perfect!* He put the car in reverse, pleased with his conquest in the "battle of the buttons," as he liked to call the method of getting a fare off the computer. *Omigosh!* he suddenly realized. *I forgot to push the "accept" button!* He slammed on the brakes and punched in his acceptance. *Whew! That was close!* He finished backing out of his parking spot and headed up Riverside drive, toward Dublin.

When he was close to the pickup address he began to coach himself. *Remember, this time, play up your engineering background-- let her know the taxi thing is only temporary. And give her time to warm up to you…don't expect her to fall in love in five minutes.*

Thad stopped in front of 2643 Summer Drive and waited for "Ginger" to walk out to the car. There was no need to blow the horn since she was sitting on the front porch. He got out of the car and opened the trunk.

"I can take those if you like," he said. As he took the bags from her, he glanced at her left hand. *Whew, no ring!* He lifted her two suitcases into the trunk.

"Thank you."

"Don't mention it."

After they both climbed into the taxi and fastened their seatbelts, Thad put the car in drive and headed down Sawmill Road. "Sure is nice weather today, eh?" he asked.

"It's beautiful," Ginger said. "And it's supposed to be good the next few days."

"Glad to hear that!"

"So, how long have you been driving a cab?"

Golden! thought Thad. *I didn't even have to break the ice myself this time.* "Oh, only about ten months, actually," he said. "I'm only doing this temporarily, until I can get a better job." He let the remark hang in the air.

"And what type of job might that be?" asked Ginger.

Thank you, Sylvester! said Thad silently to his guardian angel. "I have a degree in Aerospace Engineering, but I haven't worked in that field for a few years. I, uh, have had a little problem with insomnia--a health issue--and I haven't been able to work a full-time, pressured job."

"Really!" said Ginger, a concerned look on her face.

Let's not let this thing get out of hand, Thad cautioned himself. *Best to calm her fears right away.*

"Yeah," continued Thad, "it's not really all that bad. I will probably be getting back into engineering in the next few months. I sleep fine now--see, that's why I took this job as a taxi driver, to experiment to see if I could handle a full-time job. I've been working full-time for almost a year now, and my sleep is good, so the next step is a full-time engineering job. I want to see if I can handle that. I should say my sleep isn't *perfect* yet, but it's getting there. When it improves a little more, I'll get another job."

"Oh, I used to have a boyfriend who was an electrical engineer," said Ginger. "He really liked his work."

'Used to'? thought Thad. *That's a good sign.* He turned briefly around and asked, "And what work do you do?"

"I'm a financial analyst for Nestle."

"Oh, that's that place off of Route 161, right?"

"Right. It's a nice place to work, although I don't like all the traveling I've had to do recently."

"How often is that?" asked Thad.

"Basically, it's been at least once a week."

"That is a bit much." Thad pointed out the right side of the car. "Ah, don't you love that smell?" They were passing the Busch brewery which often emitted the pleasant aroma of hops.

"Ha, typical male," said Ginger. "Beer, beer, beer!"

"I'm lovin' it!" said Thad as he gave her a quick smile.

Maybe a little erudite show of force, thought Thad. *Give her one of my 'Thad theories'...* "I have a theory--I like to call it the 'technological merry-go-round phenomenon.'"

"An engineer with a theory," Ginger said smilingly. "How appropriate!"

"Here's the thing," began Thad. "I believe that what goes around comes around--in the technological world. For instance, take writing. It used to be, before the invention of the telephone, that everyone would write letters to each other. Then when everyone had telephones, they would simply phone each other. But now we have e-mail and everyone writes each other again!" Thad waved his hand with a flourish and glanced back at Ginger.

"Bravo," said Ginger, "lavish logic, if I may say so."

"And another thing," continued Thad, "you ever thought about the names we use? In ages past, people were generally known by their first names and what village they were from, like 'Helen of Troy,' or 'Theresa of Avila,' or, heck, even, 'Jesus of Nazareth.' Then it became the custom for everyone to have a last name, so we had 'Christopher Columbus,' 'George Washington,' and all that. But nowadays, with instant worldwide news and communications, some people are back to one-name names. When you say 'Tiger,' everyone knows you're talking about Tiger Woods; when you say 'W,' everyone thinks of George W. Bush; or 'LeBron' refers to LeBron James. What goes around, comes around."

"I think you're a little weak on that one," said Ginger. "I mean, I think famous people will always be known by a special moniker, no matter what era we're in."

"Well, like I say, it's just a theory...I haven't published it yet. One more aspect of that theory: What about CDs? You know, we used to have records, then cassette tapes, but now we're back to records again. CDs are basically little records."

"All right," said Ginger, "I can see that."

The conversation stopped for a few minutes as each were lost in thought.

Time to close the sale, Thad thought. "So, I hope the weather is as good where you're going as it is here!"

"Probably about the same," replied Ginger.   "I'm going to Spain."

"You don't say!" Thad couldn't repress the broad smile that came to his face. "That's great! I know a little about Spain actually."

"Do you know someone there?"

"Have you ever heard of Garabandal?"

"Uh, can't say that I have. Have you been there?"

"Not yet--but I plan on going there after the Warning...to see the Miracle!"

"The Miracle?" asked Ginger with a blank expression.

"Well, have you heard about the Warning?"

"The Warning? Whaa?"

"Yeah, you see, the Miracle's going to be awesome!" said Thad excitedly, not seeing Ginger's reaction.   "I've got tickets already booked for it! But, the funny thing is, only one person, Conchita, knows the exact date of the Miracle. She will announce it to the world eight days before it occurs. It's supposed to occur on a Thursday evening sometime in March, April, or May in this little town called Garabandal in Spain. I can't wait! I already have some theories as to what the Miracle will be: you know, maybe something like a giant image of Christ in the sky, or a picture of Mary."   Thad pulled a Garabandal brochure out of his briefcase and turned to give it to Ginger. Only then did he see her vacant stare. "Oh...is something wrong? I just thought you might like this brochure on Garabandal."

After a moment or two, Ginger said softly, "Not right now...thanks anyway." She looked out the window and folded her arms.

"Oh, I didn't mean to offend you. Is it something I said?"

Ginger didn't reply, just kept staring at the passing scenery.

Dog-GONE-it! thought Thad. *I blew it again! I shouldn't have come on so strong about the Garabandal stuff.   Aww, shoot! Something turned her completely off. Chalk that up to experience.*

They rode the rest of the way in silence, broken only by Thad's asking for the name of the airline on which she was flying. Though not expecting much, Thad did get a decent tip, so all was not lost on the trip.

****

Dexter was still sitting in his living room watching hockey on TV, but couldn't seem to shake the small voice in his head.

"I believe the priest's phone number is on that card in your wallet," whispered the little voice.

"I thought I told you to shut up," replied Dexter in the secret recesses of his mind.

"The phone's right beside you."

"I don't give a crap. Go play in traffic!"

"Oh--okay Dexter--as long as you know what you're doing."

"Darn right I know what I'm doing." Dexter returned his focus to the TV. The Blue Jackets had just scored another goal, giving them the lead. *I've got nothing to worry about*, he consoled himself.

He watched TV for another half hour, did some work on a project he had brought home from the office, ate dinner, and then went to bed, without waiting for his girlfriend to come home. He woke up the next day at his usual time and explained his near-death experience to Daphne over breakfast. She passed it off as a "lucky break" and told him not to worry about it. He spent the rest of the day doing some yard work, and then Monday morning, because his car was in the shop, Dexter was forced to use Daphne's car. He drove her to her office in the Polaris area on the far north side of Columbus and then headed for his office. He drove down High Street rather than take the freeway since he wanted to stop at Graceland for some batteries at the store there. When the traffic light at Selby and High changed to yellow, Dexter decided to brake to a stop instead of trying to beat it. He always lamented the fact that some people seemed to be running red lights more often, upping their chances of a serious accident. *What was the big deal, anyway*, he wondered. It was good now and then to be able to take a break from the grind of driving. It gave one time to look around and see the city. He unconsciously swiveled his head to take in his surroundings when his eyes fell upon--*oh, come on!* He complained to himself. He happened to be stopped right in front of Saint Michael's Church here in Worthington. He remembered from the card that the taxi driver had given him: this was the church at which *that priest* lived! *Son of a bitch!* He softly swore to himself. *Why can't I get rid of this B.S.? I don't want to get into another tug-of-war with that stupid voice in my head!* When the light turned green, he pressed the accelerator to the floor and let the engine squeal the tires. Only when he was two blocks away from the dreaded church did he let up on the pedal and return to the legal speed.

"I believe your cell phone is already turned on," began the little voice.

Dexter decided the silent treatment was the only effective treatment this time.

"Ahem."

Dexter kept his eyes on the road and his mind *off* his conscience.

"You'll never win, you know Dexter. Just like Luke in 'Star Wars'-- it is your destiny!"

Silence from Dexter.

"Another one bites the dust, another one bites the dust, and another one goes and another one goes, another one bites the dust!" The old rock song kept running through Dexter's head.

"Nice try," said Dexter to his conscience.

"A-HA! Got you to talk!"

"GET--THE--HELL--AWAY--FROM--ME!"   shouted   Dexter inside the car.

"555-7873," said his conscience in a sing-song voice.

"AAARRRGGGHH!" shouted Dexter. He slammed on the brakes and turned into the first parking lot he came to. Without stopping to consider what he was doing, he unclipped his cell phone from his belt, got the priest's card from his wallet and punched in the number to Saint Michael's Church.

"Hello, Saint Michael's Church," said a pleasant voice.

"I'd like to speak to the priest please," said Dexter in an irritated voice.

"Which one, sir?"

"Oh, hell! The one who---just a minute!" Dexter looked down at the card in his hand. "I'd like to speak to Father Rankin, please! And I'm only doing this because I'm being forced to. It wasn't my idea!"

"Ohhh, uhh, okay," said the woman, "one moment please."

This is just so much bullcrap, Dexter thought to himself. *I'll talk with this church-boy once and then forget I ever saw him.*

"Hello, this is Father Rankin."

"Uh, yeah, Father Rankin, my name is Dexter Griffith and I--oh, hell!" Dexter momentarily thought about hanging up and forgetting the whole thing.

"You sound pretty upset, my friend," said Father Rankin gently. "Is there something you'd like to talk about?"

"Not really! Well--I mean--look! I met your brother riding in a taxicab and he gave me your card because--anyway, he suggested I talk with you about stuff. It'll probably be just one short visit. I really don't have much to say, so, uhh..."

"Oh, you must be talking about Thad, right? Yeah, my brother the taxi driver! So he's out making sales calls for me! Well, sure, I think I can fit you in one of these days. When would be best for you? Days or evenings?"

Dexter shook his head and let out a noise of irritation. "Pssshh! You know, Father, with all due respect, I think I'll just cancel this whole thing. I really just did this spontaneously without giving it much thought. So, thanks for---"

"Now, you must have had a good reason for taking the trouble to call me. Besides, knowing Thad he probably made a deal with you, right? You have to hold up your end of the bargain."

"Well, he did say that I could repay him by visiting you."

"There! See? Look, I'll make a deal with you too. You see me for one visit and if you don't want to set any more appointments, we call it quits right then--deal?"

"Welll, do you think we could do, uhh, just one short visit?"

"Right," said Father Rankin. "One visit--no more than one hour."

"Welll, I suppose," said Dexter, making a face.

"How's Thursday at eight sound?"

"Let me check my calendar for a second." Dexter pulled out his appointment book and checked the date and time. "That's fine. I'll see you then."

"Great! Say hello to Thad if you happen to see him."

"Hopefully never--only if my car breaks down again."

"I see. Bye."

"Bye."

****

It was classic Ohio State football once again. Anyone who knew anything about college football knew that, for the past two years, OSU was the master of the close game. In the last few seasons, the Buckeyes had won an astonishing ninety-three percent of their victories by seven or fewer points. On the rare occasion that Ohio State did lose a game, the usual expression around Central Ohio was "Live by the close game, die by the close game." The game with Penn State was proving to be no exception. The score was twenty-eight to twenty-seven, in favor of the Nittany Lions, and as Kevin looked up at the clock for the hundredth time that quarter, he could see that there were just over two minutes left in the game. When he saw Coach Panaski signal for a timeout, he handed the ball to the ref and walked over to the sideline.

"They won't be expecting it now," said Panaski when his players had formed a circle around him. "We use the option now and we win the game."

Kevin gritted his teeth and let out an audible gasp. "We don't know it well enough, Coach! Let's just pass to Platwood!"

"We can do it, Kevin!" said Jason, the running back. "I won't mess up, I promise!"

"I'll get open if you need me!" said Platwood, the Buckeyes' leading receiver.

"Case closed," said the Coach. "We run the option. "Now let's go kick some Nittany ass!" He slapped two players on the behind. "Just like practice!" The number of times the option had been run in Ohio Stadium could be counted on the lower three keys of a piano. It was fourth and eight and the Buckeyes needed a first down if they were to have any chance of winning the game and keeping alive their hopes of a national championship. Long gone from the OSU players' minds was the thought of a quality win to boost their standings in the rankings. They would be satisfied with a one-point victory now, or even a half-point win, were that possible. Kevin took the snap from under center and rolled left. The Penn State defensive line was taken completely off guard. Kevin looked for Jason and found him in perfect position! He pitched the ball to him, and then blocked one of PSU's linebackers. A lane wide enough for a Hummer opened up and Jason took advantage of it. He sprinted across the line of scrimmage and gained fifteen yards before being tackled by the Penn State safety.

"Yes!" yelled Jason as he rolled to his feet and pumped his fist in the air. He ran up to Kevin and slapped the side of his helmet. "Awesome block, dude!"

"Awesome run, dude!" replied Kevin, giving his running back a high-five. The players lined up quickly, the center hiked the ball, and Kevin threw it to the ground, giving them time to set up their next play. The ball was on the fifty yard line, so they would need a minimum of about seventeen yards to get a chance at a long field-goal attempt. In the huddle, the tight-end told Kevin what play Panaski had called in.

"Platwood, you ready?" asked Kevin. Kyle Platwood rarely dropped passes and Kevin wanted to make sure his star ball-handler was in top form.

"All present and accounted for, boss!" said Platwood.

"Good. I'm going to hit you across the middle about ten yards out."

"Got it, boss."

Kevin looked at the other nine players in the huddle. "The ball will be snapped on the third 'hike.'" Several players voiced their understanding. Kevin slapped the two players on either side of him. "All right, people, we only have a minute, ten left, so let's get this done!"

The OSU offense lined up with Platwood on the left and Kevin in the shotgun.

"Hike, rabbit five, hike, HIKE!"

Kevin immediately saw that it was a blitz. He was about to throw the ball out of bounds when he saw Platwood open across the middle. He cocked his arm, but just as he threw the ball a Penn State linebacker hit him. Platwood lunged for the pigskin, but it was picked off! A Penn State safety scooped the ball up and looked for an opening. He was hit simultaneously from both sides by two Buckeye players. Just when it looked like the play was over, the ball popped out! Platwood dove on it and the Buckeyes retained possession!

"That's not good for my heart!" yelled Coach Panaski from the sidelines. "Let's score some points and quit goofing around!" Panaski sent in a player to tell Kevin to run the same play over again.

"He's gotta be kidding!" said Kevin, in the huddle. "It's third down--this is four-down territory!"

"We don't have any time, Kevin!" said Platwood. "The play clock's down to thirteen!"

"Okay! Let's do it!"

They lined up again and this time the play worked as designed. Penn State wasn't expecting them to run the exact same play and they didn't blitz either. Platwood caught the pass in stride and was brought down on the forty yard line, a ten yard completion, giving OSU a first down.

In the huddle, a player told Kevin the play Panaski had given him. "Panaski says we're to run J-52. Jason should get about five yards out of it."

"You hear that, Jason?" Kevin asked him.

"I line up on the right, right?"

"No, the left! You best hit the books a little more next week!" said Kevin heatedly.

"Give him a break, boss," said Platwood. "He just confused it with K-52."

"Fine. Let's get this over with."

Kevin took the snap and slammed the ball into Jason's stomach. Jason used all the power of his two hundred and twenty pound frame to run--straight into a Penn State tackle. He gained a total of zero yards, keeping the Buckeyes forty yards from the end zone. Kevin looked up at the clock and saw there were only thirty-two seconds left in the game. Panaski sent the play into the huddle.

"Again?" asked Kevin when the incoming player told the quarterback of Panaski's instructions. "He wants us to run the same play *again?!*"

"No time to argue!" said one of the tight ends.

They lined up and Kevin took the snap--just as the whistle blew and a flag fluttered onto the emerald-green turf.

"He was in the neutral zone!" Panaski pointed to one of Penn State's linebackers as he yelled at one of the referees.

The zebras congregated in the middle of the field, then the one in the white hat signaled offsides against Ohio State.

"You gotta be kiddin' me!" screamed Panaski. Some of Ohio State's assistant coaches calmed their head coach down as the referee moved the ball back five yards. That made it second down and fifteen to go for a first down.

On the next play, Kevin hit his tight end for a gain of nine yards. Back in the huddle, Kevin set up the play which had just been called in.

"Platwood, this one is all yours. Make your guy bite ten yards out and then run a post across the middle. We want to set this up just fine for Whinney." Whinny was OSU's kicker, his nickname coined from the trademark sound he made when he complained about the position of the ball he had to kick.

"HIKE, HIKE!" Kevin dropped back and saw Platwood in perfect position. He released the ball and it flew straight and true right into his receiver's hands--and then right out again.

"No! NO!" yelled Kevin. "How could you drop that?" Kevin was so busy complaining that he didn't see Panaski signaling him to call for a time out. The game clock wound down to five seconds, then four... Finally one of the linesman saw the coach and gave the referee the "T" sign! It was fourth down, there were two seconds left in the game and OSU had the ball on their opponents' forty yard line--a fifty-seven yard field goal would be needed!

Kevin jogged to the sidelines and watched as Whinney walked onto the field. *I've done all I can do,* Kevin thought. *I've given my best. I hope you give your best, old Whinney, old pal.* Whinney looked over at Kevin and gave him a slight nod. Kevin gave him the thumbs-up sign.

Whinney stood next to the holder and started his routine. *Right foot back, left foot back, right foot back, left foot back. So far, so good,* he coached himself. *Left foot sidestep, move right foot next to left. Left foot sidestep, move right foot next to left. Good. The hard part's over.* He looked up at the goalpost, then over at the flags flying on the rim of the stadium. *Slight left-to-right breeze, probably about ten miles per hour. No problem. Remember, the national championship rides on--No!* he scolded himself. *Just another day at the office! Just follow your routine and everything will be fine.*

Whinney had actually kicked a fifty-nine yard field goal before, but it had been in practice. His longest in-game kick so far had been a forty-nine yarder against Rice in the second game of this season. He had not missed a field goal in seventeen attempts, going all the way back to the Michigan State game during last season. Although plagued by a sore knee from a touchdown-preventing tackle in the first game this year, he had been regularly splitting the uprights, usually with ten or more yards to spare.

Whinney waited while the holder got into position and the rest of the offensive line set themselves up. The holder held up his hands, and the center snapped the ball to him. Whinney paused to make sure it was a good snap, then ran forward. Left, right, left, kick! The ball rocketed forward, its low profile almost being spoiled by the outstretched hand of a PSU defender. The crowd rose to its feet as one man. At first the ball seemed to be heading off to the right, then it curved so it was just inside the right goalpost. End over end it tumbled while the audience held its breath. No one made a sound as the projectile descended toward the ground. A loud gasp! was heard as it hit the horizontal bar. The ball bounced up, still flipping end over end. It hit the bottom bar a second time--and fell forward! Three points!

"Whin-ney! Whin-ney! Whin-ney!" chanted the Buckeye players and crowd as the kicker was carried off the field by his teammates.

"I thought I told you guys to quit giving me heart attacks!" yelled Panaski as he joined the jostling players. "Once a day is enough!"

"You love it!" said Kevin as he gave the Coach a bear hug. Kevin went over to congratulate Whinney, who was being mobbed by fans for his autograph.

"Way to go, Whin-man!"

"Hey, I just scored three points! The rest of you scored twenty-seven!" protested the ecstatic kicker.

"Put a cork in it, bro! Absorb the glory!" Kevin grabbed Whinney and gave him a shake. "Awesome!"

"Kevin, yo!" said Chad, coming up behind the quarterback. "I've got something for you!" The tight end put a ring in Kevin's hand.

"Hey, we haven't won the championship yet!"

"That's not a championship ring, Kev! Take a look!"

"What the heck?" Kevin held up the object to take a closer look.

"It's a wedding ring, guy. You're one step closer!"

"Gag me with a spoon, Chad." Kevin's smile disappeared.

"Hey, I thought you'd appreciate it, man!"

"Well, you can keep it for now." Kevin gave the ring back to his friend. "Hey, not to be a downer. I'll talk to you later," Kevin said. His classic ear-to-ear grin returned and he punched Chad on the shoulder pad. "Time to party, pardner!"

Kevin and Chad joined the rest of the team for their jubilant jaunt back to the locker room.

****

As he drove up High Street on his way to see Thad's brother, the priest, Dexter considered calling the whole thing off. *I'll just get out the cell phone and give him some excuse. This is the most idiotic thing I've done since the Millennium began.* Dexter pulled into the parking lot of Saint Michael's Church and shut off the engine. *Shoot, in for a penny, in for a pound...I might as well get this over with.* Dexter tilted his head back and gritted his teeth. *I can do this*, he prodded himself. *One hour and it'll be over. My debt to that taxi driver will be paid.* He got out of his car, walked up to the rectory door and rang the bell.

"Yes?" said a voice over the intercom.

"I'm here to see Father Rankin."

"Oh, Dexter...I'll be right out!"

Well, at least he's not behind schedule or something, thought Dexter.

A minute later, a tall, thin man appeared at the door and let Dexter in. Father Rankin had kindly, brown eyes and a demeanor which spoke of the proper blend of severity and mercy, depending on the state of the person with whom he happened to be dealing.

"Good to see you," said Father Rankin. "Have any problem finding it?"

"Oh, no. You're right here on High Street; I've driven by a lot, although it wasn't until a few days ago that I actually recognized the name."

"Fine, fine. My office is just down this corridor."

Father Rankin and Dexter entered a modest, yet clean and well-kept office. Dexter shut the door and sat down on the chair in front of the desk.

"So, in the next fifty-nine minutes, what can I do for you?" said Father Rankin with a smile.

"Well, maybe I should first explain how I found out about you-- have you talked with your brother recently?"

"Let's see," Father Rankin said pensively, "I don't believe I've talked with him in about two weeks."

"Oh, well, then let me explain." Dexter related his first meeting with Thad on the trip to the airport and the subsequent, coincidental meeting on the freeway.

"Oh, so you really *are* being forced to speak with me."

"I don't know if *forced* is exactly the right word, but let's just say I don't plan on making a habit out of it. You see, I never really thought much about religion until a few days ago--I don't know if your brother told you, but I almost died the other day! I was helping Thad fix some antenna on top of the Lincoln-Leveque and I almost fell off the stupid thing! Now I can't seem to silence my conscience about all this after-death stuff. I never really thought it was something I needed to worry about until I was retired. Maybe then I'd start going to Church on Sunday...I don't know...I'm just your plain, ordinary 21st Century Man. I really don't see the need for religion or God or anything that's not *real*. You know: the economy, national defense, freedom, women's rights, racial equality. That's all that matters! I just feel lucky to live at this point in time and in this country. It's Pax Americana and I feel fine! As far as religion goes--well, what difference does it make? Heaven? Fine! Hell? I don't know about that. Like God is really going to be that mad at someone to make him burn forever. My parents never talked much about religion, and neither have I. Maybe society has advanced to the point where organized religion is no longer relevant. I don't really have much of an opinion on it. I guess you really don't have much of an opinion on something until it affects you personally."

"Let's start from the beginning," said Father Rankin, leaning back in his chair.

"Such as...?"

"Family, education, any religious training..."

"I was born here in Columbus, went to public schools, got a Bachelor's in Electrical Engineering from Stanford and am now running my own robotics company. As far as religious training, I went to Sunday school a few times when I was a kid, but my parents were not of any religious denomination. I only go to Church for a wedding or funeral."

"Have you been baptized?" asked Father Rankin.

"Yes. I do remember my Dad telling me that a few times."

"So are you an atheist, Dexter?"

"I'm not really an atheist, I just don't see the point in organized religion, to tell you the truth."

"What *is* the point of organized religion?" asked Father Rankin.

"*You* are asking *me*? You're the priest, you tell me!"

"Hmm, I'm trying to think what Aquinas said about that..."

"Aquinas?"

"Aquinas was a theologian; lived in the 13th Century."

"Oh, now I know we must be talking Catholic stuff since you're referring to the Dark Ages," said Dexter with a disparaging look.

"Yes, but dark for whom?"

"For everyone! All those popes and dukes and whoever ruled with an iron hand, suppressed everyone's freedom."

"Maybe it was dark for the devil, since the Church flourished during that time period."

"Look, I may be just an illiterate engineer, but I have heard of the Spanish Inquisition, the Crusades, indulgences--you're saying that was all *good*?"

"That reminds me of a joke," said Father Rankin. "You know what you call it when a mother asks her ten-year old if he's eaten his vegetables at dinner?"

"I'm sure you'll tell me."

"The Spinach Inquisition!"

"That's hogwash!" replied Dexter, not even bothering to laugh. "Thousands of people were killed in the Spanish Inquisition and the Crusades, and you make a joke out of it!"

"All right," said Father Rankin, turning serious, "do you know how many people were killed in the Spanish Inquisition?"

"I don't know," said Dexter with a toss of his head. "At least half a million, I would think--which would be a lot for those days, considering the whole population of Europe was probably only about twenty million."

"Try eight hundred."

"Oh, *right*! What loony-tune Catholic history book did you get that from?"

"Try any serious historian of the period, my friend."

"I have a hard time believing that," said Dexter, shaking his head.

"What's more," said Father Rankin, "the Catholic Church didn't execute anyone. The Spanish government did. The Church would try the accused in court and then hand them over to the government for punishment."

"Oh, great, so some lackeys of the Church did the dirty work while the cardinals looked the other way."

"Lackeys my ass!" said Father Rankin.

A look of shock crossed Dexter's face. "Priests cuss too?"

Father Rankin dismissed it with a wave of his hand. "Hey, even in the Gospel Christ said, 'If your ass falls into a ditch on the Sabbath, wouldn't you pull it out?'"

"Somehow I think that was different."

"Look who's being all high and mighty now! Anyway, no, they weren't lackeys of the Church. They were bona fide civil servants, unconnected to the Church."

"I'm going to have to do some reading up on that before I buy any of this," said Dexter.

"Dexter, the main thing to remember about the Inquisition was that it was directed against individuals who were destroying the very fabric of society. The Catholic Faith was so much a part of the warp and woof of medieval life that any attack against it was construed as an attack against the general populace itself. Look at the 9-11 attack against the Trade Towers in New York City. Do you see anyone crying out for the rights of the poor terrorists?"

"Father Rankin, that was *totally* different! We're talking about three thousand dead people, not just some silly religious rituals."

"But that's just it," said Father Rankin. "In those days, people didn't just think of it as some 'silly religious rituals.' They thought of it as the *spiritual* death of millions of people. In their eyes, the heretics were 'killing,' if you will, many, many souls. Besides, it is an historical fact that the Spanish Inquisition was much more lenient than some of the witch hunters in England and Germany. I read somewhere that 30,000 were burned at the stake in England and 100,000 went to the stake in Germany."

"What about that Torquemada guy?" asked Dexter. He was a real piece of work. He must have killed a boatload!"

"Well, I can't remember exact numbers, but I do seem to remember that he executed something like only three percent of those who were judged by his courts. And another thing--I was reading recently that the Spanish Inquisition was considered the most merciful court in Europe. Sometimes convicts would deliberately blaspheme, just so they could be put into the prisons of the Spanish Inquisition."

"All right, all right, look--I'll have to read up on some of this. I really don't have much knowledge on the subject. But I do know a little about the Crusades. Now, tell me, Father, you really aren't going to defend them, are you? Half of Europe marches to the Middle East, kills hordes of people, ransacks cities, all in the name of regaining some holy sites."

"I have a question for you, Dexter: is anything worth dying for?"

"Sure, truth, justice, and the American Way."

"So you would die for your country?"

"I really haven't given it much thought. To tell you the truth, I'm glad I didn't have to serve in the military."

"All right, put it this way: do you think it is a noble thing for one to give one's life for his country?"

"Yes, I do. I had a friend who died in the first Iraqi war. I thought he was a cool dude. I was sorry he didn't come back."

"Well, the Crusaders gave their lives fighting for the Holy Land. Why can't we honor them for their heroic sacrifice?"

"I don't know, I mean, Iraq *invaded* Kuwait. They were torturing and killing people and stuff. The US came to right a wrong. And then in the second Iraq war, we were toppling a really evil man--or at least that's the stated reason for the war."

"Well, the Crusaders came to right a wrong also. They held the Holy Lands to be very sacred ground. The Crusaders simply wanted to keep the route to Jesus' places open for pilgrims. They too were righting a wrong--that's just it! Most people don't realize it, but the Crusades were actually a *defensive* war. For three or four hundred years before the First Crusade, Islam had been conquering country after country. By the end of the Eleventh Century, Muslims had taken two-thirds of the old Christian world. You know what really brought about the Crusades? The emperor in Constantinople called for help from the Christians of western Europe after the Turks conquered Asia Minor."

"What exactly is 'Asia Minor'?" asked Dexter.

"'Asia Minor' is modern-day Turkey."

"You still can't fool me, Father," said Dexter, shaking his head back and forth. "So, the king of some country calls on all Catholics to come to his aid. Therefore, some fat slobs from France decide to go collect a little war prize and do a little plundering along the way."

"Dexter, Dexter," said Father Rankin, a little patronizingly, forming a tight smile with his mouth. "How you *do* get suckered into the usual propaganda. The truth is that not only did the Crusaders fail to *gain* fortune on the Crusades, they often *lost* or *spent* a great deal of their treasure on the effort. It wasn't cheap to send an army three-quarters of the way across the known world. They did it as an act of faith and love in order to store up treasure for themselves in Heaven. Maybe you need to read an article by this Italian journalist I came across a few years ago: 'Messini,' or 'Messo,' something like that--no--'Messori,' yeah, that's it. Anyway, he maintains that the dark legend of the Crusades was fabricated by the architects of the Enlightenment to discredit the Catholic Church."

"Father, you say he is an Italian? Wouldn't it stand to reason that he would be a little biased in favor of the Church?"

"You'd be surprised at some of the things you read by reputedly good Catholics, Italian or not. No, from what I could see, Messori had some pretty logical things to say. One of the main points he makes is what I alluded to just now--that in Christian-Muslim conflicts throughout history, it is usually the Muslims who are the aggressor and the Church who is the defender. You know, all of North Africa was once Catholic. In the 7th Century Islam conquered those areas which had been the home and hearth of such notables as Saint Augustine. As a matter of fact, the Muslims advanced all the way up to the walls of Vienna, Austria before being turned back. You'll hear a lot of vitriol about the massacre of Muslims in Jerusalem in 1099, but many forget about the equally horrific actions of Mohammed II in Otranto, Italy in 1480."

"Ancient history," said Dexter. "What about today?"

"Glad you asked. Barbaric things are going on in northern Africa today as well. There's been a civil war in Sudan for years now, with the Christians in the South enduring most of the suffering. I've heard of slavery there as well."

"Hmm," said Dexter, "food for thought. To be honest, that's not the train of thought you get from the mainstream American media today. Let me think it over awhile."

"Pagan's privilege," said Father Rankin with smile.

"Thanks for the encouragement, guy."

"You don't have to stay a pagan forever, you know."

"Whoaa!" Dexter said, holding up both hands. "Let's not get ahead of ourselves here. This is my first time ever talking to a priest--

remember, I'm only doing this to repay your brother for his help on the freeway."

"As you wish."

They talked for another twenty minutes, then Dexter rose from his chair and walked to the door.

"Well, see you later, Dexter."

"We'll see," said Dexter as he walked out of the priest's office.

Chapter 4

"Helllll-oh!" said Kevin as he picked up the phone in his apartment. He had inherited silly ways to answer the phone from his Dad. When he had sons of his own, Kevin would expect no less from them.

"Yo, QB-boy," said Chad from the other end. "What up?"

Kevin put down the bottle of pop in his hand and sat down on the couch. "The Dow-Jones average I hope!"

"Business-boy!" replied Chad. "You don't care about Wall Street! You're a History major--cheesh! You should be hoping Barnes and Noble book sales are up."

"The more people have, the more they'll buy books. Ergo, the hopes for the stock market."

"Logic-boy! What now--philosophy?"

"Try economics."

"Enough of the idle banter…it's time you tell me about the ring."

"The ring?" Kevin wore a blank look. "Refresh my memory." He took a swig of pop and put his feet up on the coffee table.

"I offered you a wedding ring after the game--for Anne! You remember!"

"Ohhh, *thaaat*. Yes, I said I would explain."

"Bingo, bub."

"Just a second." Kevin took another drink of pop and collected his thoughts. "I'm not really sure if I'm ready for marriage."

"But you *promised* her!"

"I know, I know."

"What--are you going to lose a game just so we don't win the title, just so you don't have to marry her?"

"We're going to win the championship, Chad! Marriage or not, that title is *ours!*"

"Well why won't you take the ring I offered you? Anne would love it!"

"What if I go to the NFL next year?" asked Kevin. "I don't want to be tied down to just one girl."

"Oh, so now Anne's not good enough for you, huh?"

"That's not what I mean, it's just--nnnph! I'm only twenty-one years old! My Dad didn't get married till he was twenty-nine!"

"Kevin, chicks like Anne don't come along that often. She's a rare blend of interior *and* exterior beauty."

"True, true," said Kevin. "I can't fault you there."

"So..."

"So, why do I have to rush things? I read somewhere the other day that the average age men get married at today is twenty-seven; I've got six years left."

"Look, Kevin, if you don't think Anne is the girl for you, I'll gladly take her off your hands."

"No, no, that won't be necessary," said Kevin, shaking his head. "She's a fine woman. I'll get my act together one of these days."

"Do you love her?"

"Yes, yes...yeah, I...guess I love her. It's just that--"

"How can you *not* fall in love with someone like Anne?"

"You're right, I know."

"Kevin," said Chad, "I wish you would stop playing 'yes man' and start giving me some straight answers."

"Understood. I really like Anne, but I hesitate to say I 'love' her."

"Well, at least we're finally making some progress."

"That's why I can't accept your offer of the ring right now."

"I see."

There was silence for a few seconds.

"Don't tell that to anyone," said Kevin.

"It's in the vault," replied Chad.

"I just honestly don't know if I have the right feelings toward Anne, enough to want to marry her."

"Have you ever been in love with any girl?" asked Chad.

"Puppy love once, in high school. Nothing beyond that."

"You sure this isn't going to affect the way you play football." Chad said it without an inflection at the end.

"Definitely not. You know, this thing isn't a legal document. I said it to her once, during dinner at Baja Sol."

"So you lied to her."

"You don't give up, do you Chad?"

"Just making sure you're all right is all."

"Well, we're going to win the national championship; you can bet on that. I'll worry about marriage after that."

"Sounds good. You think Michigan is going to blitz as much as Panaski thinks they will?"

"No. They know we're expecting that."

"I hope so," said Chad. "I gotta run. See you tomorrow in 'Stones.'" Chad was taking a Geology course with Kevin, popularly known as "Stones for Drones."

"Great. And, Chad, thanks for offering the ring. Maybe I'll take you up on it next spring."

"Okay, Mr. Decisive. Let's just hope you make up your mind more quickly when you're getting blitzed this Saturday."

"See you later."

"Over and out."

****

Shen checked his AK-47, just to make sure he had a full clip. After putting on his boots, he emerged from the tent and walked over to the field table where his sergeant was poring over a map.

"If you don't mind my asking, Sarge, just exactly where are we?"

"Getting a little anxious, eh, Shen? Can't wait for the Chinese People's Liberation Army to get its act together, huh?" Sergeant Moy asked with a smile. "Don't worry, you'll be in the land of milk and honey soon enough -- but to answer your question: we're exactly thirty-two kilometers miles north of a little town known as 'Caborca,' if that means anything to you."

"Yeah, I uhh...thanks." Shen turned on his heel to see if there were any leftovers in the mess hall.

****

"Mornin', Jerry!" said Dexter as he followed him into Grobotics at the beginning of a sunny November day.

"At least you didn't say 'Good'!"

"I never pass up a chance to be honest!"

"Ain't that the truth," said Jerry.

Before heading back to the lab, he turned to Dexter. "Boss, I think I know the first step we need to take to 'cure' Bobby's vision problems, but it'll take a little travel on your part."

"Groan, sigh," said Dexter. "Give me the damage. How long, how far."

"Well, I was on the internet last night and I found a place called Sightsim."

"Exactly how do you think they can help us?" asked Dexter.

"It's the same problem as always," said Jerry. "First we went after local optimization techniques and we got stuck in irrelevant, localized details. What we're using now to help Bobby see is an exhaustive search and it simply requires too much computer memory. It looks like Sightsim can provide us with an ingenious search sequence so we don't go spraying innocent bystanders like we did at Woodward the other day."

"How much memory are we talking about eliminating?"

"We might be able to reduce it by as much as forty percent."

"Bonus!" said Dexter. "Now we're talking! Now, what about that dual lens setup you were talking to me about?"

"Oh...right!" said Jerry. He walked over to a nearby table and picked up a magazine. "I saw it in one of the trades...right...here-- yeah. The idea is to hookup two lenses for each of Bobby's eyes. It works just like the human eye: one lens focuses on the big picture, while the other focuses on the center of the image. The technical name is..." Jerry turned the page and scanned it. "Let's see, in humans, it's called the 'fovea centralis'--the part that gives precise focus in the center of the retina, and the part that gives the overall picture is the 'parafovea.'"

"Does this Sightsim place know about all this?"

"Most definitely! When I checked out their website, I made sure they were up to snuff on this stuff."

"Well," said Dexter, handing the magazine back to Jerry, "make it so. Anyway, should I call them? That's just like it sounds? One word: Sightsim?"

"Yes, yes, yes. You should have no problem finding it on the net."

"Where are they located?"

"Traverse City, Michigan," said Jerry.

"What good can come out of Traverse City, Michigan?"

"What good can come out of Columbus, Ohio?"

"You're on dangerous ground, sir," said Dexter.

"Oh, I forgot--the Buckeyes!"

"How 'bout the banana split? Did you know it was invented here?"

"Now *that's* a claim to fame!" sneered Jerry.

"Hey, the world is a brighter place because of the banana split."

"Anyway, I hope Bobby is a brighter robot because of your trip. You gonna do any fly-fishing while you're up there, Dexter? Might catch some big ones."

"Do they have that up in that part of Michigan--and at this time of year?"

"You're asking the wrong guy, boss. The only fish I ever caught were minnows--and that was with my bare hands on a Boy Scout camping trip."

"Well, I probably don't have the time for it anyway." Dexter turned around and headed to his office.

"Verin Bagh!" he said to Mrs. Downing when she put the phone down.

"What?!"

"Aha!" exclaimed Dexter. "Gotcha! Bet you don't know what language that was!"

"No fair!" said Mrs. Downing. "*I'm* supposed to give *you* the 'Good Morning' puzzle!"

"You phone, you groan, my little receptionist!" said Dexter devilishly.

"Well, I never!" said Mrs. Downing in fake indignity.

"You've got till five today to figure out what language."

"How do you spell it?"

"Just like it sounds: Verin Bagh." He spelled it out for her then walked into his office. After studying Sightsim's website, Dexter gave the head of engineering at Sightsim a call and set up a time to see him the following week.

He picked up the phone and dialed Mrs. Downing's extension. "I'll be flying to Traverse City, Michigan next Tuesday and Wednesday, returning Wednesday. Better book me into a hotel for Tuesday night."

"Fine," she said. "You sure you spelled Verin Bagh right? I can't find it anywhere!"

"How soon we give up, milady! Do you think I would give you an easy one?"

"Why do I deal with such men!" She pretended to slam the phone down.

Dexter chuckled and turned to his computer to investigate Sightsim a little more closely.

****

The Michigan game. *The* Game. It defined Columbus as did no other event in the Capital City. Every football team had its archrival, but few contests reached the level of intensity of the OSU/Michigan "event." Already over one hundred years old, the contest was often called the greatest rivalry in college sports--even the greatest rivalry in *all* of sports. This year it would be played in venerable Ohio Stadium, the beloved horseshoe-shaped arena affectionately known as "the Shoe." Prognosticators were predicting an attendance record, with some soothsayers projecting a crowd of over one hundred and seven thousand. The Buckeye fans were out in force this November Saturday, covering the Ohio State campus like bees on a hive. With OSU ranked first and Michigan third in most of the national polls, all eyes were focused on this matchup, since the winner would undoubtedly end up in the national championship game in January. The weather added its vote of confidence by giving Columbus a clear blue sky and strong golden sunlight.

The kickoff came as advertised at precisely ten minutes after noon, and the long awaited gridiron game was underway. The Buckeyes returned the kickoff to their thirty-five yard line and Kevin Conaway trotted out to begin his last game in Ohio Stadium.

"All right, guys," he said as the team huddled around him, "Panaski's feeling cocky today. First play is gonna be Alpha Strike Five to Platwood."

"He wants to throw a bomb on the *first* play?" asked Chad, astonished.

"You got it," said Kevin. "Everyone ready?"

The OSU offense broke from the huddle and lined up, trying not to smile as they looked into the faces of the Michigan defense.

"Fifty-five blue, HIKE!" yelled Kevin. He took the ball and dropped back, staying in the pocket until he saw his talented receiver break inside, thirty yards away. Just as a Michigan tackle was about to sack him, he threw the ball toward Platwood. Platwood reached out, snagged the pigskin without having to break stride, and ran into the end zone! Pandemonium would be too tame a word to describe the reaction of the merry multitude of crazed Buckeye fans as Platwood crossed the goal line! A group of about twenty students even tried to run onto the field before being chased away by some state troopers. The OSU offensive line swarmed around Kevin and practically carried him off the field on their shoulders.

"We still have fifty-nine minutes to go!" he kept telling his players. "Not so fast!"

Kevin high-fived Platwood when he got to the sideline, then thanked Coach Panaski. "You're a genius, Coach! How'd you know they'd fall for that one?"

"Hey, thank Coach Dunter," replied Panaski, pointing to the Offensive coordinator. "It was his idea!" He slapped Kevin on the helmet. "Don't relax yet, we've only begun to fight!"

Michigan came back and scored on their first possession, which quickly quieted the crowd. It became a tug-of-war after that, with each team responding in kind when the other scored either a touchdown or a field goal. With ninety seconds left in the game, the score was OSU 20, Michigan 21. Ohio State had the ball on the Michigan twenty-four yard line. When Kevin lined up to take the snap, he could sense a blitz and called a timeout, leaving his team with only one for the rest of the game.

"What's the problem?" asked Panaski when Kevin reached the

sideline.

"They were going to blitz and I didn't think we were set up right."

"Why didn't you audible?"

"We only had one guy in the backfield--I didn't want to risk it."

"Remember, just don't turn it over. It's a chip shot for Whinney right now. OSU's field-goal kicker was second in the nation in completion percentage and had saved the Buckeyes more than once that season.

"Right-I got it," said Kevin. "What do you say we do now? How 'bout a quarterback draw? They'd never expect it."

"Maybe on third down. Right now, go with the option. They won't expect that either."

"But we haven't used it since last week!" protested Kevin.

"Therefore it'll catch them off guard."

"All right. Jason," Kevin turned toward his trusted running back. "You okay with that?"

"Rock on," said Jason. "Just like in practice!" They ran back onto the field and got into their stances.

"Twenty-two, hike, HIKE, HIKE!" Kevin grabbed the ball from the center and rolled left. He looked downfield for Platwood, but neither he nor any other receiver was open. He looked behind the line of scrimmage, and--*there he is!* Kevin dumped the ball off to Jason and watched as the talented running back chewed up twelve yards, getting a first down before being manhandled to the ground by two Michigan players.

"It *worked!*" shouted Jason, grinning from ear to ear as he joined the huddle.

"Like a knife through warm butter!" said Kevin. The ball was now on the twelve yard line and the clock was stopped at forty-four seconds. A player came running out from the side of the field with the play from Panaski.

"Coach said run a trap to the right--nothing fancy, keep it in the middle of the field."

The trap gained two yards and the next play, a simple "up the gut", gained three more. It was third and five with thirty seconds left. The coach called a timeout and motioned the offense over to the sideline.

"We're going with Landmark Seven," Panaski said matter-of-factly.

"Coach!" cried Kevin. "It's too risky! All we need is a field goal!"

"We can't give them the chance to beat us with a field goal when they get the ball back--they still have two timeouts left," replied Panaski evenly. "Now, let's go. Landmark Seven."

Kevin snapped his chinstrap on and jogged out to the line of scrimmage. Chad lined up on his left.

"Deck one, deck two, hike, HIKE!" yelled Kevin. He handed the ball off to Chad, who then dropped back to pass. Chad pump-faked to Platwood, who was double-covered in the right corner of the end-zone. All alone in the left corner of the end-zone was Quinn, the other tight end. As if he had been doing it for his whole career, Chad floated the ball to Quinn, who hauled it in and scored the touchdown!

Kevin and Chad ran over to Quinn and they all shared a triumvirate-bear hug!

"Chad for President! Chad for President!" shouted Kevin.

"Quinn is King! Quinn is King!" Chad was meanwhile yelling into the tight end's ear.

"Out of the end-zone, you meatheads!" Quinn shouted back, pushing his teammates toward the bench. "There's still twenty seconds left!"

After the extra point, the score stood at OSU 27, Michigan 21.

Michigan wasn't through quite yet, however. They took the kickoff to their forty-five yard line, gained twelve yards on their first play, then immediately called a timeout.

"Now you see why I didn't want to settle for a field goal?" the head coach said to Kevin.

"You are all-knowing, Coach!" said Kevin.

On the next play, with twelve seconds left, Michigan threw the ball to their receiver, who caught it, and stepped out of bounds, stopping the clock. There were now only three seconds left. The ball was on the eleven-yard line. Michigan went to a spread offense and hiked the ball. Their quarterback lofted the ball into a jumble of jostling players in the end zone. A Michigan player got a hand on the ball, knocking it up. It was headed right for the hands of another Wolverine, when an OSU cornerback reached in and batted it to the ground!

Not since Lindbergh landed in Paris did a crowd go as wild as did that in Ohio Stadium that afternoon! The goalposts were spared since a group of pepper-spraying state troopers surrounded each one. This didn't dampen the enthusiasm of the Buckeye minions as they crowded onto the sardine-packed field. The OSU band had somehow managed to start playing 'Carmen Ohio' and one hundred thousand fans joined in for a tone-deaf rendition of the beloved Buckeye ballad.

****

   "I like your dress, Anne," said Kevin after they had ordered from the menu. They were at Spain Restaurant, a cozy little place on Dublin-Granville Road, which Kevin had first learned about from his Entertainment coupon book. Kevin would often take Anne to dinner on Saturday nights, after which they would usually go to a team victory party.
   "Thanks," said Anne, brushing the hair out of her eyes. "My Mom made it for me."
   "Really! Nice job! How does she find the time? She still works at that marketing company, right?"
   "That's right. Oh, I don't know, since I'm the youngest, she doesn't have any more kids to take up her time."
   "I see. Huh…kids," said Kevin.
   "What about kids?"
   "I would like four kids, myself, so we can play bridge."
   "Well, if both of us play, then we only need two kids."
   "Or we could go for the national average and have two-point-three kids."
   "That sounds fine with me," said Anne, nodding her head.
   "Naw, four minimum."
   "First things first," said Anne with a smile. "How about we have the reception at Confluence Park?"
   "Uhh." Kevin took a drink from the water glass and broke off a piece of bread."
   "'Uhh' what?"
   "Well, you know, we're not really engaged yet--I don't want to jump the gun."
   "Look who's jumping the gun, Mr. 'four kid minimum.'"
   "That was just theorizing…statistics."

"Now kids are just 'statistics'?" asked Anne.

Kevin held up his hand. "That didn't come out right. Kids are important, don't get me wrong."

"All right, then how 'bout we honeymoon in Hawaii?"

"Hawaii? That's pretty expensive, isn't it?"

"You're going to be making a million dollars in the NFL, aren't you? I would think you could afford Hawaii."

"That's true...yeah...uh, but Hawaii, you sure you'd like to go *there*?"

"Yeah, I would like to go to Hawaii," said Anne with a little dismay. "What's wrong with you anyway? You seem a bit hesitant about all this."

Should I tell her? Kevin asked himself. *No, a smokescreen will do.* He grinned at her and touched her hand. "Sorry, Anne, I'm just a little preoccupied with winning a national championship. You know how it goes."

"*That's* the Kevin Conaway I know," Anne said triumphantly.

I can't keep lying to her like this, Kevin thought to himself as he gave her a weak smile. After dessert and coffee, Kevin paid the bill and then they went to a party at one of the players' apartments.

****

A week had passed since Dexter's first talk with Father Rankin, and Dexter had, on a whim, decided to pay the priest a second visit, more out of curiosity than anything else. Dexter walked up to the office door at Saint Michael Church, rang the doorbell, and was ushered in by the parish secretary. After exchanging pleasantries with her, he strode to Father Rankin's closed office door and knocked.

"Come in!" said Fr Rankin, tidying up the papers on his desk before turning his chair toward the couch.

"It's just me," said Dexter, closing the door behind him, "the lost and black and wandering lamb."

"Ahh, but aren't they the most interesting!"

"Interesting, yes. Valuable, no."

"Spoken like a true black sheep."

"Baa-ahh-ahh."

"Anything of note happen this week, Dexter?"

"Actually, I took up pole vaulting and set a world record. However, since there were no witnesses, my name won't be in any official records."

"Surely you videotaped it?"

"Oh, of course, but the rules committee doesn't accept digital 8 tapes, only regular 8 millimeter."

"Pity."

"What about you, Father? You set any world records--in preaching, maybe?"

"I heard Confessions for twenty-eight hours straight, but, just like you it wasn't accepted."

"No videotape?"

"That would break the seal of Confession."

"Tsk. Hey," said Dexter, sitting up straight, "I was thinking: I told you all about myself last week--what about you? Were you born with a black suit on and that white thing around your neck?"

"Oh," said Father Rankin, "you mean this Roman collar?"

"So that's what they call it. Yeah, what church pew did you fall out of? You were probably one of those kids who never even farted when he was young, right?"

"Ah, my misguided man, far from it! I rumbled with the best of them when I was young. I had a sports car, girlfriend--I even had my own airplane!"

Dexter shook his head back and forth. "Huh? *You*? I thought you had to take the virtue of poverty."

"The *vow* of poverty. Actually as a diocesan priest I only take the vows of chastity and obedience, although I would have taken the vow of poverty had I joined Mother Theresa's order of priests."

"I thought she died a few years ago. Wait a minute, she had *nuns*, not *priests*!"

"Most people don't know it," said Father Rankin, "but she started an order of priests as well, the Missionaries of Charity Fathers. I was a seminarian in that order for eight years."

"Eight years? Weren't you made a priest by then?"

"The word is ordained. No, I left before I was ordained and became a diocesan priest instead."

"Why weren't you ordained in that order?"

"Looking back, it wasn't meant to be. I'm much happier being here in my hometown, and besides, the United States is in dire need of priests as it is."

"So what's this about the airplane and girlfriend?"

"I worked at Ford as an engineer for ten years before entering the Missionaries of Charity. I bought a house, a car, and all the rest that goes with a young American male."

"Was she pretty?"

"The girl? Darn right she was pretty! And gracious as well."

"What kind of plane did you have?"

"A Mooney 201."

"A Mooney! All I've got is a Cessna!"

"Oh," said Father Rankin, "you've got a plane?"

"Yeah, a Cessna Skyhawk."

"Ever crashed?"

"Huh?"

"Have you ever crashed in it?"

"No, why?"

"I came close once. Before I had my instrument rating I flew into some clouds up around Toledo. I almost didn't come out of that alive."

"What did you do?"

"Luckily, I remained calm. I flew on instruments and landed at the first airport I could find."

"Lucky you."

"You got a motorcycle?"

"Huh? What is it with this interrogation mode?"

"I just wondered if you owned a motorcycle."

"Actually, no. I never was attracted to one."

"I had a beauty--a Harley-Davidson Softail with an Evolution engine. I rode to Alaska on it one summer."

"Really?"

"Really. I think most of the time I was in my twenties I was just searching for more meaning in my life. A motorcycle trip to Alaska seemed a good substitute for the priesthood at the time."

"Speaking of searching for meaning in life, that brings up this week's topic." Dexter pulled out his appointment book and sat up. "One word this week, Padre, one word."

"Guilt?"

"We'll get to that. This week: Hell."

"Curious," said Fr Rankin. "I was wondering when that might come up."

"Well I generally don't like to think about it, but I thought I'd get it off my chest."

"Hey, I know where you're coming from, Dexter. Most people would just as soon deny the existence of Hell, or at least deny that there are more than eight people there. That reminds me of a poll I heard about. They asked people in Iowa if they thought they themselves were going to Hell. Only five percent said yes. Then they asked them if they knew *anyone else* who was going to Hell. This time, *ninety-three* percent of the respondents said yes! It's sort of hilarious when you think about it."

"Sounds similar to another story I heard about," said Dexter. "They did the same type of poll but this time the question was about peoples' lawyers. First they asked the people what they thought of lawyers in general. Most of the pollees agreed that the great majority of lawyers were evil. Then they asked each person what they thought of *their own* lawyer. 'Oh, he's great!' just about all of them said!"

Fr Rankin chuckled and nodded his head in agreement. "That's good, that's good Dexter."

"So anyway, what about Hell?"

"Well, what about it?"

"Well," said Dexter, clenching his teeth and pressing his lips together, "I don't think anyone should go to Hell! I thought 'God is love' and all that. What's the point? What--does God say: OK, you've been bad, now get away from me, you idiot!"

"Let's begin with official Church teaching," said Fr Rankin. "What does the Church teach about who's in Heaven and who's in Hell? Well, to begin with, the only thing we know with absolute certainty is that a person who is canonized a Saint by the Catholic Church is definitely in Heaven. That's all we know for certain."

"Great! So no one is in Hell!"

"I didn't say that."

"So there *are* people in Hell."

"The Church simply states that we don't know. However, what we know from private revelation and the lives of the Saints is another story."

"Help," said Dexter in a weak voice.

"Hold on! Some of it's good news! Don't lose heart. Have you heard of Medjugorje?"

"What's that?"

"Medjugorje is a small town in former Yugoslavia. The Blessed Mother has been appearing there since 1981."

"You mean, like, a bright light and choirs of angels singing?"

"Not quite like you might see in the movies. She appeared to a group of quite normal teen-agers. Well, anyway, she told one of the visionaries about Heaven and Hell and Purgatory."

"What was that?"

"Oh, yes, Purgatory. It's basically the doormat to Heaven. It's the place where you are purified before entering Heaven. Anyway, the Blessed Mother revealed to this guy, it was a boy if I'm not mistaken, that the majority of souls go to Purgatory, the next greatest number go to Hell, and a small number go straight to Heaven, without passing through Purgatory first."

"So," said Dexter, "some people *do* go to Hell."

"Well, I should tell you about some of the saints. For instance, Saint Theresa of Avila said she had a vision of quite a number of souls falling into Hell. I forget her exact words, but it was something like 'I saw souls falling into Hell like leaves from a tree in autumn.' I get her confused with another Saint who compared it to snowflakes in winter."

"That's all I needed to hear. Thanks for the cheery news."

"Would you rather have learned that now or a hundred years from now?"

"I wish the whole thing would just go away. I wish--you know what I wish? I wish it was just complete annihilation, just one big wipeout when we die. With your way, the good people go to Heaven or Purgatory and the idiots go to Hell. Look, please answer my question-- what is the point of Hell? I'm still not satisfied."

"Let's see," Fr Rankin said as he arose from his chair. "I believe it was Garrigou-Lagrange that said it." He walked over to his bookcase and pulled out a medium-sized paperback.

"Gary Goo?"

"Reginald is his first name; Garrigou-Lagrange is his last name. Famous Dominican writer who died around 1960. He wrote this book-- it's titled 'Everlasting Life - A Theological Treatise on the Four Last Things - Death, Judgment, Heaven, Hell.' Here it is! On page one-oh-seven, he says: 'First of all, we admit that this eternity of suffering cannot be demonstrated apodictically.' Apodictically means logically.

He goes on to say: 'Why? Because it is a revealed mystery, a mystery of justice which is the consequence of a mystery of iniquity, namely, of mortal sin that remains without repentance.'"

"Uhh, what was that?" asked Dexter.

"Basically, Garrigou is saying that the eternity of Hell cannot be demonstrated logically, like a math equation. He says that it is a mystery which God has shown to us."

"You know, are we really going anywhere in this discussion?" asked Dexter. "Just about the time I thought I was going to get a good answer to my questions you pull out the 'mystery' thing."

"You mean what I just read from Garrigou?"

"Right! How's that supposed to help me? I want answers, not mysteries!"

"Dexter, did you see the Lord of the Rings movies?"

"Yeah."

"Do you remember the scene in 'The Fellowship of the Ring' where Gandalf was talking to Frodo just before they entered the Mines of Moria?"

"I only saw it once--you'll have to fill me in."

"I have a friend who's seen every Tolkien movie like, five times, or something, and we were talking about it just last week. Anyway, Gandalf was responding to Frodo's complaints about all the hardship they were experiencing. Gandalf had some very interesting things to say. My friend was quoting it to me almost verbatim, but the gist of it was that we cannot decide what happens to us; we can only decide what to do with the time that is given to us. I think our age has too much of a tendency to question everything instead of simply trying to do the Will of God."

"Father, the guy who wrote 'The Two Towers' was a Catholic-- whaddya expect from him?"

"True, but, see--now you're questioning again."

"Enquiring minds need to know."

"How about 'humble minds need to serve'?"

"What's that from?"

"I just made it up."

"So where does that leave us?" asked Dexter.

"Well, I think the point is that we will never fully understand the logic of the eternity of Hell, at least in this life. I suppose the point is to try like Hell to avoid Hell."

"Don't you mean 'try like Heaven to avoid Hell'?"

"Very good, Dexter," said Father Rankin with a smile. "You're learning."

"Well, that helps a little, but I still can't quite accept sending someone to Hell forever."

"I'll tell you what, Dexter. Pray to the Holy Spirit for enlightenment."

"What if I don't believe in the Holy Spirit?"

"Oh boy," said Fr Rankin. "Looks like we have next week's topic already set."

"Oh, Lord, make me a Catholic, but not yet," mumbled Dexter.

"Very good, Dexter!" said Father Rankin with a big grin. "How did you know Saint Augustine said that--or a version of that?"

"Hey, bro, I've read a few things besides engineering textbooks in my life."

"Well, that's a start. You can't deny Saint Augustine existed. It's an historical fact. You can pray to him!"

"Heck, *prayer*," said Dexter, slightly derisively. "Opium for the masses."

They touched on a few other issues, then Dexter stood up and gathered his notes.

"Just keep on praying to the Holy Spirit, okay?" asked Father Rankin.

"It's a deal, holy-man," said Dexter on his way out the door. "I just might see you again after Thanksgiving."

"Bye, Dexter."

Dexter drove home and went right to bed. He was up at six and put in a call for Thad to pick him up in twenty minutes. He had just finished a quick bowl of cereal when he heard the taxi's horn. Dexter grabbed his suitcase and walked out to the curb.

"Glad you could give me a ride on such short notice, Thad," said Dexter as he handed his bag to Thad.

"I just happened to be sitting around in Arlington when you called; I wasn't far away." Thad put the suitcase into the trunk and climbed into the driver's seat. He turned around to face Dexter, who had just slammed the back door. "Sorry for the inconvenience, but you might want to check your door--sometimes it doesn't shut right."

Dexter pushed on the door and it flew open. "Whoa! Good thing you told me that."

"Yeah," said Thad, "just push the inside door release to the closed position and it should latch."

Dexter followed his instructions and the door closed tightly. "There. That should do it."

"Great! You might want to put on your seat belt, too, just to be extra safe." Satisfied that his passenger was secure, Thad backed out of the driveway and headed in the direction of the highway. "Just curious--why don't you just drive your own car up to Don Scott? Isn't parking free there, since it's the Ohio State airport?"

"Uhh," began Dexter, "Daphne--that's my girlfriend--needs to use my car when I'm gone, since her license tags expired. She forgot to renew them."

"Oh--just wondering," said Thad lightly. "Oh, yeah--I hear from my brother that you chatted with him the other day."

"Hey, a deal's a deal, pal," said Dexter with a trace of irritation. "Thanks for the help on the freeway, but I don't really know if I'll be making a habit out of talking with a priest, even though he's your brother."

"Hmm," said Thad with a trace of a smile on his lips, "my brother made it sound like you'd be meeting him again."

"Well, yeah, I didn't exactly slam the door in his face, but we'll see what happens."

"Did you get a chance..." Thad paused to slow down when someone pulled out in front of him. "Did you get a chance to read that brochure I gave you?"

"What bro--oh, uhh, no I didn't get a chance..."

"Did you throw it out?" asked Thad innocently.

"Whaa?"

"No problem, here's another." Thad passed a brightly colored brochure back to Dexter, who reluctantly took it.

"I think you'll find its contents quite informative, really," said Thad. "Garabandal is a small town on the northern edge of Spain, near France. The Blessed Mother appeared there from 1961 to 1965 to four young girls. She told the girls that there would be three great events in the 'near' future. I say 'near,' but that means roughly a span of about fifty years. She said there would be a Warning, which could happen anytime. Next will be the Miracle, and after that the Chastisement."

"Exactly what did she predict about this 'Warning,' as you call it?"

"She predicted a worldwide illumination of consciences. I believe I also remember the term 'correction of the conscience of the world.'"

"Sounds like a recipe for mass hallucination," said Dexter.

"Well, there won't be any mistaking the Miracle; everyone will believe that. Mary said that every person will *know* that the Miracle is of divine origin."

"Fine, you can tell me all about the Miracle sometime, but back to this Warning thing. You say it will correct the conscience of the world? What exactly is wrong with the world's conscience? Are we really all that bad?"

"I suppose it all depends how you view the world," said Thad. "From the Catholic point of view, we've got a lot of work to do."

"Name names," said Dexter.

"Abortion, euthanasia, sins of the flesh, for starters."

"Oh, come on, guy! Get with the program! There have always been abortion and--whatever name you gave to those sins."

"Not on the scale we've got today! We abort thirty-four hundred babies *every day* in this country. And that's not counting the rest of the world."

"They're *fetuses*, not *babies*!"

Thad turned onto Riverside Drive and turned around to glance at his passenger. "Look, Dexter, what about *you*? What needs to be corrected about *your conscience?*"

"Ahh, hell," said Dexter, pressing back into his seat and joining his hands on top of his head. "I don't know if I really want to discuss that right now."

"I respect your privacy and all that, but I just want to point out that the Warning could be somewhat shocking, right? I mean, you can at least admit *that*...?"

"Yeah, yeah," Dexter sighed. "Maybe, maybe," he said in a low voice.

There was silence for a minute or two, each man lost in his thoughts, watching the trees along the Scioto River slide by the windows.

"So, on the lighter side, where are you headed?" asked Thad.

"I'm going to Traverse City, Michigan, of all places."

"What's in Traverse City?"

"Well, you see, our company makes robots and I'm going to check out a company which specializes in vision systems. I talked with one of their engineers and he thought it best if I visit their factory to hammer out the details of some custom components we want them to make for us."

"Which components?"

"Huh?" asked Dexter.

"I was just curious what parts you need."

"Are you sure you're not an industrial spy?" Dexter asked with a smile.

"Yeah, actually Orange Cabs wants to replace all of us drivers with robots. I thought I'd help them along a little." Thad grinned back at Dexter. "Actually I have a degree in Engineering, so I have some interest in these types of things." Thad briefly explained his insomnia/disability problem to Dexter.

"So you don't expect to be driving a cab permanently?"

"No," said Thad. "I hope to get back into my field one of these days."

"Terrific! Anyway, the vision system we now have has trouble distinguishing the bad guy from the innocent bystanders. We're trying to get Bobby to lock onto one person and stay locked on. Last time we demo-ed the robot he accidentally sprayed this pepper solution at two women who were watching."

"Who's Bobby?"

"Oh," said Dexter with a chuckle. "I tend to forget when I'm not talking with a company colleague. Bobby is the name of our security robot--'Robocop' if you will, although that name's been taken."

"I get it! Like the police in England--they call them 'Bobbies,' right"?

"Very good, Thad! You drive a taxi in London too?"

"No, my uncle took me to Europe when I graduated from high school. I just remember a few of their slang terms."

"I see."

They lapsed into silence again and in a few minutes were on Case Road, which led to the Ohio State University Airport.

"Which building?" asked Thad.

"Those low-slung blue T-hangars over there." Dexter pointed in the general direction of the control tower.

Thad pulled up to the hangars, stopped the meter, went back to the trunk and deposited Dexter's suitcase on the sidewalk.

Dexter handed Thad thirty dollars. "I presume that'll cover it?"

"Hey, thanks!" said Thad. "You're quite the generous tipper today!"

"Don't mention it, my friend."

"I won't."

"You won't what?" asked Dexter with a quizzical look.

"I won't mention it."

"Back in your cab, joke-boy! With the tip I gave you I should be spared such deleterious humor!"

"Enjoy your flight," said Thad with a laugh and drove off in his cab.

Dexter's flight to Michigan was routine and he landed at Cherry Capital Airport ten minutes ahead of schedule, thanks to a lighter than expected headwind. He took a cab to his hotel and spent the next day with Chip Booster, Sightsim's Head of Engineering. Dexter was impressed by Sightsim's expertise in search algorithms and promised Chip that he would get back to him soon--he just had to check a few things with Jerry back in Columbus. Chip gave Dexter a ride out to the airport, where Dexter couldn't help but give him a quick tour of the airplane, his pride and joy.

"Nice set of wings, Dexter! I just might ask our board if I can get my hands on one of these. I'll just have to cook up a few numbers to show how much money we can supposedly save."

"The hassle you save at the airport is worth it, let me tell you," said Dexter.

"I can believe it. Good luck with those search routines!" He waved to Dexter and drove off in his car.

Dexter opened up the airplane's side door and deposited his suitcase inside. After checking the oil, he called the fuel truck. While waiting for the gas he looked over his sectionals to make sure he had all the proper frequencies he would need for the three hour flight. The truck filled his tanks and he paid with his credit card. Next he preflighted the plane, taking special care to check for water in the fuel. Too much of that could cause the engine to stop. Satisfied that his Cessna 172 was ready for flight, he climbed into the cockpit, flipped a few switches and looked around to make sure no one was near the propeller.

He opened his side window and said "Clear!" in a loud voice.

The starter motor whirred and the engine purred to life. It was one of the events of a flight Dexter liked most--the engine had started and now flight was only a matter of time. He taxied to the active runway, called the tower and was given clearance to takeoff. He taxied onto Runway twenty-eight and applied full throttle. Twenty seconds later he was off the ground, climbing at seven hundred feet per minute. He turned to a heading of one-sixty, as dictated by his GPS unit and leveled off at his cruising altitude of three thousand, five hundred feet. He thought he would fly low and enjoy the scenery. After turning on the autopilot Dexter pulled out the issue of The New York Times that he had brought from Columbus and settled in for the trip back. Occasionally he checked the heading and altitude, just to be sure the autopilot was working properly. Once near Detroit and again near Toledo, he had to check in with each city's approach control. The weather was picture-perfect-clear and the flight was uneventful until he was passing over Lima, Ohio. The engine began to sputter and the tachometer dipped dangerously when Dexter looked at it.

"What the h-?!" he said aloud as he tossed the newspaper onto the passenger seat.

The engine coughed once and then just as soon ran smoothly.

Dexter paused briefly to make sure there were no other problems, then visibly relaxed.

"There, that's better," he reassured himself. He picked up the paper and was about to finish the article on arctic geology that he had been reading when the engine gave a loud belch and then stopped completely!

"Son of a bitch!" Dexter yelled. He instinctively turned on carburetor heat and pushed the mixture to full rich.

"Hell, what now?" he said, wracking his memory for the correct procedure for an emergency landing. He slowed the airplane to best glide speed, eighty knots, then pressed the "Nearest" button on his GPS. It pointed him to Wyandot County Airport, which Dexter surmised was near the town of Upper Sandusky. *Let's see,* he reasoned, *it shows that Wyandot County is five-point-two miles away...what's the best glide rate a 172 can do? Twelve to one? That means I can glide--*"Wheee!" Dexter's thoughts were interrupted by the blare of the stall horn, warning him he was on the edge of losing lift under his wings. He quickly pushed the nose of the plane down and watched as the airspeed indicator crept back up into the green arc.

Watch it, Dexter! he scolded himself. *You can't afford to stall the wings with your engine out! Now...where was I? I'm...how far up am I?* He shot a glance at his altimeter. *Shoot! Now I'm only three thousand feet up! The elevation around here is about one-thousand...that means I'm actually only two thousand feet above the ground...so two thousand feet of altitude multiplied by a glide ratio of twelve...I can glide twenty-four thousand feet, which is about... a little less than five miles.* He wiped the sweat off his face and dried his hands on his shirt. *And the GPS says I'm...let's see...shoot! I'm going the wrong way! Now I'm five-point-four-miles from the nearest airport! I can't make it!* He spotted a smooth and relatively long farm field off to the left. *Looks like I'm going to have to put it down right there,* he concluded. He circled around to lose altitude, but just as he turned "final," when he was up about five hundred feet, the engine suddenly burst back to life!

"What is going on? This is crazy!" he shouted to the empty cockpit. *What the hell?!* thought Dexter. *I might as well try to make it back to Columbus.* He brought the flaps up and established a ninety-knot climb. *What if I had been flying on instruments?* he wondered to himself.

"You'd be dead meat," his conscience told him.

"You might be right," he replied.

"Single engine, single chance," his conscience replied.

It was only after he was safely back at altitude that he took the time to reply to the air traffic controller who had been calling him. Dexter explained the reason for his unorthodox loss of altitude and assured the controller that he would not be declaring an emergency.

Dexter monitored the GPS for the rest of the trip, taking note of the airports closest to his flight path. He landed safely back at the OSU airport and taxied back to his hangar. When he got home that evening, he called Bill Long, his trusted mechanic and asked him to weigh in on the engine failure.

"Sounds all the world like your fuel filter," said Bill.

"You've seen this before?" asked Dexter.

"At least three times, yeah. Most recent time I remember was in 2007. A 152 did exactly what you did, only his engine quit over downtown Columbus. You're lucky yours quit out in the boonies."

"What happened to that guy?"

"Same as you--engine restarted just in the nick of time."

"What happens if you're in the clouds and the engine quits?" asked Dexter.

"Hey, that's why I fly a twin, bud. They come with a built-in insurance policy."

"Well, give me a ring when you've given it a look," said Dexter. "I left the keys with the FBO people."

"Right. Have a good Thanksgiving…you doing any traveling?"

"You too, Bill…no, I'm staying right here."

"See you later!"

"Bye."

Chapter 5

Although things were hopping at Grobotics after the long Thanksgiving weekend, Dexter was able to slip away for another meeting with Father Rankin on Monday. It wasn't so much that he was falling for any of "that religious idiocy" as he'd come to call it, but that he liked the mental sparring he could do with this man of the cloth. As Dexter drove onto the entrance ramp to the freeway, he pressed the accelerator to the floor and let the Charger's 6.1 liters rocket him into the fast lane of Route 315. *It sure is nice to have the power when you need it,* he comforted himself. He remembered a friend of his back in college who lamented the "mouse power," as he termed it, of his small Japanese import. *Yep*, Dexter concluded, *there are few problems in the world which can't be cured by a day of driving a Charger.* He liked to use that expression when people complimented him on his car--he didn't think he needed to reveal to them that he actually appropriated it from a bumper sticker he once saw in California which promised the same medicinal help from a day of surfing. *Maybe I* should *try surfing sometime*, he suggested to himself. *Maybe on my next vacation, I'll---*. His thoughts were interrupted by the ringing of his cell phone.

Dexter unclasped it from his belt holder and glanced at the incoming number. "Restricted," it read.

"Hello?"

"Is this the robot magnate?"

"This is Dexter Griffith, who's this, please?"

"Is this the owner and CEO of Grobotics?"

Dexter didn't like the way this was going. "Before I give out anymore information, could I please ask who I'm speaking to?"

"At the present that won't be necessary, Dexter. We just wanted to let you know that we admire the work you do and we've concluded that you're probably worth a lot of money."

"Sir," said Dexter, changing the phone to his right hand and slowing down to get into the right lane, "if you would like to talk about a robot you might possibly need, that's fine. Could you please tell me your name and company?"

"Oh, yeah. My name's Mr. Trepidation and my company is Swindle, Incorporated."

Dexter had had about enough. "Look, Mr. --whatever your *real* name is: if you want to talk to me seriously, call me at my office number, OK? I'm busy right now."

There was no reply.

"Hello? Hello?" Dexter pulled the cell phone away from his ear and pushed the "end" button.

"Great," said Dexter. "All I needed was a crank call to get me in the right frame of mind to talk to this priest."

Five minutes later he turned into Saint Michael's parking lot and found his way into Father Rankin's office.

"Greetings," said Father Rankin, closing the door behind Dexter.

"Greetings, yourself."

"Anything new in the world of robots I should know about?"

"I just had a crank call on my cell phone on the way here...I'm still trying to figure it out...but, yeah, Bobby is coming along just fine, though we still have a long way to go."

"Have a seat," said Father Rankin, gesturing to the one by his coffee table. "What's this about a phone call? You do seem a bit absent-minded at the moment." Father Rankin put his pipe in his mouth and lit it, then sat down across from Dexter.

"I really don't know what it's about, to be honest," said Dexter. "This guy gives me some fake name--at least I'm pretty sure it was fake--and then he tells me how he likes Grobotics and that I'm worth a lot of money."

"Was it a potential customer?"

"That's what I thought at first, but I have a bad feeling about the guy. His tone was sort of, of, sort of cynical, would probably be the best adjective I could give to describe him."

"Did you possibly recognize his voice--hey! Maybe it's in your list of called numbers on your cell!"

"No," said Dexter dejectedly, "I already checked and it was a totally untraceable call."

"Hmm." Father Rankin lit his pipe again and took a few long pulls on it till he was convinced it would stay lit. "But at least the robots are coming along fine, you say."

"Yeah," said Dexter, scratching his head, "we've got another demo coming up in a week or so. Hopefully this time we manage to spray the bad-guy-targets instead of some innocent bystanders."

"I take it it didn't go so great last time?"

Dexter explained to Father Rankin the demo wherein Bobby accidentally sprayed two of the women in the crowd at the Woodward Company. He also explained the origin of the 'Bobby' moniker.

"So you expect 'Bobby' to do better this time?"

"Well, we've installed a new vision system in him, so I don't know what else could go wrong."

"The melding of mind and machine has only the Creator seen," recited Father Rankin.

"What's that from?"

"An obscure poet from the 20s--David Albertson, British. You've heard of him?"

"Uhh, can't seem to recall the name. What was the name of the poem?"

Father Rankin took a pull on his pipe before replying. "The name escapes me, but I do know he wrote it in reaction to Karel Capek's stage play *R.U.R.*"

"Rossum's Universal Robot's!" said Dexter excitedly. "You really *are* a well-informed cleric, if I may say so. Capek's play is basic philosophy for a roboticist like me."

"Hey, you hang around enough engineers for ten years like I did, you tend to pick up this kind of stuff."

"Bet you can't tell me the name of the starring female character."

"Helena Glory, right?"

"Mighty impressive, padre! I thought all you altar-types knew about was the Bible."

"Hey, priests kick ass, my friend! Grace builds on nature," said Father Rankin. "A sound mind in a sound body. Christ was an excellent carpenter long before he ever started preaching."

"Speaking of the Bible, I have some questions." Dexter opened his notebook and flipped through the pages.

"We're getting to the main event so quickly!"

"I believe your quote is 'humble minds need to serve'? I'm just trying to be a humble mind."

"That reminds me of a joke," said Father Rankin, leaning forward and putting his pipe on the coffee table. "There's this bishop who keeps hearing edifying reports about this very humble nun who lives in his diocese. He keeps hearing so much praise for her that one day he decides to visit her convent and see for himself just how humble she really is. He knocks on the door of the convent and a nun opens the door a little and asks, 'Can I help you?' The bishop asks if he could speak to the humble nun he's heard so much about. The nun swings the door wide open, lifts up her arms and exclaims: 'That's me, Bishop!'"

"Heh-heh, that's pretty good," said Dexter with a chuckle. "She must have been awfully 'proud' of her humility."

"But not to interrupt your humble mind trying to serve," said Father Rankin, gesturing toward Dexter's notebook. "Hear, hear, let the questioning begin!"

"The Rapture."

"The Rapture," echoed Father Rankin.

"Surely you've heard about it."

"Oh, yes, yes, I have a bit of knowledge on that subject. I suppose you ran into one of our 'separated brethren' in the last few days?"

"Brethren?" asked Dexter. "What--a black guy?"

"No, no. By 'separated brethren' I mean a Protestant; a Christian who is not Catholic."

"Yeah, this guy was a Pentecostal, I think. Anyway, this guy has me convinced that I'll be flying up to Heaven before any of the bad stuff starts down here on earth. That is, if I accept Jesus as my 'personal Lord and Savior'--he kept repeating that phrase. Is there any Biblical basis for this?"

"Yes and no. First, let's be clear. The Rapture is the belief held among a majority, if I'm not mistaken, of Protestants, that Christ will 'rapture' or 'instantly pull up' to Heaven all righteous people right before the end of the world so that they will not have to suffer the tribulations that the Bible predicts for that period of time."

"Right on the money!" said Dexter. "Only this guy I talked to made it sound like I would be left here on earth."

"'Left Behind,' I believe is the term?"

"Huh?"

"That's the name for a series of novels written about the End Times. I should point out that there are differences of opinion among Protestants about when the Rapture will occur--before, during, or after the Tribulation. The Tribulation is the period of persecution of the Church before the end of the world."

"Well, anyway, what *does* the Bible say?"

"The Protestants," began Father Rankin, "misinterpret one or two passages from the Book of Revelation, or Apocalypse." He reached over to the New Testament that was lying on the coffee table. "Let's see if I can find it without a whole lot of searching..." He laid his pipe on the ashtray and thumbed through the pages. "It's first or second Thessalonians...I always forget...ah! Here it is: First Thessalonians, verses fifteen to eighteen. 'For this we say to you in the word of the Lord, that we who live, who survive in the coming of the Lord, shall not precede those who have fallen asleep. For the Lord himself with cry of command, with voice of archangel, and with trumpet of God will descend from heaven; and the dead in Christ will rise up first. Then we who live, who survive, shall be caught up together with them in clouds to meet the Lord in the air, and so we shall ever be with the Lord. Wherefore, comfort one another with these words.'"

"Sounds pretty convincing to me," reasoned Dexter. "'Meet the Lord in the air'?"

"True," said Father Rankin, putting his pipe back into his mouth.

"What does the word 'Rapture' mean anyway?" asked Dexter.

"Now that you ask I'm not really sure...hmm." Father Rankin looked at the passage again. "Oh, well, thank goodness for footnotes. It says here that it comes from, uh...that's a bit ironic...'rapture' comes from the Latin verb 'rapiemur,' meaning 'we will be caught up.'"

"Latin?"

"Yeah--I didn't think the Protestants who came up with the Rapture would be using a Latin bible."

"Well, anyway, what's the Catholic take on the Rapture?" asked Dexter.

"Surprisingly enough," began Father Rankin, "the Catholic view is the same as the Protestant Reformers and most traditional Protestants today: we believe that the millennium is the present reign of Christ in heaven and on earth through his Church."

"The 'millennium'?"

"The 'millennium' is a span of time talked about in the Bible during which Christ will reign on earth. There's a whole bunch of discussion going on among Protestants about that, as well. Suffice it to say that the Catholics believe that the millennium has been the period from Christ's life on earth up to the present day. I should mention, though, that I've read that some apparitions claim that there actually will be a thousand year Reign of Christ on earth after the period of tribulation ends. As far as the Rapture goes, I guess you'd have to say we believe the Rapture will occur on the last day of the world, when all faithful believers will be taken up to heaven. But, see, The Blessed Mother has said several times that we are not now at the end of the world; we are at the end of this *age*. The main point is that there is no mention in that passage that I just read about those who will be 'left behind' on the earth. Catholics have many, many apparitions from the last seven or eight hundred years about what, in general, will happen in the end times. The Protestants have two or three Bible verses which they misinterpret and blow out of proportion. Well, they also have Edgar Cayce, but that's just one guy. As a friend of mine likes to say: 'it's not that the bad people will be "left behind," but rather that the good people will he "right in front"!'"

"Name names," said Dexter.

"What names?"

"You said Catholics have many apparitions."

"Oh." Father Rankin shrugged and took the pipe from his mouth. "There's Lourdes, Fatima, Knock, Beauraing, Banneaux. Those are the better known ones. There's also Akita, Garabandal, Medjugorje, Elyria, Betania. Now not all of those are completely approved by the Church, but I don't think any of them have been condemned."

"You say 'apparitions.' Who appeared?"

"All of those I just mentioned were by the Blessed Mother. But there have been others by Jesus, even by God the Father. I also heard that there's some man living in Australia who's been to Heaven, Purgatory, and Hell."

"Yeah, right," said Dexter. "Like it wouldn't be on the six o'clock news."

"Hey, if he comes to town again, I'll let you know. You can go hear him speak."

"I don't know if I'm quite ready for that, but you know ever since I started talking with you, I expected you to bring it up, but you haven't," said Dexter.

"Bring what up?" asked Father Rankin.

"Well, I told you, didn't I?"

"I know one thing for sure, and that's that I can't read minds...why don't you refresh my memory."

"I, uh, right now I'm...I'm living with a girl!"

"I take it from your tone that you're not married to this 'girl.'"

"Right."

"Hmm." Father Rankin took a long pull on his pipe and blew out the smoke. "What do you think about it?"

"What does it matter? You're the priest--you tell me."

"Oh, don't worry, I'll tell you, I was just curious about your angle on the situation."

"Hell, I'm only doing what the rest of the world is doing...maybe I'll marry her someday...what's wrong with a little test drive before I buy the car?"

"Hmm...go on."

"Well...there's not much else to say. Man. Woman. What else is there?"

Father Rankin gave a small snort. "Sheesh, man, I was hoping to hear a little of the 'L' word?"

"'L' word? L word, L word...uhh...'Legal' situation? Nothing doing, this is a 'no hassle relationship.' We made that clear from the beginning."

"Dexter," Father Rankin said with a paternal smile. "Not 'Legal.' 'Love.'"

"Love?"

"Love."

"I love her! I mean we've lived together for two years! Don't you think we love each other by now?"

"That's precisely what I'm asking," said Father Rankin.

"What do you mean, 'Do I love her?' Why else would I have anything to do with her if I didn't love her?"

"How long did you know her before you lived together?"

"How long? Let's see." Dexter tilted his head back and looked toward the ceiling. "I'd say about three months."

"You can fall in love in only three months?"

"Father, you can fall in love in three minutes!"

"What is love, Dexter?"

"Why do you ask all these goofy questions? Am I getting a PhD in Philosophy?"

"Have you ever thought much about love?"

"I don't know…love is…love is that special care you feel toward someone, right?"

"Ah," said Father Rankin, taking the pipe out of his mouth and setting it on the coffee table. "*Feeling.*"

"That's right, *feeling.* Is there something wrong with *feeling*?"

"How about this definition of love: Love is the willingness to endure pain for the sake of another."

"Prairie-dung!" said Dexter.   "Back to classic Catholic crap! Guilt, pain, suffer, suffer, suffer!"

"Ever read Saint-Exupery?*"*

"More Catholic trivia? Have I ever read--" Dexter leaned back in his chair. "Sheesh! All right! Go ahead! Brainwash me!"

"Uh, first of all, I don't know if Saint-Exupery was a Catholic. I guess he was French, so he probably was--oh! I see, you thought I was quoting a *Saint*! No, no. That was just this guy's name. He's not a canonized Saint, he's a writer. Anyway, in this story that he wrote he told of an aviator who crashed in the Andes, in South America. This was back in the 20s or so, when there wasn't much in the way of sophisticated electronic tracking equipment. So this aviator is lying there on the side of a mountain and he knows he's going to die, but he realizes he has to move himself to a place where his dead body will more likely be found by searchers so that his wife will be able to collect the insurance money. This guy is all banged up, broken bones and what-not, but by a supreme act of the will he drags himself to a more visible location on the side of the mountain. Now *that's* love."

"I suppose you'll relate this to Christ or something?" asked Dexter.

"*I* didn't mention Christ, now did I?"

"I was just pre-empting you."

"I just told a story from literary classics."

"Fine, so the aviator loved his wife. Can't I love my girlfriend even though I don't get into a plane crash--even though I'm not married to her?"

"Sure, you can love her--do you?"

"I'm *attracted* to her, yeah! She makes me feel good--hell, you know what I'm talking about."

"But, oh!" said Father Rankin in mock surprise. "But I'm a priest! How can I know what you're talking about?"

"Nice try, guy," said Dexter. "I'm not *that* ignorant of the Catholic religion. You hear it all in the Confessional."

"Point taken," said Father Rankin, nodding his head.

"All right, let's get back to my original question. We got into all this 'love' B.S. and we got sidetracked...what about my living with my girlfriend? Her name's Daphne."

"Oh, that's nice to have a girlfriend with a name," said Father Rankin with a smile.

"Yeah, right. So what is the deal with living with someone if you're not married--and don't ask me what I think! You're not a therapist, you're a priest. You should be telling what the Catholic Church teaches!"

"Well, let's not get ahead of ourselves here. Among other things a Catholic priest *is* a therapist. You're right, he's not *primarily* a therapist, but part of being a good Confessor is to heal the sinner's wounds. A friend of mine used to say that if there were enough people going to Confession, the psychiatrists would go out of business. I'm always amazed at people who go to see a shrink for $200 an hour when Confession is free. So, anyway, you want to know what is taught about your situation. The truth is that the Church has always stood by the sixth commandment."

"I assume that's the one about adultery."

"Right."

"I can see that," said Dexter. "I mean, adultery can really hurt people, but what I'm doing--pssshh! It's like what a friend of mine from LA said once. A guy and a girl living together is like two little deer running around in the forest. Neither one is attached to anyone, it's just plain fun!"

"Aha!" said Father Rankin.

"What? Oh, give me a break! I know--*fun*, right? I said the dreaded anti-Catholic word."

"Hold up a minute--is fun really that antithetical to the Catholic religion? Have you heard the definition of Puritanism?"

"Try me."

"Puritanism is that sneaking suspicion that somewhere, someone is happy."

Dexter gave a half-smile. "Pshaw! Sounds more like a definition of Catholicism."

"Aha, again!" said Father Rankin. "Maybe you haven't heard the one about a group of Catholics?"

Dexter just stared at him.

"Wherever there are four good Catholics, there's always a fifth."

"Hmmph," replied Dexter, suppressing a smile. "Catholics and alcohol! Isn't that the truth."

"There's nothing wrong with drinking alcohol," said Father Rankin. "It's just the quantity that matters."

"Oh, I see. Point zero-oh-eight blood alcohol, right? Anything over that is a sin? Is that the way it goes?"

"There's no hard and fast rule. I remember a fellow priest telling me a few years back that we should drink to the point of hilarity and not beyond."

"What's that supposed to mean?"

"I'll explain in a minute. I just want to tell you about a guy I used to know in college. He had this thing called the 'Catholic ounce.' Basically, he would never drink more than eleven ounces of beer at one sitting. He used to say it made him 'tipsy.'" Father Rankin shook his head back and forth, looked at the floor and chuckled. "Yeah, that was the expression he used, 'tipsy.' So he would have a twelve ounce bottle of beer for dinner, and there would always be about an inch of beer left in the bottom of the bottle when we left."

"Who cares?" said Dexter.

"Oh, so anyway." Father Rankin snapped out of his reverie and looked up at Dexter.

"You were saying 'to the point of hilarity and not beyond,'" Dexter reminded him.

"The Catholic philosophy of drinking is basically that alcohol should make us happier, not sadder."

"Duh."

"All right, all right. I know that sounds a tad obvious. Somewhere in the Old Testament it says that God gave man wine to 'cheer his heart.' The reason getting drunk is wrong is that it shows a fundamental defect in that person's life. What I mean is that we should be happy without needing to get wasted! Alcohol should be a lubricant, as the expression goes, but it shouldn't be a, a...flood, or the whole tank of gas. Think of a car..."

"Here we go again with the analogies," said Dexter.

"I just happen to love cars! But, yeah, think of a car...the lubricant is only a small part of what the car needs to operate. There's also the gas, the coolant, the transmission fluid..."

"And your point is?"

"My point is that for someone who's truly happy, alcohol is only an add-on to their happiness. Life should be a bundle of joy and gaiety and we shouldn't need alcohol to be that joyful. My Dad used to give us kids a little wine to drink while we were growing up so that we wouldn't think it was some forbidden thing that we just *had* to try when we got to be eighteen. And he was right! When we did leave the house, we drank only in moderation, because we already experienced the thrill of it."

Dexter rubbed his eyes and looked at his watch. "Look, before we run out of time, can we at least finish this thing about adultery? We always seem to go off on these tangents. I said something about how living with Daphne was fun, and you were all up in arms about that."

"Yes, I remember what you were saying. I guess I was just trying to point out that the Church is not against fun per se. What I mean to stress is that--"

"Father Rankin?" The parish secretary's voice rang out on the office intercom. "I need to speak to you right away!"

"Excuse me, Dexter." Father Rankin turned to his desk and picked up the handset. "Yes Peggy? Riverside? 6701? Fine, yes, right away. Thanks." He hung up and stood. "Sorry, Dexter, but it looks like I have to go on a sick call to Riverside Hospital. We'll have to continue next time."

"Is someone dying?"

"Looks that way. I better get over there right away." He put on his jacket and walked toward the door. "Next week, same time?"

"I guess...good luck."

Dexter followed the priest out to the parking lot and entered his car for the drive home. As he turned onto High Street his cell phone rang.

"Hello."

"Yeah, Dexter?"

"Right here."

"Hey, this is Bill over at Don Scott. I just wanted to tell you what I found out about your Skyhawk."

"Is it what you thought, the fuel filter?"

"Exactly that. There were some small stones and what not in your fuel line leading up to the filter. You were lucky you got the engine restarted up there."

"Huh," said Dexter. "How did I get a restart if there was that stuff in there?"

"Beats me," said Bill. "Did you do any wild maneuvers or something? That could have dislodged this stuff."

"Uhh, I don't think so...I was too busy trying to find a landing strip."

"Were you carrying a rabbit's foot or something?"

"No, nothing special."

"Well, anyway, I cleaned it all out and put in a new filter. I'll send you the bill as usual."

"Great. So it's ready to fly?"

"Anytime you like."

"Thanks a bunch, Bill! Bye."

"Later."

As he drove down 315 Dexter went over what he had discussed with Father Rankin. *I wish he had told me what he thought about Daphne and I.*

"You know what he would say," replied his conscience.

"I can't tell that to Daphne!" complained Dexter. *Hmm, what would Father Rankin say?* wondered Dexter. *Should I tell Daphne? Would she listen? Would she care what a priest thought?*

Dexter drove into his company's parking lot, took his briefcase out and walked in the side door. He nearly bumped into Jerry, who was pushing an unwieldy cart past the doorway.

"Whoa!" said Jerry. "Didn't mean to run you over, boss!"

"Sure you didn't! You just want to take ultimate power at Grobotics, that's all!"

"Aaah, I'll wait till we go public till I turn all the robots on you."

"At least I can trust an engineer to be honest," smiled Dexter.

"So...Dexter, what's the word from Sightsim?" asked Jerry. "Did they solve all our problems?"

"I brought back some software solutions that just might do the trick, Jer. The first is a genetic algorithm. It apes the evolutionary process of nature. The guy was explaining it to me, something about simulating chromosomes. I'll have to study the material he gave me. I'll make a copy for you."

"Did they demo it for you?"

"They did as much as they could. They did set up that dual vision thing you were talking about. It worked pretty well and it was able to lock onto one of the men while he walked through the office."

"What else did they show you?"

"Two other search sequences, which might work better for Bobby when he has to pick out a target against a moving background. The genetic routine used a fixed backdrop, so we'll see how Bobby handles it."

"And the fly fishing? Was it up to snuff?"

"The short answer is that I didn't have time. The real reason might have to do with the fact that it was too cold."

"Surely you're not saying that you wimped out?"

"Oh, no, nothing like that. I just readjusted my priorities."

"Fine, so you wimped out."

"That'll be all, my fickle friend."

"Ha! I knew it!" Jerry laughed and walked back to the lab.

Dexter spent the remainder of the day at Grobotics, briefing his engineers on his findings from Sightsim. He stayed till six and then decided to call it a day. A couple of the engineers, the two unmarried ones, Dexter noticed, were still in the lab as he walked toward the door.

"Be sure to set the alarm when you leave," he reminded them.

"You got it," said the one in the white shirt.

****

Thad was glad he'd had the heater fixed in his cab last winter. It was unusually cold for the second week of December and he had the heat on full blast as he arrived in front of an address in Powell, an outlying suburb on the north end of Columbus. The figure of a lithe woman walking out to the car warmed his heart even more. He couldn't believe his luck--she was a blonde, and not bad looking, besides.

"You headed out on business or vacation?" he asked after he put her bags in the trunk and got into the car.

"Hopefully a little of both," she said. "I'm going to a conference in Phoenix, but I have a friend from college who lives there and she invited me to stay for the weekend."

"Not bad…good time of year to be going to Arizona."

"Right."

Don't say anything too radical this time, Thad told himself. "So, what's the conference about?"

"Environmental Science industry. I work for Battelle, you know, down by campus."

"Oh, yeah, over there on King Avenue, right?"

"That's the place," she said. "Just south of OSU."

"Are you an engineer?" asked Thad.

"Yes, I got my degree in Chemical Engineering. I do a lot of work with pollution control research, that type of thing."

"Sort of like me; I used to work in research."

"A cab driver who does research!" she said in mock surprise.

"Hey, don't take the average guy in the street too lightly! I have a degree in Aerospace Engineering and I worked on the National Aerospace Plane project back in the eighty's." Thad merged into the traffic on 315. "The airport, right?"

"Yes. Southwest Airlines."

"Great."

"So you retired and now you're a taxi driver, huh?" she asked.

"Not really retired. I'm on a temporary disability. I have recurring bouts of insomnia. I get them from stress--you know, like stress from a full-time, pressurized job."

"Where did you go to school?" she asked.

"Notre Dame."

"You have to be the only Notre Dame graduate driving a cab in the country!"

"Mightn't you say 'the world?'"

"Curiouser and curiouser."

"Lewis Carroll, 'Alice in Wonderland,'" said Thad.

"My, my, an engineer who's well read!"

"My Mom always quoted from that book."

"I see," she said.

Thad drove onto the Outerbelt and fought his way across the traffic trying to exit to Route 23. *I'm not doing too bad so far*, he coached himself. *I checked and she has no ring--that's good. I won't talk about Garabandal right now--unless she brings it up. What can I ask next? I wonder where she went to school.*

"So where did *you* go to school?" he asked.

"Brown."

"Oh, yeah, Gordon Gee."

"How did you know that?" she asked.

"He was president of OSU before he went to Brown and now he's back at OSU. Witty guy, huh?"

"Yes, he is. I remember at our graduation he said we would have to start doing our laundry more often and it would be the end of 'the smell test.'"

"Same here!" said Thad with a chuckle. "I went to my sister's graduation from OSU and he said the exact same thing at *her* commencement."

"It sure is a small world!"

"Yeah, 'tiny globe' as my brother likes to say."

"I just wondered if you could tell me something about cab driving," said the woman. "Exactly how does the meter work? It seems like sometimes it runs fast and other times slow."

"Ah, the mystery and magic of the money meter," replied Thad.

"Boy, an engineer who also knows how to alliterate!"

"Hey, you know what they say about Notre Dame: we're number one and we're not too bad in sports either."

"You *used* to be number one in football, you mean," said the passenger.

"It's about time for another championship for us."

"That simple, huh?"

"Precisely," said Thad, nodding his head. "Anyway, as regards the meter: when the car is moving, it's forty-five cents for every two-ninths of a mile, and when the car is stopped, it's forty-five cents for every minute."

"Why that makes perfect sense," she said sarcastically.

"Hey, don't ask me where they got the 'two-ninths' of a mile; 'Ours not to wonder why, ours but to drive and,' uhh--"

"Sigh."

"That'll work--yeah, 'drive and sigh.'   Heaven knows I do enough of that when the traffic gets bad."

They passed by Easton and in a few minutes were on International Parkway, leading to the airport terminal. Thad knew he had precious little time to get her phone number.

"Well, I hope you enjoy Arizona," he said.

"It should be fun, I think."

"Try not to get bitten by any snakes or anything."

"Oh, I know. My friend was telling me she found a tarantula by the sliding door in her living room one day."

"Eah!" said Thad, scrunching up his lips. "I'll take Ohio any day!"

"Even when it gets to be subzero in a few weeks?"

"Hey, like I always say---oh, I'm sorry, I forgot. Did you say American?"

"Southwest, actually."

"Okay." Thad drove the cab up to the curb and put it into park. "Yeah, like I always say, except for a few weeks in the summer and a few weeks in the winter, Columbus is a great place to live."

"You might have a point there. I really like this time of year, with Christmas and parties and all that. How much do I owe you?"

Thad looked at the meter. "The meter says forty-three, twenty-five, but you can take four dollars off that. I'm running a special for blondes!"

She laughed and handed Thad fifty dollars. "Keep the change, funny man." She scooped up her purse and got out of the car.

Thad pocketed the bills and raced for the trunk. *I've got to get her last name,* he thought. He had read her first name on the computer screen in the cab and figured he could get her last name from her credit card. *The dispatcher said that she was going to pay by credit card.* He stepped around to the rear of the taxi and fumbled with the lock.

"These things are sometimes a bit tricky," he said, glancing up at her. Finally he popped the lid. "There." *You can't just get her name out of the phone book and call her up!* he thought. *You've got to get her to give it to you* now! Thad lifted her bag out of the trunk and set it on the sidewalk.

"Thank you, I enjoyed talking with you," she said with a smile.

"Oh, no problem, thank *you!*"

They stood there a second and then she started to walk away.

"Have a good flight!" Thad said.

She waved and was swallowed up in the crowd in front of the luggage kiosk.

Thad, you idiot! he screamed inwardly. *Why didn't you ask her for her phone number? At least you could have given her one of your business cards! Everything went great on the trip here...she* would *have given it to you!*

"Bird crap," he said as he slammed the trunk lid. He got into the cab and drove off. He didn't notice his passenger-woman looking at him as he left.

****

It was five minutes past midnight and Kevin wasn't making any progress on his paper. As a history major, he was used to writing papers, but this one had given him writer's block. He was writing a paper on the politics of those European nations which had remained neutral during World War I.

Hmm, let's try this again. Go to Google...type in--no, this time I'll type in "Portugal 1917" just to see what that tiny country was doing at the time. Kevin deftly moved the mouse around on the desktop and pecked away at the keyboard. He sat patiently while the circle revolved in the upper left hand corner. *Must be a lot of other students on the Net tonight. I guess I'm not the only one who puts off papers till the last minute.* A list of websites appeared on the screen. Kevin double-clicked on one about a place called "Fatima." Just then a new screen appeared on the monitor. *What?* asked Kevin, scratching his head as a picture of a Rosary popped up on the computer. "Victories of the Rosary - Portugal - 1917," read the title at the top of the page. *This is news to me...must be some fringe group.* Kevin read the paragraph under the headline:

In 1917, Portugal was verging on totalitarianism after the revolution of 1910. The revolution had decreed a sharp separation of Church and state, Church property had been confiscated, and religious congregations had been ordered dissolved. The intelligentsia and ruling classes were anti-religious and decisively anti-clerical. The ruling cognoscenti were contemptuous of traditional religious beliefs often describing these beliefs as mere superstitions in the newspapers and journals they ran. Even rural areas normally immune to the intellectual fads of the cosmopolitan centers were affected by church closings and a cautious wariness about any outward expression of religious belief. Despite this, strong religious faith still took root in the simple peasants of the rural countryside. In this environment, a series of apparitions by the Blessed Virgin occurred to three small children from the rural village of Fatima over a six month period starting in May of 1917.

Kevin scratched his head again and bit his lower lip. *Why haven't I ever heard of this? Is this some radical conspiracy theory?* He scrolled down the page and read a little further:

During the last apparition, on October 13, 1917, the Lady of light revealed herself to be Our Lady of the Rosary. The 70,000 rain-soaked pilgrims who came to witness Mary's final appearance saw the sun spin out of its orbit, emitting a rainbow of color as it gyrated; finally, when this display ceased, the sun was seen plunging toward the earth causing the pilgrims to scream in terror. When the sun eventually resumed its normal behavior about twelve minutes after it began this inexplicable display, many of these rain-soaked people found their clothing completely dry. Further, a number of pilgrims who came with medical problems found their ailments either completely healed or significantly alleviated. In addition, the more than ten thousand people in the surrounding villages who chose not to go to the apparition site also saw the sun dance in the sky.

Kevin chuckled, sat back in his chair, and took a swig of the Mountain Dew he had next to him. *What a crock of--spit! Who wrote this?* He scrolled down to the bottom of the article. *Ha! That figures…no writer's name is given, just "Our Lady's Helpers." Some spineless bird who doesn't want to stick up for a wacky theory.* Kevin swallowed a little more Mountain Dew and shook his head back and forth. *Why haven't I ever heard of this? Of course, who's to say this miracle didn't really happen? I'll have to ask my professor about this sometime.*

Kevin drained the last of the pop and sat up straight. *Enough of this flimflam! I've got a paper to write. I can't quote this stuff in my paper. I've got to research some real history.* He tossed the empty soda container at the wastebasket. It bounced off the rim and landed on the floor. *I better do better than that in the Fiesta Bowl or else we'll lose the National Championship game in three weeks.*

****

It only took Dexter five minutes to drive from his office to his home. As soon as he walked in the back door, he sat down at the kitchen table and began reading the "New York Times." When he heard Daphne's car pull into the driveway, he felt butterflies in his stomach.

A minute later, his girlfriend came through the door.

"Hey, hunk," said Daphne cheerfully, "what up?" She put her key chain on the kitchen counter, walked over to where Dexter was sitting at the table, and gave him a kiss on the forehead.

"Uh, not too bad, Daphne...I, umm." He kept looking at the newspaper, not returning his girlfriend's gaze.

"Trouble at work, hon? How are the robots these days?" Daphne sat down at the table opposite Dexter. "Are they going crazy as usual?" She smiled at him.

"Everything's going OK, I guess," he said quietly, still keeping his eyes on the paper.

"Well, I'm doing just fine, thanks for asking," said Daphne, a little irritation showing in her brown eyes.

"Oh, yeah," said Dexter, half-heartedly. "How *is* work?"

"Couldn't be better, actually. Sales are up for the quarter and that makes everyone happy. Hey!" she said suddenly, slapping her hand down on the newspaper. "Can't you at least *look* at me when I'm talking?"

Dexter jumped at the sound and put the paper down, looking around the room, taking short glances at Daphne.

"We have to talk," he said matter-of-factly.

"Oh, no, what's it this time?" lamented Daphne. "All right! I'm not being neat enough, right? I'm leaving the milk out on the table? Something I said?"

"Daphne, I, uh--." Dexter shifted in his chair, straightened up the pile of newspapers and put his elbows on the table. "I've just been talking with--"

"Not your mother again," said Daphne. "Look, Dexter, if I've told you once, I've told you a million times, that woman--"

"Not my mother."

"Who? That secretary at your office? She never did like me."

"Actually, I've been talking with a, well, this guy that a taxi driver told me about."

"*Taxi* driver?"

"I've been to see a priest a few times," Dexter said quickly.

"A *priest*?"

"Right."

"Are you some long-lost Catholic and never told me?" asked Daphne.

"No, I just promised this taxi driver I would talk to his brother."

"Why did you do that?"

"The cabbie helped me out on the freeway once and he suggested I talk to his brother."

"Suggested?"

"Well, then I had the near-death experience on the Lincoln-Leveque and it sort of scared me."

"So go see a shrink if you have to...why a priest? I didn't think you needed religion. You getting soft in your old age?"

"Not really, it's just that I've been talking with this priest and I've sort of started to think about what we've discussed."

"Dexter," said Daphne, sitting up in her chair, "tell me the truth: are you going to become a Catholic or something?"

"No! No, no," said Dexter reassuringly. "I've just thought about how I'm living with you and, uh..."

"What about living with me?"

"It's just that we've been together for so long and we're not legally..."

"Married? Is *that* what you're so hung up about?!"

"Look, Daphne," he said, holding out one of his hands to her. "I'm not trying to say anything's wrong with you."

"I get it! This priest has told you we shouldn't be living together unless we're married! Right!??"

"He hasn't said anything about us...yet. We were just about to get to that last time I was there. I just started thinking about--"

"*You* started thinking...! Now you're some Holy Joe or whatever? What's wrong with us living together before we're married? Is there something wrong with trying out a relationship before you make it official?"

"Once in a while I get a little guilty when I talk with Father Rankin."

"The truth finally comes out!" jeered Daphne. "Catholic guilt! So *that* explains it!"

"Hey, honey, I'm not Catholic," said Dexter. "I'm not saying we can't live together. I just wondered what *you* thought about all this. Look, I didn't really mean that about feeling guilty. Maybe I'll stop seeing this priest anyway."

"You're darn right you're going to stop seeing that priest! Ever since that bullcrap started your head's been screwed up! What's wrong with you anyway?"

"Not to worry, not to worry," said Dexter, holding his hands up in submission. "It's decided--I've decided. I don't know if I was really getting much out of it anyway."

"I should say so," said Daphne, shaking her head with a grimacing look. "Aren't you taking this 'near-death' thing a little too seriously? All right, I know it was pretty intense at the time, but--it's over, you know?"

"True, true. It's just that sometimes I can't seem to shake the memories it resurrected in my mind."

"What memories?"

"Well...you know...stuff that happened when I was in high school and college--uhh, stuff that I feel a little..."

"Oh, *come on*," said Daphne. "I thought we just agreed you would get over your little guilt trips. You remind me of a bumper sticker I saw a few years ago during the whole hype for that movie 'Titanic.' It said, 'The ship sank. Get over it.'"

"Point taken," said Dexter. "I'll do my best."

"Now *that* sounds like the winner I *used* to know. What do you say we whip up a little spaghetti for dinner and top it off with some White Zinfandel?"

"I suppose," he said unemotionally.

"Hey, bucko, care to be a little more excited?"

Dexter broke into one of his trademark grins and stood up. "Say no more, babe! Point me in the direction of the marinara sauce."

"Finally! Intelligent life returns to Urlin Avenue!"

The couple enjoyed a savory dinner and soon retired to the bedroom. They didn't get a whole lot of sleep that night.

Two days later, Dexter called up Thad for a ride, and was surprised to see him stop in front of his house after only a short five-minute wait.

"You must've been awfully close, Thad my man," said Dexter, climbing into the backseat.

"Who's to say I wasn't far away and broke the speed limit to get here?" asked Thad.

"Sigh, why couldn't I find a *normal* taxi driver?"

"There *is* such a thing?"

"Sigh again."

"Where to *this* time, my most revered robotics renegade?" asked Thad as he turned on the meter.

"The Paint Patrol at Kenny and Henderson," said Dexter. I'm getting a few rust spots taken care of on the Charger."

"What model is it?"

"It's a Charger SRT8; it has 6.1 liters of pure power under the hood, and I love each and every one of them."

"As you wish, sir. You know, you can get rid of all your rust spots if you go to Garabandal for the Miracle."

"Huh?" said Dexter. "Is that in that pamphlet you gave me? What do you mean, 'get rid of your rust spots?' And what exactly *is* the Miracle?"

"Touché!" replied Thad. "Call it poetic license. By 'getting rid of your rust spots' I mean that Mary said whoever attends the Miracle will be cured of all their illnesses, physical and spiritual. Take that and put it in your blender, pal!"

"Touché yourself! Explain yourself, cabbie! What *is* the Miracle?"

"Mary said the Miracle will occur at Garabandal, Spain and will be able to be seen by everyone around the world on TV. It will be able to be seen and photographed, but not touched. She also said that a visible sign will be left on the spot as a reminder of the Miracle. The sign will remain till the end of the world."

"Boy," said Dexter, shaking his head from side to side. "What will they have you Catholics believing next?"

"Hey, Mr. Worldly, there have already been miracles at Garabandal to back up all this."

"Such as?"

"How 'bout a Communion Host appearing out of thin air on one of the seers' tongues?"

"How 'bout trick photography?" said Dexter.

"Diamond heart!"

"Is that an insult?"

"You just have an extremely hard heart, Dexter. You're cynical to the max!"

"How 'bout you're gullible to the max?"

"Just wait till the Miracle, is all I can say...you'll see."

"Just like Charlie Brown waiting for--oh, I guess saying that would be hard hearted of me."

"Scrooge has a heart!" said Thad. "You actually checked your language! Can I sign you up for the flight?"

"What--you're actually booking flights to see this dog and pony show?"

"Doggone straight! The Miracle will happen on a Thursday at 8:30 in the evening on a feast-day of a martyred Saint for the Eucharist, but not on a feast-day of Our Lady or Our Lord. It will happen in the month of March, April, or May, between the eighth and sixteenth of the month but not on the eighth or the sixteenth."

"You sound like a travel guide, bud!" exclaimed Dexter. "You got this thing memorized or something?"

"I'm totally excited, guy! This is going to be *the* event of the century--or of the Millennium! Anyway, the Miracle will be seen around the area of the Pines, as it is called."

"'The Pines'?"

"'The Pines' is a place near Garabandal where there's a clump of pine trees. The great thing is that the Miracle will be visible from all the surrounding hills--the mountainside will serve as a natural amphitheater--millions will be able to fit in the area!"

"You've got to be kidding me! Don't tell me you're serious! You actually believe all that superstition? 'Between the eighth and the sixteenth of the month.' Do you get bonus points if you guess the right date?"

"Hey, bud, it's Heaven's timetable, not mine."

"Sheesh," said Dexter with a smirk on his face. "It sounds like something out of a Darren King novel."

"What's so odd?" asked Thad. "People have to know when to go, so they can get there in time for the Miracle. It's going to be fantastic! The valley there will probably be packed to the max!"

"One second, Thad. Just how *are* people going to know when to go? Sounds like there will be several Thursdays to choose from."

"Aha!" said Thad with a grin. "A crack appears in the façade of our granite unbeliever's cliff-face."

"Just *supposing* all this is true," said Dexter.

"One of the visionaries, Conchita, knows the exact date of the miracle and will announce it eight days before it occurs...so everyone will have plenty of time to get to Spain."

"Well isn't that just peachy. And how is little old Garabandal going to handle a double-decker Airbus 380 from New York?"

"Madrid will handle most of the big planes, while Toledo and other nearby cities can handle the rest."

"Son of a b!" said Dexter. "You've got all this figured out, haven't you?"

"I've been following this whole deal since I was a kid, my friend. I first heard of Garabandal when I was in sixth grade. I purchased my plane ticket to Garabandal ten years ago."

"You really *are* into this, huh?"

"When you had parents like I did, religion is second-nature, if not first-nature."

"So, Thad, you've had thirty years to think about it...what do you think the Miracle is going to be?"

"Maybe something to do with the pine trees at Garabandal. Some of the apparitions occurred around some pine trees there and for a number of years there was a magazine called 'Needles.' Maybe the trees will spontaneously burst into flame--I don't know..."

"How about if all the Popes reappear all at once, floating in the air?" asked Dexter.

"Golden!" said Thad. "They could all be seated on their thrones!"

"Oh, help!" moaned Dexter. "I'm actually getting sucked into this silliness."

"Bring it on! You're becoming 'one of us.' One-of-us! One-of-us!"

"Gag me with a spoon, guy. Ah, luckily we're here." The taxi pulled into the parking lot of the paint shop. "How much do I owe you?"

"Ten-eighty," said Thad.

"Here, keep the change," said Dexter, handing Thad a twenty dollar bill.

"Such generosity from someone with a heart as hard as a diamond!" said Thad jokingly.

"Now you can buy lunch on your flight to Garabandal."

"Thanks a lot, Dexter."

"I'll be seeing you."

"Bye."

Chapter 6

A clear dawn greeted Dexter as he drove down Third Avenue on his way to work. *At least it's not a red sky*, he thought. *Not bad weather with Christmas just a week away. It might just stay clear all day long. Sometimes winter in Columbus can be monotonously gray. Maybe that's why Ohio State University's colors were scarlet and gray. But what did the scarlet mean? Red sky in the morning, sailor take warning? Hmm. Something to ponder*, concluded Dexter.

His thoughts were interrupted by the ringing of his cell phone.

"Hello."

"Dexter, I missed you yesterday!" said Father Rankin on the other end. "I thought we had an appointment for one o'clock."

"Oh, yeah," Dexter said weakly.

"One of your robots blow up or something?"

"No, I sort of…I just, uh, thought that…" His voice trailed off.

"Cat got your tongue?"

Dexter steeled himself and gritted his teeth. "Father Rankin, I've decided to stop seeing you…I fulfilled my promise to your brother--I spoke with you several times and I--I think that's enough. Not to be rude, but I don't think I'm getting much out of it anymore."

"What's the real reason, Dexter?" asked Father Rankin in a slow voice.

"Might as well tell him the truth," coaxed his conscience.

"No!" Dexter protested silently.

"It just isn't what I need right now," said Dexter in a tight voice. He pulled into the parking lot of Grobotics and came to a stop. "Look, I just got to work--I have to go."

"Door's always open," said Father Rankin.

"Bye, Father Rankin."

"Bye."

Dexter sat in the car a few moments.

"Bad move," said the little voice.

"I know what I'm doing," he silently replied.

"The priest is good for you, guy."

"Stay away from me!" thought Dexter.

"Have it your way, then."

"Darn right," thought Dexter. He walked into the building and made the usual small talk with his secretary and a few of the engineers whom he passed. The first item was to set up another demonstration of Bobby. He called Paul at the Woodward Company and was surprised when Paul answered.

"Paul! It's Dexter. What--did you fire your secretary? I didn't expect to get you right off the bat."

"She's just running a little late," said Paul. Don't you think CEOs are capable of doing secretarial work?"

"Hey, not so loud. If *my* secretary hears that, I'll be answering all *my* calls too. But, anyway, I just wanted to set up another demo of Bobby. I don't think you'll be disappointed this time. We just installed some new software from Sightsim and Bobby's lookin' good!"

"Glad to hear it!" said Paul. "When can you come over?"

"Whenever you like. Next week sometime?"

"The sooner the better!"

"Okay, how about tomorrow?"

"That'd be great--what about today?"

"Today?" asked Dexter, swallowing once. "Uhh, just a second, let me ask Jerry." Dexter put Paul on hold and rang Jerry's office.

"Hello, this is Jerry."

"Jerry, do you think we could demo Bobby *today*?"

"Today? Wow, I just finished installing the software yesterday."

"Have you tested him yet?"

"Actually, yeah, I did it last night after you left."

"And...?"

"Bobby did just fine! Sure, let's do the demo today!"

"Great! I'll tell Paul--he's on the other line."

Dexter punched a couple of buttons on the phone. "Paul?"

"Right here."

"Sure, we can demo today. How 'bout we come over about two?"

"Good deal," said Paul. "See you then."

"And we won't spray any of your employees this time either."

"Oh, yeah?" laughed Paul. "None of our employees, just some of our customers, if any show up, right?"

"The truth is out," said Dexter morosely. You caught my ploy."

"See ya at two, Charlie Brown."

"Bye." Dexter hung up the phone and began to organize the papers on his desk.

After lunch Jerry helped Dexter load their two-hundred pound robot into the company van, then both men and machine headed out of the parking lot.

"This time I think Bobby will be seeing twenty-fifteen," said Jerry as he merged into traffic on I-670.

"You mean twenty-twenty?" asked Dexter.

"Better than that…twenty-fifteen."

"I never did understand that--what does twenty-fifteen mean?"

"Ha!" said Jerry. "That reminds me of a friend I had once in Houston. He wanted to be an astronaut but his vision was awful. He was always trying to improve his eyesight, but it never worked. He'd have carrot juice for every meal and wear these pinhole glasses. Anyway, twenty-fifteen means that what the average person sees at fifteen feet, the guy with incredible vision can see at twenty feet."

"You're that confident in the big metal guy, huh?"

"Hey, Sightsim has been in this business from the beginning. I think they know what they're doing."

"Can anything good come from Traverse City, Michigan?"

"Cherry capital of the world," said Jerry. "Don't knock it."

"'Cherry capital of the world'?"

"It's exactly that. They produce something like three-quarters of the cherries grown in the United States."

"What are you, a walking encyclopedia or something?" asked Dexter.

"My grandfather grew up there. He told me all about it."

"Well, it's a small world, huh?"

"How did a robot vision system company end up in Traverse City?"

"Beats me. How did Microsoft end up in Seattle?"

"Seattle is Bill Gates' hometown."

"Could be something similar with Sightsim," said Jerry,

Ten minutes later they pulled into the Woodward parking lot. Woodward was located on the east side of Columbus, off the outer belt, just north of Broad Street. Dexter and Jerry unloaded Bobby, setting him down next to the table that had again been erected in the parking lot.

"Dexter! Jerry!" said Paul as he came out the back door of the building. "Good to see you!" He gave each of the Grobotics men a vigorous handshake. "You should have let me know," he said, gesturing toward the inert robot. "I could've had a few of our guys help you manhandle that thing."

"Not to worry," said Dexter. "Eventually we want Bobby to need only one or two people to set him up."

"Alright. Well, anyway, we've got your power lines all set up here, just like last time. You still don't need Internet access, right? We only gave you one hundred twenty volts AC today."

"That's fine," said Jerry. "Let's just hope our results are not 'just like last time.'"

"I heard that!" Paul said jokingly. "On that point...uhh, I hope you're not offended, but the peanut gallery might not be as big as last time, considering what *did* happen last time."

"No apologies necessary," said Dexter. "We goofed big time on the last demo. I don't blame your employees for avoiding us--at least this time."

"I've asked those few who are here to wear eye protection at least," said Paul.

"Good idea."

Within ten minutes Dexter and Jerry had Bobby ready to go. Jerry was glad that it was a cloudy day since Bobby wouldn't be fooled by any shadows that might confuse his otherwise improved sight.

"Ready when you are," said Paul. He was in his yellow plastic protective suit and had just placed the helmet on his head. He walked toward Bobby and stopped about twenty feet away.

"Just a minute," said Jerry. "Dexter, initialization complete with you?" They had brought two computers with them this time, using one of them solely to monitor Bobby's "eyes."

"Roger, that," said Dexter. "I've got seven hundred by seven hundred DPI on each eye. It's your call."

"Alright, Paul!" said Jerry. "We're active in --three, --two, --one, GO!"

Bobby stirred to life, swiveled his head from left to right and took a few tentative steps forward. Paul stepped back and waited for Bobby to finish his startup sequence.

"Yeehaahh!" yelled Paul and began to serpentine around the empty parking lot. Bobby "noticed" Paul's rapid movements and began to trot toward the moving target.

"Paul, go over by the bystanders like last time!" shouted Jerry. "See if Bobby gets confused!"

Paul jogged over to the edge of the loading dock area and stopped in front of a line of Woodward employees, who had taken Paul's advice and were wearing various forms of eye guards. Bobby followed Paul and stopped about ten feet away. Paul stayed perfectly still, as did Bobby. Paul leapt away from the robot and ran along the line of people. Bobby stood still for a moment, then rotated his head from side to side.

"Oh, no," said Dexter. "Not again!"

"Hold on!" cautioned Jerry. "Bobby can do it!"

Bobby turned his head in the direction of Paul's running body, locked on, and immediately took off running toward the yellow figure. No matter how many times Paul ran in front of the line of bystanders, Bobby did not spray any of them.

"Give him a voice command to close in," Dexter said to Jerry.

"Bobby--five, five, seven--close to five feet!" shouted Jerry. Bobby would not respond to any voice commands without a password, or a pass number, in this case.

Try as he might, Paul could not elude the feverish robot. Bobby was just about to spray Paul with pepper spray when the machine's right leg started to emit a cloud of acrid smoke! Bobby slowed to a walk, and then stopped altogether.

"What's going on?" shouted Dexter. "He was closing in for the kill! Jerry?!"

"From the smell of it, I think Bobby just burnt up a motor," said Jerry.

"Dog-gone it!" yelled Dexter. "I'm getting tired of this hunk of metal!" He kicked the chair next to him and walked over to Bobby.

"Hmm, let's see," said Jerry, kneeling down by the side of the robot. "Looks like that new motor from Tranerix, in the upper leg. Sheesh! It fried the connecting wires as well!"

"That's it!" said Dexter. "I'm going to Motorflux tomorrow. I told you we should have used Motorflux, Jerry! Tranerix just can't give the endurance like Motorflux."

"Motorflux will increase power consumption by at least five watts, though, boss."

"What seems to be the problem?" asked Paul, walking up to the robot and trying to catch his breath. He had just peeled off the plastic suit and the helmet and was winded from his "dance" with Bobby.

"Stupid motor fried," said Dexter. "Can't take the strain."

"Wow," said Paul, looking over Jerry's shoulder. "That does look messy."

"Why didn't this happen before?" asked Paul.

"The short answer to that is probably that we've rarely had demos go this long," said Dexter.

"No pun intended," said Jerry, under his breath, "you know, *short* circuit."

"No pun *requested*!" said Dexter, visibly irritated.

"Just trying to raise the emotional temperature a little, boss."

"Ah, hell, I know," said Dexter, shaking his head back and forth. "I'm just getting tired of this constant *testing*! I want to *make* robots and then *sell* robots! R&D is fine, but how long does this have to go on?"

"Bobby did fine as far as it went," said Paul. "Don't get too down on yourself, Dex--at least it looks like your vision problems are over."

"Yeah, you have a point there. Maybe if I raise my head up a little I will see the light at the end of the tunnel."

"Remember," said Paul, you get Bobby in fighting shape and I can guarantee you a *minimum* of two hundred purchase orders."

"Right, right. I'll definitely keep that in mind. Thanks for being the target again today, Paul," said Dexter. "And thanks for all the setup work your people did."

"No problem, Dexter," said Paul. "You sure you don't need any help loading Bobby back in the van?"

"We should be just fine...thanks for asking."

"Great! Call me when you're ready for another demo."

"Will do, Paul. Let's just hope that it's the *last* demo."

"I heard that!" Paul said with a chuckle. "Bye!"

"See ya later!" Dexter turned to Jerry, who had just finished backing the van up to the inert robot. "Jerry, I'm serious. I'm going to Motorflux *tomorrow*. I'm not even going to wait for a commercial flight--I'm flying the Cessna up on my own."

"Boss," said Jerry, "not to be a stick-in-the-mud, but why not wait till after Christmas? Everyone's going to be winding down now for the Holidays. You can fly to Chicago in January."

"Well..." Dexter stood looking at Bobby defiantly, his arms akimbo.

Jerry looked up at the clouds. "Besides, look at this weather...I don't think we're supposed to get any sun for the next few days."

"Shoot, I didn't get my instrument rating for nothing, pal. I've flown in worse conditions than this. But, hey! Maybe you're right about the Holidays. I guess Motorflux can wait till January."

They loaded Bobby into the van and headed back to Grobotics.

****

"You really think I can go first round, huh?" Kevin asked Chad, who was busy packing a bag on his bed in their apartment. It was a few days before Christmas and Kevin and Chad were about to leave Columbus for home, a four-day respite from the grueling grind leading up to the Fiesta Bowl.

"Definitely!" said Chad, as he shoved his dirty laundry into his duffel bag. "You've got some of the best stats in the nation right now, bud. Granted, your interception count is a little high, but nobody's perfect. Any team in the National Football League would love to have you on their roster."

"But I can't throw the long bomb consistently."

"Bomb, splomb--who cares? You're a winner, guy! You make the first downs when it counts. You make the completions when it counts. We can't all be Doug Flutie, you know."

"So I go out every Sunday and make fifty-thousand fans happy," said Kevin tonelessly.

"And ten million more fans on TV too."

"Right. And I'll earn five million dollars every year."

"And two million more per year on endorsements," said Chad.

"Right again! But will I really be *doing* anything?"

"What do you want: to be President of the United States or something?"

"Just between you and me, I've thought of that...does the President really accomplish much?   I mean a heart surgeon--*he* accomplishes something."

Chad chortled and threw up his hands. "Fine, then be a heart surgeon!"

"Ehhh, just an overpaid plumber," said Kevin.

"You don't give up, do you, big guy?"

"All I know is we've gotta win the championship. After that, who cares?"

"Well at least you have your priorities straight, K-man."

"What about you, Chad?   What are you going to do after graduation?"

"That's easy...find a way to become eighteen again--so I can continue playing college ball."

"You have a shot at the pros, don't you?" asked Kevin.

"I don't know.   There's something about college football that you just can't find in the NFL." Chad pulled his duffel bag shut and set it by the door. "I'll worry about all that after the Fiesta Bowl. Right now I just hope my Mom is serving up her 'yam-wiches' tomorrow."

"Sweet." Kevin picked up his bag and walked out into the hall. "See you in Arizona, pal."

"Later, Mr. 'Q-B.'"

****

It was a slow day for Thad so far. It was already one in the afternoon and he hadn't even broken even. He had to pay about seventy dollars a day for gas and two hundred bucks a month to the bank for his car payment. He figured he would need about ten more dollars till he started making a profit. *At least it's challenging*, he consoled himself as he sat in the cab with the engine running to keep warm. *Beats getting paid a boring hourly rate, at least. I never know how much, or how little, for that matter, I'll make each day. I just would've thought that it'd be a little busier today with Christmas just around the corner.* He had his hands poised over the computer buttons, ready to pounce on the next good fare that popped up. There were three fares sitting on the screen, all east-siders that no one wanted. Since Thad was sitting at Bethel and 315, his "taxus nexus" spot, as he liked to call it, he was hoping to be the first to book into one of the lucrative airport runs from the Northwest side. Suddenly zone ninety appeared on the screen! Thad snapped to attention, pressed "9", then "0", then "send." Four agonizing seconds went by, the computer clicked once, twice, then it spat out "Zone 90, Position 3." *Rats!* he thought. *I thought I would've beaten everybody on that one. Probably some guy sitting downtown.* He waited to see if the guys in positions one and two would give it up...no such luck. Thad was about to relax when zone eighty-eight popped up. *Now, this one is mine--I'm sitting* right in *zone eighty-eight.* He pressed all the buttons and was rewarded with the fare. *Let's see, going from Powell to--yes! The airport!* He pushed the "accept" button and looked up the address on the map. As he drove out of the parking lot, he glanced at the name of the fare--"Cheryl."   *Why does that sound familiar? Powell...Cheryl...hmm.* He headed up Route 315 North. *The sooner I get there, the bigger the tip.*

When he saw "Cheryl's" house, he couldn't help but let out a loud "Yelp!" It was the very home of the beautiful blonde he had driven just a week or two ago!

"This is too good to be true!" he said aloud in the cab. "Thank you, St Raphael!"

He hopped out and opened the trunk, just as the woman came out her front door.

"Hello again!" he said cheerfully as she approached the car.

"Oh..." It took her a second to recognize Thad. "Oh! It's *you* again!" she said with a wide smile.

"Service with a smile!" Thad lifted her bag into the trunk and then sat behind the wheel. "Cleveland airport, right?" he turned to smile at her.

"Why not just make it St Louis, since that's where I'm headed."

"Great! That'll be two dollars a mile, so...what? About seven hundred dollars?"

"Chicken feed for a lab researcher," she said.

Thad backed out of her driveway and got onto Route 315. "By the way, my name's Thad...Thad Rankin."   He turned slightly and looked at her.

"Well, *Thad,* my name's Cheryl. Cheryl Estevez."

"Ah, an Irish first name and a Mexican last name."

"You gotta a problem with that?" she said in mock indignation.

"As long as I don't have to guess how your parents met."

"On a blind date, like any good self-respecting American. My Dad was studying at Washington University in Saint Louis and my Mom was working at McDonnell Douglas, also in Saint Louis--and Cheryl isn't exactly an Irish name...it's a combination of Sharon and Carol."

"So, anyway, an Irish girl gets a security clearance to work at a defense contractor?"

"She had an office job and didn't need any clearances. She never dealt with sensitive material. How'd you know she is Irish?"

"Just a lucky guess, but what about your Dad?" asked Thad. "What was he studying?"

"Electrical Engineering--again--like any good self-respecting American."

"You sure are big--just a second." Thad paused a few seconds to get around a semi truck while getting onto the outer belt. "You sure are big on the 'self-respecting American' thing."

"I'm just a little tired of being mistaken for some lazy Hispanic or drunken Irishman."

"'Irish-person', you mean."

"Now you're talking my language!" she said, brightening up. "I assume you too are not a fan of the politically correct crowd?"

"Darn straight," he said. "Language is meant to be forthright and forthcoming, as Jefferson used to say."

"Did he really say that?"

"No, I just like to sound like I'm well read."

"But I thought you *were*, you know, 'Alice in Wonderland' and all that?"

"That's about it. I'm not like my brother, he's a bountiful biblioteque."

"What's that?"

"Just my pet way of saying he's a voracious reader."

"Really. Is he a professor or something?"

"Actually he's a priest."

"No kidding?" asked Cheryl, leaning against the front seat. "I'm a Catholic, too--I mean, I assume you're Catholic, right?"

"You got that right," said Thad, nodding his head. "What do you think about--" he abruptly stopped. *Don't ruin this now with the Garabandal stuff,* he remonstrated himself. *Just let it be for now.*

"About what?"

"About Saint Michael's?" said Thad, quickly changing the subject of his question.

"What about Saint Michael's?"

"Well, uh, that's where my brother is in residence as a priest. Have you ever been there?"

"A few times. My local parish is Saint Joan of Arc."

"And how do you like that? By the way, you hear they're thinking about shooting some more deer in Sharon Woods?" Thad asked as they passed the metro park at the corner of I-71 and the Outerbelt.

"Yeah, I did read about that. Looks like there're too many again." She fell silent.

"So...Saint Joan of Arc?" Thad asked again.

"Oh, yeah," she said, turning her head from the window, "It's OK, I guess."

Thad said nothing, wondering if he should press the issue. *What's she thinking?* he asked himself. *Should I mention Garabandal?*

"What do you think about the Warning?" she blurted out.

"Yes!" said Thad loudly, pumping his fist up and down.

"What?" she asked.

"I was just debating whether to ask you the same question."

"Welll," she said cautiously, "then do you know what I mean by the 'Warning'?"

"Double yes!" said Thad, clenching his teeth together and giving a wide grin. "You're awesome, girl!"

"Garabandal?" she asked.

"Triple yes! I can't believe this!" Thad picked up his clipboard and handed it back to Cheryl. "All right. Here you go. Write it down," he said matter-of-factly.

"Whaa? Write *what* down?"

"Your phone number, Ma'am," Thad laughed. "We've got some talkin' to do!"

"Is that an order or a request?" She started to look in her purse for a pen.

Thad glanced back at her. "There's a pen at the top of the clipboard. It's hidden behind the metal part. And it's an order, by the way. You're enlisted."

"Enlisted in what?" she asked as she wrote down her number.

"Rankin's Religious Roustabouts--RRR."

"How big is the 'RRR'?" she asked, handing him the clipboard.

"Oh, hundreds and hundreds."

"Really? How long has 'RRR' been going on?"

Thad looked at his watch. "Precisely seven point two seconds."

"Ohh," she said, nodding slowly, "I get the picture."

"Actually, I'm promoting you to vice president right now."

"And you're president, right?"

"I was elected!" he said. "It was unanimous!"

"By 'hundreds and hundreds,' right?"

"That's just projected membership; right now we're a little smaller."

"Like two?" Cheryl asked.

"Only one officially right now. I'm waiting to hear from another potential member," he said as he smiled at her.

"Wow, you could double your membership!"

"Oh, I know, I'll just take it all in stride."

Cheryl sat back in the seat and wondered. *Is this guy for real? He seems to know about Garabandal, but he's a* taxi driver, *for crying out loud! Can I really get interested in someone who isn't earning much money? Is he really an engineer?* She watched as they took the exit for the airport. *Well, he already has my phone number. I'll talk to him after Christmas.*

"Which do you think is higher in the order of creation?" asked Thad. "Chocolate milk or White Zinfandel?"

"Where did *that* come from?" she asked. *This guy really is flipped out,* she thought.

"I just can't decide which I like better. I like to prioritize everything, but that one has me stuck."

"Well, if you must know, I guess I would pick chocolate milk," said Cheryl.

"And your reason?"

"You can drink more chocolate milk at one sitting than White Zinfandel."

"True--as long as it doesn't make your face break out. By the way, which airline?" asked Thad.

"Southwest again."

"Okay, Southwest. Yeah, but what if you *could* drink as much White Zinfandel as chocolate milk--then which would be higher?"

"Look, Socrates, I'm a researcher, not a philosopher. I know they both end with 'h-e-r,' but that's about as far as it goes. Just drink your chocolate milk and don't complain."

"As you wish, Cheryl. The customer is always right." He stopped the car in front of the Southwest sign, put the car in park, and stopped the meter. "That'll be forty-two, eighty, if you please?"

"No discount for blondes this time?"

"Actually, it'll be five dollars more, if you include your first month's dues for Rankin's Religious Roustabouts."

She handed him fifty dollars. "Consider the extra to be a tip. I'm still undecided about the 'RRR' thing."

"Of course, milady."

After taking her bag out of the trunk and putting it on the sidewalk he slammed the trunk lid and walked over to the curb where she was sorting through her purse for the tickets.

"So when will you be back?" he asked her.

"Before New Year's. I'm going to visit my folks in Saint Louis."

"Well, I'll be calling you when you get back. Be sure to consider joining 'RRR.'"

"Merry Christmas, Thad."

"Merry Christmas."

He watched her walk up to the baggage check-in stand, then got into the cab and drove off.

                    ****

"Shen! Could you pick it up a little?" said Sergeant Moy.

"I'm trying, sir," replied Shen. He broke into a run and caught up with Moy, who was standing with arms akimbo alongside the dirt path.

"These new boots are a little uncomfortable," Shen said as he shifted the pack on his back. "I wish we could have kept the ones we got back home."

Sergeant Moy laughed derisively. "Oh, *'uncomfortable'*? I suppose 'home' for you is some plush suburb of Beijing, huh? Sorry to ruin your vacation here in the desert, soldier! Now get a move on -- when we cross the border, you'll *really* have something to be *uncomfortable* about!"

****

Luckily Coach Panaski had given the team an extra day off, so Kevin was able to head up to his parents' house in Rocky River, a suburb on the west side of Cleveland. Although it was the twenty-first of December, this would still only give the football players a precious few days around home and hearth for the holidays, since they would be leaving for the Fiesta Bowl on the day after Christmas. As he drove into town on Detroit Road, Kevin mentally reviewed all the friends and relatives he planned to visit before he had to head back to Columbus. When he saw Bob Stetka's barber shop, just before he got to Wright Avenue, he reminded himself that he had best get a haircut tomorrow or Saturday since there was a good chance he'd be interviewed on national TV in the media hype surrounding the upcoming game. By the time he pulled up to his parents' house, he had just about mentally filled up his social calendar for the next three days. Then he caught sight of the banner hanging over the front porch. "Welcome Home, Champ" it read in foot-high scarlet and gray letters. *Not yet, Mom and Dad,* he thought to himself. *It's going to take a lot of work before that sign is true.*

Just then his Dad came out the front door and walked around to Kevin's side of the car.

"Welcome home, champ!" he said as Kevin climbed out of the car and gave him a bear hug.

"Hey, not so fast, Dad. There's still a little contest down in Arizona that has to happen before you can say that."

"You beat Michigan, Kevin. Face it, you're a champ!"

"Sigh, some things never change."

"Let me help you get your bags, son. You're just in time for dinner. Your mother has cooked up a wicked pepper steak for us--

chow's on!"

"Sounds good. I'll put my stuff up in my room and be right down."

The dinner was filled with all the latest news about the Buckeye football program and the various tidbits of happenings around Rocky River. Kevin spent the next three days visiting his friends around town and all too soon it was Christmas day. Kevin was sitting by the Christmas tree in his parents' living room and thought he would take the time to read the latest John Grisham novel, since the house was quiet, at least until his young nieces and nephews showed up later on. Just as he settled into his favorite chair his mother called to him from the kitchen.

"Kevin, would you be so kind as to give Mitty a walk? The vet said it's good for him to get some exercise everyday to help heal his leg that was hurt last week." Mitty was the family dog, a mix of Collie and German Shepherd, so named because of his white paws that resembled catcher's mitts.

"Well, I was hoping to catch up on my reading a little, but, fine, I'll do it."

He went to the basement door and grabbed the leash, the sound of which brought Mitty galloping to him at full limping-speed.

"Calm down, now, Mitty," he said, as the dog pranced around, whining with excitement.

"You might want to stop by the Leiterson's and say hello," his Mom suggested when Kevin opened the back door.

Kevin let out a short laugh. "Mom, I have a girlfriend in Columbus, and she's just fine. I long ago gave up any thoughts of dating Jennifer Leiterson."

"Okay," she said in a lilting voice, "but you never know."

"Thanks, Mom." He herded Mitty through the door, around to the front of the house, and started walking down the sidewalk. Kevin had always liked the neighborhood his parents had chosen, since it was close to the center of town, not out in some newly developed subdivision on the edge of the Cleveland megalopolis. *There's a sense of belonging here*, he thought. *The typical suburb is like living on the Moon or something. You had your "domestic pod," your "retail pod," your "sports pod." You couldn't walk between anything out in the suburbs; you had to take your "spaceship" to get anywhere. Here in the city, or town, everything was connected to everything else--with sidewalks. Like Heinen's here,* he reasoned as he passed the local supermarket. *Or like Ten Thousand Villages over there. Bet you get a lot more personalized service there than you get at most of those huge mega-stores way out in the 'burbs.*

Mitty had stopped to smell a fire hydrant and didn't want to leave it.

"Come on, Mitty! Time to go! There'll be plenty of other things to smell before we have to go home." Kevin didn't notice an unkempt man in a wheelchair who had rolled up behind him on the sidewalk.

"Typical dog," the man said. "Can't pass up a good fire hydrant."

"Huh?" asked Kevin as he spun around and faced the stranger. Kevin noticed the man's left leg was missing below the knee and that he hadn't shaved in a few days.

"I said your dog is like any other dog--they just can't pass up a good fire hydrant."

"Oh...right, right," said Kevin, tossing his head back with a chuckle. "You new in town? I don't ever remember seeing you before."

"Oh, I guess I sort of stick out with my wheelchair, huh? Didn't know there was a cripple in good ol' Rocky River, right?"

"Oh, no, I didn't mean *that*," said Kevin. "I, uh, just meant that-- well, you see, I don't live here full-time anymore..."

"I know who you are, bud. Kevin Conaway--star quarterback for the Ohio State Buckeyes."

"Right," said Kevin, with a trace of embarrassment in his voice. "I didn't know you could get the games on TV up here."

"Heck, with all the new satellite channels, I don't think I missed a single game this season," said the man.

"Well, you know *my* name; what's yours?"

"Like you really care, chief. You're a national treasure; I'm the town bum."

"I don't know if I'd go *that* far."

"How far *what*? That you're not a national treasure, or I'm not the town bum?"

"Well, uh," stumbled Kevin. "I meant that *I'm* not exactly a national treasure."

"Oh, great! So I'm still the town bum."

"No, I didn't mean that either. You're just a, a--"

"Go on," said the man.

"Well, I don't know anything about you--what *is* your name?"

"Jason Bricker. Everyone just calls me 'Jake.'"

"Nice to meetcha, Jake." Kevin held out his hand.

"Oh," said Jake sarcastically, "I get to shake the hand of the mighty *Kevin Conaway*. Maybe I'm not worthy! Is my hand clean enough? What do you think?" He held up his palm for Kevin to see.

"Looks fine to me," said Kevin, moving his hand closer to Jake's.

"Naw, I don't think so. I'm not *good enough* for you."

"What's the problem, Jake?" said Kevin, withdrawing his hand. "What did I ever do to you?"

"It's what you *didn't* do--it's what *all* of you didn't do," snapped Jake. He turned his head aside and spat on the ground. "I went to Kuwait in the first Gulf War and had my leg blown off and I got that Gulf War Syndrome from Saddam's chemicals or whatever and what do I get? I'll tell you what I got--squat! I live in a hole in the wall, fleabag apartment and get a lousy two hundred dollars a month to live on! Look at *you*--quarterback for Ohio State, college education…hell, you've probably got women begging to meet you, right? Right?"

"Well, I uhh, have a girlfriend…"

"Just *one*? Hell, if I were you…Ah, forget it! Why do I even bother?" Jake made a motion to move on down the sidewalk, but Kevin stood in his path.

"Just a minute, Jake," said Kevin timidly. "Can't you get a job anywhere? What about your family?"

"Family," Jake said disgustedly. "Both my parents are dead and my sister died in a car wreck two years ago. I got nothin'!"

"What about a job?" asked Kevin as he restrained Mitty from chasing a passing cat.

"Who's gonna hire, me, champ? Haven't you noticed? I'm a *cripple*, for crying out loud!"

"Couldn't you work on a computer or something? Surely there's *something* you can do."

"Hell," said Jake, shaking his head and spitting on the ground again, "as long as I get my two hundred dollars a month, why should I work?" He reached in the bag hanging on one side of the wheelchair and pulled out a bottle. "Besides, old Jack Daniels here keeps me company when I get lonely." He unscrewed the cap and took a long drink.

"What are you doing for Christmas? Are you going somewhere for dinner, at least?"

"No one in this town will have me, big guy! Look, nice talkin' at ya, but I think I'll be going." He moved toward Kevin, who stepped out of the way.

Kevin stood transfixed for a moment, then started following Jake. "Wait a minute, Jake!"

Jake continued down the street and didn't reply.

"Jake, why don't you come over to my parents' house for dinner this evening?"

Jake stopped and spun his wheelchair around. "You can't go inviting me over to your old man's house with out asking them first, bud. Look, they probably know about me and wouldn't appreciate you doing that."

"They'll okay it, Jake. They're good people."

"Aww, forget it." Jake turned his wheelchair and started rolling again. "You don't know nothin' 'bout me," he said over his shoulder. "I've got a reputation around this town, and that includes your parents."

"Jake, wait," Kevin put his hand on the wheelchair and stopped it. "Give it a shot, whaddya say? C'mon, it's Christmas!"

Jake hung his head and didn't speak. Kevin waited for a reply and watched as Mitty raised his leg on a nearby pole.

"I'll tell you what," said Jake. "You first go back home and ask your parents--when I'm not around. If they say yes, I'll come. You can come get me--I live in that building right over there." He pointed to a run-down duplex about a block down the street.

"It's a deal, Jake. I'll stop by for you in about an hour. I'm sure they'll say yes."

"Good. Later."

"See ya, Jake." Kevin walked Mitty for another half hour, then returned home. As he expected, his parents had no objection to having Jake over for dinner, so Kevin wasted no time in going to pick him up.

"Told you they'd agree," said Kevin when Jake came to the door of his apartment.

"They must not know about me, I guess," said Jake.

"Oh, no, they said they have seen you around and had wondered about you. My Mom said she is looking forward to meeting you."

"Are your parents weird or something? I get the impression that most people in this burg hate my guts!" Jake wheeled himself out the door, then locked it behind him.

"Maybe that's not true, Jake. Maybe you just need people to get to know you."

"I've only been here for about two months now."

"Well, give people a chance to meet you. You might be surprised."

"We'll see."

The dinner at the Conaway's lasted till seven and Jake regaled them all with his real-life stories of his experiences in the first Gulf War. Under a clear and cold winter night sky, Kevin pushed his new-found friend back to his apartment.

"Now that wasn't all that bad was it?" asked Kevin.

"Kevin, I haven't enjoyed myself that much for years. I really want to thank you for your hospitality."

"Glad I could be of help. We'll have to do it again sometime."

"You just make sure you win that game--ya hear, Kevin?"

"I hear ya, Jake." He fell silent for a moment, but then blurted out: "Anne definitely wants me to win."

"Who's Anne?" Jake asked, but then turned around and smiled up at Kevin. "Ohh, *Annne*. She's that girl you were talking about at dinner, right?"

"Right."

"What exactly do you mean, she *definitely wants* you to win? Of course she wants you to win, right?"

"Aw, shoot! I shouldn't have told you anything."

"Something on your mind, Kevin?"

"I got a *lot* on my mind."

They came up to Jake's front door and Jake used his key to open it. "Hey, Kevin, I've got a beer or two in the fridge. Why don't I return the favor and you come in and we'll chat a bit?"

"Uhh," said Kevin, glancing at his watch, "you know I have to leave early tomorrow."

"Just for a little bit...I want to hear about this girlfriend of yours."

"Well," stammered Kevin. "All right. But not for long."

"Great!" Jake wheeled himself through the door and closed it after Kevin had entered.

"Cozy little place you've got here, Jake," said Kevin looking around.

"It's warm so far, I guess. Would you like a beer?"

"Actually, how 'bout a Coke or something?"

"Sprite?"

"That'd be fine."

Jake moved out to the kitchenette and came back with the soft drink.

"All right, big guy," said Jake, "let's have it."

"About Anne?"

"Heck yes, about Anne. Look Kevin, I may be in a wheel chair and all that, but I'm not a *complete* idiot. I know when I hear strain in someone's voice."

"Whew!" said Kevin, exhaling and leaning back on the couch. "'Strain': you nailed it!"

"She wants to break up with you or something?"

"Actually, just the opposite--she wants to get married."

"Aha! You're trying to avoid the ball and chain."

"I might as well tell you the real secret: I promised her that if we won the national championship, I would marry her."

"Yikes!" said Jake. "Now, that *is* a problem!"

"What's a guy to do?" asked Kevin, shrugging his shoulders. "When I promised her, we were ranked tenth in the nation and I really didn't think we'd make it to the title game."

Jake nodded his head and took a swig of his Coors. "Well, do you love her?"

"I've dated her for almost three years!"

"Yeah, but do you *love* her?"

"I love all good-looking babes."

"You think you'll find a better woman when you're in the pros, right?"

"Sometimes I don't know what I want."

"You can make it into the NFL, can't you?" asked Jake.

"It's not whether I *can*, it's whether I *want* to."

"Whoa," said Jake with a laugh. "You don't *want* to be a millionaire?"

"It's not just money. Look, Jake, why did you join the Army?"

"I wanted to serve my country."

"Are you glad you did?"

"I'm glad I did, I'm just not glad I got this bum leg."

"I feel the same thing a lot of the time," said Kevin. "I think there's something more I can do besides play football and earn money."

"You've got a problem, bub. Why don't you join the Navy and see the world--or the Peace Corps or something."

"The Peace Corps? Is that still going on?"

"Yeah, I saw something on that in the paper about a month ago."

"Hmm," said Kevin, scratching his head, "I never thought of the Peace Corps. That was started by Kennedy, right?"

"I really don't know. It just seems like something you could do if you don't want to join the military."

"Right."

"You know, Kevin, if I've learned one thing from my life, it's gratitude. I know I might come across as being a real bitching slob, but underneath I'm glad that the good Lord at least kept me alive in that war. I'll get my act together here pretty soon. I'll stop drinking so much--maybe I'll even go back to school or something. But I just hope you're grateful for everything you've been given. You're at the apex of college sports--don't let it go to your head."

"Thanks for the advice, Jake...yeah, I'll keep it in mind." Kevin looked at his watch. "Well, I guess I really better get going."

"Ha! I imagine you really might have a lot to do to get ready for the biggest event in college sports."

"You speak truth, guy." Kevin put the empty soda can on the coffee table and walked to the door. "I'll stop in next time I'm in town, Jake. Do you have e-mail?"

"You mean am I into the yuppie culture--no, I don't have e-mail, but that's another thing I might look into. I think I could use the computers at the library for that."

"Yeah, that'd probably work--here." Kevin pulled a pen out of his pocket and looked for a piece of paper. "I'll give you my e-mail address."

"Just write it on that newspaper there. That'll do for now."

"Okay," said Kevin, kneeling down to write on the coffee table. He straightened up and handed the paper to Jake. "There you have it."

"Thanks a lot, Kevin. You know it's not everyday you get to

meet someone and then see him on national TV the following week."

"Well, just pray that we win, all right?"

"You got it, bro."

Kevin opened the door and faced Jake. "I hope you do some of those things you talked about, Jake."

"We'll see, Kevin. Good luck!"

"Thanks, bye."

Chapter 7

Some comedic historians hold that by 2800 B.C. the ancient Sumerians actually were quite adept at the game of football. As a matter of fact, evidence suggests that they dominated the known world in the biennial world championship. The question has often arose as to why this gridiron game fell into disuse for more than 4700 years, i.e., why the game had resurfaced on American college campuses around 1900 A.D. Modern archeology has determined that the game was actually banned worldwide by a coalition of nations because of the detrimental effects it was having on the civilized world. Entire Saturdays were given over to preparing for, watching, and then discussing the football game. The hype began to spill over into the workweek, causing farmers to start spending less and less time on agricultural output. Finally King Enmebaragesi forbade it in the Sumerian empire, followed closely by the rest of the known world.

Gameday at the Fiesta Bowl was turning out to have ancient Sumeria written all over it. No fewer than twenty-five Airbus 380s had been chartered from Columbus to Phoenix and thousands more had arrived on regularly scheduled flights. Since Ohio State graduated about ten thousand students every year, there were few cities around the country where there was not a large, *vociferous* Buckeye brigade to cheer on their beloved players. Hotels were booked as far away as Tucson and Flagstaff, not to mention the greater Phoenix area. In an age of telecommuting and instant communication, fans nonetheless just wanted to *physically be where* the national championship game was being played. By noon of game day Tempe police had already closed University Drive and South Rural Road to car traffic, because of the multitudes of people walking around the stadium area.

Conditions in Columbus in the week prior to the championship game had even been "worse." Central Ohioans were used to the excitement of big football games, but for some reason this particular matchup had caused a stir unlike any other. Three days before game day four giant screen TVs had been set up on each side of the statehouse downtown and rare was the afternoon when several thousand fans were not standing in the cold watching replays of classic Ohio State games, most noticeably the 2002 National Championship game with Miami. In like manner, the PBS TV station had been showing old games all week. The Honda plant in Marysville even delayed its post holiday startup till after the game because they were afraid lack of attendance and/or concentration would severely hinder product quality.

At the start of the game, eight pm, the weather couldn't have been better in Phoenix: 65 degrees with clear skies and an almost-full moon rising in the east. Kevin and Chad, the two Ohio State captains, walked out to midfield for the coin toss. Opposite them stood the three team captains from Southern California.

"Good luck, boys," Chad said as he shook each player's hand.

"Yeah, right," said the USC player on the left. "Good luck to you, too."

"All right, men," said the referee. "Let's get this show on the road. Ohio State, you will call it in the air." He tossed the coin in the air and pointed to Kevin.

"Heads," Kevin said.

All eyes followed the coin as it spun on the ground and came to a rest.

"Tails," said the ref as he picked up the coin. "Southern California, it's your call."

"We want to receive," said the tallest of the USC players.

"Sweet!" said Chad, clapping Kevin on the shoulder.

"Southern California has won the toss and has elected to receive the kickoff," the referee announced over the PA speakers. A roar of approval went up from the OSU sections of the stadium.

"Way to use that double-sided coin!" Chad joked with Kevin as they trotted off the field.

"Heck, it wouldn't have mattered if I had! Why didn't Southern

California want to kickoff?" Most football teams would rather defer receiving the kickoff at the start of the game, so that they would receive the kickoff after halftime.

"Woody's up to his old tricks again," concluded Chad. It wouldn't be the first time the ghost of Woody Hayes, Ohio State's legendary coach, had been credited with a turn of the Buckeyes' fortune.

"Well, let's hope he keeps it up for about four more hours."

USC returned the kickoff to the twenty-eight yard line and moved the ball only six yards on their first three plays, forcing them to punt. Rodney Brooks, one of OSU's best special teams players, caught the punt and made it to the forty-five yard line before being bushwhacked by a bunch of USC Trojans.

Kevin, Chad, and the rest of the Buckeye offensive players ran out to the middle of the field and huddled up.

"All right, you birds," said Kevin with a glint in his eye, "Panaski says it's the option to the right--right now, first play."

"You've gotta be kidding me!" said Chad. "Not the first play!"

"What have we got to lose?" asked one of the tackles.

"Our asses, that's what!" shot back the center.

"Look, boys," said Kevin, "this is the last thing they'll be expecting, and, besides, we've got fifty-nine minutes left if it doesn't work."

"Always the optimist," groaned Chad.

The OSU players lined up, strong side to the right.

"Turquoise five, five, hike, HIKE!" said Kevin in a loud voice. The center snapped the ball and Kevin took a few steps back and rolled out to the right. He looked behind him--and Jason was right where he was supposed to be. But then a little voice said to look downfield. Kevin hesitated a millisecond and then turned his head. There was Platwood *completely wide-open*! Kevin didn't allow himself the time even to rejoice. He lofted the ball down the right sideline and, true to form, Platwood hauled it in and kept on running. The Southern Cal safety was about ten yards away, closing fast, when he and the other OSU receiver collided! Platwood ran another twenty yards--right into the end zone--untouched by Trojan hands!

Complete and utter pandemonium rocked the stadium! In a repeat of the Michigan game, a small group of OSU students burst onto the field and headed for one of the goalposts before being waylaid by a swarming mass of Arizona state troopers.

"It's Woody again!" shouted Chad as he high-fived anyone in sight. He ran up to Kevin and jumped on his back. "You're a Greek god, you jackass!"

"Who's this Woody you're talking about?" shouted Kevin.

"You weren't even hit and you've already got a concussion!" said Chad, knocking Kevin up the side of his head.

"If plays like that give me a concussion, I'll take ten more!"

"Now I know you got a concussion!" shouted Chad as he and Kevin trotted over to the sidelines, where, after about three minutes the rowdiness finally came down to a level at which they could concentrate on the remaining fifty-eight minutes of the game.

USC, playing like the number-two-ranked team they were, marched down the field after the ensuing kickoff and were able to at least score a field goal against the crushing Ohio State defense. The ball traded hands for the rest of the first half, with each team scoring a couple of times so that by halftime, the score was OSU 21, USC 17.

In the locker room at halftime, after all the OSU specialty coaches had talked with their players, the Buckeyes gathered for a pep talk by Coach Panaski.

"You boys don't know how much this championship would mean to me," said Coach Panaski. "And you really don't know how much it will mean to you, either. Forty years from now, when you're sitting around your television with your children and grandchildren watching the national championship, you'll be able to say: 'I played in that game once.' And your children and grandchildren will tell all their friends that you played in that game. Now, we're ahead by four points, and in two hours, I want to be ahead by *twenty*-four points. Enough talk. You seniors..." He looked around the room, his eyes settling on Kevin's. "You have to leave it all on the field. This is the very last time you'll wear the scarlet and gray in a football game. If you *want* to win this game, we will. If not, we won't. And I'm telling you right now, you *do* want to win this game...So let's go out and kick some Trojan butt!"

The Buckeye players rose to their feet, clapping their hands and cheering powerfully. They exploded onto the field and ran to their sideline.

"Kevin Conaway for President!" teased Chad as they watched the players line up for the kickoff.

"You can be my minister of propaganda, you loudmouth!" said

Kevin. He walked over to Coach Panaski and looked down at the list of plays on the card strapped to his arm. "What'll it be, Coach? The option again?"

"Not so fast, Kevin," said Panaski. "You can bet they won't get fooled on that again. No, this time, three yards and a cloud of dust."

"Classic Ohio State football, huh?"

"That's what we want USC to *think*, at least," said Panaski with a grin. "Our game plan might just change, however." He winked at Kevin.

"Oh, might I be privy to this late-breaking development?"

"I'll let you know. Right now--the first play will be a sweep to the left. Depending on how that goes, the next play might be a quarterback draw. And then--well, why ruin the surprise?"

"I do happen to be quarterback, you know," said Kevin. "Some people actually think that the QB should know what's going on in a football game."

"I'll send you an e-mail, if it's necessary," said Panaski smilingly.

Coach and quarterback watched anxiously as Southern California kicked off. Ohio State caught the ball in the end zone and ran it back to the twenty-five yard line.

"I'll be waiting for that e-mail," Kevin said to Panaski.

"I might just send you a note by courier pigeon."

Kevin jogged out to the huddle and told his offense of the first two scripted plays by Panaski. On the sweep, Chad gained two yards, followed by the quarterback draw which netted only three more.

Kevin looked over to the sidelines and saw Panaski giving the play to one of the receivers, who then came sprinting out to the huddle.

"Copperfield fifteen," said the receiver to Kevin as the players formed around him.

"Oh, nooo!" said Kevin. "That'll never work!"

"Refresh my memory," said one of the tackles. "What exactly is that?"

Kevin reviewed the play and made sure all his players knew their routes. He crouched down behind the center who then hiked the ball. Kevin immediately turned to face the goalpost, and walked a few steps toward it, cradling the ball in his arms. Five OSU players were all downfield, waving their arms frantically. Two Southern Cal linebackers broke through and ran straight for Kevin. They sacked him violently, throwing him to the ground like a penalty flag. But--he didn't have the ball! Fumble! The linebackers searched the field--where was the ball?

Meanwhile, the center was running backward, the ball against his stomach, covered by his beefy arms! By the time the USC defense realized that they had been hoodwinked, the OSU center had crossed the line of scrimmage and made a first down. A USC safety zipped over and easily tripped up the Buckeye center.

The crowd roared its approval and jubilation again set in on the OSU sideline.

"Don't say it!" shouted Kevin, as Chad came running up.

"Hey, that wasn't the ghost of Woody, that was the spirit of Panaski!" laughed Chad, giving his quarterback a shove. "I'm surprised that play was even legal!"

"Hey, dude, the center handed me the ball and I handed it back to him—we just did it so quickly that no one noticed."

Eight plays later, Chad lunged across the goal line and scored another OSU touchdown. The game went much like the first half, with each team trading touchdowns and field goals several times. With three minutes left in regulation, the score stood at OSU 38, USC 40. The Trojans had the ball on their own thirty yard line and were trying to run the clock out.

Kevin and Chad were nervously pacing the sideline, trying to stay out of each other's way. As they ran into each other for the third time, Chad abruptly stopped Kevin.

"You better not be thinking about that promise you made to Anne!"

"What should I be thinking?"

"Look, Kevin, I don't know whether you want to marry that woman or not, but I'm telling you right now, you *do* want to win this game!"

"I didn't even think about Anne till a minute ago," protested Kevin.

"I know," replied Chad. "I saw you staring off into space--I *thought* that was it!"

"I know, I know," said Kevin, shaking his head up and down.

"Kevin, get a grip! You don't have to marry her if we win! It was just a whimsical thing you said. It's not like you signed a contract or something."

"Uhh...right."

"You *didn't* sign a contract, did you?"

"I didn't *sign* anything...I..."

"You what?"

"I got her an engagement ring--but I haven't given it to her yet," said Kevin sheepishly.

"I thought you didn't want to marry her?"

"I know, I know."

"You sure must know a lot."

"Chad, it's not like I said--" Kevin was cutoff by a sudden roar from the crowd.

"Fumble!" said Chad, jumping up and down. "And we got the ball! Let's go, K-man, we got some work to do!"

Kevin got some hurried instructions from Coach Panaski and then sprinted out to the huddle.

"All right, boys," Kevin told the players as they gathered around him, "Coach says we get ten more yards and then it's a chip shot for Whinney. We're gonna run Jason right up the gut, and then we'll go from there."

The Buckeyes lined up with Jason in the backfield. Kevin took the snap and slammed it into the running back's stomach. Kevin continued his route, pretending to still have the ball when he heard a word which turned his stomach.

"Fumble!" someone yelled.

White and red jerseys were converging on the ball. Just as it appeared that Ohio State had recovered the fumble, the ball came flying out of the pile and bounced around the center of the field! Again, a mass of players descended on the pigskin. A USC player stretched out his arms and put his hand on top of the ball. He was desperately trying to get his other hand on the ball, when an OSU player accidentally let his foot kick the ball! The ball leapt up from the ground and sailed toward the center of the goal posts. The ball was just about to pass over the crossbar when--pssss!--it suddenly exploded in mid-air! Like a lame duck, it fell straight down--beyond the crossbar.

"What the hell?!!" shouted Chad, throwing his helmet to the ground. "That was good! We won! What happened to the ball?"

The crowd was a jumble of shouted questions and angry bursts of temper. A hush slowly spread over the masses as an accented voice boomed over the PA system.

"If we can so accurately hit a football in flight, think of what we can do to your head! You shouldn't have bought all those CD players that we made for you. We used that same technology to perfect our rifle scopes."

"Who is this joker?" asked Kevin, walking over to Coach Panaski. "We won, right?"

A subdued ripple of laughter washed over the crowd as fans pointed to the press box where a man dressed as a Chinese soldier was holding a microphone. Then without warning, a burst of machine-gun fire hit the scoreboard and it went dark. People dove for the ground and shrieked in horror.

"It's some terrorist asshole!" said Kevin after he had hit the grass.

"Who are *they*?" asked Panaski, as he rolled onto his back and pointed at the stadium entrances. An unbroken stream of Chinese soldiers jogged onto the field and into the stands. All carried AK-47s.

"Is this some kind of joke?" Kevin looked over at Panaski and then Chad. "Is the FBI doing some mock attack thing?"

As if in answer to his question, several machine guns fired high up in the stands and a group of five dead fans fell, cascading down the seats.

"Resistance is pointless," said the Chinese voice over the PA system. "We simply ask that you go out to your cars and head home."

"There's not many of them yet," said Chad. "We should all just swarm them!"

As if reading his mind, a group of fans on the far end of the field tried to do just that. The Chinese soldier there saw them coming and calmly swung his rifle in a circle in full automatic mode, creating a perfect circle of dead and dying USC fans.

"Please don't cause anymore unnecessary suffering," said the general over the loudspeakers. "Just exit the stadium and you can go home."

A pair of athletic trainers rushed to help the victims lying on the field, under the unblinking eyes of the Chinese soldiers, who continued filling up the playing field.

"This isn't happening!" moaned Kevin. "*Chinese!?* What in the name of hell are *Chinese* soldiers doing at the Fiesta Bowl?"

"You quiet!" shouted one of the soldiers, walking over to Kevin and pointing his rifle down at him. "You no speak!"

A helicopter swooped over the stadium and shone its light on the crowd, then abruptly flew off in the direction of downtown Phoenix.

After a half hour, the stadium had emptied, and Chinese soldiers stood guard as the lights were extinguished.

After showering and riding the bus out to the airport, the OSU players boarded the plane for their late night return to Columbus. The airplane captain addressed them over the plane's speakers: "Okay, fellas, I thought I would pass on what I know before we get underway. As unbelievable as it sounds, our sovereign nation has been *invaded*, I repeat *invaded* by members of the People's Liberation Army of China. They have given us permission to return to Ohio, but I don't know what's going to happen after that. From the scattered reports I've heard, the Chinese are now moving into the Southwest and Pacific Northwest, as well as the Great Lakes region. Don't ask me how all this happened. So many of our troops are scattered around the world, I don't know if the President has the ability to repel this."

"Kevin," said Chad, leaning across the airliner's aisle. "I honestly don't believe this--*really!* I thought we were the only remaining superpower and all that! We have B-2 *bombers,* for crying out loud! We have smart bombs and stealth fighters! It's impossible that this happened!"

"Hmmph," muttered Kevin, looking at the floor, and slowly shaking his head back and forth.

"What?" asked Chad, wondering how his quarterback could be so calm and collected at a time like this.

"I was just thinking," said Kevin with a concerned look in his eye, "it's just like ancient Rome."

"Always the history major, huh?"

"No, really! I read somewhere that when the barbarians finally arrived at the outskirts of Rome to take it over, most of the Romans were in the Coliseum watching the games. They couldn't bring themselves to believe that they were actually going to be conquered. And, inside of half an hour, the exact same thing just happened to us."

"Oh, come on, Kevin," said Chad, throwing up his hands. "Look at us! Does it look like we're *conquered*? I mean, we're on an airliner, heading home--heck, we'll probably be served roast beef in twenty minutes. You call that *conquered*?"

"Look at Poland, when the Nazis took over at the beginning of World War II," replied Kevin. "Yeah, it was blitzkrieg, but it still took them a few days--or weeks--to consolidate their power."

"Fine, let them consolidate all they want, as long as life goes on, who cares?"

"Don't count on playing football next fall, bud."

"Let 'em try to stop us," said Chad.

"Reality check, Chad.   Just hope you don't go to a concentration camp."

"Yeah.   One day I'm playing in the NCAA National Championship game and the next day I'm in a concentration camp."

Kevin was about to reply when the flight attendant reminded everyone to fasten their seat belts.

****

Having wallowed in idleness for most of the Christmas break, Dexter was eager to get back into the swing of things. The second Monday of the new year, January eighth, found Ohio State University airport teetering on the edge of minimums, with a four hundred foot ceiling and two miles of visibility. Scattered showers were predicted as well. So far the "peacekeeping" Chinese troops had not affected Dexter in the slightest. He read recently in *The* Dispatch that, for now at least, the Chinese were only interested in controlling the military bases and the utilities. Harsher measures, said the article, might come later. He drove to the airport and simply ignored the Chinese soldier he saw in front of the terminal building. *Best to let sleeping dogs lie,* he thought to himself. He was not going to be deterred in his objective to fly to Chicago and back to get the new motor from Motorflux. Dexter could have had the motor overnighted by Fedex™ but he wanted to get a first-hand look at Motorflux's production line to clear up a few questions he had. He started the engine on the Skyhawk at 5:50 am and went through his pre-takeoff checklist before taxiing to the active runway. Usually he avoided using the OSU airport before 7:00 am in order not to bother the residents in the area, but his impatience got the better of him. He lifted off from runway nine at precisely 6:05 am and reached his cruising altitude of nine thousand feet twenty minutes later. Tops were at five thousand, so he enjoyed the beautiful vista of blue sky while munching on a hastily prepared breakfast of yogurt, grapes, and fruit juice.

The trip was routine, save for a slight course change over Indiana to avoid a commercial jet climbing out of Indianapolis. He had decided to land at Lansing Municipal Airport on the southern edge of Chicagoland to avoid the hassle of navigating through the congested airspace over Midway. A twenty minute cab ride took him to the well-landscaped building occupied by Motorflux in the shop-worn suburb of Dolton. The president of Motorflux, Chuck Mangold, met Dexter in the lobby and was more than happy to accompany him to the shop floor, where a demonstration of the M147, Motorflux's latest ½ horsepower motor, convinced Dexter that it would be more than adequate to power his robot's leg. Dexter joined Chuck and a group of Motorflux engineers for lunch at a nearby restaurant and was back in the air by 1:30 pm.

All in all, the business trip had been a success, though Dexter would have to run some numbers by Jerry before he could be certain everything was okay. Luckily he had been able to clear Chicago airspace before it became too busy, so the first part of the trip home was uneventful. He was glad the Cessna had an autopilot as he was able to review some of the figures the people at Motorflux had given him. Cloud tops were still at five thousand, so Dexter again had an awesome view of the blue sky on the way home. The ceiling in Columbus, though, was reported as being at only three hundred feet, so he would have his hands full making a landing on instruments when he got to OSU airport. Passing over West Liberty, Ohio he turned off the autopilot and began a gradual descent into the clouds. He listened to the ATIS for the OSU airport: "Ohio State information Tango. Two One Two Three Zulu weather. Wind zero eight zero at ten. Visibility five. Sky condition: ceiling one thousand two hundred overcast. Temperature: twenty-five. Dew point: thirteen. Altimeter two niner niner two. ILS runway niner right approach in use…advise on initial contact you have information Tango."

As he fumbled with the radio to tune in the OSU Tower, Dexter glanced at his airspeed and noticed he had let it build up close to the yellow arc. *Watch that, buddy*, he scolded himself. *It's not nice to rip the wings off your own airplane.*

He keyed the mike and said: "Ohio State Tower, Cessna Five-Oh-One-Niner-Foxtrot-Whiskey is twenty-five miles northwest, with Tango, to land."

After a few seconds came the reply: "Cessna Five-Oh-One-Niner-Foxtrot-Whiskey, Ohio State Tower, fly straight in, runway niner, altimeter two niner two."

"Roger, straight in," said Dexter.

"Cessna Niner-Foxtrot-Whiskey, be advised of winds gusting to twenty," added the OSU Tower.

"Roger," said Dexter. *What's the maximum crosswind allowed for a 172?* wondered Dexter. He considered looking it up in his aircraft handbook, but instead called the Tower again. When they assured him that the gusts were rarely more than thirty degrees off the centerline of the runway on which he'd be landing, he decided he would be fine. *What's the sine of thirty, anyway? Nah, not enough to hassle me...*

Following the controller's instructions, he set himself up on a course to land on OSU's Runway nine right. Dexter put the mike down and wiped the sweat from his palms. Although he had earned his instrument rating over two years earlier, he still didn't feel too confident of his abilities in adverse weather. He would sheepishly admit that he often chose to fly only in VFR, or Visual Flight Rules weather, rather than in IFR, or Instrument Flight Rules weather. The truth was, he had done no more than about twenty total flights in IFR weather in his flying career, although he had done eight approaches within the last six months, two more than the minimum required to stay current. However, during those few flights rarely had the ceiling been any lower than about two thousand feet. Today, as had been forecast earlier, the clouds were only three hundred feet above the ground. So there was good reason for Dexter's palms to be sweating. It takes a special type of nerve to watch the altimeter unwind through one thousand feet above ground level and not be able to see the hard surface of the earth because you are still wrapped in a blanket of cloud vapor. What happens if you break out of the clouds and oops! There just happens to be a power line a hundred feet in front of that spinning prop. It all came down to trusting in good ol' electronics. You trusted that your GPS said you were where indeed you really were. You trusted that your artificial horizon said you were flying straight and level. You checked your map and made sure your final approach was above the highest obstacle in that area and then you committed to the landing. *It all sounded so simple when I read about it*, thought Dexter. It was just the *execution* that produced the sweaty palms.

The radio blared, stirring Dexter from his reverie. "Cessna Niner-Foxtrot-Whiskey, revise landing sequence--you are number two to land, following the Beech Baron now on long final."

"Roger, OSU Tower, number two behind aircraft on long final." Dexter adjusted his flight path a little to ensure he would land well after the Beech Baron. Although the Baron wasn't that big of an airplane, Dexter didn't want to take any chances with wake vortices flipping his plane over. Wake vortices are the invisible waves of air that follow behind any wing producing lift, much like the wake behind a ship at sea.

Dexter turned onto final when he was about twelve miles from the runway and began his last check before landing. He checked his altimeter...he was only up about four hundred feet, and he still couldn't see the ground. *I guess the weather report was right*, thought Dexter. *I probably won't break out until three hundred feet above ground level, just like they said.*

Dexter was about to lower the flaps when his ears picked up a slight increase in wind noise. *That's funny*, he thought. He looked at the airspeed indicator. Whoa! He was up to one hundred knots! He had been at eighty knots just a few seconds earlier. Next he looked at the vertical velocity indicator. Son of a -----! It showed seven hundred feet per minute *down*! As soon as he looked at the artificial horizon, a chill went up his spine. It had tumbled! It no longer told him if his wings were level or if he was headed up or down!

"Cessna Five-Oh-One-Niner, this is OSU Tower, you are falling far below glide slope, recommend coming up a little." Dexter had no time to respond. His mind flashed back to small headlines he occasionally saw in various newspapers: "Local man succumbs in private plane crash."

He didn't know whether to pull on the yoke or push in. He could only see solid white outside the windows. His inner ear told him he was in a right bank, but the turn and bank indicator showed him in a severe left bank. Too many things were competing for his attention in his mind! Mixed somewhere therein was a brief glimpse of him hanging from the top of the Lincoln-Leveque Tower.

"So you're helpless again, Dexter, eh?" asked a little voice in his head.

"Help me! Please!" he screamed inside the cockpit.

Going against everything his senses were telling him, he

slammed the control wheel to the right, and watched as the turn and bank indicator now tilted to the right. But now the airspeed was almost at one hundred and fifty knots! Ten more knots and he would reach Vne, velocity-never exceed, the speed beyond which he might rip the wings off!

"Ah, so you want to live some more?" asked his conscience.

"Yes, yes, yes!" he said. "Please get me out of this alive!"

Just then he broke out of the clouds and saw the ground. The nose was pointed straight at it! Involuntarily, Dexter let out a ghastly scream and began to pull back on the yoke to raise the nose. He was only about three hundred feet above the ground and was going close to one hundred and sixty knots! Using all the strength his two hundred pound body could muster, he was able to slowly pull the yoke out. He never knew it would be this hard! Just when he thought he was going to level out, he heard a sharp cracking sound. In disbelief he watched as the control yoke cracked in two! *This isn't happening!*, he shouted interiorly. Again the plane dove for the ground. Dexter grabbed the metal shaft and the remainder of the plastic handle and again pulled with all his might. He was only two hundred feet up when he saw the nose come up. Still, he didn't know if he had made it or not. He saw the ground rapidly filling the windshield, but there was nothing he could do! He had pulled the yoke out as far as it would go.

Two seconds before impact, he realized he had forgotten to shut down the engine. Although it had only been at low rpm, it still might cause a fire. *Too late now*, he realized. Just as he leveled out-- slam! The plane contacted the soil of a farm field and burrowed its way along for about two hundred feet before coming to a stop. The seat belt had luckily saved Dexter from any serious injury, although he did cut his wrist on the jagged edge of the broken yoke. Dexter tried to open the door, but the plane was too far buried in the earth. He was forced to climb out the window, knowing that at any moment he could end up in a fireball. He had enough presence of mind to shut off the electrical system before clambering through the narrow window opening.

"You okay?" shouted a man who was running across the field toward Dexter. A small group of motorists had stopped their cars by the side of the adjacent road and were making their way toward the stricken aircraft.

"Yeah...sure...I...uhh." Dexter shook his head and only then saw that his right wrist was covered with blood. He stumbled over a clump of mud and sprawled on the ground.

"Hey, you better take it easy," said the man, crouching down to help Dexter. "Let's have a look at that arm of yours."

"I think it's OK, you know, I just sort of..." Dexter trailed off and rolled onto his back.

"Here, use this," said a woman who had just walked up, holding out some paper towels she had pulled from a bag she was carrying. The man took the towels and began to clean Dexter's wrist and hand.

"I'm a nurse, I think I can help him," said the woman.

"Oh, fine," said the man. "What should I do now?"

"Direct pressure on the wound, until the bleeding stops. Here, use this." She handed him a fresh pad of paper towels.

"I want to thank--you--all of you...for--" said Dexter.

"Now just take it easy," said the nurse. "After what you've been through, you can't be expected to be writing thank you cards yet."

As he lay there, Dexter couldn't believe how close he had-- again--come to death. He glanced over at the road nearby and saw other cars passing by, people going about their normal day-to-day activities. *That* used *to be me*, he thought. *Why can't I just go about my normal routine? What is all this* death *stuff? I can worry about that when I'm eighty, not when I'm thirty.*

"I see you're on your back again, feeling helpless," said the little voice in his brain.

"*Who asked your opinion?*" Dexter silently replied. *That's another thing*, Dexter thought, *why am I all of a sudden talking to my brain? What is going on?* Immediately images of that girl he had known briefly on prom night; the bitter fights he had with his father; the time he had abandoned his once best friend after high school. *This is a pile of bullcrap*, he silently sneered to his "alter ego," or whatever the hell it was that seemed to be his constant traveling companion now. "I didn't sign up for this," he muttered in a low voice. "Leave me alone!"

"You all right?" asked the nurse. She stopped treating his wound and looked at Dexter's face. "You seem like you're off in space right now."

"Well, I did just about buy the farm, lady!" Dexter started to sit up, but just as quickly lay back down. "Look, I'm sorry; I didn't mean to be a jerk. I'm just a little pissed off at my life right now."

"Well, you just take it easy, guy--you could still go into shock.

You might be wise to get checked out at Dublin Methodist."

Dexter made a sarcastic face and shook his head. "You know, I appreciate your help, but I really don't want to go to a hospital. All I actually did was slide along the ground and come to an abrupt stop. I think I'll be all right."

"It's up to you, but if you get checked out now, it'll be easier to deal with your insurance company if you develop any medical problems later on as a result of this crash."

"I feel just fine, so I think I'll be heading out," said Dexter, slowly getting to his feet.

"Just one second there, fella," said a policeman as he walked up to Dexter. "You're going nowhere till you fill out an accident report from the FAA and talk to one of their people."

"Accident report," Dexter said sarcastically. "What is this, a routine traffic stop?"

"You think you're just going to sweep up the broken glass and walk away?" asked the policeman. "Look, I called Port Columbus on my radio and someone is on their way right now to process this situation.

"Does anyone have a Coke or something?" Dexter asked the assemblage. "I was planning to eat dinner as soon as I landed. I feel pretty dehydrated."

"I've got a few snacks in my car," said the nurse. "I'll be right back."

"I appreciate it."

The policeman cordoned off the crash site with some yellow ribbon and a few wooden stakes he had in his trunk. Five minutes later, an emergency squad pulled up, but left after failing to convince Dexter that he needed medical attention. Dexter signed two forms releasing the squad from any liability. Just as he finished the pop and cookies provided by the nurse, a portly gentleman walked across the field from the road and introduced himself as the local accident investigator from the FAA.

"Jim Saio, FAA," he said, shaking Dexter's hand. "I assume you're the pilot?"

"Right--look will this take long? I've got some things I want to do."

"Whoa Nellie! Aren't you the suave accident victim! You're lucky you came out in one piece," he said, gesturing toward the airplane. "That was one lucky accident, my friend." He ducked under the yellow tape and approached the airplane. "Mmm--mmh. Ten feet lower and you'd be in the hospital. Twenty feet lower and you'd be in the vital statistics section of tomorrow's paper! Mmmmph!" He peeked inside the cockpit. "I assume the artificial horizon failed?"

"How could you tell?" asked Dexter.

"An educated guess, really. I can see that it's tumbled and everything else looks normal. I assume you don't have vacuum backup, eh? Or electric?"

"I had meant to do that, actually. I just read an article in *Flying* about that."

"Well, let me fill out a few forms and de-brief you and I'll be finished. You're lucky I just happened to be driving in this area. Normally, I'd be out at Port Columbus this time of day. By the way, has anyone contacted the owner of this farm?"

"No." Dexter turned to the group of people. "Are any of you the owners of this land?"

"Right here," said a man with a weather-beaten face and wearing a baseball cap.

"Sir," said the FAA investigator, "you'll need to fill out this form. Will you be filing for damages?"

"Gosh, I don't know. Not a whole lot of damage done."

"Well, I'd appreciate it if you could complete just this one page." The farmer took the form and began to fill it out.

"So what do I need to do?" asked Dexter.

"Yeah, I was just about to tell you," said Jim. "Just fill out these two sheets now and you can do more tomorrow. I'll get a few photos of the crash site and we can come back tomorrow to finish up. I understand you must be feeling a little shaken now."

"I would appreciate going home," said Dexter.

After all the requisite paperwork was finished, and after setting up a time to meet the FAA man the next day, Dexter accepted a ride home from the nurse. She insisted on getting his phone number, just in case he needed medical advice or attention. Dexter resisted at first, but eventually acquiesced by the time they pulled into his driveway.

"Thanks again," he told her as he closed the car door.

"Just remember to change that bandage tomorrow. It won't be good for more than about twenty-four hours."

"Okay, Mom," he said, giving her a big smile.

The first thing he did after entering his house and checking the phone machine was grab a wine cooler from the refrigerator. He plopped down in an easy chair in the living room. He was actually glad his girlfriend wasn't home yet. She had left a message saying she'd be working late. He briefly considered calling her up to tell her about the crash, but decided against it since she said she'd be home by ten anyway.

"Glad to have a little time to think things over, hmmm?" asked the little man in his brain.

For once, Dexter didn't react negatively to his alter ego. He even admitted to himself that he was glad to have a chance to think things over. *What had it been now--two months? Let's see, the Lincoln-Leveque thing had happened around the first of November and it was now--well, New Years Day had been a week ago. So it's been about two months since I-- since I--*

"Since what?" asked his conscience innocently.

"You know darn well since what!" thought Dexter *"--since I almost--died!"*

"Ah, the 'D' word," said the little man.

"You know something?" Dexter silently asked his conscience. *"I think maybe it's time you got a name. How 'bout…uhh…how 'bout-- Albert? Yeah! Albert. I dub thee Albert!"* Dexter took a swig of his wine cooler as a toast.

"So, it's only been two months," "Albert" reminded Dexter. *"That's a pretty short time within which to almost die twice."*

"Well, I'm alive, aren't I?"

"Barely--What if you had been twenty feet lower today?" Albert silently asked.

"I don't want to go there," answered Dexter.

"No pun intended?"

"I don't want to go there either."

"But for twenty feet and you'd be in eternity, my friend."

He's got a point, thought Dexter, putting Albert on hold for a few minutes. *I never thought I'd have to worry about this till I was eighty, or maybe seventy if I had a bad heart or something. None of my other friends seem to worry about death too much. I have been too busy to think too much about it, but I have to face facts. It was* true, as my conscience told me: I have come very close to death twice now. And it seemed that both times it happened I flashed back to "things" in my past.   That's right--just when I realized the artificial horizon had failed in my plane I remembered that prom night with Sarah Menski. Is God trying to tell me something? Who the hell is God anyway? I've never darkened the door of a church, except for the occasional, obligatory wedding or funeral. I'm a decent living guy, all things considered. I pay my taxes, I've helped out at a soup kitchen a few times. What do I have to be afraid of? I'm not some mass murderer or child-molesting-pervert. Sure, I live with my girlfriend, but I love her, and that's what really matters, right? I'll marry her someday, when the time is right. Both of us are just too busy right now.

"Too busy for eternity, huh?" asked Albert.

"I've got plenty of time for eternity, why should I rush things?" Dexter said to Albert.

"You only had about eight seconds left when you were in that power dive just a few hours ago," whispered Albert in the deep recesses of Dexter's mind.

Dexter didn't have a reply for that. He just pursed his lips and admitted, perhaps, his conscience had a point.

****

Thad was nervous. He sat by the phone in his apartment and fiddled with the pen that was lying there. He hadn't called a girl in over a year. His disability had curbed his confidence so he didn't feel as pumped up about dating as he might have ten years earlier. Just about the time when he had been planning to marry rolled around, he developed this annoying insomnia problem. He had gone on a few dates in the past three years, but most ended after the woman learned of Thad's disability. Thad felt convinced that the new medicine he was on would lead to his soon being able to return to a regular job. Now all he had to do was convince Cheryl of that theory.

He picked up the phone and steeled his nerve. *What's one more rejection anyway?* he asked himself.

After three rings, Cheryl picked up the phone. "Hello?"

"Hey, Cheryl, this is Thad, the taxi driver."

"Oh, hello!" said Cheryl excitedly. "Good to hear from you!"

"Likewise! Did you enjoy your stay in Saint Louis?"

"It was great! How was your Christmas?"

"Just about perfect, thanks for asking," said Thad. "How's life among the test tubes?"

"Test tubes?"

"Your research at Battelle."

"Oh, that. Actually, I tend to work more on a computer, but I do do a little work with test tubes. Yeah, it's going well. How's the cabbie life?"

"It's fine. I always say there's really nothing to dislike about taxi driving, but I guess you could say I yearn for more at times. I really think I might apply to Battelle, you know."

"That would be cool. Do you think you could handle it?"

"Heck, I've been trying to answer that question for ten years. My doctor has me on some new medication, and that might just do the trick. I have been sleeping better in the past month--actually I'm starting to remember more of my dreams--isn't that a sign of deep sleep?"

"I seem to remember reading that somewhere, yeah."

There was an awkward silence for a few seconds. Finally Thad asked, "So was your whole family there?"

"For Christmas? Yes, all present and accounted for, thank goodness...all eight of us."

"Where do you fall in the family lineup?"

"Well, there are four boys and two girls: I'm the second girl, fifth out of six kids."

"Just like me," said Thad. "I'm the third out of four kids. Two boys and two girls...I'm the second boy."

"Well, isn't that the coincidence of the year!"

"Hear, hear!" said Thad with a laugh. "So anyway I was just calling you up to see if you changed your mind about chocolate milk and White Zinfandel."

"Excuse me?"

"You remember, which is higher in the order of creation: chocolate milk or White Zinfandel?"

"And that's the reason you called?"

"Uh, ahem," said Thad, "That is *one* of the reasons."

"Let's skip to the second reason."

"All right, I uh, was just wondering if, well, if you--how would you like to go out to dinner this Saturday?"

"I thought you would never ask. Sure, I'd love to!"

"Splendid! Or--great! How about I swing by at six?"

"Suits me."

"Excellent. Have you seen that new movie with Tom Cruise in it?"

"You mean the former seminarian?" asked Cheryl.

"Huh?"

"Tom Cruise was a seminarian when he was younger."

"I never knew that."

"Facts are facts."

"So have you seen it?"

"No, but sounds like it would be a good one."

"All right, I'll see you at six--and how 'bout if we dress 'business casual' as the expression goes?"

"Fine by me -- but, uhhmm, Thad?"

"What?"

"These Chinese -- do you think they will bother us? This is so weird -- they've invaded and here we are discussing the finer points of a Tom Cruise movie. Shouldn't we be in prison or something?"

"I know what you mean," said Thad. "It's what's called a bloodless takeover--it's a kinder, gentler overthrow of the good ole USA. They aren't doing it the traditional way, with tanks rolling down every street and mass executions--not yet anyway. It's all part of a master plan. First it started off when they took over the Panama Canal, then the port of Los Angeles, then the port in Boston. Meanwhile, they've set up deep-water ports in the Caribbean. Now, they've invaded from Mexico and Canada--but they know what they're doing. They've gained control of all our important military bases and our power plants. Heck, so many of our armed forces are overseas taking over *other* nations, it's logical that we don't have many soldiers left to guard our *own* borders. Lenin said it so well years ago: 'the West will fall into our hands like overripe fruit.'"

"Well, I guess it all makes sense somehow," said Cheryl.

"And remember," said Thad. "The show ain't over yet. We may still be in for some harder times in a few months."

"I heard that."

"All right, see you Saturday."

"Aren't you forgetting something?" asked Cheryl.

"Uhh." *I knew I should have rehearsed this call first,* Thad said to himself.

"Does 21 Fawn Meadow Court ring a bell?"

"Oh, the address!" *Whew!* Thad wiped his brow. "I know I picked you up there in the cab, but, yeah, good thing you gave me the address, so I can write it down. We don't keep our trip sheets, so I would have been up sh--I would have been out of luck."

"Well, now you can write it down, 21 Fawn Meadow Court, in Powell."

"Okay, I got it. Thanks a bunch."

"Bye."

"Bye."

****

The next morning Dexter called up Father Rankin.

"Hello."

"Father Rankin, this is Dexter."

"Hello, Dexter!" said Father Rankin. "Glad to hear your sonorous voice again!"

"Yeah, I'm glad--it's good...I think I want to talk to you again--I don't know for how much longer, but at least one more time." Dexter spun the salt shaker around while sitting at his kitchen table.

"Such an about-face!" said Father Rankin cheerfully. "Sure, just say when and I'll make sure I'm here."

"How 'bout tomorrow at four?" Just then Dexter heard several clicking sounds on the line. "What was *that*?"

"Did you hear that too?" asked Father Rankin. "Sort of a clicking sound..."

"Yeah, that's odd..."

"Huh. Maybe someone's working on the line."

"Maybe someone's tapping the phone."

"Actually," said Father Rankin, "I was reading something the other day which said that that's old hat: if someone's tapping your phone these days, you'd never know it."

"Yeah, could be...anyway, see you tomorrow."

"Sounds fine…see you then."
"Adios."
"Bye."

****

Since it was the last day of the work week, Dexter left his office early and arrived at Saint Michael's a few minutes before four. As usual, he rang the doorbell. The administrative staff went home at two-thirty, so Father Rankin himself let Dexter into the rectory.

"I saw in the paper that you almost purchased the ranch, Dexter," said Father Rankin as he closed the door behind Dexter.

"What? 'Purchased the ranch'?" asked Dexter.

"You know--'bought the farm.'"

"Oh, yeah. Such clever phrases--yeah, that's right, but I made it alright, didn't I? At least you didn't read about it on the Obituary page."

Father Rankin followed Dexter into his office, sat down and tamped tobacco into his pipe. Dexter waited silently until the pipe was lit.

"How did your theories hold up this time?" asked Father Rankin, taking a long draw on his corncob pipe.

"What's that supposed to mean?"

"Well, last time we talked you were telling me about, let's see…I believe it was…what? The 'Rapture'?…

"Actually, we had just begun to discuss my living situation; what does that have to do with my 'theories holding up'?" asked Dexter, a confused look in his eye.

"I'm talking about the nine seconds before you hit the ground."

"How do you know it was nine seconds?"

"Dexter, look. You just had a near-death experience. You know what I'm getting at. What were you thinking about when you almost died? That's the reason you decided to see me again, right? Nothing like a little 'eternity-viewing' to sharpen the conscience."

Dexter leaned back and let out an audible sigh. He looked down at the ground and paused a few seconds. "Yeah, I guess. Maybe I don't want to say…it's sort of--personal."

"That's your prerogative; you don't have to tell me. I just know what a sailor once told me after he had a brush with death. He said he had streams of thought on two levels at the same time. On the surface, he said images of his family rushed through his head---"

"No pun intended," Dexter interjected.

"Huh?"

"On the *surface*? Sailor? Water?"

"Oh...so sly, Dexter--anyway, he said on a deeper level--yes, yes--pun intended--he said he had images of what might lie ahead of him if he did drown. I just thought something similar might have happened to you."

"Hmm, did he mention having a conversation with a little voice in his head?"

"He didn't talk much about that; he mainly stressed the images that streamed through his head. Maybe he did have some talk like that. How do you suppose the conversation might have gone?"

"Nice try, Father Rankin, but like I told you, I don't think I'll tell you about my chat right now. I've got some issues I've got to clear up before I can be comfortable talking about that type of stuff--which is a great segue into what we were discussing the last time we talked. You were about to tell me what you thought about my living with Daphne."

"Ah, yes, that's right," said Father Rankin. "What you have to understand about the Church's teachings on living together before marriage is that they are meant to protect the sacrament of Marriage--"

"Sacrament?" asked Dexter.

"The textbook definition of a sacrament is an outward sign instituted by Christ to give grace."

"Example?"

"Baptism,   Confession,   Holy   Communion--those   are sacraments."

"Go on," said Dexter.

"Right. See, the point is that relations between a man and woman before marriage can actually *hurt* the prospects of a long marriage more than they can help it."

"But the whole idea is to test-drive your mate before committing to any long term relationship!"

"I understand where you're coming from," said Father Rankin. He took a pull on his pipe and looked at Dexter. "Believe me, I've heard it all from the couples in our parish. The point is that premarital sex is a glue which bonds the man and woman together and can obscure their vision."

"What are you talking about?" asked Dexter. *"Obscure their vision*? Huh?"

"I know you know that I'm not talking about their eyesight. What I mean is that the purpose of dating should be for each person to determine if the person they are courting is a suitable mate for life. Sex clouds their judgment of the other. The courtship should be basically an impassionate twelve-month long interview."

"Twelve month? What--we can't date anyone for more than twelve months?"

"I'm just repeating the thoughts of a few spiritual writers I've come across. There's no hard and fast rule. It's just that the purpose of dating is marriage and it shouldn't take more than about a year to determine if someone would make a good spouse. Heck, my own parents 'dated' for about seven years."

"Why so long?"

"Actually, they met each other when they were each about twenty-six years old. They dated a little while, then broke up. My Dad went into the seminary, my Mom went into the convent. After a year or so, before taking any vows, they both left the seminary and convent, dated some more, and eventually married when they were thirty-three."

"Far out! No wonder you're a priest."

"We definitely grew up in a religious house, as I'm sure you can tell from my brother Thad."

"I heard *that*," said Dexter.

"I once heard a bit of wisdom about dating and marriage--I forget the exact source--it might have been Reader's Digest. Anyway, someone once wrote that you shouldn't marry anyone with whom you couldn't spend three straight days sitting next to on a trans-European train trip."

"Does it have to be European?" asked Dexter with a slight grin.

"Absolutely," said Father Rankin. He took the pipe out of his mouth and pointed it at Dexter. "Central European, too. No exceptions to the rule."

"So, *glue*, huh?" asked Dexter.

"What?"

"You just said that premarital sex is a *glue* that bonds the man and woman together."

"Oh, yeah, well, uh, not just *premarital* sex, but sex between married spouses does the same."

"And your point is…?"

"The whole point is that you shouldn't glue something together until you're sure they are compatible."

"You can always use some acid or something to remove the glue," suggested Dexter.

"Precisely!" said Father Rankin excitedly. "That's exactly what divorce is--it's *acid*! It eats away at marital love and society in general."

"Hold the phone! Who said anything about *divorce*?" Dexter wore a perplexed look on his face. "If Daphne and I break up, there's no divorce--it's just a parting of the ways."

"But the glue is still there, Dexter. It'll be painful to break that bond whether you're married or not."

"Great! So we should stay together and avoid the pain."

"That is, if you're compatible together."

"So, say we stay together and get married later on?" asked Dexter.

"Well, from what I've read, you would then have about a fifty-fifty chance of staying married more than five years."

"Says who?"

"Says the *facts*, my friend. And that's not just someone's opinion, either. It's common knowledge now that about half of couples who live together before marriage end up divorcing each other within several years of the wedding day."

"Fine." Dexter threw up his hands and leaned back in his chair. "So we get divorced! Big whoop! My parents were divorced."

"Look, Dexter," said Father Rankin, spreading his hands apart. "You know from personal experience how tough it is on the kids when parents divorce. Do you really want to go through that whole show *again*?"

"That's why Daphne and I haven't married yet. Neither of us want to repeat our childhood experiences."

"Dexter," said Father Rankin, shaking his head back and forth, "now we're back to square one."

"So you really think we shouldn't live together." Dexter said it more as a statement than a question.

"Just from a very practical level I would have to say no. I can tell you from a spiritual level that it's also not a good idea, but, like I say, even from a purely sociological standpoint, I think you would be better off not living with her until you're married."

"*Helllllll*," said Dexter in a low, muttering voice. He looked out the window and thought a few seconds. Turning to the priest he said, "But what if I love her?"

"*Do* you love her?"

"Of course I--" Dexter hesitated, biting his lower lip. "Yeah! Yeah, I love her!"

"Do you buy her flowers often?"

"Huh?"

"Do you buy her flowers a lot?" asked Father Rankin, matter-of-factly.

"What does that have to do with it?"

"Just asking," said Father Rankin innocently.

"Yeah, I love her," said Dexter again. He looked out the window again, concern showing in his eye. Father Rankin said nothing, just gazed at Dexter.

"Actually, no," said Dexter.

"You don't love her?"

"No I don't buy her flowers."

"Ever?"

"I don't know if I've ever bought her flowers."

"Why not?"

"Look, Father Rankin, what's so bad about living with her?! I enjoy being around her. She thrills me--she excites me! Just like I thought! Fun is bad--right? I don't know if I love her, OK? I just like the pleasure she gives me. Do I have to plan out my whole life right now? I'm only twenty-eight. She's mine for now. Maybe I'll marry her, maybe not. *Someday* I'll settle down and have kids."

"That's good to hear." Father Rankin tapped the ashes in his pipe into an ashtray on the coffee table. "Always good to have *some* type of game plan."

"Why did I ever have to meet you anyway?" asked Dexter dejectedly. "If I'd never met your brother in that taxicab, I never would have had to run into all this religion stuff. My life used to be so...uncomplicated!"

"'Oh, for the days of milk and honey, when all the world was silk and money!'" said Father Rankin.

"Who's that, Wordsworth or someone?" asked Dexter grumpily.

"David Albertson. That same guy I quoted earlier."

"Yeah, 'silk and money.' That just about sums it up. I used to just worry about which silk tie I should wear and how I could make more money. Now I'm bogged down worrying about living with a perfectly fine woman."

"You're a free man," said Father Rankin. "No one's forcing you to do anything."

"Somehow I feel like 'Animal Farm': some animals are *more free* than others."

"You mean you feel more free now than you were before?"

"No, I feel *less* free than I did before."

"Ah, so *something's* changing inside you, eh?"

"Now *that's* about the only thing I know for sure," said Dexter.

"As you wish, my fledgling aviator."

"Fledgling! I've got two hundred hours built up!"

"Hey, Chuck Yeager has over eleven thousand hours in, like, a hundred and fifty different types of airplanes. Trust me, you're a fledgling."

"Yeah, well maybe I'll *evolve* faster than Yeager did."

"Ding!" said Father Rankin, pretending to strike a bell with his pipe. "I think I feel an incipient intellectual issue!"

"You want a piece of this?" said Dexter. "You afraid you can't stand a withering attack on 'evolution' from one of Stanford's best and brightest alums?"

Father Rankin put the pipe in his mouth and rubbed his hands together. "Ah, the trumpet calls the troops to arms! Evolution it is!"

"Evolution, my ass!" said Dexter sarcastically. "You'll probably pull out the old 'missing link' B.S. You Catholics can't handle evolution. It's just like a friend of mine said in California: when science comes up with a new theory that slams Catholicism, the pope simply changes the dogma to match the theory."

"Ah, we reach the perfect starting point," said Father Rankin. "First, let me say something that might be obvious, but it hit me the other day...all our arguing won't change a thing about evolution or creationism. What happened, happened and we can't change it--what I'm trying to say is some things need to be argued because they are about the present or future--like abortion. We can still change the laws about that...but the origin of the world? Hey! Let the chips fall where they may! If our study of history proves that evolution really happened--great! If our study of history proves that creation happened--still great! As long as we continually strive to uncover the truth we can't go wrong."

"Uhh, yeah," said Dexter. "Like you say, that is obvious, but, uhh…I never really thought about it that way."

"Okay, how 'bout we start by defining terms…the Church allows its members to believe in evolution, but not *evolutionism*. You see, evolution, as it relates to biology, refers to a process in which animals and plants change over time so that their descendants are different from their ancestors. The Church sees no problem with that. Evolutionism, though, is a little more dangerous. That theory is more of an ideology which sees the whole universe as being in a continual process of development. It doesn't recognize any spiritual or supernatural reality, but sees everything in solely material terms. It doesn't stop at biology, but tries to explain science, history, and economics as well."

"Fine," said Dexter, "Webster has spoken. Now we can put the dictionary away and get down to business; Point number one: you don't believe in the Big Bang, right?"

"Rebuttal number one," said Father Rankin, "Who do you mean when you say 'you'?"

"You, the Church, the Pope--what does it matter? You all have to believe the same thing, right?"

"Aha, the thot plickens! Point number two: no. We don't all have to believe the same thing. Pope Pius XII gave some general guidelines in this area in the 1950s and that's all we're required to believe."

"Such as?"

"Well, the first point he made was that Catholics can form their own opinions on the origin of man's body. They should just make sure they listen to the Church on issues that have to do with Revelation."

"So believe anything you want, but we'll tell you what to believe when it suits our fancy," said Dexter.

"Now don't jump to conclusions, Dexter. Hear the Pope out. The second thing Pius XII said was that we must believe that the human soul was created immediately by God. And lastly, he said that all men have been descended from one man, Adam, not from a group of original humans. That's it! Any and all theories can be held except when they conflict with these basic doctrines. See--that's not so bad, is it?"

"Eaah, dogmatic doo-doo, if you ask me," replied Dexter. "When did that come out--the 50s, you said?"

"Early 50s, if I'm not mistaken."

"Hasn't there been a lot of development since then? I mean some white-haired old theology expert tries to tell the whole scientific world what they can and cannot believe and I'm supposed to bend the knee and listen? Horsecrap!"

"But that's just it," said Father Rankin, holding his hands apart. "Pius XII said the Church *requires* no specific beliefs in this area. You can believe Adam came out of a Coke can, if you want. As long as we all came from Adam alone, believe whatever you want!"

"I don't know, Father Rankin. It all sounds too facile for me. What about these guys you hear about from time to time who study the Bible and conclude that the world began in such-and-such a year, ten thousand years ago."

"Good point, they do make the news now and again. Some minister will announce that God created the world on an exact date six thousand years ago at ten in the morning. You must always remember that those types of theories can only be attributed to that particular man, not to the Church. I will posit my own theory, if you will allow me..."

"Call it Rankin Rule Number One?" suggested Dexter.

"So be it."

"That's a good drink."

"Huh?"

"You know, SoBe--the fruit drink?"

"Never had it. Anyway, I say that the world has existed for millions of years but man--man with a soul--has only been on it since 4000 B.C."

"Care to explain your reasoning?"

"A couple of years ago I heard about this woman in Italy who lived from about 1880 to 1940. Her name was Luisa Piccarreta. She was very holy and it is reported that she survived solely on Holy Communion for some forty years."

"Holy Communion," stated Dexter. "That's that wafer thing you eat?"

"Correct. The Body and Blood of Christ."

"You mean you *believe* it's the Body and Blood of Christ."

"Well if it really *is* the Body and Blood of Christ, it doesn't matter if we believe it or not, right?"

"Hmm, let me consider that. Go on about the Italian woman."

"Right. Well, anyway, besides that she sat up in bed in the same position for forty years. They had to bury her in an L-shaped coffin."

"And your point is..."

"It was revealed to her that there elapsed exactly three-thousand, nine-hundred and seventeen years from the Garden of Eden till the birth of Jesus."

"*Revealed* to her?" asked Dexter. "Huh?"

"She had a supernatural experience. Christ revealed many wonderful things to her."

"What do you mean, the Garden of Eden? Isn't that just a Biblical myth?"

"I might be mistaken, but I think various archeologists and historians point to an area around modern-day Iraq as being the cradle of civilization."

"I can see that, yeah--Mesopotamia and all that--but the Garden of Eden, what's that?"

"Well," began Father Rankin, stroking his chin, "Maria said it was four-thousand years from the *Fall* till the Incarnation."

"Fall? Incarnation?"

"The Fall is Adam's eating of the apple. The Incarnation is Christ's becoming man."

"More theological mumbo-jumbo," said Dexter. "Archeologists have physical evidence of ancient peoples. I haven't heard anything about a clay jar from 'The Garden of Eden.'"

"You expect any artifacts to have a barcode on them, or to say 'Made in Mesopotamia?' How do we know some of those old clay water pitchers *aren't* from the Garden of Eden?"

"How do we know they *are*?"

"Hmm," said Father Rankin, "we appear to have a face-off."

"How do you know so much about this anyway?" asked Dexter. "I didn't think priests knew much outside of churchy stuff."

"Hey, remember, I *was* an engineer at Ford for ten years. I know a bit about science and the like."

"And you still believe man has existed for only six thousand years?"

"Like I said, this is only my own personal theory. I'm still investigating that Italian visionary lady to see if she's legit. And, remember, even that lady's apparitions are only private revelation. She has not been approved by the Church and no Catholic is obliged to believe what she alleges she has been told. But, yes, I do realize there may be some problems with believing that man is only six thousand years old, but here too remember that I am referring to man *with a soul*. It is entirely possible that God created human creatures two million years ago, and didn't infuse a soul into him until six thousand years ago."

"Why do you say two million years ago?" asked Dexter.

"It's just some reading I've been doing recently on EWTN's website."

"EWTN?"

"Eternal Word Television Network. It's a Catholic TV station on cable. You should watch it sometime. Anyway, I was reading that from the 1920s to the 1970s researchers believed that man evolved from a small ape-ish creature they called 'Australopithecus.' Fossils showed that this animal lived more than a million years ago and evidently was able to use tools. Apparently he walked upright some of the time. His use of tools, so the theory went, led to the evolution of a larger brain through natural selection. You'd see textbooks of the period showing 'Australopithecus' standing next to 'Homo Erectus,' sort of like you see a picture of a '65 Mustang next to a 2009 Mustang in a book on car history. The surprise, though, came in the 1970s when researchers discovered remains of 'Homo Erectus' from *two* million years ago. And they had tools with them as well. This meant that 'Homo Erectus' lived at the same time as 'Australopithecus' and possibly even before him. Some therefore concluded that the tools found among the ape-man fossils actually belonged to 'Homo Erectus.'"

"So where does that leave us?" asked Dexter.

"Well, as far as I know, the issue is still being debated. I'd like to know if there have been any new developments. The main point of this theory, though, is that upright man existed *before* ape-man. Therefore, there was no progression from ape-man to upright man."

"What does the Church say?"

"She says just what I said earlier: those three guidelines of

Pius XII are still in force."

"It's all a crock of spit," concluded Dexter.

"Mr. High and Mighty Stanford has spoken!" said Father Rankin mockingly.

"Don't take your average Secular Humanist so lightly, buddy!" said Dexter. "You think I was born yesterday?"

"Dexter, why are you so contrary to all my arguments when it comes to Catholic doctrine?"

"It's just what I said earlier! The Church is a chameleon--it'll change the color of its doctrine to match the color of the latest scientific theory."

"But that's just it! There *is* no conflict between the Church and Science, between Faith and Reason. Sure, it might appear at first glance that the Church is like some wimpy yes-man who changes his opinion every hour to agree with his bosses. Maybe a better analogy is--well, I don't know--maybe like a--husband and wife. Do you call the husband wimpy because he changes his attitude to fit his wife's? Do you call the wife spineless when she submits to her husband's wishes? It seems to me that the happy married couple works together to achieve marital peace--not only for their own good but for their children. Think about science and religion in the same way. If indeed God did really create the universe, how can the study of its laws conflict with the way he wants his creatures who are in that universe to live?"

"Eeeeeehhh!" said Dexter, imitating a game show buzzer. "Logical contradiction! You just supposed that God created the Universe--I thought our whole discussion was about that point!"

"Well," said Father Rankin, "we can ask the court recorder if necessary, but I believe we began this discussion on the subject of evolution, not creation."

"Puhleease, Father! Logical contradiction number two! Creation? Evolution? You can't have your cake and eat it too! They're mutually opposed to each other. Take your pick, but not both."

"What about the big 'ID' theory? Do you give it any merit?"

"Intelligent Design, you mean? Creationism in wrapping paper! From what I've heard, it's nothing new."

"Ah, but it allows for evolution *and* creation. You *can* have your cake and eat it too."

"Look," said Dexter, "what is wrong with believing the universe has always been here and always will be here? Isn't that what it all comes down to? In the final analysis, the argument is over the existence or non-existence of God. Sure, Intelligent Design allows for evolution, but it still insists on God, right?"

"I don't know," said Father Rankin. "I've read a few things on the Internet that led me to believe that Intelligent Design doesn't necessarily require a Divine Being."

"Well then what's the point? What's the 'Intelligent' in Intelligent Design stand for? Intelligent asteroids?"

"Like I say, it's just something I happened upon a few weeks ago--I have to study it some more. But anyway, you're right about the existence or non-existence of God. I always like to use this illustration: say you wake up one morning and find a bike on your front lawn. Do you say to yourself: I wonder where that bike came from. Or do you say to yourself: 'it just appeared there. No one put it there, it's just there.' What if the same thing happened again and again, a different bike each time? After the twentieth time, would you still say 'Well, another bike appeared there, oh well!'? I think each time you would become increasingly interested in just how a bike kept 'appearing' on your front lawn. You would probably camp out on your front porch to find out what was happening. You would know perfectly well that some person was putting a bike on your front lawn in the middle of the night. Why does the existence of the universe have to be so terribly different? Everyday we wake up and there's a whole universe on our 'front lawn,' so to speak. Are we really that dull-witted to say, it just 'appeared' there? It seems like we have one mind for everyday life, and a completely different mind when it comes to the origin of the universe."

Dexter shook his head back and forth. "You're comparing a bike to the universe? Reality check? Isn't that just a little too simplistic?"

"Hey, it's my own personal example. I just want to point out that often we use common sense in our everyday life, but then omit common sense when it comes to big important questions. Don't take it for dogma yet. At least not until I'm declared a Doctor of the Church."

"Doctor of the Church? I think you mentioned that once. What is that?"

"A doctor of the Church is a man or woman who is held in special reverence by the Church for his/her enlightening teachings and writings."

"Well, maybe you'll become a Nurse of the Church."

"I'd be satisfied to just be a Nurse's Aid of the Church."

"So where does that leave us?" asked Dexter.

"Seems to me," said Father Rankin, "that it's pretty much settled: God created the universe six billion years ago, and created the first soul six thousand years ago."

Not missing a beat, Dexter replied: "You're right, it looks like we're pretty much in agreement: the universe has always existed, and the first man evolved from slime two million years ago."

Father Rankin grinned and held out his hand. "Great! Pleasure doing business with you."

"Don't mention it," said Dexter, shaking the padre's hand. After a few closing remarks, he gathered his belongings and headed for the door. "See you next week, I suppose."

"Count on it, my friend, count on it."

****

It was the best party Kevin had been to since the championship game. The Chinese occupation troops had pretty much left him and his friends alone, at least for the time being. Chad was hosting the party at his parents' home in Muirfield, the upscale housing development built around Jack Nicklaus' golf course to the northwest of Columbus. Chad's parents had moved to Muirfield after Chad finished high school in Rocky River, Ohio. Kevin was making the rounds with Anne, playing the part of the sociable quarterback when he bumped into Tony Tornelli, an old friend from high school.

"Tony! Long time, no see!" Kevin said, pumping Tony's hand.

"Kevin Conaway for President! To think I knew you when you were nobody!"

"Hey, you have to be nobody before you can be somebody, right?"

"Is that how that works?" asked Tony. "Looks like I've made a good start I guess!" He glanced at Anne, who was looking off to the side.

"Enough about me, dude," said Kevin, "what have you been up

to?"

"I have ten patents to my name, two best-selling novels, and I'm up for re-election to the Senate this fall!"

"Whoa, big fella! I think you have to be at least twenty-five years old to be in the Senate."

"So I'm off by a few years--they'll get over it!"

"Is *anything* that you said true?" asked Kevin.

"Well, I am working on a novel, but it's a long way from being a bestseller. So, look, who's--" Tony was about to motion toward Anne, but at that moment she drifted off toward another group of partiers.

"Oh, this is--" Kevin turned to Anne, but stopped talking when he saw her walk away.

"What's the deal?" asked Tony in a low voice. "That's your date, right?"

"Yeah, that's my--" Kevin bit his lower lip and shook his head slightly. "That kid is beginning to piss me off."

"Woman problems, huh?"

"It's a long story...maybe I can explain sometime." Kevin looked again in Anne's direction and saw she was talking with some guy whom he vaguely recognized.

"So, what's up with you after graduation?" asked Tony. "The pros?"

Kevin snapped his head around to look at Tony. "Huh? I mean--sorry, I'm just a little distracted--yeah, the pros. Maybe...do you think we'll be having football? Look, what I mean is--Tony, this is insane! We're slowly being occupied by the Chinese and no one cares! Sure, we can come to a victory party like this, but how much longer will we have our freedoms?"

"It does seem a little strange," agreed Tony. "I just heard on the radio when I was driving here tonight that it's being called the 'kinder, gentler takeover.'"

"Yeah, for now," scoffed Kevin. "Remember what happened to those students in Tiananmen Square in China back in the 80s. That wasn't exactly 'kind' or 'gentle.'"

"What did happen to them?"

"To tell the truth, I'm not really too sure--I think they were imprisoned, I don't know. Were any of them executed?"

"Couldn't tell ya."

"So what are you studying, Tony? You say you're writing a

novel?"

"As luck would have it, I'm an English major, and, yes, I am writing a novel."

"You're at OSU, right?"

"Right."

"What's the novel about?" asked Kevin, after he took a swig of his beer.

"Well, the working title is 'Narthex.' It's about a boy who finds he wants to be an astronaut by taking hiking expeditions in the woods with his dog."

"What's a 'Narthex'?"

"A Narthex is just the Latin word for the lobby, or vestibule, of a church."

"What's that have to do with being an astronaut?"

"I'm working on that," said Tony. He took a bite of the chocolate chip cookie he was holding. "But suffice it to say I don't want to give away the plot."

"Speaking of church, remember that nun we had for algebra back at Saint Ed's?"

"Yeah, Sister Rosemarie!"

"I heard she just moved out to Mohun Hall at Ohio Dominican."

"Man, she must be about ninety or something by now."

"Right!" agreed Tony. "She was old when she was teaching us."

Kevin adopted a pensive look, then said to Tony in a low voice. "You much into the Catholic thing--you know, Saint Ed's and all that?"

"I'm pretty much of a C & E Catholic, if you get my drift."

"'C & E'?"

"Christmas and Easter Catholic."

"Oh," smiled Kevin. "Huh. Never heard it put that way."

"Yeah, me and the Lord, we got a deal worked out."

"What's that?" Kevin asked with a chuckle.

"It's simple. He lets me know a day ahead of time when I'm going to die, and then I go to Confession and settle accounts with him."

"Hey, where can I sign up for that plan?" asked Kevin. "Sounds like you can have your cake and eat it, too!"

"It's called the Las Vegas option. You see, it does involve a slight degree of risk."

"Such as you might die in a car wreck on the way home

tonight."

"Very perceptive of you, my friend," laughed Tony.

"Without any chance of going to Confession before you die," said Kevin.

"Doubly perceptive, Mr. C!"

"I got an 'A' in religion at Saint Ed's."

"Oh, aren't you the theological maestro, therefore."

"Actually, I memorized the 'Summa Theologica.'"

"Uh, look, we 'C & E' Catholics are a little ignorant of this stuff."

"It's a book written by some scholar back in the Middle Ages," explained Kevin.

"So, are you some religious buff or something?"

"Hardly. My parents are pretty good Catholics. I suppose a little rubbed off on me."

"You still go to Sunday Mass?" asked Tony.

"I try to. I miss every now and then."

"Not to change the subject, but you don't sound too sure about what you're going to do after graduation."

"Now it's time for you to be perceptive, dude. Yeah, you could say that. First, who knows what's going to happen with this Chinese stuff, and second, I'm not too thrilled with playing pro ball."

"Four million dollars is a little hard to live on, huh," said Tony sarcastically.

Kevin looked down at the floor and gave a tight smile. "Hell, that's what everyone says. Sometimes, I just think there's more to life than money and fame."

"You sure you didn't get hit too hard in the Fiesta Bowl? Maybe you're suffering delusions, guy."

"I know, I know…it does sound a bit stupid. Just ignore me--I'll figure this all out."

"You go, boy!" Tony said with a laugh, giving Kevin a slap on the back. "If you have trouble accepting all that cash, consider me as a worthy charity."

"I heard that!" said Kevin. "I'll see you around…looks like I better go find my woman."

"Can't live with 'em; can't live with 'em."

"The truth of life! You said it, Tony."

Kevin spent the next half hour mingling with the steady stream of well-wishers who continually congratulated him on his storied OSU football career. He caught sight of Anne sitting on the couch with *that* guy and started to wander in her direction. Just then the front door of the house burst open and a large group of Chinese soldiers walked in, all carrying snub-nosed assault rifles.

"Wu hui qi! Wu hui qi!" they began shouting. "Party finished! Party finished!"

Chad's mother stormed up to one of the soldiers and shouted: "Who do you think you are? This is *my* house! We're not breaking any laws!"

The Chinese infantryman held his rifle out in front of him and simply pushed the woman back into the crowd.

"Now, ever-body is quiet," said the lead Chinese sergeant in broken English. "No need for you make trouble. Ever-body go home. Party over!" He looked around the room but no one moved. "I say party over! Move!"

Several people started to put on their coats and hats, but a group of football players stood defiantly looking at the sergeant.

"I have OK to shoot!" shouted the Chinaman as he unbuckled his pistol and pulled it out with his right hand. "MOVE!"

"C'mon, Kevin," said Tony, pulling on his sleeve, "let's get outta here."

"Yeah, right." Kevin turned to face the group of football players. "You guys, let's not make any trouble, at least not now."

A few of the players grumbled, but eventually picked up their coats and filed out the front door.

Kevin walked up to Anne after they had both walked outside. "Need a ride?" he asked.

The young man standing with Anne gave Kevin a dirty look and motioned to his car. "Anne, why don't I give you a lift home?"

"That won't be necessary," said Kevin, stepping toward the college student, who was about an inch shorter than Kevin.

"That'll be all, children!" said Anne, loudly, looking sharply at the two men. She turned toward her new acquaintance. "Josh, I came with Kevin here; I guess I better go home with him too."

"Maybe I'll see you on campus, huh?" Josh asked, starting to walk away.

"Yeah, I'll be there," she said, looking all the while at Kevin.

Kevin and Anne walked silently to his car and both climbed in. After driving for a minute or two, Kevin opened his mouth to speak.

"Don't even ask," she said crossly.

Kevin drove onto the outer belt and headed for the OSU campus. "Care to tell me what all this is about?"

"You didn't even introduce me to your old high school friend you met!"

"Like I had a chance! You walked away before I could tell Tony about you!"

"Yeah, I guess it's only right that I'm like the fourth topic of conversation that comes up."

"Anne, what *really* is the problem? You've been a bit tense ever since I picked you up tonight."

"The question is: what is wrong with *you*?"

"All right, I give up; what *is* wrong with me?"

Anne said nothing. She looked out the window and noticed that Antrim Lake was completely iced over. Kevin tapped the steering wheel impatiently.

"You won the championship." Anne finally said.

"True."

"So, what about it?"

"Ohh," said Kevin, "so *that's* what this is about."

"You said you'd marry me if you won. You haven't said word-one about it and it's been a whole week now."

"Well," Kevin said, scrunching up his face, "give me a chance. You know, it's not something you take lightly."

"Well, a promise is a promise."

"All right...I know. Tonight just wasn't right. You know, we went to a party. I'll work it out."

"You promise?"

Kevin hesitated, then laughed. "Sure, honey. I'll get my act together."

Kevin dropped her off in front of her sorority house on Fifteenth Avenue and drove home.

****

Father Rankin had been able to clear a spot on his usually busy Sunday schedule and had just shown Dexter into his parish office for another session.

"I was surfing the internet when I came across this site about salvation and the Catholic Church," said Dexter. "It was B.S., man! They claimed that you can't be saved unless you're Catholic! That really bothers me!"

"I believe you're referring to 'Extra Ecclesiam Nulla Salus,'" said Father Rankin.

"Uh, you sure you're not confusing that with 'E Pluribus Unum?' Father, I never took a day of Latin, if that's what you're speaking."

"No Salvation Outside the Church."

"Yeah! I remember that phrase. They can't be serious, can they?"

"You have to understand the meaning of the expression. Basically, it means that *if* someone is saved, they are saved by grace *from* the Catholic Church."

"Oh," said Dexter feebly. "That's quite a bit different from what I thought."

"Not to worry," said Fr Rankin. "The first time I heard it I ran around confused for about three weeks till a priest set me straight. Like some other things in the Catholic Faith it can be easily misunderstood."

"What exactly *is* grace?"

"Grace is a sharing in the very life of God. It is spiritual energy--it's spiritual 'good vibes' from God himself."

"So who gets grace?"

"God gives grace to every human at one point or another."

"So non-Catholics can be saved?"

"That is correct. I remember a sermon I heard once. The priest said: 'We know that there is no salvation outside of Jesus Christ. What can we say of others who do not know and follow Christ? The only thing we can say is 'We have no idea.'"

"What's the deal with that song "Amazing Grace?" asked Dexter. I hear it from time to time…I believe one of the lines says that 'grace saved a fool like me.' So all we have to do is get grace and we're saved?"

"Now we get to the thermodynamics of salvation," said Father Rankin. "I say thermodynamics because salvation theology can sometimes be a little too theoretical, a little too hard to bring down to brass tacks, like the study of heat flow. You took thermo, right?"

"One course--I see your point.   Thermo as opposed to mechanics, right? You can *see* levers and rods, but not *heat*."

"Precisely.   Anyway, I would describe the Catholic doctrine of salvation and grace thusly: We are saved by grace.   If we are damned, we are damned by our works. God chooses to reward us for our good works. The end."

"So we are 'saved by grace,' like the song says," said Dexter.

"Whoa," said Father Rankin. "The proper wording for that song 'Amazing Grace' is really: 'that *is saving* a wretch like me'--not 'that *saved* a wretch like me.'   While on earth, we can never be sure of our salvation--only if we die in the state of grace will we avoid Hell. As long as we are still breathing we can lose our friendship with God. Put it this way. I remember reading this from some priest--I forget the title of the book, but he said 'God, who created us without our help, will not save us without our help.'"

"Sooo, we are not saved by grace alone."

"Welll, this is why I compare it to thermodynamics, Dexter. You get into some terminology about which whole books have been written. Don't get me wrong--the Council of Trent said--it was held around the year fifteen-fifty--they said that God alone provides the grace for salvation. They were very clear on that point. Where Catholics and Protestants diverge, is our *response* to that grace. Catholics believe that we can *cooperate* with God's grace, and thus save our soul. Protestants tend to talk about faith alone and that type of thing. Luther believed in the total depravity of man, that we were basically piles of bullcrap that had to be completely covered over by the 'snow' of Christ in order to be saved.   The Catholic view gives a much more 'optimistic,' if you will, view of man."

"Hmm," said Dexter. "Food for thought."

"Dexter, my friend, there is a grocery of food for thought in that. And you know, let me add to that.   Some people are fond of saying that Catholicism is a 'both/and' religion, which is true--we tend to look at the big picture. But, regarding what I just said about 'will not save us without our help,' I've been thinking recently about that.   For the whole salvation thing to make sense I really think it must involve the free will of the soul in question. I heard that Christ told a Saint once-- Saint Faustina--she lived back in the 20s and 30s--that only those souls who want to actually go to Hell."

"Now, come on, Father!" said Dexter.   "Like anyone really

wants to go to Hell."

"Well, let me tell you what this one Bishop said once on his TV program. He compared salvation to the situation in which you owe someone five thousand dollars. You're walking along the street and you see your creditor coming toward you on the sidewalk--what do you do? Well, you probably cross to the other side of the street so you don't have to meet him that day. I really think that is how salvation works. If we die with so much sin on our soul that we can't bear to meet Christ, well…we throw ourselves into Hell."

"It's starting to make a little sense, but what about Muslims? They don't know Christ. They just believe in Allah and the Koran."

"We can really only leave that up to God," said Father Rankin. "I just try to get as many people as I can to become Catholic and let the good Lord worry about the admissions criteria. There is a reported apparition of the Blessed Mother to some Muslims about, uh, I think it was forty years ago. We can only hope they follow the dictates of their conscience and follow the light of truth that is given to them. My Dad used to say that only those who know the Catholic Church is the true Church but remain outside of her are in trouble."

"Then why should anyone become Catholic if you don't need to be one to be saved?"

"In the end it all comes down to the individual and God. I've met some Mormons who, as far as I could tell, truly believed they were in the true Church of Christ. In the Bible at one point, God says: 'If you are neither hot nor cold, I will begin to vomit you out of my mouth.' And the other thing to remember is that people don't always follow their consciences. I met a guy in Houston once who said that someone once asked a gun-for-hire, a hitman, if it was hard to kill someone. The guy replied: 'it gets easier after the first time.' That's really the case with so many people…they deaden their consciences, till after a while they can no longer hear the 'little voice' speaking to them."

"I once heard that thing about God vomiting from a guy I knew in Boy Scouts," said Dexter. "Exactly what is he getting at there?"

"Basically, it means God looks for people who are zealous--for good or evil. It's the apathetic ones that anger him the most."

"Like me, for instance."

"Hey, you made the effort to come and talk to me, right? That's gotta count for something."

"Great, so I'm saved!" said Dexter.

"Just keep on the path you're on."

"So Hitler was saved, right? He sure was 'cold'!"

"The classic example of hot versus cold is Saint Paul. He persecuted the Christians and then later became one. There were no halfway measures with him."

"That was two thousand years ago--anything more recent?"

"Let's see," began Fr Rankin, stroking his chin, "how about Doctor Bernard Nathanson."

"The only doctor I know about is Doctor Who."

"I guess you haven't followed the pro-life movement too closely."

"That's a whole other topic."

"Bernard Nathanson was a hard-core abortionist who converted to the Faith and is now a leading champion in the pro-life movement. He is another classic example of someone who, at various times in his life, was 'hot' and 'cold.'"

"So Europeans can be saved," said Dexter.

"What?" Now it was time for Fr Rankin to be perplexed.

"It's the way they build their sinks over there. A friend of mine was telling me that, instead of having one spigot like we do here, they have two separate spigots on either side of the sink, one for hot and one for cold. When you try to wash your hands, you're either burned or frozen."

"Ah, so," said Fr Rankin. "Would that their souls were the same."

"So, tell me," said Dexter, "how many do you think make it in?"

"Make it in?"

"You know--make it into Heaven? Percentage."

Fr Rankin smiled. "Maybe I'll tell you in a little while. What's your guesstimate?"

"You're asking the wrong guy here, Father. As of now, I'm trying to decide if I'm still an atheist or not. If it were up to me, I'd let everybody into Heaven."

"Ah, a universalist."

"Huh?"

"Universal salvation," said Father Rankin. "That's the name they give to the belief that everyone is saved."

"Where can I sign up? Sounds like I could be a card-carrying member."

"Well, in a sense we can all be universalists, Dexter."

"Whaaa? You don't seem like you're that type, Father."

"We can all *hope* that all men will be saved, but we shouldn't say we're *certain* that all men are saved."

"Somehow I don't see the distinction."

"To be honest," said Father Rankin, "I really don't see much point in it either. I was just repeating what I heard once from someone."

"So, really, Father, how many *do* you think make it into Heaven?"

"I'd have to agree with what Mary said at Medjugorje, i.e., what I told you previously: the majority go to Purgatory, the next greatest number go to Hell, and the rest go directly to Heaven--but, you know, to be perfectly honest with you, I go from universal salvation to universal damnation sometimes...depending on my mood. I really have to be more merciful in my judgments and 'send' more people to Purgatory than Hell. Well--no--I shouldn't judge anyone to Hell, only Purgatory, at the worst."

"What exactly is Purgatory? I heard a friend of mine say that it's the place you go to after you die and you stay there until you say you're sorry.

"Well, his theology is a tad askew. Purgatory is the place you go to after you die, but you go there to make up, or 'atone,' as the expression goes, for your sins. You have hopefully already said you're sorry while you're still here on this earth."

"Why can't we just pop right into Heaven?" asked Dexter. "Seems to me we suffer enough while we're here."

"Now do you really think that when Mother Teresa died and John F. Kennedy died they both deserved the same treatment? Do you think they should all just 'pop' right into Heaven?"

"Who says JFK went to Heaven anyway?"

"Funny you should mention that," said Father Rankin. "Just last week I was talking with a brother priest over in Zanesville and he was telling me that he heard it first hand that Kennedy went to confession in Dallas on the morning of the day he was shot."

"You sure he didn't read it in 'The National Inquirer'?"

"Hey--take it for what it's worth. I choose to believe it."

"So now we know JFK is in Heaven," said Dexter.

"Well," said Father Rankin, "of course we can never judge, but I'd say it's a pretty good bet that ol' John 'F' has passed the Pearly Gates by now. But, my point is--take any average bloke--everyone dies in a different state of 'goodness' and 'badness.'"

"So that's your reasoning for the existence of Purgatory?"

"That as well as several Scriptural references."

"I really don't want to hear a bunch of Bible quotes at the moment."

"Just suffice it to say that Purgatory is the 'doormat' to Heaven."

"Hmm, 'doormat'…interesting concept," said Dexter.

"You don't sound like you're convinced."

"I'll take what you say under advisement, Father."

"You sound like Mark Twain."

"How's that?"

"Mark Twain once said that he didn't have problems with the passages in the Bible that he didn't understand. He said he had problems with the passages that he *did* understand!"

"Yeah, right. Was Mark Twain a believer?"

"To be honest I don't know what religion he was."

"So he's in Hell, too."

"Whoaa, Nellie!" said Father Rankin. "Dexter, I think I'm going to have to name you Boanerges."

"Like I really know what you're talking about."

"Boanerges! *Sons of Thunder*! It's what Christ named the Apostles James and John. Those two were always quick to condemn people who didn't immediately agree with them."

"Hey, you're the one condemning people…all this talk of 'Medjurgorje' and 'next greatest number goes to Hell' and 'Purgatory.' What ever happened to a Loving and Merciful God and all that?"

"Whoaa, Nellie, again! Now we're back into Universalism and all that! The Golden Mean, my friend, the Golden Mean! God *is* all loving, but he is all *just* as well. I still remember how my Dad used to say that God is all mercy on this side of death, and all justice on the other side of death."

"Fine," said Dexter, "he's all mercy in this life. Let him just suck me up into Heaven in this life, and I won't have to worry about anything on the 'other side of death,' as you put it."

"Tsk, tsk," said Father Rankin. "Presumption in a nutshell."

"What is it with all these 'terms,' anyway? Can we just talk plain language? All right, 'presumption.' Let's go back to the 9th Century and hear the definition of 'presumption.'"

"That's just it, Dexter. Yes! The 9th Century! All these theories have been hammered out over centuries. Theology has a history of development just like any other discipline. But, anyway, 'presumption' is the certainty that one is saved before he dies. We can never be certain we are saved until after death. 'Presumption' is the opposite of despair, which is the belief that we are damned and can do nothing about it."

"What about 'annihilism'?"

"'Annihilism'?" asked Father Rankin.

"I just made it up--the belief that after death we are simply annihilated. What's wrong with that?"

"Well, I can tell you what John Milton said in his poem 'Paradise Lost.' The way he tells the story, after Satan loses the battle with Michael the Archangel, he finds himself in Hell. Looking around him, Satan says, 'Well, at least I still exist.'"

"Uh," said Dexter, "not to slight a great poet, but I'd rather not exist than burn in Hell. Anyway, that's one poet's belief, what does the Church say about annihilism--surely it's a belief that's been around before."

"Oh, I do believe it is a belief which has appeared from time to time in history, but what's wrong with it? Hmm, well, first off, what about Christ's Passion and Death? What was all that about if there is no Heaven or Hell? Another of my pet theories is that religion is boring without Hell."

"So it's a pious belief that some people hold onto when they need a role model to get over the tough times in life."

"Now, one minute," began Father Rankin, "the resurrection may be a pious belief but the crucifixion of Christ is a documented, historical fact. Cornelius Tacitus was an historian in first-century Rome and he documented Christ's life. And--wait! Lest I contradict myself--I shouldn't have said the resurrection is just a pious belief. He was seen by over five hundred people before he ascended into Heaven. And, remember, all twelve Apostles were martyred for their belief in Christ. Sort of hard to be put to death for a made-up story."

"All right, so some Jew hangs on a cross for a few hours and dies. There were plenty of people that died by crucifixion in Roman times. I'm supposed to be impressed by that?"

"You might not believe it, but it has been revealed to various Saints throughout history that Christ suffered an infinity of pain during his Passion. Christ used his Divinity to keep himself alive so his Humanity could suffer all the more. A normal man may have died much sooner than he did."

"Still, three hours is three hours," said Dexter. "Wasn't that about all the time that Christ was on the cross? I seem to remember that from that Mel Gibson movie on the Passion."

"Oh, but Dexter, you have to realize that Christ's Passion began the night before with the Agony in the Garden and lasted up until his last breath on Good Friday afternoon."

"Okay, so it was, what?--eighteen hours. The Nazis tortured people for longer than that."

"I've read certain authors who allege that Christ suffered interiorly all throughout his life--as did his mother, I might add. You have to remember that pain can come in different levels of intensity. Remember Christ's cry from the Cross: 'My God, my God, why have you forsaken me?' That was probably the worst suffering he had to endure. Or, actually, I take that back--I heard someone say once that Christ's worst suffering while he was on the Cross was to be able to look into the future and see that, for some people, all his horrible suffering would be in vain, i.e., that some people would still ignore him and go to Hell despite all he suffered for them."

"What's so bad about interior suffering?" asked Dexter. "We all have our bad days."

"Think of how you feel when someone intentionally humiliates you, or slights you, or betrays you."

"Well, I do remember this guy I knew in high school. He basically went from being my best friend to being my worst enemy, just because I beat him out of the starting spot in wrestling."

"Multiply that hurt by a million times--that's what Christ felt. He was not only abandoned by the Apostles, but by God Himself! That's what he meant by 'My God, why have you abandoned me?'"

"Christ said that?" Dexter asked.

"It's one of the seven last words of--well, seven last *phrases* that Christ spoke on the Cross," said Father Rankin.

"Seven, huh? Isn't that some sort of perfect number thing?"

"It's just what is written in the Gospels."

"So what's your point?"

"My point is that God sustains everything and keeps it in being. Imagine how Christ must have felt to be abandoned by God himself! No life force at all--just total emptiness and nothingness."

"C'mon, it couldn't have been that bad! After all he *was* supposed to be half-God, right? He could take it."

"First of all," said Father Rankin, "he was *not* half-God. He was fully God and fully human. Furthermore, he suffered in his humanity just like any man suffers. Actually, he suffered *more* than any man suffers. As I said just now, he used his divinity to keep his humanity conscious so that he *could* suffer more."

"All right, whatever. How did we get on this topic anyway? I came in to ask about 'No Salvation Outside the Church'--remember? I saw that website that claimed that everyone who's not Catholic is going to Hell."

"Well," said Father Rankin, "you do understand what I said...?"

"You said something about grace coming from the Catholic Church."

"Right--we believe that when someone is saved, they are saved by grace coming from the Catholic Church."

"That sounds pretty bigoted if you ask me," said Dexter, shaking his head back and forth. "So with one sweep of his pen, some Pope relegates all non-Catholics into irrelevance."

"You must be referring to Pope Boniface VIII."

"I don't know--it was some Pope back in the 12th Century or something. What difference does it make?"

"I'm not the greatest Church Historian around," said Father Rankin, "but I believe it was around the year 1300. What I really think you need to read, Dexter, is the book 'The Glories of Mary,' by Saint Alphonsus Ligouri."

"Mary? She's the mother of Jesus, right? Now you want me to start believing in all that?"

"Look," said Father Rankin, leaning forward in his chair, "salvation is more than just a courtroom ritual and a guillotine reserved for most of humanity. The Blessed Mother is responsible for saving many, many souls through her intercession with God."

"'Intercession'?" asked Dexter.

"It means her influence, her *'pull'* with God."

"'Pull'? You mean we bribe Mary to tell God to look the other way when we want to do something bad?"

"More like we ask her to put in a good word for us. I remember a sermon I heard a few years ago in which this priest said that it would be good on Judgment Day if Christ could at least say to us: 'I don't know you too well, but my mother has said good things about you.'"

"I don't know about all this," said Dexter, scratching his head and scrunching up his nose. "I came in here to talk about non-Catholics going to Hell and now we're discussing various nuances of brownie points, as far as I can tell."

"Why don't you just ponder a few of these points until we meet again? This isn't a calculus lesson. These types of things need time to ripen before they can be 'eaten,' if you will--and remember this: for most people death is just a theoretical exercise that they think of once a year and then immediately decide to avoid thinking about till they're eighty years old. Try pressing a loaded gun against someone's head and see how 'calm' they are about the ultimate destiny of their soul. I know from personal experience."

"What are you talking about?" asked Dexter.

"While I was on that Alaska trip, I was stopped by some miscreants while riding in the wilds of that state. They did indeed put a gun against my head and demand my money."

"What happened?"

"Well, thanks be to God, a bus of tourists stopped just about the time he was getting ready to shoot me."

"Lucky you."

"You can say that again!" said Father Rankin. "Anyway, for the two minutes that I had the gun against my head, I said about fifty Acts of Contrition. I think you'll find that most people get *real* interested in religion when their life is in imminent danger."

"Tell me about it," said Dexter. "I know the feeling." Dexter rose from his chair and put on his coat.

"Same time next week?" asked Father Rankin.

"Uhh, I'll let you know."

"So long."

Dexter abruptly left the room without the customary handshake. He got in his car and headed down High Street, surprised to see so much traffic around Graceland Shopping Center. *Must be that new department store that opened yesterday,* he thought. *Maybe I can open my first robot store here...might be good demographics for it.* He arrived home fifteen minutes later and grimaced when he saw

Daphne's car already in the driveway. He was hoping she might have to work late and he could avoid talking to her for at least another day. He pulled his Charger behind her car and plodded into the house.

"I hear footsteps!" said Daphne in a lilting voice from the kitchen. "How does corned beef sound for dinner, Dex?"

"Yeah," said Dexter.

"I can't *hear* you!" said Daphne melodically.

"Sounds good," he said a little louder as he walked into the kitchen. He filled a cup with water and drank it.

"Don't I get my usual 'Good Evening' kiss?" asked Daphne.

"Uhhnn," Dexter said between swallows.

"How romantic of you, my dear."

Dexter poured the unused water into the sink and pretended to straighten up the dishes.

"I know that act," said Daphne. "Let's have it: you lose a contract or something? One of your engineers quit?"

"No, nothing like that." He opened the refrigerator and spent a few seconds surveying its contents. He closed the door and faced his girlfriend. "Daphne, we have to talk."

"Holy crap!" she cried. "Just when I thought it was going to be a perfect day, this happens." She put the pan she was holding back on the stove and looked over at Dexter.

Dexter leaned against the counter and looked down at the floor, avoiding her eyes. "Daphne, I know we've discussed this before, but I just--"

"Wait one second!" Daphne said. "I know guilt when I see it! This is that *priest* again, isn't it? I thought you were done with him! Have you been talking with him again?"

"Now, Daffy..."

"Don't try to sweet talk me on this one, bubba!"

"Yes, I have been back to see Father Rankin."

"Oh, so he even has a name. *'Father so-and-so.'* Aren't you the pretty little altar boy!"

"Daphne, he told me that it isn't good for a marriage to live together."

"Oh, there's logic at its best! Now it's somehow wrong to try out a product before you buy it! Who does this priest think he is anyway? Our relationship is *ours*! *We* should decide what's best for us, not *him*."

"But he said that over half the marriages end in divorce when the couple lives together before they are married."

"And what about the half that end up in perfectly fine marriages?" asked Daphne. "You ever think about them?"

"I never thought about it that way."

"What *else* didn't you think about, Dexter?"

"It's just that he didn't seem to think we should be doing this."

"Ohhhhhh!" screamed Daphne, pulling on her hair, turning away from Dexter. "Why is this happening to me? What is *wrong* with you?" She turned back toward Dexter and walked up next to him. "Dexter, you're not Catholic! You don't have to listen to this *priest!*" She spat out the word 'priest.' "Or *are* you a Catholic? Have you converted or something without telling me?"

"No," said Dexter. "I've just been to see this guy about four or so times. It really has to do with the--the plane crash more than anything."

"*Again* with the plane crash thing?" she asked. "Is this déjà vu or what? I thought we had this same conversation about two weeks ago or whenever."

"Well, you see I had that plane crash and it really got me thinking about death and stuff."

"Dexter when are you going to drop this whole religion idiocy? Religion is for losers and weaklings! You have everything going for you! Don't waste it all on this--don't listen to some weird priest. Please!"

"But Father Rankin doesn't strike me as being a loser or weakling. He was an engineer before becoming a priest. You know what? He rode up to Alaska on a motorcycle--all by himself!"

"This is insane!" yelled Daphne, tearing off the apron she was wearing. "You want to do something all by yourself, too? 'Cause I'm going out to eat dinner tonight. You can finish cooking dinner 'all by yourself' too. You better get a clue, Dexter. You're losing it!" She picked up her purse and walked out the door.

Dexter just stood there and watched her go. After a few minutes he was jarred back to reality when he smelled some food burning on the stove.

Chapter 8

Thad hadn't been this excited in years. As he pulled up in front of Cheryl's apartment he remembered that quote he read once in high-school: "If you don't think there are any frontiers left in the world, just watch a young man walk up to the door of his first date." *Well, it's not my* first *date, for crying out loud,* he reasoned. *But I guess it might as well be, as nervous as I am.* He approached the front door and rang the doorbell.

"Six o'clock on the dot!" said Cheryl as she opened her front door. She was wearing a light blue blouse with a darker blue skirt. Her golden hair came down to just below her shoulders, and framed her high-cheek-boned face.

"'Reliable Rankin,' that's me!" said Thad with a grin.

"Or 'Thoughtful Thad'!"

"I'd have to concur with that," said Thad, nodding. *I don't deserve this girl,* he thought. *She reminds me of that "ABBA" lyric: "I am the girl with golden hair."*

Cheryl put on her coat and locked the front door.

"Your car sure is sparkling for such a slushy winter's day as this," she said to Thad. Thad had washed and waxed his car, a Ford Taurus, for the occasion, and Cheryl motioned to it in her driveway.

"I don't want to give Tauruses a bad name, you know how it goes." He opened the passenger door for Cheryl, then closed it once she had entered.

"That's one more thing I like about Columbus," he said as he climbed in the driver's side. "Rather gentle winters."

"Oh, I know," said Cheryl. "All the benefits of southern weather, without the bugs."

"I heard that." Thad backed out of the driveway and headed toward Powell Road. "One time I was in Florida and there was this huge 'thing' on my pillow one night. Scared the daylights out of me."

"Just goes to confirm my 'Misery Factor' theory," said Cheryl.

"Do tell--incidentally, I thought we'd go to the 'Refectory,' on Bethel Road, if you'd like."

"Oh, sounds good. I've never been there, but I've heard good things about it from friends of mine."

"So, what's this 'Misery Factor'?" asked Thad. He waited for a truck to pass, then turned onto Powell Road.

"Oh, yeah. I suppose someone else has published it somewhere, but anyway I think that everyone has the same amount of misery wherever they live. LA has great weather year around, but they have smog and congestion too."

"And wildfires every now and then," added Thad.

"That's right, wildfires. Or Florida: they have great weather in the winter, but it's hot in the summer--and they have the occasional hurricane too."

"And Columbus?"

"That's what's great about Columbus," said Cheryl excitedly. "It really is the golden mean of misery. It's like Goldilocks' porridge, not too hot, not too cold. Just about the time the hot weather starts to get annoying in the summer, it starts to cool off--and the same is true of the cold weather in the winter. Columbus is just below the snowline, so it's rare when we get any heavy snow."

"So what *is* there to be miserable about in Columbus?" asked Thad.

"Besides Buckeye fans?" she asked with an impish smile.

"Hey, that's what makes Columbus the vibrant city it is!"

"I don't know if *vibrant* is the proper adjective for a Buckeye football fan."

"You're right--'cultured' might be a better term," said Thad.

"Yeah, right."

"So basically the job at Battelle brought you to Columbus, huh?"

"Right," said Cheryl. "This is my first job out of school. I had two job offers, one in Chicago and one here."

"You chose Columbus over Chicago?"

"Chicago's a great place, but I just thought it might be too big and too cold."

"I guess I could see that--but it must be nice to live right next door to Lake Michigan."

"Yeah, and it doesn't hurt that the Cubs finally won the World Series last year."

"Oh, they must have gone nuts up there."

"So I heard."

Ten minutes later, Thad parked the car behind the Refectory and in short order they were sitting in a corner booth in the restaurant.

"What's your favorite wine?" he asked Cheryl.

"No question there--Lambrusco."

"Oh, a sweet-liker, huh?"

"At least my favorite isn't as pedestrian as yours."

"How do know my favorite?"

"Don't you remember your question in the cab: 'Which is higher in the order of creation, chocolate milk or White Zinfandel'?"

"Oh, right, right," said Thad. "Good memory...that's good. Pedestrian, huh? What makes you say that?"

"It's only offered at ninety-five percent of the restaurants in this country, that's all."

"Sort of like Snickers."

"How so?"

"Well, Snickers, I guess, is the most popular candy bar in the US--it's my favorite as well."

"Wow!" said Cheryl. "Our first date and we're getting to know all our deepest secrets!"

"You'll never find out my favorite ice cream--at least that secret's safe!"

"That's easy--Dove bar."

"Mum's the word," said Thad. "It's in the vault."

They were interrupted by the waiter, who explained the specials of the day.

"I'll have the Spiced Duck Breast," said Thad. "Cheryl, you ought to try it, it's delicious. Half is spiced, and half is not spiced."

"Hmm...not to be contrary, but I think I'll try the Filet Mignon," said Cheryl.

"Very good," said the waiter. "I'll be out with your salads

shortly."

"Thank you."

"Mary, Mary, quite contrary, huh?" asked Thad with a smile.

"Actually I tried duck at a restaurant near Brown and I didn't care for it too much."

"Well, that's because it was 'Brown Duck.' This is 'Orange Duck.'"

"Typical Notre Dame humor," replied Cheryl. "Nice try."

After a sumptuous dinner and then a dessert of Apple Crepes, they sat lingering over cups of decaf coffee.

"You really believe this Garabandal stuff, then?" asked Cheryl.

"I've been following it since the sixth grade. My parents took us kids to a film about Garabandal down at the Ohio state fairgrounds when I was about eleven. It really made an impression on me. How about you, Cheryl? When did you first hear about it?"

"I had heard a little about it from one of my brothers a couple years ago, but I never paid it much attention till the last few months. Sometimes I--" Cheryl stopped abruptly and took a drink of her coffee. "Oh, I don't know..."

"What?" asked Thad, peering into her face.

"I really don't know who to ask."

"Hey, I know as much about Garabandal as anybody."

"It's not really about Garabandal as--well, you know about the Chastisement, right?"

"Riiight," said Thad slowly.

"I guess what I mean--what I'm trying to say is, what's it all worth if all these people are going to die? Don't most of the prophecies say something about two-thirds to three-quarters of the world's population is going to die?"

"That's right--you're worried that it might be you?"

"I guess what I'm worried about, or maybe more to the point, what I have to fight against is apathy. Why do anything if some big comet's headed our way? Even if we live the earth is going to be one big cinder!"

"Look at it this way," said Thad, holding out one of his hands. "If you're living right and you die in the Chastisement, fine. You go to Heaven, maybe bypassing Purgatory altogether. If you live through the Chastisement, the prophecies say the earth will be a great place to live. It's gets a little confusing at times, but some visionaries have said stuff like cold climates will become temperate, and that the soil will be so fertile that there will be twelve growing seasons per year!"

"Really."

"Honest. I can try to find the sources if you'd like."

"I'll take your word for it right now," said Cheryl. She drank the last bit of coffee in her cup. "Still, I'm not enthused at some of the things I've read--about some of the suffering we might have to endure."

"I also read somewhere--I've read so much I forget where it comes from--that those who live through the Chastisement will live their Purgatory on earth."

"Ohh." Cheryl shivered slightly from some unseen draft. "All right, enough svart gihil! Onward to Tom Cruise and the cinema!"

"'Svart gihil'?" asked Thad with a puzzled look.

"It's a Swedish, or German term my Dad likes to use. It means 'black moods.'"

"Okay, huh--svart gihil. I'll have to remember that. All right, Tom Cruise. One of my taxi passengers said it was a great film. I hope they're right."

Two hours later, on the way home from the movie, Thad pointed out the right side of the car. "I grew up right over there, on West Longview."

"Oh, yeah, Clintonville, right?" asked Cheryl.

"Right. It's a cozy little section of the city."

"So, did you think Tom Cruise stole the diamond when the movie just started?"

"I figured he couldn't end up being *that* bad, but I knew that's what they *wanted* us to believe," said Thad.

"Yeah, they almost fooled me too, but it's hard to see Tom Cruise as a thief."

"Right. How'd you like that woman actor--Parnips, or something?"

"Jackie Pearson. Yeah, she was good, I don't know about Oscar material, but she has potential."

"Nothing like a little 'PMA' to figure out a plot," said Thad.

"'PMA'?"

"Post Movie Analysis--you'll have to pardon my acronyms. It's just a latent longing for the military, I guess."

"All right, Mr. 'RRR.' That'll be enough!"

"Thanks for reminding me! Did you want to sign up now to join

Rankin's Religious Roustabouts?"

"I'll wait till I can go swimming in Alaska, I think," Cheryl said laughingly.

"Aww...now you're making fun of the Chastisement--I'm telling!"

"Who you gonna tell, taxi-boy? Your dispatcher? Does he believe in Garabandal too?"

"Double aww-whammy!" said Thad in mock surprise. Now you're making fun of Garabandal too. You'll get in dutch with the Blessed Mother!"

"'*In dutch*'? Where did you pick up that expression? Some 1930s movie?"

"My august father, I'll have you know. And it means to get in trouble, for your information."

"'My *august* father'?" said Cheryl, shaking her head. "I haven't heard that term since I took the SAT!"

"Oh, you poor, underprivileged Ivy League-ers," said Thad. "If only you knew the value of a variegated vocabulary." He looked at her with a toothy grin.

"Oh, yeah, Notre Dame! Bastion of college football! I bet you get a *really* good education there!"

"Hey, Notre Dame is God's highest creation--you know: 'Notre Dame'...French for 'Our Lady.'"

Cheryl chuckled, at a loss for how to reply to that one. They pulled up in front of her apartment and Thad put the car in park.

"I hope you enjoyed yourself, Cheryl." He leaned over and kissed her on the cheek.

"All except for the part about Notre Dame."

"Oh, you mean you were *over*joyed about that part."

"Oh, spare me!" She opened her door and stepped out. "Yes, Thad, a good time was had by all, if you must know."

"Same here, Miss Estevez, I'll be calling you, if that's all right with you."

"I'll be waiting by the phone, taxi-man!"

"Goodnight."

"Goodbye."

****

Dexter didn't want to admit it, but he was actually beginning to enjoy his chats with Father Rankin. He drove into the parking lot at Saint Michael's and walked to the door. *Where is this all going, I wonder.* He pushed the doorbell and turned to see some kids having a snowball fight at the other end of the schoolyard. *It's nothing I can't handle. This priest doesn't have anything on me. The important thing is to keep an open mind.*

"Hello, Dexter!" said the parish secretary warmly as she held the door open for Dexter. "A bit cold out these days, no?" Dexter had gotten to know the office staff at the church and had become accustomed to a little small talk with them.

"I can't disagree with that, Dorothy...I assume Father Rankin's in his office?"

"Oh, yes. You can walk right in."

"Father, I'd like to discuss Hell a little more," said Dexter after he greeted the priest and sat in a chair.

"You want to discuss the Hell out of Hell, eh?"

"Hell, I want to discuss *me* out of Hell!"

"Ah," said Father Rankin with a short laugh, "but I thought you didn't believe in Hell?"

"I'm not so sure, actually," said Dexter with a wistful look in his eye. "Ever since the plane crash, I haven't looked at things the same way."

"Maybe you've been thinking about the Warning?"

"Would you get off that 'Garb-dal' stuff, please," said Dexter, scrunching up his mouth.

"You mean *Garabandal.*"

"Fine, so my Spanish is a little rusty. Look, that Marian apparition stuff is a bit flaky, you know? I thought you or someone told me it's not official Church doctrine, so why do you keep pushing it?"

"Now, Dexter, we are free to believe anything as long as it hasn't been condemned by the Church--and officially Garabandal is still under investigation and has never been condemned -- or I should say, if it ever was condemned, it is now back under investigation."

"Well, the JFK assassination is still under investigation too. Most people have forgotten about it."

"Mary predicted the Warning over forty years ago."

"I'm sure something like the Warning has been predicted by all kinds of soothsayers as well."

"I have yet to hear of one besides Mary."

"Whatever the case, for now I'd like to stick to basic theology, like Hell--I'm still not satisfied with our previous discussion about it."

"Exactly what are you questioning?" asked Father Rankin.

"Well one thing that's been bouncing around in my head is something I remember reading in a Philosophy class back at Stanford: why should Hell last forever if our sins last only a short time? Doesn't it make more sense for the punishment to fit the crime? Say a guy is a murderer for twenty years; why not punish him in a 'temporary Hell' for twenty years, or maybe for forty years--but forever? C'mon!"

"Funny you should mention that," said Father Rankin, taking the pipe out of his mouth. "I asked the exact same question back in a theology class up at the Josephinum about five years ago. Then again, I suppose more people wonder about this than you might think, at first. Now, you just mentioned the JFK assassination: do you think Lee Harvey Oswald should have been given the same punishment as a kid who stole a candy bar from a convenience store? Both 'crimes' only lasted a few minutes, right?"

"First, do we really know that Oswald did it? And, second, Oswald was shot to death."

"Fine, pick any generic assassination attempt and any generic candy theft. Surely you don't think they deserve the same punishment?"

"Welll," said Dexter, "you're sort of comparing squirrels to ducks, apples to oranges."

"Or, am I? I think the issue here is that of confusing the duration of a sin with its gravity. If a man goes to Hell, it is because of the seriousness of his unrepentant sin or sins, not just how long they happened to last. Look at our own legal system: an act of treason, which may only last as long as it takes to hand a foreign spy an envelope containing top secret materials, can get you the death penalty or, maybe in some countries, lifelong exile."

"Hmm, I'd have to ponder that...actually I never heard that argument, but, uh, well...gravity versus duration..."

"What you also want to keep in mind," said Father Rankin, "is that mortal sin is actually *infinitely* grave, since it is an offense against an *Infinite* Being."

"Sort of like dividing any number by zero."

"Huh?" asked Father Rankin, thrown off for a change.

"You were an engineer and you don't understand that?" asked Dexter with a laugh. "No wonder Ford is the last of the Big Three."

"Ohhh, you mean *infinity*! Right, any number divided by zero equals infinity. You had me there for a second. By the way, Ford is still the best car company in the world. And hey! I can still solve diff e-q's with the best of 'em, bub!"

"Now you want a piece of a Stanford math genius? Father, I think you had better stick with theology."

"Any textbook, any chalkboard, bro," said Father Rankin with a gunslinger's look in his eye.

"I can solve that equation. I'm the best there is," mimicked Dexter.

"'Firefox!' Clint Eastwood!" said Father Rankin. "That's good, Dexter!"

"Ah, a priest who's well video-ed. I'm impressed!" Dexter nodded his head up and down with approval, then glanced down at his notebook. "But, anyway, I'm not finished with you yet, Mr. Priest-slash-Engineer. How 'bout this: if Hell is eternal, then everyone there receives the same punishment, no matter how terrible their crimes were."

"You've never read Dante's Inferno, I presume?"

"It's not on the Bestseller list, last time I checked."

"The simple answer to your question is that there are degrees of punishment in Hell. All punishments in Hell are eternal, but they're not the same. Matter of fact, Dante puts the Devil at the bottom of Hell, encased in ice."

"Fine," said Dexter, "we can discuss the source, or lack thereof, of that doctrine some other time--what about the fact that an eternal Hell is completely out of proportion with the pleasure gained by the sinner? I mean, I'm going to Hell forever just because I have brief periods of fun with my girlfriend?"

"The answer is similar to your earlier question about the duration of the sin. The point here is that the punishment is not proportional to the amount of joy felt by the perpetrator, but by the size of the offense against God."

"And I would assume you would say that living with someone you're not married to is a pretty big offense?"

"If the person knows full well what he is doing, yeah, it is. The question is, how much culpability does the average guy have today?"

"You know, Father Rankin," said Dexter, sitting up straight in his chair and running his hand through his hair, "I'll tell you what I really can't get out of my head. I think I mentioned this last time we talked. It seems to me that God will annihilate the bad guys and let the good guys into Heaven. I still don't see any point to Hell--forgive and forget, right?"

"Yes, Dexter, I can see where you're coming from and I understand how you might think that, but you must understand that the doctrine of the eternity of Hell comes solely from Divine revelation alone. Remember, I said a few weeks ago that Garrigou-Lagrange wrote that Hell could not be demonstrated logically, like a math equation. I believe it was he who made the point that our understanding of this mystery can never be fully understood, much as a polygon inscribed in a circle will never fill the circle, no matter how many sides it has."

"So we believe it because the Bible tells us to," said Dexter slightly sarcastically.

"We believe it because Christ told us to!" said Father Rankin, getting a little angry. "You think Christ was some kind of misguided fool? He spoke of Hell *eleven times* in the Gospels! Should we just sort of ignore that, show Him into the parlor where He won't disturb the dinner guests? Don't you think he knows what he's talking about?"

"And why should I believe Christ?" asked Dexter.

"C'mon, Dexter, pssshh!" exclaimed Father Rankin. "We've been talking all this time and you still doubt Christ's Divinity?"

"Sorry to upset your precious timetable, Father, but I like to work with logic and reason and normalcy! I have a couple of near-death experiences, I meet an eccentric taxi-driver who spouts Mary worship and now you tell me I have to accept an illogical belief simply because some guy talked about it two thousand years ago...forget it!"

"All right, all right," said Father Rankin, holding up his hands and bowing his head a little. "Maybe I got a little too hot under the collar there -- under the *Roman* collar. I have to remember sometimes that I'm dealing with people who were brought up in, basically, a completely different world than I was. I remember my father used to tell the story of a French farmer who was once asked if it was possible that God did not exist. Looking out over his verdant fields ripe for the harvest, the farmer simply replied emphatically: 'It's impossible! It's impossible!' He actually said it in French, but my Dad did a better imitation than I can do."

"My parents were divorced," said Dexter.

"Oh, I do remember you saying that previously."

"Heck," said Dexter, "my Dad was only interested in making money and making impressions. His second wife was your typical 'trophy wife,' as the expression goes. He talked about God about as much as he talked about my Mom, which was never."

"Sorry to hear that, Dexter."

"Yeah, well, you get over it—there're only about fifty million of us in this country."

Father Rankin shook his head back and forth and pursed his lips. "That's really sad. I never had to deal with divorce."

"What," said Dexter, "I suppose you came from 'Perfectville, USA,' right? Wise father, gracious mother, poster child siblings?"

"You might say that, I suppose. My Dad is a good man, religious, happy, congenial, but not too concerned about financial matters--from what you just said, it sounds like your Dad and mine are opposites. My Mom was also a good person, though she died a few years ago. I remember a priest down at Saint Pat's once said that she had very 'kind eyes.' She was very warm and cheerful--and not just a superficial 'womanly' kind of cheerfulness. It was a genuine joy she had all the time, and people knew it, too. During the last three years of her life, for various periods of time, she had to 'eat' through a tube in her stomach; she couldn't swallow food or liquid, lest she aspirate it. Yet she never complained, and I mean *never*."

"How 'bout your siblings?" asked Dexter. "I suppose you never said a cross word to each other?"

"Yeah, right," said Father Rankin. "My brother and I had World War III for about ten years, although it was all in good fun. We'd wrestle each other after school several days a week, but like I say, we liked to work out our frustrations through an innocent rumble now and then."

"Any sisters?"

"Two."

"Older or younger?"

Father Rankin couldn't help but smile. "Definitely younger. I am the oldest of four children: boy, girl, boy, girl. I got on pretty well with both of my sisters, although with Beth, the older one, there was the occasional verbal attack. She couldn't stand it when I'd call her 'screech pig,' anytime she shouted out about something. With Anastasia, the youngest, well, I really was too old to argue with her most of the time; I'm eight years older than she."

"Sounds like 'Perfectville' to me," said Dexter, nodding his head.

"Hey," said Father Rankin, "like my uncle likes to say, we tend to 'halo' the past. Sure I had a good upbringing, but we did weather some difficult times."

"Doesn't sound as bad as I had it."

"Was it really that bad?"

"Shoot, I lived with my Dad and his second wife most of the time. I had a step-sister, from the second wife's original marriage. We never lacked for material goods, but I always wanted a real brother and sister. The pain of separation from my real Mom always bothered me--it still does. Sure, I can see her now, but it's just not the same as having my true Mom and Dad together."

"Sounds like so many stories I hear around the parish," said Father Rankin, shaking his head back and forth. "I really should be more grateful for the upbringing I had."

"Yeah, well, maybe I'll get over it someday," said Dexter. "Anyway, you were saying something about how we have to accept the doctrine of Hell because it's in the Bible--or, right--because Christ said so--well, I was wondering about--"

"Excuse me," said Father Rankin, "if I could interrupt, I just wanted to add that if he wanted to, God could annihilate, but he chooses not to. When a soul is created, it lasts forever. And one more point about annihilation: it would mean all offenses would be equally punished. You see, the sinner longs for annihilation because he doesn't want to have to face God."

"But what about God's love and mercy?" asked Dexter. "Isn't it part of Catholic doctrine that God *is* love, that he is all-loving, all-merciful?"

"The short answer to that is that God's mercy is regulated by his wisdom. His wisdom forbids mercy to devils and devilish men. But even in Hell, God exercises his mercy, by not punishing the damned as much as they deserve."

"Hold on a second," said Dexter. "First of all, where do you get all this stuff? Can you point it out in the Bible?"

"Catholic doctrine is based on the Bible *and* Tradition. Tradition is—well…" Father Rankin scratched his chin. "Tradition is the revealed truths that were taught by Christ and His Apostles—those things that were handed down by word of mouth and not written down. Or rather, they *were* written down eventually, by the Fathers of the Church--by men such as Ignatius of Antioch and Polycarp. But what I was just saying…let me add something my Dad used to say--I think I told you this previously: on this side of death, we find God's mercy; on the other side of death, we find God's justice."

"See, that's the type of stuff I didn't have growing up. My Dad would have said something like: on this side of age sixty, you should be saving in precious metals; on the other side of sixty, you should be investing in stocks--or maybe the other way around."

"Did he ever go to Church?"

"Only when absolutely necessary."

"Hmm," said Father Rankin, "I begin to see your situation."

"Okay," said Dexter, "back to what you were saying--if God is so merciful, why don't the souls in Hell just call on God's mercy?"

"Because the condemned soul doesn't ask pardon or mercy, it always looks on itself as hopeless. Its hatred of God is complete. I remember reading a book by Saint Faustina on the subject of Divine Mercy. I believe I mentioned her in one of our earlier talks. Jesus told this woman once that basically the only souls that are damned are those who want to be damned."

"Well, son of a bitch!" said Dexter. "Good news for all of us!"

"Now don't go overboard, here," said Father Rankin. "Remember that Christ often talked about the fact that he will come like a thief in the night, when we are least expecting it. There are plenty of other stories from the lives of the saints that are pretty clear that the number of souls in Hell is not small."

"Shoot, back to square one," joked Dexter.

"Hold on, my friend. The one thing that Catholicism has going for it is balance. Virtue abhors the extreme. Most often Catholicism is not either/or, but both/and."

"Fine," said Dexter, looking at his watch.   "I don't have much time left and I only have about one or two more questions, for now." He read from his notebook: "Why does God allow suffering, since it is an evil--what I mean is how can he allow *eternal* suffering? I know that good can come from temporary suffering here on this earth, but *forever*?"

"Well," said Father Rankin, "you're right in pointing out that suffering can be medicinal, as a criminal may avoid crime after serving ten years in prison. But some punishment is meant to be purely punitive, as in lifelong imprisonment or the death penalty. Now, the death penalty *can* be medicinal in that it scares other people away from crime, and such is the case with Hell. I clearly remember Garrigou-Lagrange saying that the fear of Hell is the beginning of wisdom. Maybe you've heard that phrase stated as 'the fear of the Lord is the beginning of wisdom,' but I really think that the *beginning* of a conversion often starts with the simple fear of Hell. I'm inclined to say that the *perfection*, or the *final stage* of a conversion is the fear of the Lord."

"Isn't that pretty juvenile, though?" asked Dexter. "I mean when you're a kid, you don't play in the street because you're afraid your Dad will give you a spanking. Now you're trying to tell me I should be afraid of a 'spanking' from God? How can you expect a mature adult to think that way?"

"Ah, but Dexter, we are to be *children* of God, as Christ clearly says in the Gospels. But in a sense you're right, and that's the distinction I was trying to make just now. Often, the first step in getting to Heaven is realizing that you will do all in your power to avoid Hell. Then, after you've progressed in the spiritual life, you begin to fear offending God because you love him so much, sort of like going from negative to positive numbers, if that means anything to you."

"It's all fear, isn't it?" said Dexter with a perplexed look on his face.

"The technical terms are 'servile fear' and 'filial fear,' actually," said Father Rankin. "'Servile fear' refers to the fear a slave has for his master, while 'filial fear' refers to the aversion a son has for offending his father."

"It's still all fear!"

"Dexter, I repeat myself again…this stuff can't be swallowed in a few minutes, like a mechanics problem. I invite you to think it over awhile…it might take months before you really appreciate these things."

"Well, Father, if there's one thing you've said today that I would agree with, it's that the doctrine of eternal Hell is not logical--I can definitely agree to that."

"Now don't put words into Garrigou-Lagrange's mouth. He said that divine revelation alone can enlighten us about the logic of eternal Hell. There is some logic to saying that any offense against an infinite Being deserves an infinite punishment."

"So if I steal a lollipop that deserves Hell?"

"That leads us into mortal and venial sins, but that's another topic."

"Doesn't sound too complicated..."

"True," said Father Rankin. "A mortal sin is that which cuts us off completely from the grace of God, whereas a venial sin only lessens the grace of God in our soul."

"I don't know if I accept all that stuff," said Dexter. "What, you classify sins like a grocery store or something?"

"It's not something I can explain in a single sentence." Father Rankin glanced at his watch. "I really had better get going; I have to prepare a catechism class for tonight."

"You mean 'brainwashing session'?"

"Always the secular humanist, eh Dexter?" said Father Rankin, half-seriously.

"That's exactly what a friend of mine wrote on a postcard to congratulate me on being accepted to Stanford. He wrote just one line: 'Now you're a secular humanist!'"

"And you're darn proud of it, I suppose?"

"Hey, where would the world be without us?"

"Ha! There's a subject for a bestseller," said Father Rankin. He rose from his chair and patted Dexter on the shoulder. "Keep trying, my son. Someday you'll crawl out of the philosophical pit into higher realms."

"Pit!" said Dexter, standing up and walking to the door. "The only pit I know about is 'The Pit and the Pendulum,' from your Inquisition history."

"Ha again!" said Father Rankin. "What *did* they teach you at Stanford?"

"All I know is voltage equals resistance times current..."

Fr Rankin sighed. "Engineer, heal thyself."

"Sayonara, Father."

****

The next morning Dexter was in his office at Grobotics entering some data in a spreadsheet.

"Call for you on line three," Mrs. Downing said over Dexter's phone intercom. "It's from Herb Nalber--he says he sent you some info last week."

"Thanks, I'll take it right now." Dexter turned from the computer and snatched the phone with his right hand.

"Hello, this is Dexter Griffith."

"Dexter, this is Herb Nalber, I'm with Tevercon? I just wondered if you got that literature that I mailed you last week."

"Uh, Tevercon, Tevercon...refresh my memory, what's your product?"

"We're in the motor business. I sent you a brochure on our new stepper motor. Did you get a chance to look at it?"

"Oh, yeah, I do seem to recall something about that. What kind of amperage are we--" Dexter stopped abruptly when he heard a series of clicks on the line. "Excuse me?"

"Yes?" said the salesman. "You want to know about amperage?"

"I just heard some clicks on the line...did you hear that?"

"No, I didn't...what did you hear?"

"Hmmph, I don't know exactly--just some clicking noises. You didn't hear anything on your end?"

"No, just silence."

"Oh," said Dexter. "The same thing happened to me a week or two ago. I wonder if I'm being bugged or something."

"I've heard that the clicking sound is outdated. If someone wanted to bug you, you would never know it. Anyway, why would anyone want to bug you?"

"Maybe I'm just imagining things...and, yeah, someone told me the same thing a little while ago...anyway, where were we?--motors...yeah, uh, what kind of amperage are we talking about with these stepper motors?"

"The amperages range from three hundred milliamps to three amps. What kind of current are you looking at?"

"That's in the ballpark. We need somewhere around 500 milliamps, with spikes up to one-point-two amps."

"What kind of timeframe are we talking about?" asked Herb.

"I'll tell you what. Get back with me in about two weeks and I'll know more then."

"Great! In the meantime, if you have questions, you can read that brochure I gave you. It's pretty informative."

"Fine," said Dexter. "Talk to you later."

"Bye."

****

Thad had just dropped off a passenger at Doctor's West Hospital and was driving his taxi north on the Outerbelt to pick up a call at Tuttle Crossing Mall. He knew it was a bit of a stretch to drive this far, but he figured he would probably get a good tip from someone in a wealthier area such as Tuttle. He had just passed over Roberts Road when he saw lights flashing in his rearview mirror. *What? What did I do?* He thought it might not be he who was in trouble, but when Thad looked again, the police officer was motioning with his hand for him to pull over. *I was only doing seventy! Heck, there were other people passing me!* Resigned to his fate, though, Thad slowed and stopped alongside the highway. He watched as not one, but *two*, police officers walked up to his cab. It was only then that Thad saw that these were not your garden-variety native cops--they were *Chinese soldiers!*

"What you do?" shouted one, standing outside the driver's window. "You go very fast!"

Thad rolled down his window and looked up at the husky man. "I was only going with the flow of traffic, sir. I really don't think I was going that fast."

"We saw you!" said the second cop, who was standing by the other side of Thad's cab. "We have radar! We know you go fast!"

"Look, uh, I don't mean to cause any harm. If you want--"

"You get out car!" said the taller one, on the driver's side. "We talk to you!"

Thad turned to unbuckle his seatbelt when the shorter soldier pounded on the passenger door.

"Hey! Open! Open! Is lock!"

Thad hit the electric unlock button and the soldier opened the door. He slapped Thad's briefcase which was lying on the passenger seat. "Move! Move! I sit down!"

"Okay, okay," Thad said, pulling his briefcase toward him.

"Out! Out!" yelled the other soldier.

"You guys are *nuts*," Thad said under his breath. He waited for a break in the traffic, climbed out of his door, and walked around to the rear of the cab.

"What this?" said the shorter soldier, emerging from the passenger side of the car, holding up a Rosary.

"That's a prayer thing," said Thad, bringing his hands together. "You know--God, pray, Jesus?"

"We *know* that, Mister *Rankin!*" said the soldier at the rear of the car, giving Thad a shove.

"Hey, how do you guys know my name? What's going on here?"

"We know about your *praying* games, taxi-man," said the shorter soldier derisively. He walked around to join his colleague at the back of the car. "You stop pray, you understand?" He held up a Garabandal pamphlet in his other hand. "We not like this thing! You no give out." He lifted his boot and stomped it against the lights at the rear of the car, shattering the red plastic. "Now you drive without good light. We give you ticket!"

"Hey!" Thad screamed. "That's my cab! What are you guys doing!" He spun around to face the Chinaman but both soldiers pulled out their nightsticks and stood defiantly looking at Thad.

"You can't do this to me!" Thad sputtered.

"We do anything we want," said the taller soldier evenly. "You not like, that too bad."

"Uhhmf!" grunted Thad, throwing up his hands and pacing back and forth. "This is bullcrap! You guys are supposed to be the *police*?"

"You listen to us...you stop religion activities...NO MORE!" shouted the shorter Chinaman. "WE in control now! You not stop-- bad things happen to you!" He turned to his comrade and put away his nightstick. "C'mon Hu, let's go." The other soldier holstered his weapon and they walked back to their cruiser. "Remember what we say!" said the taller one just before he lowered himself into the car.

Thad watched as the police car merged into the traffic and sped away. *This can only get worse, I guess,* he thought to himself. *So much for "peace-keeping" troops...these Chinese mean business.*

Thad bent down to inspect his shattered tail light. *Well, it's going to take more than a little busted light to stop me practicing my religion.* He called the Orange Cab radio room, cancelled the fare that was still waiting, then drove the cab back to the company garage to get the light fixed.

****

Dexter's talks with Father Rankin had turned into a weekly habit now, and Thursday afternoon found Dexter once again in the priest's office.

"What's the deal with the Chinese?" asked Dexter, shaking his head. "You think they're going to turn the thumbscrews one of these days?"

"It's definitely strange, I'll give you that," replied Father Rankin. "I keep thinking one of these days a tank will come crashing through the church walls when I'm saying Mass. So far, they seem content to 'live and let live.' Although I've heard some dark rumors floating around."

"Such as?"

"Such as there are unconfirmed reports of some people disappearing."

"Who?" asked Dexter.

"No one that I know first-hand--just vague assertions right now."

"It sure does seem an odd way to take over a country."

"Well, we can't let it stop our little discussions," said Father Rankin. "What might you have on your mind today?"

"Thad keeps telling me to 'offer it up,' when I complain about something," said Dexter. "What is he talking about?"

Father Rankin took a few puffs on his pipe before replying. "You into baseball?"

"Well, yeah, the World Series, I guess. I don't watch much during the season."

"So you've heard the term 'sacrifice fly'?"

"Right--say a runner's on third, so the batter pops up to right field so the guy on third can score a run."

"Well, there you have it," said Father Rankin, smiling.

"All right, no more of the 'Dr Enigmatic' stuff. Let's have the explanation."

"Why don't you explain what happens in the 'sacrifice fly'."

"I just did."

"I mean philosophically."

"Father Rankin, you're the one with the degree in philosophy."

"Give it a try."

"Well, the batter realizes it's going to be an automatic out, but he hit's the pop fly anyway because..."

"Yeessss?" interjected Father Rankin.

"Because he realizes some good will come from it--he realizes his team will score a home run."

"So what does he do with the automatic out?" Father Rankin put the pipe back in his mouth and stared at Dexter.

"He *sacrifices* it...Oh, I see what you're trying to get me to say...he *offers it up*."

"Once again, there you have it."

"But that's baseball, what about real life? Thad told me I should offer up traffic jams. I mean huhh?"

"Sacrifice," said Father Rankin, "is as old as man. It goes way back into the Old Testament. Abraham once offered his son Isaac up when God asked him to do so. He was on the verge of killing his only son, when an angel stayed his hand and told him God said he didn't have to sacrifice Isaac."

"Hey, first we talk baseball and now we talk about ancient Mesopotamia or whatever. Could you bring this down to traffic jams on the freeway?"

"What Thad meant by that is that you should essentially talk to God thusly: 'Dear God, I really hate this traffic jam. I'm late for my next appointment and I didn't get much sleep last night. But I present all this pain to you so that you will do some good for a friend of mine who needs a lot of grace to straighten his life out.' God accepts your sacrifice, he is pleased, and therefore gives some graces to your friend."

"I thought that was called 'bribing.'"

"Hmmm," said Father Rankin, looking at his bookshelf, "where's my dictionary? Ah, yes, here it is." He rose from his chair, grabbed the book and sat down again. "Let me read to you the definition of 'bribing.'" He thumbed through the pages, then said: "'Bribing:

anything promised or given as illicit payment.' Ah, here's where I suppose we run into trouble. Let me read the second definition: 'anything given or serving to persuade or induce.'"

"Certainly sounds like 'offering it up' fits definition number two," said Dexter.

"That's true, but I think most people think of bribing in a negative way, like in the first definition."

"Well, it's right there in the dictionary--'persuade or induce.'"

"A better term might be 'a negotiation with God,'" said Father Rankin, as he pounded the ashtray to knock the ashes out of his pipe. "Besides, what's wrong with making a deal with God? We promise things to our family and friends and business associates all the time. We see no harm in that; why should a 'deal' with God be any different? By offering things up, any evil thing can be turned to something good. It's a win-win situation. Evil can be turned into good by 'offering it up.'"

"I don't know," replied Dexter. "Sometimes I like to just cuss when I'm mad. A good string of profanity sometimes really lowers my blood pressure, especially when I'm cut off in traffic or something."

"Ah, yes, the 'natural man,'" said Father Rankin.

"What, I'm not allowed to cuss?"

"The 'natural man' is just a term an old friend of mine and I used to use. Before I became a seminarian, I suppose you could say I was a 'natural man.' 'Natural man' as opposed to 'supernatural man': man before he turns his life to God and man after he turns his life to God."

"Count me in!" said Dexter, raising his hand. "I'm a 'natural man' from the get-go."

"Like you said a little while ago...'Oh Lord, give me purity, but not yet,'" said Father Rankin.

"Saint Augustine's my man, Padre."

"I'm glad you see the benefits of the saintly life, Dexter!"

"Saintly life! Spare me! How the hell am I supposed to have any fun? According to you, I can't drink, can't have sex, can't cuss..."

"You can do all that, at the proper time. You can drink in moderation, have sex with your wife, should you get married. You can even cuss from time to time."

"Huuhhh?"

"The only thing you can't do is use the name of God in vain. Other than that cuss all you want, it's not a sin."

"I thought religion was supposed to be dull and boring."

"Perish the thought," said Father Rankin. I think it was Hilaire Belloc who once said something like: 'Wherever the Catholic sun doth shine, there's music and laughter and good red wine.' Or maybe you need to read a little Chesterton--I know, I know," said Father Rankin, raising his hand before Dexter could speak. "You have no idea who Chesterton was. G.K. Chesterton was a Catholic writer who lived in the first part of the 20th Century. He was a convert from Anglicanism. He had many classic quotes attributed to him, but the one I thought I'd tell you is this. He said it before his conversion, when he was about thirty years old: 'I have run the whole gamut of pleasure and I am thoroughly disgusted.'"

"Golly gee," said Dexter, "I've experienced a lot of the pleasures of life, and I'm thoroughly satisfied!"

"Then why are you here talking to me?"

"Because of my near-death experiences--whatever you want to call it. My conscience won't leave me alone. Weren't you ever affected by something like that sometime in your life?"

"Definitely," said Father Rankin. "I've had some things to atone for in my life."

"But you're a priest! What could you possibly have to be guilty about?"

"We all have room for improvement, my friend. I've stepped up some of the penances I used to do. Or, rather, I recommended some of the penances that I had stopped doing."

"'Penances'?" asked Dexter. "What, you flog yourself hourly to appease the gods?"

"Some small things, some bigger things. Sometimes just delaying a drink of water."

"You get all worried about drinking too much *water*!? C'mon, Father! Look, what is all this about? How do we know all this B.S. is true? Maybe all your religion is just so you don't have to face the real world like the rest of us! You've got your nice little office here, your nice little church...maybe it's all just a chimera."

"Big Stanford word," said Father Rankin. "What exactly does it mean?"

"Chimera--you know--daydream, non-reality."

"To begin with, your question is four thousand years old. Long ago, the prophet Elijah was asked the same thing by some people who worshipped the god Baal. They declared that Baal was the real god and that Elijah's God was fake. Elijah called their bluff and set up a test. Each camp would erect an altar of wood on which they placed a sacrifice. Each party would then call on their god to send down fire and consume the sacrifice. Everything was set up and the Baal-ians went first. They danced and prayed and danced some more, but nothing happened. Elijah laughed at them and told them they needed to pray harder. Nothing worked for them. When it was Elijah's turn, he soaked the wood of the altar in water and prayed to God to send down fire to consume the sacrifice. Bingo! Fire fell from heaven and up went the sacrifice in flames. Case closed."

"Mythological mumbo-jumbo from some dusty archives," said Dexter with a dismissive wave of his hand. "Probably thought up by some monk during the dark ages."

"All right, try this on for size, my skeptical Skinner..."

"Skinner?"

"Contemporary of Freud. Anyway, back in the Middle Ages--I think it was the twelfth Century, there was a king in Europe who--"

"Error mode one--*twelfth* Century?" asked Dexter. "Could we at least move into the *Twentieth* Century?"

"Hold on, it gets better," said Father Rankin. "So---this king is a bit of a mischievous type and he decides one day that he would like to find out to what his wife, the queen, has been up."

"'Been up'?"

"Inside joke. Winston Churchill liked to use that phraseology. You're not supposed to end your sentences with a preposition. So, anyway, this king tells the queen's confessor, i.e., the priest to whom the queen goes to Confession, that he must divulge everything the queen confesses. Now, the priest, being a priest, tells the king that he cannot do that because it would break the seal of Confession. The king, by way of reply says that if the priest doesn't tell him the queen's sins, he will kill him. The priest says, 'Fine.' The king orders the priest to be tied up and thrown into the river. Such is done and the priest dies and he's buried in the ground. The interesting part is that a century later some people dig up the priest's coffin and they find that, although the body of the priest has indeed decayed, his tongue is still perfected preserved, looking like the day he died. Now , the *really* intriguing thing I want you to know, is that you can go this very day over to that country and see the tongue perfectly preserved...put *that* into your hard drive and boot it."

"It's still there, huh? Still pink and taste buds and all?" asked Dexter.

"You got it, my gracious atheist. Why don't you log onto Priceline and get some plane tickets over there right now?"

"Maybe I'll take your word for it."

"There's also the flesh and blood at Lanciano," said Father Rankin enthusiastically.

"Italy? Wasn't there some battle there in World War II?"

"Might have been, but there in Lanciano is a tabernacle containing a Communion Host which turned into visible flesh 1300 years ago--as well as a chalice containing five coagulated globules of blood."

"What's so great about that?"

"Around the year 700 in Lanciano, Italy, there was a monk who was having doubts about the Real Presence of Christ in the Eucharist. One day at Mass the Host turned into visible Flesh and the contents of the chalice into visible Blood. The Flesh and Blood are still there today, visible to anyone who visits there."

"So they preserved it with chemicals, big whoop!" said Dexter.

"Ah, but no," replied Father Rankin. "They performed an intense scientific study in 1970 and 1971 and they found that there was no trace at all of any material or agents used for preservation of flesh or blood. That's another miracle that you can see with your own eyes."

Dexter seemed a little subdued and sat on the couch silent.

"Oh, I forgot to mention Guadalupe," said Father Rankin. "Down in Mexico City there is an image of the Blessed Mother that has been around for over four hundred years. There's a whole story to how it was miraculously made, but the part I think you'd be interested in is that scientists can't explain how the image has stood up all these years. It's made on a material called ayate yet it has held up for centuries, since 1531, to be exact. Aaannnd, scientists can't figure out where the pigment that colors the image comes from."

"Wait a minute," said Dexter. "Is that the picture I see on some Mexicans' cars and trucks and stuff? Lady with a blue cloak on a bronze background?"

"That's the one, right! Mexicans are mighty proud of it, and rightly so."

Dexter sat still a few moments and then replied. "Would that be on the Internet? I just might look that up."

"Actually, I never have checked, but I'm sure it must be," said Father Rankin.

Dexter continued to sit still, turning these recent facts over in his mind. Finally, he tilted his head back and asked: "So where does that leave us?"

"Well, you came in today asking about 'offering it up.' Do you understand now?"

"I suppose there are different levels of understanding," said Dexter. "But, yeah, you've given me a little to think about."

"Great, what should be our topic for next week?"

"I'm not sure, but I am sure that something will come up by then."

"All right, same time next week--oh, wait a minute," said Father Rankin, remembering something. "We better make it two weeks from now--next week I've got a vicariate meeting to go to."

"Whatever that is," replied Dexter, a bit flippantly.

"It's basically a battle of the paper clips, as they say."

"Well, catch you on the flip-flop, then."

"Huhh?" asked Father Rankin.

"Old trucking term. See ya later."

"Bye."

As he was driving down High Street, Dexter called into Mrs. Downing and told her he would skip returning to the office, opting instead to go directly home. He turned off of Ashland Avenue onto Urlin to find a moving truck in his driveway. *Am I moving out of my house*? he wondered. He parked his car on the street and strode over the lawn. Daphne came walking out of the front door, carrying a lamp.

"You having a garage sale, Daphne?" he asked.

"Take the hint, Dexter--I'm officially out of here!"

"You're moving out?!! What's wrong?"

"I wouldn't want to upset your precious little conscience by living with you any longer, Mr. Holy Roller."

"Wait! Daphne, we need to talk, babe! You don't need to move out. Let's talk!"

Daphne put the lamp in the truck and walked back toward the front door. "That's all we *have* been doing since you started talking to your priest friend--and your cab driver friend. Apparently, I'm not good enough for you anymore, I guess!"

"Hey, honey, look…" Dexter put his hand on her shoulder.

"Keep your holier-than-thou hands off me!" said Daphne loudly.

"Something wrong, Daph?" asked a woman who appeared at the front door.

"Oh, just Mr. Perfect here thinks he can smooth everything over now," said Daphne, gesturing toward Dexter.

"Take a hint, guy," said the woman. "Doesn't that look like a moving truck to you?"

"Who are you?" asked Dexter.

"Just someone who has a little more interest in Daphne than you apparently do."

The two women went back in the house and emerged a minute later carrying a coffee table.

"That's *my* coffee table," said Dexter.

"If you'll remember, you bought it using *my* credit card and you never reimbursed me," said Daphne.

Dexter just stood there, perplexed. He watched while more items were placed in the truck. Eventually he wandered back to his car and drove to the Caribou Coffee on Grandview Avenue. He absentmindedly ordered an espresso and sat down by the side window, deep in thought. *It's over,* he tried to convince himself. *I've been with Daphne for three years, and now it's kaput. Darn! This religion bullcrap is getting out of control! I'm losing my woman over it!*

"And your coffee table," whispered Albert.

"It's all your fault, Albert!" he replied.

"You're the one who kept going to the priest," said Albert.

"You didn't stop me!" Dexter responded.

"She wasn't worth it."

"The heck she wasn't!"

"Beautiful on the outside, but not inside," said Albert.

"How do you know?"

"Angels have a way of knowing such things, Dexter," whispered Albert in the recesses of Dexter's mind.

Dexter didn't know what to do now. *Should I go try to stop her?* he asked himself. *Isn't that what they did in the movies?* Someone was supposed to walk up to him and say, "What are you doing, fool?! Go chase her!" Dexter sheepishly looked around the coffee shop to see if any such visitor was forthcoming. But then he asked himself: *I really don't want to go after her, do I? What was that old saying? "The attraction was purely physical." Yeah, I guess that just about sums it up*, he thought. *Daphne never cared about religion or philosophy, did she? We both liked the same type of music, but what else did we have in common?*

Dexter surveyed the female patrons who were sitting in the java house. *There's still plenty of fish in the sea, right?* He duly noted a couple of hot prospects up by the front window. They were both laughing over some joke one of them just told. *So what if Daphne is moving out? I can have any chick I want!* He briefly thought about approaching the two girls up by the window, but decided against it. *What was that old expression?* He wondered. *"On the rebound?"* He seemed to remember it from some black and white movies made in the 40s. *That's me, all right,* he agreed. *On the rebound--from Daphne. I wonder how many bounces I'll have before I find someone else,* he mused.

"Who says you're going to find someone else?" asked Albert.

"I could get someone else inside of an hour," rejoined Dexter to his "little buddy."

"You like your freedom too much, don't you? You've talked too much to Father Rankin, haven't you?"

"This has nothing to do with him!" Dexter said emphatically to the small voice.

"Dexter is a Catholic, Dexter is a Catholic!" sang Albert playfully.

"Shut the heck up, a-hole!"

"DA-da-da-DA-da!" continued Albert.

"All right, meathead," Dexter silently said to Albert, *"Watch this!"* Dexter walked over to the table where the girls sat. "Hey, ladies! What's happenin'?"

"Not much," replied the redheaded one on Dexter's left. She brought her hand up to her mouth, trying to squelch a snicker.

"How are you?" asked the brunette, herself trying not to laugh.

"I'm doin' great...!" Dexter said, with a bit of hesitation, a questioning look in his eyes.

The brunette's gaze met her friend's eyes and they both burst out laughing.

"What's so funny?" asked Dexter, looking from one girl to another, wondering what he missed.

"Oh, nothing, we just, uh..." the two girls twittered again, unable to contain whatever humor they shared.

"See ya later," said Dexter disgustedly and walked back to his table.

"What was it you wanted me to watch?" asked Albert mockingly.

"*Get lost, jerk!*" Dexter said to his conscience. He grabbed a newspaper from a nearby table and sat down to read. From time to time he sipped his espresso and checked his watch. *I'll give them another hour to finish moving out before I head home, he told himself.*

He ended up killing time in the coffee shop for almost two hours before he meandered back home. Only with a large dose of self-control was he able to contain his anger as he walked through his house and noted all the furniture Daphne had "liberated."

****

Kevin was in his apartment finishing up a quick dinner of pizza and Coke, which he ate while surfing the web for the latest on the upcoming NFL combine. By midnight, though, he decided he had best start researching the paper he needed to write. The professor had given only rough outlines for this assignment, merely telling his students that they should cover something about Europe around the time of the Renaissance. Kevin clicked on an article about southern Europe during the Sixteenth Century and sat up in his chair when he saw the headline of one of the sections: "Rosary Stops the Moslems." *Whaaat? Who put this out?* He scrolled down the page and saw that it was written by "Our Lady of Victory Parish." He moved back to the beginning of the article and started reading:

The title of Our Lady of Victories dates back to an historic battle between Christian and Moslem forces at Lepanto in 1571.

The Moslems had invaded much of Spain and were threatening to overrun most of Europe and de-Christianize Europe. The threat was real and it all came together at a sea battle at Lepanto. Realizing the importance of this moment the Pope, Pius V, called upon all Christians to pray the Rosary for the success of this battle. The Christian sailors prayed the Rosary together before the battle as well. The Christian forces prevailed, Europe was saved for the Christian Faith and the Moslems were pushed back to Africa. In honor of this victory, the Pope declared Mary the Lady of Victory and declared her feast day to be held on October 7 the Feast of the Holy Rosary.

Our Lady's powerful intercession has always been a belief of the Catholic Church. Next to Christ her Son, she pleads our cause with a mother's heart and concern with whatever we bring her. Confident that Our Lady's prayers are always heard we pray:

O Victorious Lady, Thou who has ever such powerful influence with Thy Divine Son, in conquering the hardest of hearts, intercede for those for whom we pray, that their hearts being softened by the rays of Divine Grace, they may return to the unity of the true Faith, through Christ our Lord.

Amen.

Kevin clenched his teeth, ran his hand over his five-o-clock shadow, and sat back in the chair. *This is just like a story I read last fall--about the Austrians praying the Rosary and the Communists leaving their country.* He joined his hands and put them behind his neck. *Why haven't I ever heard of this stuff? The one about Austria is a little "iffy"--I mean, who can say for sure what really drove the Russians from Austria? But this thing in the 1500s, with the Muslims and the Pope...hmmm...who's to say that the Christian forces wouldn't have won even if no one had said the Rosary...? Does God really intervene in human affairs like this? Was this a miracle? The people back then sure had faith, I guess...I wonder what these "sailors" were like. Goody two shoes? Or real men? I don't know, though...I've never heard even a whisper of this from my standard history textbooks...wouldn't it at least have made some sidebar about "Radical Conspiracy Theories?" After all, some credence was given to alternate theories about the JFK assassination and the supposed "surprise" attack on Pearl Harbor.   Should I write about this for my paper?* Kevin paused for a minute and looked around his apartment. *Naaa! The professor would chew this up and spit it out in a second. Best to stick to conventional material.* He searched for another ten minutes before finally settling on writing a paper about advances in printing press technology in England in the Fifteenth Century.

Chapter 9

It was one of those gray February Midwestern days that made one wonder if the sun would ever shine again before the next Ice Age. It had been over a week since he finished his paper on printing press technology and since it was a Saturday, Kevin spent the day doing errands and reading a book on the Crimean War. Just before seven o'clock, he drove his car to Anne's sorority, stopped out front, and honked the horn, hoping no car would need to get through on the perpetually crowded Fifteenth Avenue. Ten minutes later he was still waiting and a car did come down the street, forcing him to circle the block. When he stopped again out in front of Anne's house, she was waiting by the curb.

"Where did you go?" asked Anne after she closed the car door. "I heard you honk and when I came out there was nothing out here."

"I waited for ten minutes and had to circle the block because a car came up behind me. You know, I did say *seven* o'clock--it's now seven-*fifteen*."

"I was running a little behind," said Anne.

"Well, I think you shou--arvy--lam," muttered Kevin.

"*Excuse* me?" asked Anne. "What was that?"

"Oh, nothing."

They drove in silence till they got to Hyde Park, a landmark steak restaurant on Frantz Road in the suburb of Dublin.

"Who said we're going to *this* place?" asked Anne.

"I thought it would be a good place for steak."

"You could have asked, you know."

"That I could have."

When they walked in the front door, two Chinese guards stood in their way. "Driver card," one of them said.

"What?" asked Kevin.

"He wants your driver's license," whispered Anne.

"Yes," said the guard on the left. "Driver license."

Kevin pulled out his wallet and handed his license to the guard.

"Wait here," said the shorter guard. He walked over to a computer terminal on a table and scanned Kevin's license. Satisfied everything was approved he walked back to Kevin and returned his license to him. "You go eat--everthing good."

After a short wait, they were seated in a booth and ordered from the menu.

"Do you think it's going to get worse?" asked Anne.

"What? The food?" asked Kevin.

"No! I mean the Chinese thing. So far it hasn't been too bad, but that's the first time I've been stopped at a *restaurant*, for crying out loud!"

"I really don't know what to think. It's all so crazy. We've been taken over by the Chinese and here we are eating steak at a cozy restaurant--some hardship this is!"

"I've heard some crazy stuff, though, from some of my friends. Everything appears normal, but I've heard that a few people have turned up missing."

"They probably just fled to Canada," suggested Kevin.

"I don't think so, Kevin. That's where these Chinese came from. My Dad said they were up there for the last two years, getting ready to invade."

"As long as I get to keep on eating and living a normal life, they can do all they want."

"It can't go on like this, Kevin. Sooner or later, they're going to put us all into prison or something."

"Get real, Anne! There are three hundred million of us and less than a million occupation troops. They're just 'peacekeeping forces.'"

A half hour later, the server cleared away their dishes and the two were left sipping coffee.

"You realize it's been exactly one month since the Fiesta Bowl?" asked Anne.

"Hmm," said Kevin, "yeah, January 3rd to February 3rd. You're right."

"Seems like yesterday, huh?"

"You can say that twice, or three times."

"So, yeah," said Anne, looking into Kevin's eyes.

Kevin looked off to the side, admiring the painting on the back wall of the restaurant.

"Have you done any more thinking about your future?" asked Anne with a hopeful smile.

"I really don't know if the Chinese are that wild about NFL football, Anne. What kind of a future is there for a quarterback if there aren't going to be any games anymore?"

"Who says they're going to cancel the games?"

"Anne," said Kevin emphatically, "you just said yourself that you've heard of people disappearing. You think these Chinese are just here for fun? They couldn't care less about football. I heard they're making the fairgrounds into a concentration camp."

"I don't know," said Anne softly, folding up her napkin. "As long as we don't make any trouble, maybe life might go on as usual."

"Usual," said Kevin sarcastically. "What's usual anymore? You can't even get gas anymore without some Chinese pipsqueak grunt approving it."

"At least we have each other," said Anne, reaching over to hold Kevin's hand.

"Ummph," said Kevin, leaving his hand where it was, but making no effort to grip hers.

"So you've done it, Mr. QB…you've won the national championship…now you can get on with your life…with the *important* things in life." She gave Kevin a knowing look while continuing to cradle his hand.

"Yeah, like finding a job. What am I going to do with a History degree?"

"You promised," said Anne, drawing her hand away from Kevin's."

"I suppose I could get into sales or something," continued Kevin. "If I learned Chinese, maybe they'd let me sell their stuff…they sure do manufacture a lot of stuff."

"Kevvviin," said Anne slowly, "remember when we talked after that party a few weeks ago?"

Kevin glanced nervously at his girlfriend, then looked again at the painting hanging on the wall. "I need a little time, Anne," he said, without meeting her eyes. "I just think things are a little too uncertain right now."

"Kevin, we've been dating for two and a half *years*. I think that's long enough!"

Kevin had no reply. He just took another drink of coffee and adjusted the watch on his wrist.

Just then a middle-aged man stopped by their table. "Kevin! That was a great game you played! I just want to let you know I hope all the best for you."

"Thanks," said Kevin, somewhat morosely. It wasn't the first time he had been accosted in public by a rabid Buckeye fan.

"Hey," the man said, holding out a pen and paper. "Would you?"

"Sure." Kevin signed his name and handed the pen back to the man. "Thanks for your support." The man trudged off to show his prize to his friends at a table in the corner.

"Kevin," began Anne, leaning toward him, "you said--you *promised*--that if you won the national championship, you would ask me to marry you."

Kevin let out a long sigh, put his hands on the edge of the table and leaned back. "Anne, I just can't decide right now. I made that promise before all this Chinese stuff started happening. Maybe I shouldn't have made that promise."

"What's that supposed to mean?!" Anne said in a raised voice, causing the patrons at the table across the aisle to look in their direction.

"That's not what I meant," said Kevin, half-whispering, holding his hands up and shaking his head. "Let me explain."

"I'm waiting," Anne said impatiently.

"Look, when I made that promise, it was October...the sky was blue, the sun was out, the trees were changing color..."

"Kevin, do I look like a *fool*? What in the *hell* are you trying to tell me? I suppose you really didn't think you were going to win the championship, is that it? Or were you thinking that you would just sweet talk me to get me to shut up?"

"Anne, what I was trying--"

"--I think it's really pretty simple," interrupted Anne. "You were either a loser or a liar!"

"Hey, now come on, babe. There's no need to get upset. Why don't we go to Graeter's for some of that ice cream you like and we can work this out?"

"CAPITAL 'N', CAPITAL 'O'!" Anne said loudly. Then, lowering her voice, she said, "Kevin, you call me when you're ready to stop playing games. A promise is a promise. We've been together too long to keep postponing this." She stood up and put on her coat. "Goodbye!" She grabbed her purse off the seat.

"Let me at least give you a ride home," said Kevin.

"No, thank you!" She walked out and caught a cab, which happened to be waiting by the entrance.

Kevin calmly finished off his ice water, trying not to notice the stares of the other patrons. He paid the bill, drove back to campus, and decided to call it a night. Early the following morning, unable to sleep in, he phoned the one friend he knew could help him sort things out.

"Chad!" said Kevin enthusiastically when his friend answered the phone. "What up, dude?"

"Uhhn, what time is it?" Chad said groggily.

"Who knows? It's morning and that means it's time to wake up, pal."

"It's *Sunday* morning and that means it's time to *sleep*."

"Not after what happened last night," Kevin said somewhat dejectedly.

"All right," sighed Chad. "Let's have it...I figure there was a reason you called this early."

"Woman problems."

"Uh-huh."

"We were at Hyde Park last night and she walked out."

"Let me take a wild guess why she would do something like that."

"I know: same old story," said Kevin. "Things sort of came to a head."

"She brought up your promise, right? And you hedged your bets, right?"

"Right."

"You said you were uncertain about the future and she said you've been dating for three years and it was about time you got married."

"Right--two and a half years. You bugged our table or what?" asked Kevin.

"Dude, we had this same conversation back in the fall, remember? You were worried if we won the national championship you'd have to marry her--remember?"

"Yeah," said Kevin quietly.

"So what are you going to do now?"

"I don't know, should I call her? No, I don't want to call her...the ball's definitely in my court...any suggestions?"

"Why don't you decide if you're going to marry her and then act accordingly," said Chad.

"I just want a little more time, Chad. I don't feel ready to make that kind of decision."

"She's got a point, Kevin. You've been dating a while and women don't like it when men break their promises."

"I never should have made that promise."

"Yeah, and the Chinese never should have shot that football like they did at the Fiesta Bowl. Like a friend of mine likes to say: 'Life is messy; deal with it.'"

"Well, that's the thing, Chad. What's going to happen with this Chinese thing? Are we all going to be arrested and sent to a concentration camp or something? This is weird! The Chinese have invaded and not much has changed."

"The media isn't telling us everything, but I think some people are starting to disappear--and I'd be careful what you say over the phone. I hear they're starting to listen in to random calls."

"Really?"

"Really. Sometimes you'll hear a click after you start talking--that's what that 'click' is."

"Hmmph," said Kevin. "I'll have to remember that. So as far as Anne goes, I guess I'll, uhh, call her, and, well, I guess I should, uhh..."

"Kevin, it's simple--do you want to marry her or not?"

"Not now--definitely not now. I just don't know if she's my dream girl."

"All right, it's even simpler yet. The next time she asks you that, you're gonna have to tell her how you feel about it."

"Tell her she's not my *dream girl*?"

"Not *that*. Just tell her you need some more time."

"What if she doesn't ask?"

"Not to worry, big guy, she will."

"Ohh-kay," said Kevin. "I appreciate the advice--hey, you heard anything from your agent or anything--you know--about the combine in March?"

"I don't think the Chinese are going to let us have a football season next fall. No, I haven't heard anything, and I wouldn't hold your breath either."

"I got it. Thanks, Chad--see ya later."

"Ciao."

                    ****

Wednesday was grocery day for Thad. He had never really figured out why it had to be Wednesday, but somehow it had become part of his routine. His older sister occasionally kidded him about his militaristic schedule, but Thad couldn't be deterred. "Without a schedule, life is a living hell," as Pete Beck, one of his favorite authors, had written. He walked into the lobby of the Whipple grocery at Fifth and Grandview and pulled out a shopping cart, pleased to see that Whipple had bought brand new carts for the store when they had taken it over a few years ago from the now defunct Big Bear grocery chain. It was sad to see the Big Bear grocery stores succumb to the economic forces of the current decade. Big Bear had served Central Ohio for the better part of five decades, but had been forced out of business by bad management, among other rumored reasons. Thad headed first for the produce department, where he tore off a plastic bag and looked down at the selection of lettuce. *Huh? Am I that early?* Usually there were scores of heads of lettuce by this time of the morning. Now there were only three wilted heads of Romaine sitting there. *Maybe the stock clerk is running behind...I'll come back after I've done the rest of my shopping.* Thad picked up a pumpkin pie, but noticed that the shelves of the bakery department were also under-stocked. *Am I missing something here?* He had no problem finding grape juice, canned soup, and a bag or two of candy, but when he came to the bread aisle, he was again confronted with shelves less than half-full, and totally devoid of Catherine Clark, his favorite brand. *What is going on here? That settles it, I'm asking the manager.* Thad strode up to the Customer Service desk.

"Excuse me," he said to the young woman who was busy counting some bills.

"May I help you?"

"Yeah, uh, I don't know if I'm a little early or something, but I couldn't find several of the types of food I'm accustomed to getting here. Are you short of help or something?"

"We apologize, sir," said the woman, "but we're experiencing some delivery problems. You might try back later."

"*Delivery problems?*" asked Thad with a questioning look. "I've never heard of that happening."

"You could speak with the manager if you like."

"No, that won't be necessary…thanks." Thad walked away, scratching his head. *That sounds odd…'delivery problems'…*   He brought his selections to the cashier and checked out. When he got home he put all the groceries away and decided to check his e-mail. He saw one from a fellow cab driver titled "food." *This sounds interesting.* He double-clicked on the message and quickly read it:

> Thad,
>   Just thought you might be interested in a news article I came across from "TheWorldRightNow.com." It deals with the food supply. Go to their website and click on "Food Alert."
>   You driving tomorrow? See ya around!
>   Later,
>   Ahmed

Thad brought up the website and clicked on "Food Alert." The computer hesitated a few seconds, then displayed a paragraph from AP:

Chinese Adjust Food Production Schedules

By Leo Castashi
ASSOCIATED PRESS

A spokesman for the newly created American

Socialist Administration announced today that selected food processing plants around the country have been temporarily closed to facilitate "a spirit of co-operation with the current political climate." When asked how long these closures are expected to last, he replied that "the ruling politburo will decide that question after judging the people's reaction to government initiatives."

What does that mean? wondered Thad. He read it again: *"...to facilitate a spirit of co-operation..." Huh? I know what that means: they're going to periodically starve us till we fall in line!* He patted his slightly enlarged potbelly. *Well, about time I worked on getting rid of this 'spare tire,' as the expression goes.*

****

Kevin was sitting on the couch in his apartment, bending a paperclip out of shape. One part of him was telling him to drop Anne altogether; the other part was urging him to follow Chad's advice and tell Anne he just needed a little more time. After five more minutes of deliberation, he picked up the phone from its cradle and punched in Anne's number.

"Hello," said Anne as she picked up the phone, using a dish towel to keep the handset dry.

"Hey, Anne, this is Kevin. How are you?"

Anne waiting a few seconds before replying. "Fine," she said abruptly.

Kevin paused a moment, then asked, "Is this a bad time? I could call later? Are you busy?"

"I was just doing the dishes."

"Oh, sorry about that. I just wanted to apologize about Saturday night."

"You want to apologize," said Anne matter-of-factly.

"That's right, maybe I was a little cold-shouldered about all that."

"'Maybe'?"

"Well, yeah, you know, I didn't want to see you storm out of the restaurant like that."

"Then why did you say what you said?"

"Oh, I just, uhh...I just thought maybe we could discuss that."

"What's there to discuss?" Anne said impatiently.

"I just wanted to explain myself a little more clearly--look, what do you say we go out this Saturday--or tomorrow, whenever you're free."

"I think you can 'explain yourself' right now on the phone."

"True, true," Kevin said agreeably.

"I'm waiting."

"Okay, well, you wanted to know about that promise I made to you about marrying you if we won the national championship. I just wanted to ask if, uh, say, maybe you could give me a little time to think about it."

Anne pulled out a chair in her kitchen and sat down. "Kevin, this is very simple. Do you want to go out to dinner Saturday night?"

"Well, yeah, babe! Yeah, that would be great!"

"Good," said Anne. "Next question: will you be bringing an engagement ring with you?"

Kevin let out an audible gasp and leaned back in the chair in which he was seated. "Pardon me?"

"Simple question, Kevin: yes or no?"

"Uh, I-I-I...*Anne!* I've gotta think about that!"

"When you make up your mind, you can call me. Until then, good-bye!" She slammed the phone down and threw the dish towel into the sink.

Kevin was still holding the handset to his head a minute later. *What have I done? Am I a total idiot?* He put the phone back on the hook, walked out to the kitchen and took a beer out of the refrigerator. After taking a long drink, he sat down on one of the kitchen chairs. *It's like that phrase Chad always repeats: food is the only true love in life.*

****

It had been two weeks since Daphne had moved out, and Dexter had almost put his life back in order. Other than the fact that it was the first week of February--"The Month of Morosity," as his high school English teacher had called it, things were settling into a routine for the young engineer. As he sat in his office at Grobotics, Dexter still couldn't remember Thad's cell phone number and had to check his appointment book to look it up. He pressed the seven numbers and stared out the window while the phone rang.

"Columbus Custom Cab! This is Thad!"

"Thad, Dexter. What's up in Gahanna?"

"I'm not in Gahanna; I'm in Dublin."

"Just thought I'd take a wild guess--you cabbies sure must know the city."

"Indeed we do."

"So, look, Thad, I want to give you a book."

"What brought this sudden philanthropic spirit on?"

"I just thought I would do my part to spread the works of a truly accomplished writer. You ever heard of Paul Garuth?"

"Not off the top of my head, no," said Thad. "Is he still alive?"

"No, he died the end of last century. He was a somewhat popular novelist in the 60s and 70s."

"What's the title of the novel?"

"Birds of Autumn," said Dexter.

"Never heard of it."

"I think you'll like it."

"Well, I'll tell you what: I can stop by after my next fare. I'm going to be dropping someone off in Arlington."

"Good deal, I'll be here. I'll see you then."

Forty minutes later, Thad walked into Dexter's well-appointed office. "Nice crib, Mr. President," said Thad as he walked over to a cigar store Indian in the corner. "You know how to take care of yourself."

"Hey," said Dexter. He rose from his chair and walked to his office door and closed it. "It's like I read in a book of quotable quotes once: 'If you look good and dress well, you don't need a purpose in life.'"

"Ha!" laughed Thad. "Isn't that the Narcissist's Creed."

"I take my philosophy where I can get it, bro. Here you are," said Dexter, handing a book to Thad. "It's all yours."

Thad took the book from Dexter and read the title: "'<u>Dreaming of Montana</u>'? I thought you said something about 'Birds' or whatever? What's this book?...by 'Christopher Sylves'...Who's he?"

"The title I gave you over the phone was a ruse. I made it up. *This* is the book I want you to have."

"What's it about?" asked Thad, turning it over and reading the back cover.

"*This* is what it's about," said Dexter, picking up a duplicate of the book from his desk.

"Huh? What, you want to form a reading club or something?"

"No dice. These two books are now our own personal 'Enigma.'"

"Clue in the clueless, Dexter. What are you talking about?"

"'Enigma' was the secret code used by the Germans in the Second World War. It took the Allies a long time to break it, it was so good."

"The Germans do everything 'good,'" said Thad as he flipped through the pages. "But, uh...like I don't see any cipher sheets or whatever in here. Where's the beef?"

"Where's your imagination, you cabbie-engineer? All right, example: turn to page one-oh-seven." Dexter and Thad both thumbed through the book till each one had that page. "Now, let's see...fourth line, third word."

"Okay," said Thad. "It says 'fifth.'"

"Great. Now, turn to, uh..." Dexter scanned a few pages. "Go to page one-twelve, second line from the bottom, last word."

"'High.'"

"There you have it," said Dexter, smiling. "I present to you Enigma."

"There I have *what?*" asked Thad.

"Fifth and High--meet me at Fifth and High."

"Oh...I see. When do we use this? Why?"

"Ever since the Chinese arrived, I think my phone's been bugged--or at least sometimes. I've been getting clicks on it from time to time, although your brother said if someone was tapping the line, I'd never know it."

"Maybe so, but I noticed clicks occasionally, too," said Thad. "Oh, okay! So these novels are what we use when we want to communicate over the phone without letting anyone know what we're talking about."

"You got it, slick. If you can't find the exact word you're looking for, you can spell it out with individual letters, but it'll just take more time."

"Where'd you get the idea?"

"Whaddaya mean?" asked Dexter with a smile. "Don't you think I'm capable of thinking it up myself?"

"Typical stuck-up Stanford student! Intellectual pig!" said Thad with a grin.

"All right, I confess. I read about it in a book about some Wall Street tycoon back in the 1920s. He did the same thing with one of his colleagues."

"That's more like it," said Thad. "That's probably where you got all your robotic ideas, too, eh?"

"Out!" screeched Dexter. "Before you steal some industrial secrets!"

"Typical 'PUPpy'!--'Paranoid Urban Professional'!"

"Out, cabbie! Back to the streets from whence you came!"

"Later, pal." Thad opened the door and walked out to his taxi.

From his office window, Dexter watched him walk out and smiled to himself. *Something about those Rankins...which reminds me--I'm supposed to see Father Rankin at four today.* He looked at his watch, told Mrs. Downing he would be out for a while and drove up to Saint Michael Church. By three-fifty-eight, he was sitting in a chair opposite the priest, who had been reading "Popular Mechanics" when Dexter walked into the office.

"What ho, Mr. Griffith?" asked Father Rankin, looking up from his desk.

"'*What ho*'?" asked Dexter. "Isn't that a tad dated?"

"Aaaa, it's just an expression used by Wooster in P.G. Wodehouse."

"Is that that 'Jeeves' thing I've heard about?"

"Precisely. Wooster and Jeeves--they're as inseparable as Laurel and Hardy. Jeeves is the butler and Wooster is the 'bon vivant.'"

"So you're 'Wooster,' then?" asked Dexter.

"As you wish, sir."

"Before we begin anything religious, you have any more thoughts on the Chinese thing? I mean they're here, but they're not here--know what I mean?"

"I think," said Father Rankin, "that the operative word is 'peacekeeping.' The papers say that they will be here only long enough to ensure the safety of the American people."

"That sounds like a crock, if you ask me," said Dexter. "Weren't we 'peaceful' *before* these Chinamen started patrolling our streets?"

"I'd have to agree with you there...I guess it's all just the beginning of martial law."

"What does that mean: 'martial law'?"

"It means they start checking our 'papers' anytime we want to travel anywhere," said Father Rankin. "What I hope it *doesn't* mean is prohibiting people from coming to Mass."

"You think it might come to that?"

"Anything's possible, I suppose."

"Well, anyway," said Dexter, "now that we're through with the typical introductory mishmash, maybe we can actually begin some intelligent discussion."

"Righto," said Father Rankin, "but doesn't that require two intelligent people?"

"You've got a point there, Padre. Maybe I need to find someone else to talk to."

"But I thought you wanted to have an *intelligent* discussion."

"Touché! Your advantage, Mr. Priest. Indulgences, indulgences, indulgences. Thus is announced today's topic."

"Today's timely topic?" asked Father Rankin with a smile.

"Okay, you win," said Dexter, extending his hand toward Father Rankin. "Let's all give a hand to the Master of Alliteration."

"Thank you, all you theological theorists!"

"Father, please? Indulgences? Can we actually start a meaningful discussion here?"

"For a dollar ninety-seven you can buy your way to Heaven," sang out Father Rankin.

"Care to explain that?"

"Just an old jingle my Dad used to sing. I guess it was some war cry from the Protestant Reformation."

"Whatever--what about the dollar ninety-seven thing?"

"Well, I'm not exactly sure where my Dad got it, because, of course, the Protestant Reformation predated the 'dollar' by about three hundred years, but the idea was that the Catholic Church used to sell indulgences."

"Hold the phone," said Dexter, raising his hand. "Explain 'indulgence' in the first place. I just happened to see the term the other day when I was reading a history book."

"Sure," said Father Rankin. "An indulgence is the partial or complete remission of the punishment due to sin after absolution."

"Translation, please?"

"An indulgence basically cuts down your Purgatory time. We believe that the majority of people who don't go to Hell have to spend some time in Purgatory for sins that have already been forgiven while still living."

"Wait!" said Dexter. "I might have said this before, but I remember some guy in high school telling me that Purgatory is the place you go till you say 'I'm sorry.'"

"Not quite right," explained Father Rankin. "Hopefully, you will have said 'I'm sorry' while still alive, and will only need to go to Purgatory to 'cleanse' your soul before being admitted to Heaven. Purgatory supposes that you have already asked for and been given forgiveness while on this earth--for a Catholic, that means going to Confession. Look, let me give you an example, actually from personal experience. Say when you're a kid you are playing around with your little bow and arrow set. Say, additionally, that you set up your target right next to the basement window of your house. Now say that your aim isn't always perfect and you happen to miss your target and break the basement window with your errant arrow. What are you required to do?"

"This sounds like a personal story."

"Trust me, it is. The first thing you do is go up to your mother and father and tell them you're sorry. Next, you fix the window. Purgatory is the fixing-the-window-part. Confession is the apologizing to your Mom and Dad part. This is where indulgences come in. An indulgence is similar to your father saying, 'Okay, Johnny, I'll fix the window for you. All you need to do is buy the glass.' A plenary indulgence would equate to your father saying 'that's fine, Johnny, I'll do everything, including buying the glass. You don't have to do anything--your apology is sufficient.'"

"That sounds like a racket, if you ask me," said Dexter. "What-- God likes to hand out 'Get Out of Jail Free' cards?"

"Well, I should mention the fine print about Plenary

Indulgences," said Father Rankin. "The remission of punishment is not a full remission if the penitent has any attachment to venial sin. Basically, the remission of sins is proportional to the person's detachment from venial sin."

"'Venial'?" asked Dexter. "I think you told me before, but refresh my memory."

"Venial as opposed to mortal sin. Venial sin is that sin which decreases sanctifying grace in our soul. Mortal sin completely cuts off sanctifying grace in our soul."

"Hell, you mean."

"Right, if a person dies in the state of mortal sin, he goes to Hell. Venial sin simply increases our Purgatory time."

"That is," said Dexter, "if you believe in Purgatory."

"First of all," said Father Rankin, "Purgatory makes sense. Everyone dies in different stages of sanctity, that is, everyone who is not damned. Do you think the average 'Joe six-CD' dies in the same state of soul as did Mother Theresa? Purgatory is the doormat of Heaven. We all need to wipe the 'feet' of our soul before entering the infinite cleanliness of Heaven. And, if you want some Bible backup, I can give that to you too. In the book of Maccabees, one of the men therein says that 'It is a holy and wholesome thought to pray for the dead.' Also, in the Gospel, Christ at one point says that 'You will not be released till you have paid the last penny.' Many scripture scholars have concurred that these and other Bible quotes are evidence for the existence of Purgatory."

"But, I still ask, 'Where's the beef?' How does the Church get away with handing out indulgences? I thought only God can operate in the grace business."

"Think of it as a giant treasury," explained Father Rankin. "Over the centuries, the Catholic Church has built up a boatload of graces earned first of all by Christ and then by all the sufferings of the sick, the martyrs, the imprisoned. The Church simply says that indulgences tap into this spiritual wealth and distributes it--it's there for the taking. The Church is not the owner of all this spiritual wealth, just the administrator."

"Bible backup?"

"One Scripture passage that comes to mind is the parable of the unjust steward. Christ told the story of this company president, if you will, who was about to be fired from his job by the owner of the

company. Thinking fast, the president calls in the company's debtors
and reduces their debts. To someone owing a hundred jars of oil, he
says your debt is reduced to fifty jars. He does the same to some guy
who is in debt to the owner for a hundred bushels of wheat. Christ
essentially says that his followers should have the same
industriousness in winning grace from God. This is the whole purpose
of indulgences. So many people today are savvy about investing in
the stock market. If you ask me, the really intelligent people are those
who are more interested in 'investing' in their souls. Plenary
indulgences are the best thing since anti-lock brakes. I highly
recommend them."

"It still sounds like a glorified 'Get Out of Jail Free' card," said
Dexter.

"I suppose there is a similarity, only an indulgence is not just
some lottery dreamt up by the local bishop. There is a lot of spiritual
machinery behind it."

"'Spiritual machinery'?"

"Sorry, it's just my Mechanical Engineering background coming
out. I mean that it is a well-thought out doctrine solidly based on
Scripture."

"It still seems like the popes are playing God."

"You have to remember," said Father Rankin, "there has been
an unbroken line of popes ever since Peter. It is this 'apostolic
succession,' as the expression goes, that gives the Church the
authority to grant indulgences."

Dexter leaned back in his seat and shook his head. "Then why
is it that indulgences get such a bad rap? The few times I've ever
heard about them were mostly when people were laughing at the
Church."

"I understand, I understand," said Father Rankin. He relit his
pipe before speaking. "There is good reason for the lowlife reputation
that indulgences have. During the Middle Ages there were plenty of
abuses which found their way into the world of indulgences. As I said
earlier about the 'dollar ninety-seven' thing, there was a time when
lucre-minded men sought to make a profit by selling 'free trips to
Heaven' and the like. Originally, one of the good works by which one
could gain an indulgence was the giving of alms to the poor, to a
hospital or the like. Eventually, though, this degenerated to the point
that people thought that they could simply 'buy' an indulgence.

Fortunately the Council of Trent formally forbad the selling of indulgences and today there is absolutely no monetary value placed on any indulgence."

"With all these indulgences, does anyone spend any time in Purgatory?" asked Dexter.

"You know," said Father Rankin, "sometimes I like to compare it to college tuition, say at a private university. Do that many people really pay the full price up front, cash on the barrelhead? I mean there are grants, and loans, and scholarships, and work-study programs. I see Purgatory in the same way. God is so merciful that he has provided numerous ways to reduce--even eliminate Purgatory time. But, I should add that one author holds that the average person spends three years in Purgatory."

"In other words," said Dexter, "the Catholic Church is the financial aid office of the spiritual life!"

"Dex, m'boy, you're catching on! You'll be 'Pope-ing' any day now!"

"'Pope-ing'?"

"I think that's the term some Protestant churches give to converting to the Catholic Church."

"Not quite so fast, priest! I'm just investigating right now...don't jump to any conclusions."

"What's holding you back, anyway? You've been coming to see me for--what, three months now? I would've thought you might be putting the directional gyro on Rome by now."

"Who says I'm even going to become a Catholic? I'm just taking things one step at a time. I'm not too convinced one way or the other right now. Maybe I'll just go back to being a decent, law-abiding secular humanist, I don't know..."

"I thought you still were a secular humanist."

"Like I say, I really don't know...what's in between a secular humanist and a Catholic?"

"A Democrat?"

"Ha! Very funny, Mr. Republican-of-the-cloth! Just because you listen to Rush Limback..."

"And what if I do?"

"I don't know about Rush...he's sort of arrogant."

"He's just kidding around!" said Father Rankin. "You're not the first person I've heard who's said that about Rush. My gosh, he always says 'talent on loan from God.' If that's not humility, what is?"

"Well, hell, is *he* Catholic?

"I don't know…he's got to get his marital life straightened out."

"What else can you tell me about indulgences?" asked Dexter.

"What else do you want to know?"

"How 'bout you give me a concrete example of an indulgence?"

"No problem! Reading the Bible for a half-hour is a Plenary Indulgence."

"That's cool! Doesn't sound too hard."

"It's not, but keep in mind that to receive a Plenary Indulgence, one has to go to Confession, receive Holy Communion, and say a prayer for the Pope's intentions."

"Oh, so it's a little more involved."

"A little."

"What about a non-Plenary Indulgence?" asked Dexter.

"A partial indulgence? Saying the Crucifix Prayer before a crucifix gives a partial indulgence."

"I thought it was like a hundred days or something."

"The Church eliminated the numbering system of partial indulgences and says that there are just two kinds of indulgences, plenary and partial."

"How do they know how many days of Purgatory are eliminated anyway?"

"Ha!" said Father Rankin, smiling. "Common misperception number eighty-eight! The number of days refers not to the number of days of Purgatory but to the number of days of public penance. For example, an indulgence of five-hundred days remits the same amount of punishment as would five-hundred days of penance."

"Sort of sounds like the deductions you take for income tax," said Dexter.

"My Dad was in the IRS for awhile, actually."

"My Dad was on the 'outs' with the IRS for awhile, actually."

"So," asked Father Rankin, clapping his hands together, "I guess I can sign you up for four Plenary Indulgences next week, huh?"

"Right, Shuff!"

"Shuff?" asked Father Rankin.

"Just an expression this guy used to use who I ran cross-country with in high school. No. No indulgences for me right now. I've got too much living to do first, sir."

"As you wish, sir."

"Now you're sounding like *Jeeves.*"

"As you wish, sir."

"Always the comic, Father. Look, I hate to break up this tea-party, but I have to 'Head-East,' as the expression goes."

"Head-East! Great band from the 80s!" said Father Rankin.

"So you do know something outside of theology!"

"I danced with the best of them, Dexter."

"You sure you're a real priest, Father Rankin? Maybe I'll call up the Bishop and check you out."

"Uh, I think I hear someone calling me," said Father Rankin, rising from his seat.

"Uh-huh! Uh-huh!" said Dexter. "Look at the cockroaches flee when the light is shined on them!"

"Ahhhh, a pagan comparing a priest to a cockroach! I'm telling!"

"Who you calling a pagan?! I thought I was a Democrat!"

"And the difference is…?"

"Now *that's* too low," said Dexter. "Have some respect for your fellow countrymen!"

"Don't you mean your fellow country *people?*"

"Hell's bells, you never stop, do you Father?"

"If there's something you should never doubt about a priest, it's his stubbornness," said Father Rankin.

"Hear, hear!" said Dexter. "The truth is out."

"Speaking of 'out,' I thought you said you needed to head 'out.'"

"Was it something I said?"

"Precisely."

"I know when someone's trying to give me a hint."

Father Rankin sang out: "Oh, people of God go home! And leave the priests alone!"

"Your own composition, Father?"

"Actually, I stole it from a tall priest who once was pastor of Saint Pat's."

Dexter picked up his notebook, walked across the room and opened the office door. "See ya later, alligator!"

"Pretty soon, you big raccoon!" replied Father Rankin.

Dexter just shook his head and kept on walking.

****

"So basically you're making cleaner air," said Thad. He was on his second date with Cheryl and they were dining at Eastern Bay, a Chinese restaurant on Riverside Drive.

"You might say that," said Cheryl. "Battelle is trying to get more involved in environmental projects and my team is leading the way. How about you, Thad? When are you going to get back into a real job?"

"I suppose I should give it a try one of these days."

"How long have you been out of work?"

"It's been about five years so far, although I've only been driving a cab for a little over a year."

"Where were you working when you developed your insomnia?" Cheryl took a sip of water and waited for Thad to finish chewing.

"A place called P.B. Browton out in Hilliard. They make tree branch shredding machines."

"I thought you said you worked on some 'National Aircraft' project or something?"

"That's true, you're right." Thad poured some soy sauce on his rice before continuing. "It was called the National Aerospace Plane, or NASP, for short. It was basically an airplane that was supposed to fly from New York to Tokyo in only two hours."

"Two hours?"

"Right. It was supposed to be sort of like a rocket, following a ballistic trajectory."

"You seem to be speaking in the past tense," said Cheryl.

Thad took a few swallows of beer, and then set his glass down. "Yeah, it was cancelled about fifteen years ago; it wasn't making much progress."

"And that's why you quit?"

"Not exactly. I quit because of Dwight D. Eisenhower and my uncle."

"Explain yourself, Englishman!" said Cheryl jokingly.

"I'm only half-English. I'm also a quarter Irish, one-eighth German, and one-eighth French."

"Okay, you *mongrel*, let's hear it!"

"Dwight D. Eisenhower used to say--incidentally, did you know that the 'D' in Eisenhower's name stands for 'Dalmatian'?"

"Yeah, right."

"Anyway, Eisenhower used to warn against the military industrial complex that was just beginning to grow during his Presidency."

"What's so bad about it?"

"To be perfectly honest, I found it to be a form of corporate welfare! You know how sometimes you'll be driving along the street and you'll see a group of city workers toiling away on the road?"

"Yeah...they're part of the 'military-industrial complex'?" Cheryl brought her glass to her lips and took a drink.

"Not them, I'm just using them as an example. Most of the time you'll find about three-quarters of those city workers standing around doing nothing, while the other quarter does the real work. *That's* what it was like in the aerospace industry--at least the projects that I was on."

"Then how do they survive if they don't do any work?"

"Well, like I said, the NASP was cancelled several years ago. Of course I can't remember the precise reason given. Hey, how's your sesame chicken?"

"It's good! I'll have to come to this restaurant more often; I like their food. How's your pork--that's sweet and sour pork, right?"

"Right--yeah, it's good too!"

"So you went from building rockets in LA to building tree shredders in measly Columbus, Ohio."

"Hey," said Thad with a grin, "*easly* on the *measly*. This is my hometown, remember."

"Oh, okay, is 'bucolic' better?"

"Better, but not too accurate."

"You're just trying to dodge the subject...let's have it, rocket man!" said Cheryl, who then took another bite of her chicken.

"Well, there were a couple stops along the way. I went to graduate school at Stanford for six days and then sold conveyors in Chicago for two years."

"Hold on," said Cheryl, swallowing her food, "first the six days at Stanford--six *days*? What--did you flunk your first 'pop quiz' or something?"

"Well, the reason for--"

"Wait a minute! Sorry to interrupt you, but let's back up a minute. You didn't tell me what your uncle had to do with this whole thing...remember? You said you quit your job because of Eisenhower and your uncle."

"Right, right. Yeah, my uncle used to say that 'Thad is working on things to kill Russian teenagers.'"

"Come again?"

"He just meant that since I was working on defense related projects I was helping to make 'bombs' that would be used against Russian soldiers in World War III."

"But I thought Russia is our friend now."

"This was back in the 80s when the Cold War was still on."

"Oh. All right, back to Stanford and those ill-fated six-days."

"Well, you see, the only reason I wanted to go to graduate school at Stanford was to get out of the Aerospace Industry."

"What were you going to study?"

"I was enrolled in Mechanical Engineering. I really wanted to study Electrical Engineering--you know, Silicon Valley and all that--"

"You wanted to be Steve Jobs and Bill Gates, right?" asked Cheryl.

"Right, how'd you know?"

"I'm beginning to get the picture--entrepreneurship, right?"

"Precisely. Anyway, the long and short of it is that I didn't want to pay for graduate school myself. Rockwell said they would pay for my graduate school if I would come back to work for them for two years after I graduated from Stanford. I said 'no way' and moved from LA up to Stanford, thinking I would foot the bill myself. After I got to Stanford, I realized I had accomplished my goal, i.e., getting out of the aerospace industry, so I really didn't need graduate school. Ergo, I dropped out and tried to figure out what to do next."

"Which, logically, was selling conveyors in Chicago."

"There was logic," protested Thad, "there was logic. You see, I had some friends from Notre Dame in Chicago and they told me that Chicago was a good place to get a manufacturing job in the private sector, which is exactly what I wanted. If there was one thing I learned from my jobs in aerospace it was to work in private industry and to actually *make something*, not just research it."

"That's two things."

"Fine. I learned *two* things."

"But you said you were in sales, not engineering."

"Well, I had to take what I could get. There was no aerospace industry in Chicago and most of the engineering jobs seemed to be in electronics or whatever, so I took a job selling conveyors."

"Did you like it?" asked Cheryl. "Hey, let's get some coffee." She signaled the waiter and the two of them ordered decaf.

"Actually, I did, but the truth was I wasn't too good at sales."

"Why did you quit?"

"Ah, the awful truth," said Thad, dropping his voice. "I was fired."

"Oh, sorry to hear that. Were you sad to have to leave the job?"

"Mixed emotions, really. The guys at the office kept saying that 'it's like starting your own business,' which I liked, but I don't know if I'm cut out for sales."

"So you came home."

"Right. This is where my family is and I really don't want to move. I got the job at the tree shredding factory and then I developed insomnia."

"What brought that on?" asked Cheryl.

"Sixty-two dollar question," replied Thad. "The doctors think it was my career, or lack thereof."

"Name names, time times."

"Huh?"

"Give me the time context of all this, you know dates and stuff."

"Okay...I was fired from the sales job in August and had the nervous breakdown in May."

"Whoa! *Nervous breakdown*?" asked Cheryl. "I thought this was simple insomnia."

"Well, yeah, maybe nervous breakdown is a little too strong. Actually none of the doctors ever really used that term."

"Anything happen in May to trigger this--uh, 'event'?"

"I took the engineering job at Browton in April and six weeks later I was in Harding."

"That's that place on the north side, right?"

"Right, in Worthington. It's a mental hospital--actually used to be one of the top five in the nation, I guess. It changed hands a few years ago. Now it's owned by Ohio State, but back then it was simply known as 'Harding.'"

"So you took this engineering job and flipped out," said Cheryl.

"I started the job around the first of April and then started losing sleep about the first week of May. I thought I could handle it, but when you go a week with a total of only about ten hours sleep, you start to look for a cure *real* fast."

"And the cure was Harding."

"Yeah, I guess my parents suggested it…I think they noticed I was acting a bit strange."

"Strange?"

"I started to get paranoid, like thinking my apartment neighbor was causing me to lose sleep."

"Go on," said Cheryl.

"Well, I have to laugh about it now, but it was serious business then--I remember I went to Big Bear one night and bought a roll of aluminum foil because I thought that would stop the 'sleep machine,' as I called it. I spread this foil around the baseboard of the adjoining wall to try to stop the electronic rays that I was convinced my neighbor was pumping into my apartment." Thad gave a short laugh. "Oh, yeah, I also remember barricading myself behind the stereo speakers, thinking that would stop the 'sleep rays.'"

"You were a genuine nutcase!"

"I appreciate your use of the past tense there."

"Are you still nutty?"

"It's worn off over the years so that's it's practically zero now, but for a while they labeled me as a 'paranoid delusionist.'"

"And so goes the saga of Thad Rankin," said Cheryl with a smile.

"They're going to make a movie about it one of these days, just you wait."

"I thought you said you were over your delusions." Cheryl gave Thad a playful nudge with her hand.

"Can't a guy have a few delusions now and then to pass the time?"

"All right, we'll allow that one…what would you name your blockbusting movie?"

"How 'bout: 'The Secret Life of Thaddeus Rankin'?"

"I think that name's been taken by Thurber, sorry."

"I guess I'll just have to hold a name-guessing contest in the

'Dispatch.'"

"My, my, how the delusions pour when it rains! Like our newspaper would print something like that."

"I still have one more; I'm allowed three per day."

"So are you cured now, or what?" asked Cheryl.

"I'm not sure, actually. Hey, what do you want for dessert?"

"Changing the subject, are we?"

"Just needing to satisfy my sugar-body." Thad called the waiter over. "I'll take the carrot cake."

"And I'll take the banana pudding." They handed the menus to the waiter.

"So, really, Thad, aren't you able by now to work a higher-paying job?"

Thad's mouth tightened as he put his hands on the edge of the table and leaned back in his seat. "Uh, I guess what it comes down to is that I have to test out my insomnia."

"How would you do that?"

"The simple way would be to get a full-time, pressurized engineering job and see if I can handle it--see if my insomnia kicks up again or goes away. But, you see, I also get a monthly disability check from the government, and they have rules about how much you're allowed to earn per month."

"So, what are you waiting for?"

"Well, I sort of like the taxi job and I don't know if I'd like to get an office job again."

A serious look crossed Cheryl's face. "But aren't you essentially cheating the government out of their money if you're able to support yourself and you stay on the dole?"

"Nnnnmmm, uh...yeah," said Thad in a low voice.

"So?"

"I see what you're saying..."

"Well, break out the classified ads and see what you can find."

"But I'm not sure about working, really."

"You're not sure about working--what do you mean by that?"

"Well, the insomnia problem is sort of, uh..."

"I thought that was pretty much over," said Cheryl.

"Well, you see, back when this whole thing started, back when I quit the aerospace job in California, I had thought a little about--about being a priest," he said quickly.

"A priest!" she said a little too loudly. The server arrived with their desserts just then and Thad asked him for the check.

"What do you mean, 'a priest'?" said Cheryl a little more quietly. She took a spoonful of her pudding and then a sip of the decaf.

"Well, my brother had just been ordained and--"

"This is the one at Saint Michael's, right?"

"Yeah, he's assigned to Saint Michael's in Worthington."

"So you thought you should be a priest, too?"

"I was sort of rejected back then and I took it hard."

"What does that mean, 'sort of rejected'? Were you 'sort of' in the seminary?"

"No, I was never in the seminary, but I really just discovered I probably couldn't be a priest."

"This isn't really making much sense, Thad."

Thad took a few bites of his carrot cake and brushed the hair out of his eyes. "The insomnia, I think, might have been caused by my stress over thinking about becoming a priest."

"Then it had nothing to do with your job at that place in Hilliard?" asked Cheryl.

"Yes and no. Uhh, I think there was a combination of things. See, I had left my career, basically, when I quit Rockwell in Los Angeles, and that was a bit of a blow. Then I was fired from the sales job in Chicago, and then I lost the job in Hilliard. And all that time I was thinking of the priesthood." Thad shook his head and leaned back in his chair. "Ah, I don't know! The whole thing just seemed to be coming down on top of me--all at once."

"Which leaves us at the present time--why not just forget the past and get a job and move on?"

Thad looked across the room and pursed his lips. "Cheryl, I guess--" He glanced at her briefly and then looked down at the table. "Maybe I could still be a priest!"

Cheryl raised her eyebrows and let out a small gasp. "After all this, you're still thinking about *that*?"

Thad was shaking his head, his eyes averted. "Ah, I don't know, I can't figure out if it's just a delusion, or it's something I should take seriously."

"Well, if you want my opinion, it's--if everything you said just now is accurate--it's definitely a delusion," said Cheryl. She looked at her watch. "Maybe we had better get going."

Thad paid the bill after which they got into his car and headed east on Fifth Avenue.

"Do you still want to see that movie?" asked Thad as they approached Route 315.

"You know, why don't you just take me home," said Cheryl. "I don't know if I care much to see a movie right now."

"You sure? It's supposed to be a really good one--Look, I didn't mean to scare you off back there. I just have a few problems to iron out."

"'A few problems'? Thad, I think--and, no, I do *not* want to see a movie." She pointed to the left. "I would like to go home now."

"All right," said Thad dejectedly.

"Thad, I enjoyed our time together, but your attitude is just a little crazy. I mean you have a degree in aerospace engineering and you're driving a cab! You had a nervous breakdown because you couldn't, or didn't want to--or whatever--you couldn't be a priest. Now you're going out on dates and you still think about being a priest, but you're still just driving a taxi. It doesn't look like you want to get a decent paying job. I'm sorry! I just don't understand!"

"I know, I know," said Thad calmly. "It is a bit messed up."

They drove the rest of the way in silence till they reached her apartment.

"Is it okay if I call you next week?" asked Thad.

"I don't--well, maybe I just--let's just let it rest for now, okay?" said Cheryl.

"Okay. Thanks for going out tonight."

Cheryl said nothing, just climbed out and shut the car door.

At least she didn't slam it, thought Thad.

He spent the next two days nursing his bruised ego, and decided to go into work a little later on Tuesday morning, allowing a little time to go to morning Mass. When he woke up in bed, Thad rolled over and opened his eyes. *Wow,* he groggily said to himself, *it's pretty light outside for being this early.* He was about to check his bedside clock but drifted off to sleep again. Five minutes later he opened his eyes again. A little more alert now, he again wondered about the brightness shining through his window. *Wait a minute, it shouldn't be* this *bright in February...* He turned to the clock and looked at the time. *Yikes! It's eight twenty-five!* If he hurried, he could just make it to the nine o'clock Mass at Saint Margaret of Cortona on

Hague Avenue. He jumped out of bed and into the shower. He skipped making his bed and quickly shaved and combed his hair. *With a little luck, I'll make it before the First Reading.*

He opened his apartment door, threw the "Dispatch" onto his couch and locked the door behind him. Luckily it hadn't snowed overnight so he didn't have to spend any time brushing the snow off his car. Thad drove up to the intersection of North Star and Fifth Avenues, but just missed the green light. *Darn! Come on, Sylvester!* he said silently to his Guardian Angel. *You could have kept that light green just a little longer!* Finally the light changed and Thad went charging down Fifth Avenue, slowing down temporarily as he passed a police car parked along the side of the road. *Sweeet*, he thought as he made the light at Trabue and Hague. *I might even make it for the whole Mass!* He turned into the parking lot and pulled into his usual spot, right next to Mrs. Carmelo's Buick. He gathered up his meditation book and weekday Missal and walked over to the church. He opened the outer door, walked across the vestibule, opened the inner door, and blessed himself with holy water. Out of the corner of his eye, as he walked to his customary spot on the left side of the church, he thought he saw Mrs. Carmelo lying down on the pew. *What? Is she sick or something?* Then he raised his head and looked up at the altar. *Oh my God--! No...no! Jesus, help me!*

Father Rechault was sprawled out on the floor, lying in a large pool of blood! Thad looked back at Mrs. Carmelo. *Please, Jesus! Mary, help me!* Mrs. Carmelo was lying motionless on the pew, which was splattered with blood. That was when Thad cast his eyes around and took it all in: *Everyone in the church was dead!* His heart began beating very quickly and very heavily. That old man whose name he could never remember was still in a kneeling position, slumped over the pew, five bullet holes in the back of his winter coat. Thad's hands began shaking violently and he dropped his books. He looked up at the tabernacle. *At least they didn't desecrate that!   Jesus, what should I do? Dear God, don't do this to me!*

Thad picked up his books and genuflected. He stood there, trembling, running his hand through his hair. *Go!* said a strong, inner voice. *Get out of here! Don't go home! Flee to the countryside!* Thad didn't need to be told twice. He sprinted out to his car and headed west on Trabue Road. *Best to stay off the Interstates, I suppose.* He kept heading west, not knowing where to stop. *Good thing I got gas yesterday--and 'double good thing' I drove my own car this morning and not my taxicab.*

Thad turned onto Walker Road and headed north, although it was becoming harder and harder to keep track of directions. A light snow had begun to fall, thus disabling the sun from helping him with navigation. As he passed a farm on the right side of the road, he saw a chicken coop and it occurred to him that he didn't have any food in the car with him. *I'll have to solve that problem pretty soon, considering I haven't eaten since last night.* He decided he would pull over and stop to think for a few minutes. A minute later he saw a wide spot on the side of the road and slowed to a stop. *First things first: Where can I go? Should I go back to my apartment? Where can I sleep tonight? Do I have any money?*

"Whoa!" he said aloud, slapping the passenger seat beside him. "Calm down!" He took out his wallet and looked inside. *Darn! I've only got fifteen bucks! If I go anywhere I have to use cash. If I use my credit card, they can track me. Or am I being a little paranoid? Dexter did say he thought he was being bugged...if the Chinese were bugging Dexter, they for sure would be after me! After all, I'm the Garabandal-nutty-conspiracy-theory-taxi-driver. I've written many letters to the editor. Surely the Commies, or the One-Worlders, or whoever, would know about me--or am I really that important?*

Thad saw a car approaching and he involuntarily shielded his face from the passer-by. *Wow! I really am getting paranoid!...But then again, aren't all the prophecies coming true? All right, back to square-one--first things first. Where do I go now? I probably had better stay away from my apartment--at least for now. I can't stay in a motel--if I use my credit card they can track me. What about getting cash from an ATM? Possibly, but they can track that, too. I wonder if Dexter could help me somehow.* He patted his pockets, looking for his cell phone. *Don't tell me I left it in my briefcase!* Since he used the phone mainly for his taxi business, he usually kept it in the satchel he carried in the taxicab. *Oh, man, I hope it's in this car!* He leaned over and opened the glove compartment. *Yes!* he thought with a sigh of relief as he grabbed it and shut the lid of the glove box. *Thank goodness for small favors!* Thad was trying to remember Dexter's office number when his eyes fell upon the novel Dexter had given him. *Couldn't hurt to have that in hand.* He picked up <u>Dreaming of Montana</u> from the floor on the passenger side. *I might even have time to read this now that I'm "liberated."*

Thad retrieved Dexter's number from the memory of the cell phone and dialed Grobotics.

"Grobotics, how may I direct your call?" said Mrs. Downing.

"Could I speak with--" Thad began to say in a whisper, then shook his head and repeated in a normal voice: "Oh, excuse me-- could I speak with Dexter, please?"

"Sure, one moment, may I ask who's calling?"

"Just tell him a friend."

"Oh…okay."

Thirty seconds later, Dexter came on the line. "Hello, this is Dexter."

"Dexter!" Thad said with relief in his voice. "It's Thad!"

"Hey, guy, what's happening? You sound a little upset."

"Dexter, bad, bad news. I went to Mass this morning and the priest and the people there were shot!"

"What? Where was this? Did you get hurt?"

"Dexter, I'm on the run, I--no, I didn't get hurt--I got there after-- oh, hell! Dexter, they gunned down the priest right in front of the altar! And they killed Mrs. Carmelo!"

"Hey, calm down, Thad…you say you're alright? Where are you?"

"That's just it! I can't tell you any of that. Remember the book you gave me? It's time to use it."

"You mean--" started Dexter, "it was--ohh." He was silent for a few seconds.

"I got there after it happened," said Thad. "I don't believe how lucky I was! I overslept and got there late. Everyone was dead by the time I arrived."

"Oh, no…," said Dexter. "I wonder if it's on the news."

"I really don't think so. I've heard that they're keeping stuff like this quiet."

"Wait! Thad! Are you using your cell? They can track you now--they've put GPS sensors in the phone! Maybe you better end the call."

"It's OK. I've got an old phone, without the GPS. I pay a special fee each month to block my location--but you're right, they can trace my call to this general area--they can know which 'cell' I'm in."

"Are you local?"

"Suffice it to say I'm outside the city limits."

"Well out there I think the cells are pretty large. You should be okay for now."

"Dexter, I have a bit of a problem. I need shelter, and I'm getting hungry and I'm low on cash. I don't want to use my credit cards or ATM card, because they can trace that--any suggestions?"

"Thad, you sure you're not overdoing this a little? How do you know the Chinese even care about you? Why don't you just come back and live normally?"

"I've thought about that and I don't want to take the chance. There's been a few Chinese checking out everyone at the daily Mass at St Margaret's for the past two weeks. I even saw one of them copying down license plate numbers about a week ago. And, oh yeah!--a couple of Chinese cops stopped me on the highway two weeks ago. They broke my tail light for no reason."

"Hmm, you may have a point. Maybe you better lie low for now. I'm still getting those clicks on the line myself, and it seems it's more often now, too."

"What do you think I should do?" asked Thad. "I can't survive without money."

"Wellhh, uhh," said Dexter, reaching over to grab the novel, "I guess it's time to start reading <u>Birds of Autumn</u>." He began flipping through the book. "Okay, have you got it there with you, I hope?"

"<u>Birds of Autumn</u>, right in front of me."

"Good. Let's see. All right...page...two-oh-seven...fourth line...third word--now, remember! Don't say it over the phone!"

"Gotcha," said Thad as he turned to see that the word was "gold." "I got it--where might I find that word--uhh, maybe we could say the word is 'frog.'"

"Yes, yes, 'frog,' as you put it, can be found at, uh, let's see...page twenty-five...the five, six--seventh line from the top...eighth word in...and..." Dexter continued reading off the words and letters till Thad had been told, in code, that gold was at Dexter's family farm on Route 42, zero-point-six miles south of Taylor Blair Road. Dexter's family rented the farm out to a local man who raised an assortment of crops on the land. Lastly, Dexter told Thad that he was welcome to stay in the rundown shack on the farm. Thad thanked Dexter and told him he would call him after he had secured the "frog" and settled into his new "home."

Thad climbed into his car and pulled out a map. *Let's see, I take Walker Road to Patterson to Amity to Lucas Pike, and Lucas Pike...runs right into Route 42! Perfect! Now, where's this...what's it called...Taylor Blair Road? Okay, there it is--a couple miles south of Lucas Pike. No problem!* Thad folded up the map and backed the Taurus out onto Walker Road. Fifteen minutes later he turned into the driveway of Dexter's farm on Route 42. *Rustic enough,* he thought as he surveyed the primitive shack and barn that comprised the two buildings on the farm. Dexter had told him, in the awkward wording necessitated by the novel-code, that the gold was buried in the floor of the barn, directly beneath a rope that was hanging from one of the rafters. As Thad opened the barn door it gave a protesting squeak. He looked for the rope and found it after his eyes had adjusted to the dim light. Just as Dexter had said, Thad found a shovel standing up against the back wall of the barn. He was about to take out the first shovelful when he heard a truck engine come up the drive.

Thad quickly threw the shovel into a corner of the barn and stepped out into the open area in front of the building.

A man in a tan Carhartt coat and pants was climbing down from his oversized pickup. Thad noticed that a rifle was mounted on a rack behind the seat of the truck.

"Howdy!" Thad said in as rural an accent as he could muster.

"Good mornin'!" said the man, walking up to Thad and holding out his hand. "I'm Blake Townsend; I live just down the road."

Thad shook the proffered hand. "Glad to meetcha! I'm Jeff Mason." He thought it best not to use his real name till he knew who this "farmer" really was.

"I assume you're a friend of Dexter's?"

"That's right. I was just checking up on things for Dexter, because, uhh..." Thad let his voice fall off.

Blake's eyes narrowed as he looked Thad over, then turned to look at his car. "What exactly did Dexter want you to do out here?"

"Oh, you know," Thad avoided Blake's eyes and turned around, motioning with his arm. "Just make sure everything's okay. I was just in the barn there. I think things are pretty good."

"Well, you might want to tell Dexter that there were some Chinese military types out here a few days ago. I saw them when I drove by--they've been randomly stopping at farms around here I've been told."

"Really?" asked Thad. "Did they stay long?"

"I drove by about ten minutes later and their truck was gone, so, no, I don't think they were here long."

"Huh," said Thad, now looking over Blake. He pointed to the truck. "I see you have a rifle there."

"That's right!" said Blake. "And I'm keeping it there, too. None of those Chinese bastards are going to take it from me!"

"I hear ya--I don't blame you."

"Awright, well, I guess I'll be heading on. I just wanted to make sure you weren't hurtin' Dexter's barn or nothin'."

"Not at all--I'll tell him you stopped by."

"G'day, Jeff."

"See ya, Blake."

Thad watched Blake drive away, then returned to the barn. This time he closed the barn door halfway so no one from the road could see what he was doing. He looked around the inside of the empty barn. *I wonder how long I'll be hanging out here. Do the Chinese know about Dexter's gold? Of course, Blake* did *say they have been making* random *stops...maybe they have no idea what's out here.* Thad retrieved the shovel and five minutes later had unearthed a metal box, buried about eighteen inches below the dirt floor of the barn. It took all the muscle he could muster, but finally he lifted the container up to ground level. When he took off the lid, he felt a slight tinge of greed. Lying there in silent grandeur were dozens of bright, newly minted Gold American Eagles! *Now I know how explorers must have felt when they came across buried treasure!* He picked up a few of the coins and heard the reassuring "thlink!" sound they made when he dropped them back onto the pile. *Now my food problem is solved.* Thad had read in the paper that as the US Dollar was losing value, more and more businesses were accepting only precious metals for payment, that is, if they accepted anything other than the SMARTCARD, the universal credit card that would soon be issued to all citizens of the emerging global government. *This should last quite a while. Now, how to get it out to the car?* He remembered he had a few plastic bags in the trunk and used these to transfer some of the gold to the trunk of the Taurus. He was careful not to let anyone who might be unobtrusively watching see what he was carrying. It took about ten trips, but soon about half of Dexter's stash of gold was locked securely in the trunk of Thad's car.

He went back to the barn, put the half-full box in the ground and filled in the hole, covering it with straw to deter any prying eyes from seeing evidence of his "discovery." Thad quickly looked around the barn to see if there was anything of value he might use. *Nothing in here but dirt and straw…and, well, yeah…gold.* He walked out of the barn and over to the unimpressive-looking shack. *Might as well tour my new "home."* When he pulled on the outer screen door, it promptly came off its hinges, almost clobbering him on the head.

"Thank you," he said aloud. "Wonderful."

He opened the inner door and stepped into what looked like a set from some 1950s sitcom. There was an old Formica-topped dining room table surrounded by four metal tube, green-vinyl covered chairs. The wallpaper on the walls was of a faded yellow color imprinted with blue-colored birds. *At least they got my two favorite colors right,* Thad thought sarcastically. There was even an old jukebox pushed up against one wall, complete with Chuck Berry and Buddy Holly 45 RPM records. *Doesn't Dexter have enough money to fix this place up? It doesn't look like it's changed since his grandfather was here. Where am I supposed to sleep?* He cast his eyes about the one-room edifice, chuckling softly when he saw a dusty olive-drab cot standing in one corner. *This just keeps getting better! This place is fine for some kids playing "camping" in the middle of summer, but I have to* live *here!* The image of Mrs. Carmelo's body lying in the Church flashed through Thad's mind. *All right, it could be worse…at least I didn't die this morning.* He found a couple of blankets in the shack and tossed them onto the cot. *I'm going to need a few more of those tonight.*

Thad called up Dexter and apprised him of his situation. After settling a few more details he headed into Marysville to buy supplies.

****

The alarm went off and woke Kevin from a dream he was having about windsurfing in the Bahamas. He reached out and hit the snooze button, only to be awakened ten minutes later by the clock's "Defcon One" buzz, as one of his friends liked to call its annoying sound. After hitting the snooze bar a second time, Kevin was sufficiently awake to remember it was Sunday, and that he should go to church. When he glanced at the travel clock, he noticed the date: February eighteenth. *Lent is probably going to begin one of these days*, he reminded himself. He slithered out of bed and took a quick shower. Seeing that it was already past eleven o'clock, he decided he would head for the eleven-thirty Mass at Saint Christopher Church in Grandview. Although it didn't snow overnight, he did have to spend a few minutes chipping ice from his car's windows. The streets were clear and free of traffic, enabling him to arrive at Saint Christopher's ten minutes early. He selected a seat in the rear, out of the "eyeshot" of the priest. Kevin hated having the priest look at him while giving his sermon. The first part of the Mass went according to plan, although Kevin was a little surprised to see four Chinese men, at the beginning of the Eucharistic prayer, enter the side door of the church and sit in the front pew. Kevin was giving half his attention to wondering about the visitors when he brought his mind back to listening to the words of the priest.

"of my Body," said the priest, who then raised the Host with both hands, held it briefly above the altar, then brought it back down and continued reading the prayer.

What was that? wondered Kevin. *"of my Body?" "Of"? I thought it was "This is my Body"? I don't remember an "of" being in there.* Kevin brought his full attention back to the priest, who at that moment was saying:

"This is a symbol of my Blood, the blood of the new and everlasting covenant. It will be shed for you and for all so that sins may be forgiven. Do this in memory of me." The priest raised the chalice and then brought it back down to the altar.

Now, hold one minute, Kevin said inwardly. *I might not be the most faithful Catholic in the world, but what he just said did not sound right!* Kevin mentally reviewed it in his head. *"Of my Body" and "This is a symbol of my Blood." No, that's not right.* Kevin shook his head back and forth imperceptibly. *The Real Presence of Christ in the Eucharist means he should've said "This is my body." I'll have to check this out with someone.* Just as the Eucharistic prayer ended, he looked up to the see the four Chinese men exit out the same door they had used to enter. *They were here just to hear the Eucharistic Prayer...hmm...* Kevin stayed till the end of Mass and slipped out the back before the end of the closing hymn.

Chapter 10

"That'll be a hundred and twenty dollars and I'll need to scan your driver's license," the cashier said as Kevin walked up to the cash register. He hadn't bought any gas for a few weeks and just happened to stop at the Speedway on West Fifth Avenue while on his way home from the Radio Shack in Upper Arlington.

"A hundred and twenty dollars!?" asked Kevin. "I only got fifteen gallons!"

"It's the Chinese, my friend," explained the cashier, a middle-aged man with a pony tail and tattoo on his right forearm. "Not only are they rationing this stuff, they're taxing it like crazy as well."

"Yeah, but *eight dollars* a gallon?"

"Take it up with Chinky over there," the cashier said, motioning to the soldier that was standing just inside the doorway. Every gas station now had an armed Chinese guard to make sure no one exceeded their ration.

"This is getting ridiculous," said Kevin.

"We're a conquered nation, bud," said the cashier. "Just be glad we get any gas at all."

"I guess I can't argue with that...see ya later."

Kevin climbed into his ten-year old Chevy, and after stopping briefly at his apartment, headed north on Interstate 71. He didn't have any classes today, since it was a Friday, so he thought he would go home to his parents' house in Rocky River. He put in a CD of O.A.R. and settled in for the two-hour trip.

An hour later, just past Mansfield, the "check engine" light came on and Kevin felt the car start to lose power. "Aw, not now!" he said. "I'm out in the middle of nowhere!" Despite pressing the accelerator almost to the floor, he couldn't go over thirty miles an hour. He kept driving for a mile or two, and then fortunately saw a sign for a service station two miles up the road. He turned off at the exit and pulled into a station that had a repair garage connected to it. He went inside and explained the situation to the manager who came out to have a closer look at the old Chevy.

"Sounds like a fuel problem or maybe the tranny," said the manager. "I definitely don't recommend your driving it anymore right now."

Kevin glanced at the service bays and noticed the lights were off. "Any chance you could fix it today?"

"I'm afraid you'll have to wait till tomorrow--wait, tomorrow's Saturday, right? Uhh, well, let's see...no, I don't believe Frank will be in tomorrow. Have you got a way to get home? I don't really know if we can get to it till Monday."

"Aw, man! This isn't the way I wanted to spend the weekend!"

Just then a young man walked up to Kevin. "Excuse, me, but I couldn't help but overhear your conversation--well, first of all, you're Kevin Conaway, right?"

"Right," said Kevin, a little dejectedly. He'd hoped he could hide his football fame once in a while.

"Yeah! I thought so!" beamed the guy who was wearing an Ohio State coat. "I'm sure you've heard it many times, but that was an awesome game you played."

"Right."

"But, look--my friends and I can give you a ride--you're going to Cleveland, right--Rocky River--your car just broke down, I see?" He gestured to the car beside which they stood.

"Well..." Kevin looked at the station manager. "I can just leave this here over the weekend? You think it'll be ready Monday afternoon?"

"Sure, no problem. Yeah, should be no biggie getting it fixed Monday--well, if it's the tranny, it might take a couple of days."

Kevin went inside with the man, gave him his keys and phone number, then walked over to the college student's car.

"I really appreciate this, guy," Kevin said to the student as he opened the passenger door and got in.

"Hey, after what you did this season, it's *we* who should be thanking *you*! Oh, by the way, I'm Ryan, and these are my friends: Curt and Sparrow." Ryan shook Kevin's hand and gestured to a tall, lanky student sitting opposite a medium-sized, freckle-faced young man.

"Nice to meet you, Curt and uh, was that '*Sparrow*'?"

"Yeah, my real name's George, but most everyone calls me 'Sparrow.'"

"Boy, I'd hate to meet up with you in a dark alley," said Kevin with a smile.

"I tend to eat a lot of health food, you know, seeds and nuts--bird food--hence the name 'Sparrow.'"

"Gotcha."

Ryan started the car and drove out of the parking lot, then headed north on the Interstate.

"I just have one question for you," said Sparrow from the backseat. "In the third quarter, when it was fourth-and-one from their forty-yard line, why didn't you guys go for it? I mean, it was *their* forty-yard line."

"I *did* want to go for it," said Kevin, turning in his seat to look back at Sparrow. "Coach Panaski said to punt, so we did."

"Well, if we hadn't won, I'm sure more than one sportswriter would have picked up on that."

"Hindsight's twenty-twenty as they say," said Ryan.

"I would have to concur with that," agreed Kevin, nodding his head. "So, anyway, where you dudes headed? Road trip or do your folks live in Cleveland?"

No one said anything for a few seconds. Finally, Curt blurted out, "Ever heard of Elyria?"

"Yeah," said Kevin. "It's not far from my parents' house in Rocky River. What's in Elyria?"

Again there was a pause before Curt said: "The Blessed Mother's appearing there."

"*Supposedly* appearing there," cautioned Ryan. He turned toward Kevin. "Curt and Sparrow are trying to convince me that something's going on there, so I said I'd come up with them to see what's going on."

"So you guys are Catholics, huh?" asked Kevin.

"Guilty as charged," said Sparrow.

"So am I," said Kevin.

"No kiddin', huh?" said Ryan.   "I never would have guessed...well, I mean--"

Kevin gave a short laugh. "Is that a compliment or insult?"

"Hey, wherever there're four good Catholics, there's always a bingo game," chimed in Curt.

"All right, enough Catholic bashing for now," said Sparrow.

"You really think the Blessed Mother's appearing there?" asked Kevin.

"Well, *we* do," said Curt, motioning to Sparrow. "You're up front with the unbeliever."

"The Chinese allow this type of stuff?" asked Kevin. "I would think that would be the first thing they'd shut down."

"Actually, they don't even know we're going," said Ryan.

"So how'd you get your gas, you know, with rationing and all?"

"I had to tell them we were going to the Rock and Roll Hall of Fame. They had no problem with that--stinking Chinese jerks!"

"What's the deal with them anyway? It's like they're not really here, but they're everywhere," said Sparrow.

"You know, it's funny," said Kevin. "It sounds just like Russia. Last quarter I was reading about the Bolshevik Revolution in Russia in October, 1917. The same thing happened there. The commonly held view of the storming of the Winter Palace is so much fiction. The Commies took over the city of Petrograd, or Leningrad, in the middle of the night, and by morning their conquest was complete. The average Russian citizen didn't even know anything out of the ordinary had occurred. The opera and the theaters and restaurants remained open that evening. The total casualties were three officer cadets wounded. The real trouble didn't begin until a few weeks later."

"In other words," said Sparrow, "we've got about a month before all Hell breaks loose."

"Who knows?" replied Kevin. "What do you say, Curt: is it going to get better or worse?"

"Well, Mary said--" began Curt.

Sparrow interrupted him: "We should just beat 'em all up! Heck, there's only one or two at each gas station. I haven't seen many of them in one place, together."

"Someone tried that over in Indiana, I heard on the radio," said Curt. "The Chinese guy mowed 'em down before they had a chance.

Something like eight guys were killed. These Chinese guys don't have much conscience, Sparrow. They're members of that supposedly forgotten race--*Communists*--these guys believe Chinese domination-- or Communist domination--of the world is inevitable."

"What were you saying, Curt?" asked Kevin. "About something 'Mary' said? You mean 'the Blessed Mother'?"

"Right. Mary said that the Warning will come when things are at their worst."

"The Warning," said Kevin matter-of-factly. "I think I'm missing something."

"Wait a minute," said Sparrow. "You know about the Warning?"

"I know about the 'two-minute warning' in NFL games."

"The Warning is basically a worldwide illumination of everyone's consciences."

"You've seriously never heard of any of this?" asked Sparrow.

"Hey, I barely go to Mass every Sunday, bud," said Kevin, giving Sparrow a sideways glance. "I'm sort of a 'C.O.I.N. -- Catholic Only in Name.'" He turned around to look at Curt. "What, Mary's appearing at the Rock and Roll Hall of Fame?"

"Elyria, my friend," said Sparrow. "Mary and Jesus are appearing there tonight! You should come with us!"

"Hey," said Kevin, "now I appreciate the ride, but I'm just your normal quasi-Catholic. I didn't sign up for any apparition parties. I've got my parents waiting for me, sorry."

"Let the dead bury their dead," deadpanned Curt from the backseat.

"Huh?" said Kevin and Ryan simultaneously.

"Obscure Biblical quote," said Curt.

"Oh, yeah," said Kevin, "speaking of Biblical quotes, the words at Mass are from the Bible, right?"

"Well, *some* of the words," said Curt slowly. "Which part are you talking about?"

"Just something I heard last Sunday at Saint Christopher's. The words didn't sound right--you know--'This is My Body,' 'This is My Blood'?"

"Whaddya mean, they didn't 'sound right'?" asked Sparrow.

"It seemed like he said 'something something *of* My Body, and then--I *do* remember this exactly--he said 'This is a *symbol* of my Blood.'"

Both Curt and Sparrow were shaking their heads in the back seat. "I was afraid of this type of thing starting to happen," said Curt. "Up till now, I've only heard rumors, but it looks like they're true. Apparently, the Chinese are trying to set up--"

"Yeah!" said Kevin excitedly. "Oh, sorry to interrupt--but now I remember! I saw these four Chinese dudes come into the church right before the long prayer part, and then they left right afterwards too."

"Bad news, man," said Sparrow. "Just like you predicted, Curt."

"Well, I actually first heard about it on a website," said Curt. The Chinese are trying to set up a national, 'patriotic' Catholic Church here in the US, just like they have a fake Catholic Church over in China."

"So you mean I really didn't receive the Body of Christ last Sunday?" asked Kevin. "The Eucharistic Minister said the same thing when he gave me the Host, you know: 'The Body of Christ.' And I said 'Amen.'"

"I'm afraid you didn't," said Curt. "It was an invalid consecration."

"Well that's a crock of spit. Where can I go to Mass now?" asked Kevin.

Sparrow let out a laugh. "Looks like you're up--"

"--not a good choice of words," said Curt, holding up his hand to Sparrow. "Kevin, we'll have to keep in touch. It looks like there's going to be only a few Catholic churches in town that will have valid Masses for the time being."

"Which is all the more reason to come to the apparition tonight," said Sparrow. Whaddya say, Kevin? Feel like experiencing a little of the 'Hour of Power'?"

"You got the wrong guy, fellas. You go on and do your thing. I've got plenty of other things to hold my attention. I'll be satisfied with just going to Mass right now." The quartet fell silent for awhile as they watched the night-shrouded Ohio countryside roll by.

Twenty minutes later, as they were going down the turnpike, they passed over Wooster Road. Kevin looked over at Ryan. "Wasn't that the turnoff for Rocky River?"

"Hmm," said Ryan, turning to look back at Curt, "was that the turnoff for Rocky River, Curt? I've never been there."

Curt looked over at Sparrow. "You've been there, haven't you? Was that the turnoff?"

"Hey, *I've* been there!" said Kevin in a loud voice. "Yes, that was the turnoff for Rocky River, and *yes*, you should've turned off there."

"Gee," said Sparrow, "you know how these turnpikes are. There aren't that many exits."

"Well, you can take the next exit and backtrack, please" said Kevin.

"But then we'll be late for the apparition," said Sparrow. "We can't be late for the *apparition.*"

"Ryan," pleaded Kevin, "you're on *my* side, right? You'll take me home now, right?"

"I'm just as new at this as you are. What do ya' say, Curt? Will we be late?"

Curt glanced at his watch. "Shoot, it's eleven now, we really don't have any time to lose."

"Aw, c'mon, guys!" moaned Kevin. "This is all a setup! You're just trying to rope me into this Mary stuff of yours."

"No, honest," said Ryan. "I was daydreaming back there. I didn't mean to miss that exit."

Kevin looked over at Ryan. "Hey, how 'bout you drop off Curt and Sparrow, take me home, and then come back?"

"Then *you'll* miss the apparition!" Sparrow said to Ryan. "You can't do *that!*"

Curt leaned forward and spoke to Kevin. "Look, Kevin, sorry for the mix-up. Could you possibly stay for the apparition and go home afterwards?"

"But my parents are expecting me home *now*. I'm already a little overdue."

"There's a cell phone in the glove compartment," offered Ryan. "You could call them up."

Kevin shook his head, looked at Ryan, then back at Curt, then out the window. He let out a short gasp and opened the glove compartment. "All right, all right. Looks like I'm not going to win this one."

"One of us! One of us!" Sparrow softly chanted in the back.

A half hour later, the quartet was standing in a field off of Butternut Ridge Road awaiting midnight, the hour at which Mary and Jesus were supposed to appear.

"Where is she?" Kevin asked Curt.

"Not till midnight.   Mary and Jesus will both be here at midnight."

"How long has this been going on?"

"The visionary first started getting apparitions in 1985."

"Who is the person who gets the apparitions?"

"Her name is Maureen Sweeney-Kyle. She's a sixty-ish mother of four grown children and many grandchildren.   Sometimes Mary appears, sometimes Jesus. I think sometimes even Saint Thomas Aquinas appears."

"I seem to remember hearing that name before...refresh my memory," said Kevin.

"He was a Dominican priest that lived back in the 13th Century. He wrote a lot about theology and that type of stuff. His works are still used a lot in seminaries."

"Dominican," repeated Kevin. "I think I've heard of that...that's referring to Saint Dominic, right?"

"Right. He lived in, uhh, I think it was the 12th or 13th Century-- really holy, and smart, guy."

"What does Saint Thomas say when--"

Just then a hush fell on the crowd and people began dropping to their knees. Kevin followed suit and looked up toward the front of the crowd where the seer was also on her knees.

"I don't see anything," whispered Kevin to Curt.

"Look over there, to the right," said Curt in a low voice, pointing with his finger.

"What am I looking for?" asked Kevin.

Sparrow tapped Kevin on the shoulder and whispered: "Look at the *big* picture."

"Whaa?" Kevin searched the sky, which was completely clear, but saw nothing out of the ordinary. But then, he *did* notice something: very faintly he saw the outline of a woman wearing a blue gown with her hair covered by a veil.

"Far out..." he said as he took it in. The image looked to be about two stories high and of a sky blue color. It rested just above the crowd along the tree line at the edge of the field of pilgrims.

"Oh, now I see it," said Ryan, kneeling behind Kevin.

"Aren't you glad we missed that turnoff?" Sparrow whispered, patting Kevin on the shoulder.

"Awesome," murmured Kevin. "Yeah, thanks..."

The crowd stayed on their knees as the visionary received the message from the Virgin. After about five minutes, Maria stood up and gave the tape recorder into which she had been relaying the message to her husband. The crowd then also rose to their feet and excited snatches of conversation could be heard rippling through the ranks.

"Where's she going?" asked Kevin. "What about the message? I wanna hear the message!"

"Relax, big guy!" smiled Sparrow as he put his arm around Kevin's shoulders. "Her husband will transcribe the message and then the emcee will read it to us."

"Who's the emcee?"

"I really don't know. Usually some woman just reads the message. There's a priest up there too. He'll review the message before it's read, just to make sure it's doctrinally sound."

The four young men were each lost in his own thoughts for a few minutes. They stood up and stomped their feet and rubbed their hands together to ward off the February cold.

A swell of voices coming from the front of the crowd alerted all to the imminent reading of the latest message from Heaven. The emcee approached the microphone and looked down at the single page of text in her hand.

"My people…if I could have your attention. I would like to read Our Lady's message which Maria has just received. Before I begin, Maria asked me to tell you that the Blessed Mother stressed that the time draws near for all of her messages to reach fulfillment. Here, then, is tonight's message from Our Lady: 'Praise be to Jesus. My daughter, those who are here tonight must realize that I personally wanted them here. It is their responsibility to take the Holy Love that my Son and I offer them and spread it to those with whom they come into contact from now on. God gives his grace to each one to carry out his purpose in life. But each one should know that God may be asking *more* of him than he is currently doing. It is by reflecting on the Love of our United Hearts that my children will know what God wants of them. Be generous with God. The time for my messages to reach their fulfillment is near, *very* near. Remember what my special son, Paul, said: 'Pray always, and do not lose heart.'" The woman folded the paper and put it in her coat pocket. "Thank all of you for coming tonight, and next time, please bring a friend or two with you. The more people who receive the graces offered by Our Lord and Our Lady, the better." The woman stepped away from the microphone and walked over to a group of pilgrims standing by the prayer chapel.

"What is this about 'fulfillment of my messages'?" asked Kevin.

"Remember on the way here, I talked about 'the Warning'? asked Curt.

"Yeah, you know," said Sparrow enthusiastically, "The Warning, The Miracle, The Chastisement!?"

"Uhh, I haven't exactly seen this stuff on the nightly news, guys. What is the Warning and that other stuff?"

"Like I said earlier," began Curt, "the Warning is going to be a worldwide event. Everyone will see their souls as God sees them-- everyone at the same time, no matter what they're doing. This will be followed by a Miracle, at Garabandal. Then will come the Chastisement."

"'Chastisement' doesn't sound like a good thing," said Kevin.

"Well, it depends on how the world responds to the Miracle," said Curt.

"Yeah," said Sparrow, "if everyone shapes up after the Miracle, it might not happen at all--or it might be really mild."

"Actually, Mary said the Chastisement can no longer be avoided," said Curt. "It can only be lessened in severity."

"And you guys really *believe* all this stuff," stated Kevin.

"I'm on the fringe myself," said Ryan. "But after seeing that outline of the Blessed Mother, I might be coming around."

"You're golden!" said Sparrow, giving Ryan a slap on the back. "See, aren't you glad you made the trip?"

"The key word is 'fringe,' remember," replied Ryan. "I've got plenty to think about."

"That's another thing," said Kevin. "What was that part of the message tonight about 'more'?"

"More *what*?" asked Sparrow.

"Just the way she said 'more.' She said God may be asking 'more' of each of us."

"Care to be a little more specific?"

"That word just keeps bouncing around in my head," said Kevin.

"Well, fine! Then why don't you do *more*?" asked Sparrow.

"Like what?"

"Not to get all personal in public," said Curt, "but, uh, do you go to Mass every Sunday?"

"I try to go," said Kevin sheepishly, "but sometimes other things get in the way." He shook his head and scratched his shoulder. "I'm a little confused right now anyway."

"Who isn't with these Chinese breathing down our necks," said Sparrow.

"I just broke up with my girlfriend," Kevin blurted out. "I'd been dating her for *two and a half years!*"

"Ouch," said Ryan.

"'Ouch' is right," said Kevin. "Now I hear the Blessed Mother saying we should do 'more' for God. Like I'm not already confused enough."

"Well, for starters you could go to Mass every Sunday," said Curt. "It also wouldn't hurt to go to Confession, if you haven't been in awhile."

"Yeah," said Kevin, nodding his head, "I just mean the big picture--what I'm going to do when I graduate. 'More'...what does that mean?"

"There's more 'more' out there," joked Sparrow.

"Hey, I don't know about all you philosophers, but I'm getting a mite bit cold out here," said Ryan. "Why don't we head back to the car, now that the party's over?"

A few muffled grunts of approval and the four of them trudged across the frozen ground to the parking area. After waiting a few minutes for the majority of the cars to leave, Ryan pulled out onto Butternut Ridge Road, then onto Route 83 and headed north.

"Rocky River, right?" Ryan asked Kevin.

Kevin had been staring out the passenger window, lost in thought. After a moment's hesitation, he turned his head to look at Ryan. "Yeah, right. Just get on Route 57 and that'll take you close to my parents' house."

Curt leaned forward and handed Kevin a piece of paper and pen. "Here, Kevin, write down your e-mail address, I'd like to stay in touch."

"Good idea!" said Kevin. "I'd like to get yours as well."

"Maybe we can all get together for lunch on campus one of these days," said Sparrow.

"Yeah, I'll let you know," said Kevin, handing the pen back to Curt. "I might have a few more questions for all of you."

Following Kevin's directions, Ryan stopped in front of a modest house near the center of Rocky River.

"Thanks for the lift, guys--let's stay in touch!" said Kevin as he opened the door.

"You can get to your car all right on Monday?" asked Ryan.

"Oh, yeah, no problem. I'm sure my Dad can give me a lift."

Sparrow and Curt added their farewells and watched as Kevin walked to the door of his parents' house. Once he saw Kevin enter, Ryan drove off.

"Not bad, huh guys?" asked Sparrow. "Nothing like snaggin' the star quarterback of the National Champ OSU Buckeyes!" He said the last part in his trademark shrill voice.

"Truly an awesome dude!" agreed Curt. "I wonder if he believed anything we said."

"Hey, dudes," said Ryan. "That apparition thing was *real*. I mean, it wasn't like I was dreaming that whole thing. I saw an outline of Mary--it must have been twenty feet tall. He said he saw it too. I for one think we might be hearing from him."

"Oh, so 'Mr. Darwin' finally sees the light," teased Sparrow. "Are you 'one of us' now?"

"Now don't jump to conclusions," protested Ryan. "Just because I believe the Blessed Mother might be appearing in Elyria, Ohio doesn't mean I've changed my views on what happened on the Galapagos Islands."

"Darwin gets religion," concluded Sparrow.

"Sorry to interrupt the Scopes Monkey Trial," said Curt, "but, seriously, did you hear what Mary said about the time frame tonight?"

"Right, I meant to ask you about that," said Sparrow. "'My messages are about to be fulfilled.' Something like that."

"But it seems she always says that type of thing," said Ryan. "I remember you gave me something from that Father Gobbi guy back in the 90s and there were ominous sounds way back then."

"True, true," said Curt. "Only didn't she say something like '*very* near'? That 'very' word has me a little concerned."

"Well, that basically means the Warning is near, right?" asked Sparrow.

"I suppose," said Curt. "The kickoff of this game is the Warning, I guess."

"Any chance there could be a 'warning' for the Warning?"

asked Ryan.

"Wouldn't that be the berries!" said Sparrow.

"The 'berries'?" mimicked Ryan. "What century did you come from?"

"It's just an expression my grandfather likes to use. I guess it was hip when he was a kid."

"But, that would be cool when you think about it," said Curt. "A warning for the Warning. Sort of like a cop letting you off with a warning instead of giving you a traffic ticket."

"Sort of," said Sparrow, "but how do you think God would give us a warning for the Warning?"

"What, are we some privileged few who have the inside scoop on what God's up to?" asked Ryan.

"Maybe that *was* the 'warning for the Warning,'" said Curt.

"You mean what Mary said tonight in her message?" asked Sparrow.

"I guess we're the privileged few," said Ryan.

"It has to happen one of these days, I suppose," said Curt.

"Is there any time frame for the Warning?" asked Ryan.

"The only thing that we know is that the Warning has to happen within the lifetimes of the Garabandal visionaries," said Curt.

"And how old are they?" asked Ryan.

"I think they're in their fifties," said Curt.

"Hmm," said Ryan. "The clock is definitely ticking."

"Speaking of the clock, you guys goin' to the game tomorrow?" asked Sparrow.

"What does that have to do with the clock?" asked Ryan.

"Doesn't a basketball game use a clock?" asked Sparrow.

"Who we playing?" asked Ryan.

"Would anyone care to answer a question instead of asking one?" asked Curt.

"You talkin' to me?" asked Sparrow.

****

The mechanics at OSU airport had told Dexter it would take a few weeks before his airplane could fly again, so Dexter resorted to the commercial airlines for his business trips. He had just been to Boston to meet with an MIT professor who was an expert in tactile feedback control and made it to the Boston airport just in time to catch the last direct flight home to Columbus. Although he had planned to come home yesterday, Friday, he ended up having to stay an extra day to consult a bit more with the professor. Dexter was thinking of some of the advice the MIT don had given him as the plane started its final approach into Columbus.

"Good evening, this is your captain speaking. On behalf of Sunny Airlines, your crew would like to welcome you to Columbus where the temperature is a tolerable 38 degrees under clear skies. I'm happy to report that the local time is 8:29 PM which means we are arriving approximately 6 minutes ahead-----"

Why doesn't he finish his spiel? thought Dexter. *And why are the cabin lights dimming?* It might have been the glint of light off a nearby window, or maybe it was a car headlight, but something on the ground caught Dexter's eye. When he quickly swiveled his head to look out the airliner window, Dexter thought he'd lost his mind...*the airplane was not moving!* He could see the ground below and it definitely was not "moving" past the window. No, they weren't yet on the ground---yet the whole airplane was stopped---in midair! There was an eerie silence as well, Dexter realized. *The engines must have stopped!* The more he looked out the window, the more horrified he became! He could see out a few miles since the jet was still up several thousand feet. The lights down in the streets of Columbus were winking out, section by section. As a matter of fact, Dexter could see that the cars down below were also stopped. It was as if the whole area, including the sky, was having a huge power failure.

But then it started.

From somewhere in his past Dexter had heard about the experience of those who had seemingly died and then come back to life: the long tunnel with a blinding light at the end; some had even heard a benevolent voice calling to them from the void. Well, much as he tried to deny it, something similar was happening to Dexter now. He felt like, well, he almost laughed at the term he invented, he felt like he was undergoing a--"soul scan." He knew from first-hand experience what it was like to have a CAT-scan, the only difference now being that, instead of his brain being revealed, his soul was being exposed. Various scenes from his past life swept in and out of his consciousness. He had no sense of those around him or of his location; all he was aware of was--it still sounded ridiculous--his soul. But it wasn't like a movie. There was no progression from past to present, like those near-death experiences he had heard about. He seemed to be viewing the present state of his being for it's innate worth, almost the way a jeweler might study a fine diamond. What he really didn't want to admit was that he felt like his "soul" was being viewed from above and from outside his body. It felt like some supernatural force was overcoming him.

But then the episode began to change. His emotions started undergoing a roller-coaster ride. One minute he was terrified when he saw how he viciously yelled at his father the first summer he was home from college and then the next minute he was briefly filled with peace when he saw the image of himself taking a homeless guy to breakfast when he was on vacation in London. He felt like his soul was being torn in two! The evil force was pulling on his left "arm," and the angelic force was pulling on his right "arm." Over and over he kept seeing, first, images of evil he had done, then images of good he had done.

How long is this going to go on? he asked himself. *I can't take any more of this! Help me!*

****

At the same time Thad had just picked up a fare in his car and was heading down Route 315. He no longer got calls from the Orange Cab radio room, since the Chinese could find him that way. *Then again,* he thought, *I suppose they already know my license plate number and could find me if they really wanted. Hmm, well, best to stay as far away from the beehive as I can.* He was able to do a little business from old customers who knew his cell phone number. He used his own car and thus could drive around unnoticed. He had just merged with the southbound traffic when time seemed to stand still. He became aware that the taxi was not moving, but neither were any of the other cars on the freeway! Before he could turn around to check on his passenger in the back seat, he looked up at the nearly full moon and--*Am I hallucinating?* he asked himself. The white disk of the moon was replaced by an image of the face of a beautiful woman in a blue veil. *I know who that is,* he told himself. But just as suddenly he began to see more images form within the disk of the moon. The time in his childhood when he had stolen money from his mother's purse; that bad magazine he had kept under his bed in his adolescent years; the indifference and rebelliousness he had shown to his father during college. Through it all Thad felt a deep burning in his heart. Each "vignette" he saw up in the moon seemed to thrust a spear deeper into his soul. *I never imagined I was that bad! I'm sorry, Lord!* Just when he thought he couldn't take it anymore, the pictures up in the sky changed to a softer hue, and a buoyant feeling overcame Thad. He saw the face of the priest up at Notre Dame to whom he had made his confession after his years away from that Sacrament; he giggled when saw the image of the hundreds of mission Rosaries he had made during his senior year in college. He even saw the faces of a few of the destitute children in Africa who had used those same Rosaries. Next appeared in the disk of the moon two of his friends he had brought back to the Sacraments a couple of years ago. In rapid succession, he saw all the times he had received Communion at daily and Sunday Mass in the last twenty years. Then the moon started to return to its normal white color, but not before Thad caught a glimpse of a woman, who was wearing a veil. *Is that a wedding veil, or the veil of a nun? Her face looks vaguely familiar.* Thad strained to see the details of the woman's countenance, but before he knew it, the picture faded out and Thad found himself suddenly thrust back into the present moment. Bam! All of a sudden he was back to driving down the freeway, going sixty miles an hour! He swerved to avoid the car in front of him, then decided to pull off to the side of the highway as several other cars beside him were doing. It was only then that he heard the sobs of the man in the rear seat. Thad turned to see a clean-cut middle-aged man holding his head in his hands and crying.

****

Kevin had just sat down in the living room with his parents and they were watching a rerun of Prison Break.

"What are you doing sitting here at home with your parents?" his Mom was asking him. "It's Saturday night! You should be out living it up!"

"Mom, Dad, have you heard of Elyria? I went there last night with these guys who gave me a ride home," said Kevin.

Kevin's parents exchanged looks, then his father said in a patronizing tone: "Kevin, don't tell us you're into *that* type of stuff. Yes, we've heard of that place and we aren't too impressed by it."

Kevin opened his mouth to reply when his eyes were inexorably drawn to the TV screen. *What is happening?* he asked himself. *Why is my life being played out on the TV?* With a mixture of horror and disbelief, he watched scenes from his childhood begin to unfold on the TV. He was no longer aware of the presence of his parents, or even that he was in their living room. His whole being was caught up in his autobiography. He felt a searing pain begin to develop in the pit of his stomach. There in front of him was portrayed all the times he had slept in on Sunday instead of going to Mass; a sharp pain shot through his eyes when he saw images of all the impure books, magazines, movies, and TV shows he had watched throughout his life. He felt an ache in his hands as he saw played out in front of him the time he had gotten into a fight in grade school with his one-time best friend. Next, his heart felt like it was being torn in two as he viewed the cruel games he had played with some of the girlfriends he had known. But at last he saw the same image of the Blessed Virgin which he had just seen last night at Elyria. Cool, soothing waves of beatitude filled his body. He felt a smile form on his lips. Just as the images faded from view, he thought he made out the image of a person--he couldn't tell if it was male or female--but it was kneeling in front of a, a, *what is that person kneeling in front of?* Kevin asked himself. *Who is that person?* Then just as suddenly he was aware that he was back in the living room with his parents.

Both his mother and father were staring off into space, a look of grief and confusion on their faces. Kevin remembered what Curt and Sparrow had said just last night. The phrase was crystal clear in Kevin's head: "a worldwide illumination of everyone's consciences." He slapped the couch with his hand.

"That was it!" he said to his parents. "That was the Warning!"

Gradually color returned to his Mom's and Dad's faces and they became aware of where they were. His Mom looked at Kevin, but said nothing.

"That was it!" he said again.

His Dad shook his head and focused his eyes on Kevin. "You can *explain* what just happened?"

"Yes, I'm telling you! I just heard about this yesterday from those guys that gave me a ride here! That was 'The Warning'! They told me it was going to happen pretty soon, and it did--hey, are you guys all right? That was really cosmic, huh?"

His mother silently rose from her chair and went up the stairs to the second floor.

"Wow! She must have really been hit hard!" said Kevin.

"Hmm," said his Dad, closing his eyes and leaning his head forward.

"Was it really that bad for you too?" asked Kevin.

His father grunted and slowly nodded his head.

"Oh, Dad! I have to tell you, it was bad for me, but then just when I didn't think I could take it anymore, I saw the most beautiful picture of the Blessed Virgin--it was the same thing I saw last night at Elyria! She made me feel *so* happy inside!" Kevin stopped abruptly when he saw a tear drop from one of his father's eyes. "Oh, Dad, I'm sorry--here, let me get you a tissue." Kevin jumped up from the couch and brought a facial tissue in from the dining room. "Here, Dad."

His father wiped his eyes and grabbed Kevin's arm. "Help me up, son," his father said. "Here, give me a hug." The two embraced and then sat down together on the couch. "I want to apologize for all the bad examples I've given you over the years, Kevin--"

"I understand, Dad...I'm sorry for all the trouble I've caused you over the years."

"Kevin, I'm sorry if I've pushed you too hard--with football and all. Maybe I was trying too hard to live my dreams through you."

"That's fine, Dad. We've all got a lot of things to change now."

"I can tell you right now where I'm headed tomorrow afternoon," said his Dad. "Straight down to Father Begosi for confession."

"Me too!" said Kevin's mother, who had just come down from the upstairs unnoticed. She walked toward them, started crying, and buried her head in her husband's shoulder. "I never knew...that...God was so...*offended*...by what I've done in my life!"

"Hey, I think it's time we *all* went to Confession tomorrow," said Kevin's Dad.

"Shoot, I haven't been since I was in eighth grade," admitted Kevin.

"It's been twenty years for me," said his father.

"Same here," said his mother, taking the tissue that Kevin offered her.

Kevin suggested they say the Rosary together and the three knelt down and began to recite the beads.

****

"Dan, I know how you must be feeling...I can explain what just happened," Thad said gently to his fare in the rear seat of his "taxi."

"I'm...so...sorry, God!" the man said between breaths of air.

"Dan, you see, that was what is known as 'The Warning.' It happened to everyone around the world at the same time. You saw your sins just like everyone else."

"I never...realized...I was so...so...*evil*. You don't have a facial tissue, do you?" he asked Thad.

"Uh, let's see." Thad rummaged through his briefcase and handed Dan a paper towel. "This is the best I can come up with."

"Thank you," he said, taking the paper with a trembling hand. "What did you say about a 'Warning'? Did the same thing happen to you? How can you be so calm? Am I the only one who just went nuts or something?"

"Oh, no, sir. See? Look!" said Thad, pointing out the front windshield. "See all those other cars on the side of the road? The same thing happened to them. See that woman leaning against the side of her car? Looks like she's crying too."

The man gazed out the window while wiping his eyes with the paper towel. "What are you saying? You mean you *knew* this was going to happen?"

"Yeah--here, let me show you." Thad reached into the open briefcase again, pulled out a brochure on Garabandal, and handed it to the man. "This has been predicted by various mystics for years and years."

"Huh," said the man, skimming over the brochure. "Where is Garabandal? Oh--Spain...huh." He wiped his eyes again, and handed the brochure back to Thad.

"Oh, no, please!" said Thad. "You can keep it, by all means! I've got plenty more where that came from."

"Well, thanks. I would like to learn more about this." Dan stuffed the pamphlet in his coat pocket. "I suppose everyone is going to remember what they were doing when *this* happened, huh?"

"You're right on target--hey! Let's see what the radio says!" Thad turned on the radio and tuned to the local news station.

"...unknown at this point," the announcer was saying. "We have unconfirmed reports of several accidents around town, but we repeat: we do *not* know what has happened. Stay tuned to this station for all the latest--" Thad turned the radio off and turned to face Dan. "They don't have a clue what's going on. Man, I wish those idiotic Chinese hadn't shut down Saint Gabriel Radio!" Thad grabbed a stack of brochures and opened his door. "Dan, excuse me for a minute; I'm going to give some of these pamphlets to these other people stopped along the road." He sprang out of the car and gave a small stack to the occupants of four cars stopped near them. On reentering the car, he picked up another stack and held them out to Dan. "Why don't you take a few of these pamphlets and spread the word. Whaddya say?"

"Whaa, uh..." stammered Dan, rubbing his nose. "I wouldn't know what to tell people, I, I--why don't you keep them for your passengers?"

"Hey, I've got plenty of these to go around. You saw that those other people took them from me just now. C'mon, whaddya say?" Thad gave the brochures a shake with his hand.

"Okaayy, I guess," said Dan, reluctantly taking the pamphlets.

"So, where do you want to go?" asked Thad, turning to face the front and putting the car into gear. "Still want to go to the Arena District?"

"Oh, boy--whew! Not after that," said Dan, shaking his head. "You might as well take me home--where you picked me up. I'm in no mood to party tonight after this."

"I can understand." Thad got off at the next exit, got back on the highway heading north and dropped Dan off at his house.

****

Snap! All of a sudden the ground outside the plane window was rushing up and Dexter was conscious of his surroundings again. The plane began a series of abrupt movements, but within five seconds Dexter could hear the engines spooling up and the plane's path smoothed out. *The pilots must have "blacked out" or whatever too,* thought Dexter. The plane began to gain altitude. *Looks like he's doing a "go-around."* He stared at the passengers around him: no one said a single word. Out of habit, he glanced at his watch--8:45 PM. *When had it started? What had the pilot been saying? Something about the weather and being ahead of schedule...maybe I'll ask the man sitting next to me. But what would I say? 'Excuse me, what time was it when I noticed that the airplane had stopped flying?' Maybe I've hallucinated the whole thing.* But as Dexter looked around, he saw that he wasn't the only one who appeared to be discombobulated. The lady in front of him was holding her head in her hands, crying in long sobs. The elderly man two seats over stared straight ahead, oblivious to his surroundings. The amazing thing was that no one was talking. Even after the plane landed and hooked up to the jet way, the silence was palpable. People gathered their carry-on luggage and exited. Even the pilots and stewardesses failed to give their customary "adieu" at the doorway. The awful truth nagged at the edges of Dexter's conscience: he wasn't the only one who had "blacked out." Could it be possible that everyone on the plane had experienced what he had?

Only when he stepped off the jetway and into the terminal was he certain that his experience was bigger than he ever imagined. It was zombie-ville! No one was moving! It reminded him of those pantomime plays he had seen at the Palace Theater once. Someone had snapped a picture but forgot to tell everyone they could move on. He had never "heard" such silence before. He just couldn't get over it. *Was this a monastery?*

The noise of the deplaning passengers did finally start to have an effect on the people in the terminal. Blank arrival/departure screens began to glow again. Out the window Dexter could see the city lights begin to blink on as well. Slowly, the crowd around him showed signs of life. It reminded him of the behavior of a crowd that had just walked out of a sobering movie on a Saturday afternoon: lost in thought, still not fully ready to accept reality outside the darkness of the theater. As he walked past the Green Arrow Bar & Grill, he noticed the TV monitors were displaying the rainbow stripes indicating a loss of signal at the station. *So it hit them too*, mused Dexter--*whatever* it *was*. After an annoying wait for his luggage at the baggage claim, Dexter had little trouble locating his Dodge Charger in the labyrinthine parking lot.

The drive home to Grandview confirmed Dexter's earlier fears: It *had* hit the whole city. Traffic lights had switched to their fail-safe, blinking-red/yellow operation. The streetlights on a number of roads were out. Ambulances and police cars were out in force, sirens wailing. After parking the Charger in the garage, he switched on the TV in the living room. He was about to sort through all the mail that had accumulated during his business trip, when the familiar figure of the mayor popped onto the TV screen. "At this point," said the mayor, "we're not sure what happened. Yes, I experienced a blackout myself, but I don't care to share any details. All we know for sure is that several substations around the area experienced an unexplained shutdown for about 15 minutes. There are unconfirmed reports that some cars stalled as well."

The mayor continued to comment on the plethora of medical emergencies around the city, but Dexter was no longer listening. He sat on the couch and found himself staring off into space. It was time, he thought, to face the facts. He, and from what he could tell, many others, had experienced an extra-ordinary phenomenon. Wait, who was he kidding, *it* had been a----no, he still didn't want to admit it----a *supernatural* phenomenon. He had been trying to mask his conscience ever since he exited the plane, but he found it increasingly difficult to squelch the little voice inside him. Dexter mused about what had happened: everyone had seen their souls from an "out of body" viewpoint. He still couldn't fully explain it. The whole "soul-scan" had been like one of those thermo-graphic satellite pictures he often saw in National Geographic magazines wherein a city was displayed as a map of reddish-hot areas mixed with cooler blue spots. The only difference was that certain aspects of his life were displayed in those 15 eerie minutes. Dexter found he had a near-perfect memory of the whole episode. Certain experiences, relationships---even books and TV shows---he recalled, were cast in a darker light than others. Only one or two people in his present life were at all highlighted, sort of a yellowish-white hue. *Maybe this is about all that stuff Thad and Father*

Rankin have been talking about? he wondered. *What was that term they used? "The Conditioning?" "The Appraisal?" I'll have to ask them about it.*

"The Columbus Zoohoo! The Columbus Zoohoo!" The familiar commercial jingle broke Dexter's train of thought. As he rose from the couch to resume sorting through his mail, he shut off the TV and went to bed.

The next morning, on his way to work, while still trying to figure out what had happened the previous evening, Dexter got a call on his cell phone.

"Is this Dexter Griffith?" said the voice on the other end of the line.

"Yes, may I ask who this is?"

"Actually, you may not. You can't always call the shots, Mr. Big Shot. You see, I spoke to you earlier and I explained myself then."

Dexter pulled the cell phone away from his ear and looked at the caller I.D. "Private Number," it read. "Shoot!" he said, under his breath.

"Do you think we're *that* stupid Grobotics boy? We have ways of masking our identity."

"What do you want!?" shouted Dexter.

"We just wondered if you've been flying recently. We were so sorry to hear of your little mishap with your Cessna."

"Did *you* do that? Listen, asshole, I'll report you to the FAA!"

"Come now, Dexter! Where would that have gotten us? Where's the ROI on that? A dead CEO and a wrecked airplane. We're a little more interested in your stock portfolio--when you take Grobotics public, I think we might just want a slice of the pie."

"Who says I'm going to--no! Look! I can trace these calls if I want! Stay away from me or I'll get the police on you!" Dexter pressed the 'End' key and tossed the phone on the seat next to him. *What do those guys want?* he thought. *They didn't cause the plane crash, did they? No, I don't think so. My stock portfolio? Huh? How can they transfer that? Maybe my bullion...my gold bullion? Could they know about that? Or do they know about the stuff Thad has at the farm? I've told only two people that I know of...?*

Dexter made a mental note to consider moving his precious metals out of his safe deposit box at the bank downtown. Most people invested in T-bills, stocks, and bonds. Dexter, though, ever since he was eleven years old, had a penchant for keeping about a quarter of his net worth in a safe in downtown Columbus, as well as the stash out at the farm. Something about the feel of a ten-ounce bar of gold in his hands gave him goose bumps. He could behold ten million dollars in one glance, in five cubic feet. Dexter's father had obtained special permission for Dexter to store such a large quantity of gold from the governor of Ohio himself. But Dexter was unsure to where he would move so much gold. *It was probably only a matter of time before the Chinese nationalized it anyway. Maybe I'm just overreacting. After all, I've been in the paper only a few times, right? Hmm, something to think about.*

Dexter turned into the Grobotics parking lot and maneuvered his car into a spot, noticing that he was the first to arrive that morning. *I must not have been the only one "spooked" by yesterday's event.* Dexter unlocked the front door of the building and walked into his office. He sat at his desk and called Father Rankin on the phone. After the secretary answered he was put through to the priest.

"Father Rankin, was that the Warning--you know, what happened last night?"

"I'd have to say yes; I don't see what else it could have been."

"So what do I do now?"

"Uhh," said Father Rankin, "what did you see during the Warning?"

"A lot of scary stuff, what about you?"

"Well, suffice it to say, I went directly to Confession after it ended."

"*Priests* go to Confession too?"

"You better believe it, my friend. I saw some *really* scary stuff that I wanted to get rid of. You see, priests have more responsibility for souls, so I saw some large dark spots on my soul."

"And you simply go to Confession and it's all taken care of?" asked Dexter.

"Well, yeah, the sins are forgiven, but now I'm going to be doing some major penance to repare for those sins."

"Such as?"

"Oh, fasting, mainly. I might give up my favorite food for awhile. Sleeping on the floor more often."

"We need to talk big time, Father. Can I come in this afternoon?"

"I'll see what I can do. I know I have to--oh, just a second, Dexter." Father Rankin listened to his secretary for a moment, then came back on the phone. "Woo-boy," he said. "Dexter, it looks like it's beginning. I just got notice that there are about two hundred people over in the church right now, asking for a priest for Confession. I'll call you when I have time to see you...I might be busy for a bit."

"All right, Father. Good luck."

"Thank you. Goodbye."

"Goodbye."

****

"Four-fifty-three!" said the athletic trainer as Kevin sped over the line marking the end of the forty-yard dash. "Not too shabby, Conaway! Let's try it one more time--you can do better than that."

The NFL combine had been the best and worst of times so far for Kevin. He enjoyed rubbing elbows with the "crème de la crème" of college football here in Indianapolis, but the schedule was brutal. It had taken him, as well as the rest of the world, a few days to recover from the Warning. As soon as he picked up his car from the garage on Monday, he drove straight to Lucas Oil Stadium here in the capital of Indiana. The combine had started Tuesday with an examination by a doctor, followed by a cybex test, which measured the strength in his legs, to make sure one wasn't stronger than the other. This was followed by an orientation, and finally interviews with coaches and scouts. Wednesday Kevin took a urinalysis test, was given a complete body physical, had a video interview, performed weight-room strength tests, and then the infamous "Wonderlic Test," which teams use to judge a player's natural competitiveness and desire to play. On Thursday, there was another psychological test, even more detailed and complex than the Wonderlic. Finally, today, Friday, Kevin was going through the main event of the combine, the on-field workouts.

Kevin had eventually recovered from the Warning, but he couldn't figure out how it didn't seem to have the slightest effect on his fellow athletes. The few times he did try to gently inquire about it with some of the guys, he was usually quickly rebuffed. He finally gave up and only talked "shop" with his colleagues, of which there were plenty to go around, since Ohio State had sent a mind-boggling twenty-three players to Indianapolis that year. The next closest school was Miami, with twelve players sent to the combine.

"What did Erickson get?" asked Kevin as he turned around and jogged back to the trainer.

"Four-five -oh. Might want to turn it up just a notch, bud."

"Easy for you to say, Mitch," chuckled Kevin.

"I just work here," said Mitch, the athletic trainer. "I don't provide the sympathy cards too."

Kevin walked back to the start of the sprint course, taking his place at the end of the line of other players who, like him, were giving their all to impress these pro-football coaches, hoping to play on Sundays in the upcoming autumn.

I wonder if there will be any football this fall, Kevin thought to himself. He stepped out of line to grab the towel that he had left lying on a nearby bench. *Weren't any of these guys affected by the Warning?* He wiped the sweat from his face, replaced the towel on the bench and stood back in line. *No one seems to care in the slightest!* Kevin studied the faces of the two guys chitchatting in front of him. *Is there any remorse in their faces? Any guilt showing through their complacent eyes? Hmm, I guess, whatever they're feeling, they're not going to let their future employers here suspect anything in the slightest.*

"Yo, how'd ya do in the forty?" asked Chad, walking up to Kevin. Although Chad, a tight end, would normally have worked out separately, by a scheduling quirk, he had ended up doing the forty-yard dashes with his beloved quarterback.

"My best so far is four-five-three," said Kevin, with a look of chagrin.

"Not bad, bro," said Chad cheerfully. "Don't get too down on yourself."

"Erickson got four-five-oh."

"So, kick it up a bit on your next try."

"Right--what did you get, Chad?"

"My best is four-six-five."

"Not too shabby."

Chad and Kevin talked a little more while waiting their turns.

By mid-afternoon the combine was completed for the quarterbacks and they began to take their leave. Kevin was one of the last out as he had talked at length with one of the strength coaches about modifying his workouts in the coming weeks. He walked out to the nearly empty parking lot, climbed into his car and turned the key-- and nothing happened.

"Dog-gone it!" he cried, slapping the dashboard with his hand. "Not again! This is the *second* time in *one* week!" *Can't wait to get that signing bonus we were talking about, he* thought to himself. *I'll dump this junker and get a Hummer.*

Fortunately, he had his cell phone in the glove compartment. He called information and soon was connected to a tow truck company. The wrecker arrived fifteen minutes later and the driver took Kevin and his car to a downtown auto repair garage, where he learned he would need a new starter.

"Think you can fix it today?" Kevin asked the mechanic. "I'm from out of town and I need to get home this evening."

"Yeah, we can do that. Come back around five and you'll be all set."

Kevin handed his keys to the mechanic and asked him for directions to the nearest library.

"The main library is about half a mile away, but you might also want to check out the mall; it's just about three blocks down this street."

Kevin thanked the man and headed out the door. He had walked two blocks when he found himself in front of a church. *Hmm, is it a Catholic church?* He looked for the sign off to the side and saw that it was Saint John the Evangelist Catholic Church. *Might as well stop in and see what it looks like inside.* Kevin climbed the steps and pulled on the door, but it didn't budge. He tried the other doors before giving up. *You think they would keep a downtown church open during the day.* He shrugged his shoulders and turned to walk down the steps.

"All lock up, yes?" said a girl, who was standing on the sidewalk.

"Uhh, yeah--I guess it's locked up. Do you come here often?"

"Me not here long. I from Sveden."

"Huh! Really!" said Kevin as he walked down the steps. *Not a bad looking blonde, and the accent is cool.* "What brings you to little old Indianapolis?"

"Well, I travel with friends. My name is Kultida," she said, extending her hand.

"Oh--Kevin," he said, shaking her hand. "I was here for the combine, you know NFL?"

"'NFL'?" asked Kultida. "What that?"

"You know, football? American football?" Kevin made a passing motion with his arm.

"Ohh, yes," she smiled warmly. "You play this 'fute-ball'?"

"I'm trying out. I'm in college right now, but I hope to play professionally next fall."

"I see--you interview now."

"Sort of like that--but what about you? You say you're with friends? Who are these friends?"

"Well," began Kultida, "I see you come out of Catholic church here. I am--I was--Catholic, yes."

"So these friends of yours, they're also Catholic?"

"Oh, sort of. Why don't you come and see?" She gestured down the street.

"Wha, um, well, shoot! What the hey? I have to wait for my car to get fixed anyway." *This girl is so beautiful, I can't go wrong spending a little time with her.* "Sure, let's go meet your friends," Kevin said with a smile.

They walked to the center of downtown, where a large motor home was parked along one of the side streets.

"You have lunch here, yes?" asked Kultida, pointing to the motor home. "It's cold out here--warm in car."

"Fine," said Kevin. They climbed up into the vehicle and Kultida introduced him to a balding middle-aged man with thick black glasses.

"Kevin, this Doctor Klein. He's our director."

'Director'? wondered Kevin. *What does* that *mean?*

"Nice to meet you, Kevin."

"Kevin is football player--professional!" beamed Kultida.

"That's impressive, Kevin. You play for the Colts?"

"Oh, not yet. I'm just here for the combine--I'm trying out for the pros. I'm still in college."

"So is Kultida here," said Doctor Klein.

"What year are you in?" asked Kevin.

"I finish two year," said Kultida. "I take one year off, go back in fall."

"Nice motor home you've got here, Doctor Klein," said Kevin, "do you own it?"

"A group of us own it. Here, let me introduce you to some other people."

Doctor Klein moved to the back of the motor home and Kevin met Karen, a petite woman from France, and Ciaran, a suave looking college student from Ireland.

"Quite an international group you've got here," said Kevin.

"Oh, we try to represent a lot of different people," said Doctor Klein. "Would you like a little lunch? We've got a nice kitchenette here."

"Sounds good. I am a bit hungry. What's on today's menu?"

"You like peanut butter and jelly?" asked Kultida. "I make sandwich for you, yes?"

"Fine."

Kevin sat down at the dinette and smiled up at Kultida. "What are you studying, Kultida?"

"I study--how you say--Swedish book, no?"

"She's getting a degree in Scandinavian Literature at Vaxjo University," said Doctor Klein.

"Interesting."

"What you study?" asked Kultida as she placed the sandwich in front of Kevin. "Or you just play *fute-ball*?" she asked with a giggle.

"Thank you, Kultida. I'm studying History."

"How 'bout that," said Doctor Klein. "That's what my doctorate is in."

"Small world, eh?" said Kevin, in-between bites of the sandwich. "What's your period of specialty?"

"The Renaissance, particularly in Germany."

"Oh, so the Gutenberg Bible and all that huh?"

"Well, yes, among other things."

"Doctor Klein, I give Kevin tea?" Kultida asked, holding a box in her hands.

"Yes, uh, Kevin, would you like to try some of our tea? I know it's not all the rage here in the US, but you might want to try it."

"No harm in trying, sure."

"Give him some of *this* tea, Kultida," said Doctor Klein, handing her a box which he picked up from the counter next to him.

Ten minutes later Kevin had finished lunch and was just draining the last of the tea. "Much thanks for the food, Doctor Klein and Kultida. That tea is very, uh, relaxing."

"I'm glad you liked it, Kevin," said Doctor Klein. "Good choice," he said, giving Kultida a knowing glance.

"You welcome," said Kultida.

Kevin looked at his watch and stretched. "Well, only one hour and my car should be ready," he said with a yawn. "So are you guys with some organization or something? You seem like you just belong to some group, seeing as you're all from different countries."

"Yes, I'm glad you asked," said Doctor Klein. "Have you heard of the Reverend Sun Myung Moon?"

"Do you mean the Moonies?"

"Well, that's *one* of the terms that's used for us."

"Who is this 'Sun Mun Moon' guy?" Kevin asked, yawning and shaking his head. "Wow, I must be more tired than I thought."

"It's probably that food you ate--you know how you get tired after a meal."

"I guess."

"Anyway," began Doctor Klein, "the Reverend Sun Myung Moon is the leader of the worldwide organization designed to bring peace and happiness to all."

"So what about the Warning last week?" asked Kevin. "What do you think about that?" His eyes drooped and he involuntarily nodded his head. "Whoa! Man, am I sleepy. I might just take a little nap here..."

"The Reverend Sun Myung Moon actually predicted the Disturbance. We all saw our true selves."

"I was just...uh...thinking..." Kevin laid his head on the table. "Excuse...me..." He drifted off to sleep.

"That catnip does it every time," said Doctor Klein with a smile. "He'll be out for a few hours."

"What he do his car?" asked Kultida. "He said five clock time."

"Now, don't you worry, Kultida. If he misses his car, he just might have to stay overnight here."

Two hours later, Doctor Klein nudged Kevin. "Hey, Kevin, you had better wake up."

"Huh?" said Kevin, groggily. He raised his head and yawned. "How long have I been asleep?"

"Well, it's past six; you've been out of it for about two hours."

"Two hours!" Kevin looked at his watch. "Darn it! My car!" He hurriedly slid out of the booth and put on his coat. "I hope they're still open!"

"I go with you," said Kultida. "Make sure you be fine."

"That's not really necessary. I should be just fine."

"Ohh, we talk a little more when walk, no?" Kultida said smilingly.

"Well, whatever. Fine, let's go." He bounded down the steps of the motor home, followed by the Swedish girl.

When they reached the garage, it was closed.

"Oh, man!" yelled Kevin. "Now what am I going to do? Is my car fixed?" He walked up to the door, unsuccessfully tried to open it, and saw that they had closed at six o'clock. "Why didn't you guys wake me up?" he said to Kultida.

"We sorry...we no think you be late."

"Oh, man." Kevin searched the parking lot with his eyes. "Maybe they left it out here." Then he looked through the windows in the garage doors. "Aw, shoot! It's locked up inside the place!"

"You welcome stay with us," said Kultida. "We sorry we not wake you right away."

"This is just *great*!" he said sarcastically. "I have stuff to do back home."

"Look," said Kultida, pointing to the office door of the garage, "they open tomorrow eight--you come back then."

"I guess I have no choice," growled Kevin.

"What say you eat dinner with us, yes?"

"No, thanks, Kultida. Thanks for your help, but I think I'll just stay in a hotel--man, *that's* going to be expensive, downtown here."

"You can stay night our bus," said Kultida helpfully.

"No, no. Luckily, I've got a credit card or two here in my wallet. Oh man, I *hope* I put my credit card back in my wallet." He felt his back pocket. "Oh, nooo! This isn't happening!" He quickly patted his other pockets. "I must have left my wallet in my gym bag, and that's in the car!"

"All okay, there no problem," said Kultida. "We have macaroni and cheese for dinner. You like? You like macaroni and cheese?"

"Just a minute, let me think." Kevin brought his hand up to his bowed head. After several seconds, he straightened up. "All right, it looks like I have no choice. Looks like it's macaroni and cheese for dinner!"

"Good, good," said Kultida excitedly. "You will like."

After what Kevin had to admit was a very delicious meal of macaroni and cheese and baked potatoes, followed by pumpkin pie a la mode, Kevin watched as Doctor Klein set up a whiteboard and began drawing several pictures on it.

"You plan on giving a little talk?" asked Kevin.

"With your permission, of course."

"What's the topic?"

"We're going to discuss Heaven and the afterlife."

"Before we begin, I would really like to know what you think about the Warning that happened last week," asked Kevin.

"Oh, yes. I believe you mentioned that this afternoon. By the 'Warning,' as you say, you mean the 'Disturbance,' right?"

"Right. Weren't you affected by that? I mean, it blew me away! I saw all that I had done wrong in the past. I was really scared!"

"Actually the Reverend Sun Myung Moon made an official statement about all that. He said the 'Awakening,' as he calls it, was necessary for the world to see that it should turn its attention toward his saving message. We hope that the Awakening will bring many people to see the beauty of the Moonie religion."

"But what about sin? Do you guys believe in 'sin'?" What about Confession? How do you reconcile yourselves with God? Didn't you see all your sins during the Warning?"

"Now, Kevin, maybe that is a good starting point for our discussion. I draw your attention to the diagrams I have drawn up here." Doctor Klein pointed to the whiteboard. "This is us here on earth below and this is the saved in Heaven. Now Reverend Moon teaches that..." The professor began to explain the teachings of the Moonies in detail.

Three hours later, Doctor Klein was still going at it, and Kevin was getting a little annoyed. "Doctor Klein, this has all been interesting, but, hey!" Kevin pointed to his watch. "It's getting on toward midnight. Whaddya say we call it quits?"

"But there's so much more to talk about, right Kultida?" She had been sitting across from Kevin, helping to explain things from time to time.

"That right, Doctor. Kevin, not much longer--you want some tea?"

"Oh, no, not *that* again! So what's the idea here anyway? You keep me up all night and try to brainwash me with your doctrine?"

"Now, now, Kevin," said Doctor Klein patronizingly. "You don't really believe all that stuff you've heard about us, do you? We're simply here to help you understand God and life a little better. Look at Kultida here--doesn't she look happy? She was a Catholic once like you...we've really helped her see the light."

The "lecture" continued all night, with Kevin dozing off occasionally. He refused to take any more of the food offered him. As soon as it was light, he put on his coat and headed out the door.

"Thanks for the food, but I really could have done without the brainwashing," Kevin said as he walked past Doctor Klein.

"Think about what I said. It makes a lot of sense when you think about it."

"I suggest you think about the Warning, Doctor Klein. I think your religion has a lot to be desired."

"I walk you to garage," said Kultida.

"Knock yourself out," said Kevin. "I guess a little more brainwashing can't hurt."

After they were out of earshot of the motor home, Kevin turned to Kultida. "Look, Kultida, you don't believe all that crap, do you?"

"Doctor Klein good man, Kevin!" she said defensively. "He teach me much."

"Kultida, how long have you been Catholic?"

"I born Catholic."

"Well, why don't you come back? What happened to you during the Warning?"

"We say 'Awakening.'"

"Fine, whatever you want to call it, you can't tell me you weren't affected by it."

They turned the corner and began walking down Washington Street. When she was sure they could no longer be seen by anyone in the motor home, Kultida stopped and caught Kevin by the arm. "I have no one talk to about Awakening! I scared! Doctor Klein tell me to not talk Awakening." She pulled a pen and a piece of paper from her pocket. "You write you name and phone number...I call you!" she said hurriedly. "Quick! Doctor Klein may have someone follow us."

"Uhh...okay..." said Kevin hesitantly. He scribbled the information and gave her the scrap of paper.

"I call you, Mr. fute-ball." She stood on her toes and gave

Kevin a quick kiss on the cheek. "Bye."

Kevin was a little taken aback. "Ookaaay. Same to you."

She ran back the way they had come. Kevin turned and headed to pick up his car. *Not a bad kid*, he thought. *Swedish…hmmm.*

Chapter 11

Thad had taken the Warning in stride, mainly because he had been thinking about it almost everyday since he was in college. Not that it wasn't scary for him, but as his mother had always said: "forewarned is forearmed." At least it was now much easier for him to talk about Garabandal with the passengers in his taxi. He was overjoyed when Dexter had called him for a ride since he was eager to see how his compatriot had weathered this first of the Garabandal prophecies. Thad stopped in front of Dexter's house and honked once. Dexter walked out and opened the car door.

"Once again, welcome to Columbus Cab Company!" said Thad cheerfully as Dexter entered the taxi.

"Honestly, Thad, are you ever 'down'? Do you ever get depressed?" asked Dexter after closing the car door.

"Not very often, Dexter. I try to fight sadness when I feel it trying to take over."

"And how do you do that?"

"I go to Mass everyday and say the Rosary, for starters--that helps. It's getting harder, though, to find a Mass to go to—the Chinese have been closing down some churches."

"What exactly do you do at Mass, anyway?"

"The Mass is simply the unbloody representation of Christ's sacrifice on Calvary."

"And that makes you happy?" asked Dexter.

"What really makes me happy--oh, incidentally, do you have to stop at your office before I go to the airport?"

"Not today. I have everything I need right here," said Dexter, patting his briefcase. "But thanks for asking."

"No problem," said Thad. He started the engine and backed out onto Urlin Avenue. "Well, anyway, as I was saying, what really makes me happy is the thought of the period of peace after the Chastisement."

"There's that word again," said Dexter. "I thought you said that once. What is that? Is it connected to the Disturbance?"

"First of all, it's the 'Warning.' That's the name it was given way back in the 60's by the Blessed Mother herself. Anyway, the Chastisement is basically the punishment God is going to mete out on the world after the Miracle."

"The Miracle being that thing you described in Spain--at Garabandal, right?"

"Right!" said Thad, turning around to smile at Dexter. "You're really catching on!"

"I think I saw something about it in the paper a few days ago, I can't remember where."

"In the Chastisement," continued Thad, "two-thirds to three-quarters of the earth's population will die."

"What cereal box did you get that off of? Are you serious? Three-quarters of the earth?" asked Dexter.

"Actually, at Garabandal, the Blessed Mother said it all depends on how the world responds to the Miracle."

"We're all supposed to become little white-angel-puppy-dogs when God makes an elephant disappear?"

"There's more to the story, my friend," said Thad. "Mary said in subsequent apparitions in the years following Garabandal that the Chastisement can no longer be avoided, only mitigated."

"Great, so no matter how goody we become, the dung is still going to hit the fan."

"I'm afraid so."

Dexter didn't reply immediately, just scratched his chin and looked out the window. "So we're up shift creed without a paddle."

"Bodily death isn't the worst thing; it's eternal death that's the scary part."

"I believe you're referring to Hell?" asked Dexter.

"That's correct. Maybe God knows that--wait, why am I saying 'maybe'? I mean God *does* know that he can minimize the number of people going to Hell by sending the Chastisement right after the Miracle."

"Why can't God just have the Miracle, everyone comes clean, and everyone lives happily ever after?"

"Because who says everyone will *stay* clean? You know how people are...we're a bunch of backsliders."

"Yeah, but *two-thirds* of the earth is supposed to die? C'mon! That's a bit severe!"

"Hey, there'll be a lot more elbow room down here," joked Thad.

"The hell with you, buddy," said Dexter. "I don't appreciate making a joke out of a catastrophe."

"Ah-so! Then you believe it's really going to happen!"

"I never said that! It's just a nice theory, as far as I'm concerned."

"I'll tell you one thing that sticks in my craw, though," said Thad. "The Blessed Mother said to a Saint back in the twelfth century that, well, her exact quote was 'One day through the Rosary and the Scapular I will save the world.'"

"So the 'Chastisement' is a big scare tactic," said Dexter. "Just like the way the meteorologists hype up a big hurricane and it turns out to be a little tropical storm---and, by the way, what is the Scapular and the Rosary?"

"The Scapular is something worn around your neck. There is a piece of brown cloth attached to each end. Mary said that whoever dies wearing the Scapular will not go to Hell. The Rosary is a collection of beads that are used to say a collection of 'Our Fathers' and 'Hail Marys.' While you say the prayers of the Rosary, you meditate on scenes from Christ's life. But, as far as what the Blessed Mother said back in the Twelfth Century...who knows what she meant by that promise? She saved Christendom through the Rosary at the Battle of Lepanto in 1571--was she referring to *that*? Why would she contradict herself, saying the Chastisement was certain to occur, if she didn't really mean it?"

"What the heck is it with Mary anyway?" asked Dexter. "What, does she know the future or something? I thought only God knew everything."

"I'm sure Mary only tells her visionaries what God tells her to say."

"Say this Chastisement is for real--what is it going to be?"

"That's pretty much unknown in the final analysis. Some people think it will be an asteroid hitting the earth, some say it'll be nuclear war. One of the visionaries at Garabandal said the Chastisement starts with an 'A,' and that it's not an asteroid. The Blessed Mother said at Akita, an apparition in Japan, that 'fire will fall from heaven.' No one really knows."

"What do *you* think it'll be?" asked Dexter.

"My personal opinion is a big asteroid. Mary said to some visionaries back in the 90s that those asteroids that hit Jupiter were a sign of things to come."

"Prairie-shat, just when I was about to get a good robot on the market."

"Hey, bud, make a post-chastisement robot! There'll be plenty of work to do cleaning up after the asteroid. Robots would come in handy."

"Where do I plug its battery in? Will trees have ready-made electrical outlets?"

"I wonder if there will even be any trees left standing," said Thad.

"Well, boy, this just sounds like a barrel of fun! First we get hit by an asteroid, four billion people die, then we're stuck in a barren wasteland. Great!" Dexter slapped the car seat with his hand. "I guess the people left alive will then starve to death, right?"

"I forget the exact places I read all this stuff, but I do seem to remember that the soil will be so enriched by the fire and asteroid, that it will be extremely fertile. There'll be something like four harvests per year."

"Where *do* you get all this stuff, Thad? It sounds like something out of the Lord of the Rings movies!"

"I know it all does sound rather fantastic, but I could lend you a few books if you'd like. It basically all comes from various apparitions men and women have had over the past seven hundred years or so."

"How much of it is dogma?" asked Dexter.

"Basically none of it is, but that doesn't mean we can't believe it. As long as an apparition isn't condemned by the Church, we're free to believe it."

"So four billion are going to die, and no one knows it."

"Oh, word is getting around." Thad turned and glanced quickly at Dexter. "Did you see that special on Channel 5 the other night--the one on the Miracle? By the way, thanks for keeping a TV for me out there at your farm--it comes in handy."

"You're welcome, and no, I don't watch a whole lot of TV. I'm surprised the Chinese would let something like that be aired."

"Well, more and more people are finding out about the Miracle. And as far as the Chinese go, well, I always take a lot of comfort in what Sister Eunice used to say when she taught me in third grade: 'Never forget that God is always in control of the world, no matter how bad things may seem.'"

"Most people I talk to call the 'Warning' the 'Disturbance.'"

"Whatever you call it, that *event* scared the daylights out of me!" said Thad.

"*You*?" asked Dexter, leaning forward to look at Thad. "What do *you* have to be ashamed of? *I'm* the one who had the frightening experience!"

"Oh, we all have varying levels of dirt or dust in our souls. You know what? I actually think I might be called to the priesthood."

"Is that what you saw during the Disturbance?" asked Dexter. "You think you're supposed to become a priest?"

"I can't be certain. It was a little hazy, but I think God wants me to start doing a little more than just driving a taxi--not that there's anything wrong with driving a taxi--but with my background in engineering, I think I have some room for improvement. I'm going to go to the Josephinum and talk with the dean of students there."

Dexter said nothing, absorbed in his thoughts.

"What about you, Dexter? How was the Warning for *you*?"

"Painful, to say the least." Dexter bit his lower lip and shook his head. "Sometimes I think it was real, sometimes I think it was just a hallucination."

"I see. By the way, which airline are you flying today?" asked Thad as he changed lanes.

"Northern Airlines."

"All right, Northern Airlines." Thad always liked to repeat the name of the airline so he didn't forget it by the time he arrived at the Ticketing curb. "Yeah, that's true, the social psychiatrists have done their job well. A good number of people are still reluctant to attribute any supernatural cause to the Warning, but, let me tell you, there won't be any second-guessing the Miracle. Mary said there will be no doubt in people's minds that it's from God."

"So everyone will be saved!" said Dexter. "Everyone will be believers!"

"Not so fast. Even the demons in Hell are 'believers.' They believe Christ is the Son of God. It takes more than that to save your soul. You also have to have an absence of unforgiven sin and good works."

"That sounds like the big 'C' word."

"'C' word?"

"Confession."

"You *are* a bright boy, Dex-man! Are you thinking of 'hitting the box?'"

"'Hitting the box?'"

"Just an expression a friend of mine in California used to use. Hit the *Confessional* box."

"Not a chance, Thad-man. I can ask forgiveness all on my own. Why do you insist on needing a priest?"

"Aww, we'll see what happens in the next few months, Mr. Rugged Individualist, we'll see."

"'We'll see' is right."

"So where are you off to today, Robot-boy?" asked Thad. "Montana? Chicago?"

"Arizona, actually. Phoenix. There's an electronics company there that I need to talk to about the sensors in Bobby's hand. I'd fly the Cessna, but it might take too long. The weather's not the best either."

"As you wish, milord." Thad dropped Dexter off at the Northern Airlines kiosk and stopped in the McDonald's parking lot to await the next fare.

****

Dexter returned from Phoenix the next day and made it to Father Rankin's office with three minutes to spare. He plopped down in the chair in front of Father Rankin's desk and paused to catch his breath.

"Tough day at the office?" asked the priest.

"Ha! I could wish for such an easy life. No--I just got back from Phoenix. Almost missed the flight, too."

"Aww, what you go through for fame and fortune."

"Hey, if you want to make a small fortune in robotics, start out with a large fortune," said Dexter with a smile.

"Rejected!" laughed Father Rankin. "Nice try, but I happen to know that that quote comes from Howard Hughes, and he was referring to aviation, not robotics."

"I was just being creative."

"Plagiarist! You're just providing substance for your first Confession."

"It'll be a clear day in LA before I go to Confession, Father Rankin."

"'Clear day in LA?' Huuhh?" asked Father Rankin, wrinkling his eyebrows.

"You know: 'cold day in Hell.' That type of thing," said Dexter. "Once again I'm being creative! What's the deal with Confession anyway? I was talking about it with your brother yesterday."

"What do you mean, 'what's the deal?'" asked Father Rankin.

"Well, is it really necessary? I can tell God I'm sorry in the silence of my own heart. The priest seems like unnecessary baggage."

"The short answer to that is 'Then why did Christ institute the Sacrament of Confession?'"

"The short rejoinder to that," said Dexter, "is 'Who says Christ instituted the Sacrament of Confession?'"

"The Church."

"Quote quotes."

"'Whose sins you shall forgive, they are forgiven them and whose sins you shall retain, they are retained.' End of story."

"Care to quote Chapter and verse?" asked Dexter.

"Suffice it to say that Christ said it in the upper room after the Resurrection. I'm not certain of the Chapter, but it is in the Gospel of John."

"And from that you divine the Sacrament of Confession."

"Exactly."

"Why couldn't it have just been Christ giving final instructions to the twelve Apostles? Who says it extends down to your local priest two thousand years later?"

"Ah, but therein lies the big difference between Catholics and Protestants. I believe I said this in one of our earlier discussions, but it is worth repeating. Whereas Protestants believe in 'Scripture alone,' Catholics believe in Scripture *and* Tradition. We believe that not only does one need to believe in the Bible, but that one needs an authority to interpret that Bible as well."

"What's so bad about personal interpretation of the Bible?" asked Dexter. "It seems to me that it allows for a wonderful diversity of belief."

"What about the Constitution of the United States?" asked Father Rankin. "Should we just let everyone interpret it their own way? Don't we have legislatures and courts and judges?"

"But that's different. The Constitution deals with flesh and blood issues, with *real* things."

"Salvation isn't *real*?" asked Father Rankin. "Isn't the issue here that some who call themselves Christians don't want to take religion too seriously? This reminds me of something a priest friend of mine up in Cardington, Ohio used to say: 'It's easier to live as a Protestant. It's easier to die as a Catholic.' Lot of truth in that."

"Fine," said Dexter, "so there is a theological basis for Confession. Maybe some people need it--I don't think I do. I can talk to God just fine on my own."

"This reminds me of the Gospel story wherein Christ says to a paralytic man, 'Your sins are forgiven.' The Pharisees harbor bad thoughts toward Jesus, so Christ says to them, 'You doubt that I can forgive sins? Which is easier to say, "Your sins are forgiven" or "Take up your pallet and walk?" But so you know that the Son of God has the power to forgive sins, I say to this cripple, Take up your pallet and walk.' The paralytic gets up and walks." Father Rankin leaned forward in his chair. "I think the same thing applies here, in a way. Which is easier to do? Kneel down by your bed at night and say 'God, I'm sorry for my sins,' or to go to a church, enter the Confessional, and say to a priest, 'Forgive me, Father, for I have sinned'? I know I'm stretching the analogy a little here, but I think you'll agree that it's a little harder to tell your sins out loud in the presence of another man."

"Psssh!" replied Dexter, tossing his head. "So I'm supposed to go to Confession because it's the harder thing to do. What kind of reason is that?"

"Not just because it's the harder thing to do," explained Father

Rankin. "But because it's the more *realistic* thing to do. When you break the law, does the policeman just say, 'Say you're sorry, and everything will be fine'? No, he brings the perpetrator before a judge and the criminal gets a punishment. The same thing happens in Confession, though the penance is much lighter. The priest forgives sins in the name of Christ. It is almost as if Christ himself were sitting in the confessional."

"But does it really deter anyone from sinning?" asked Dexter. "It seems to me the attitude of some Catholics is to sin freely because they can always get rid of their sins in Confession."

"Yeah," said Father Rankin, clasping his hands together behind his head and leaning back in his chair, "I've heard that argument before, but in my personal experience as a Confessor, that rarely happens. I find that people usually *are* deterred from sin because they know they would have to confess it. Besides, someone who goes to Confession on a Saturday afternoon is going to want to keep his soul clean so he can go to Holy Communion on Sunday morning."

"That's another thing," said Dexter, "Holy Communion. What's the deal there?"

"We Catholics believe that Holy Communion is the Body, Blood, Soul and Divinity of Jesus Christ."

"What does it taste like?"

"The Host has all the accidents of bread, meaning it looks, feels, and tastes like ordinary bread."

"What's so spectacular about that? What proof is there that it really *is* the Body of Christ?"

"First of all," said Father Rankin, "look at it this way. If Holy Communion really *did* taste and look like human flesh, there would be no need for faith or belief--the whole Mystery would be visible before everyone's eyes. Secondly, there have been countless miracles that demonstrated the Real Presence of Christ. I remember one story where the Host was passing by a town square in medieval Europe and a donkey knelt down as it went by."

"So it felt like taking a rest just when some priest passed by," said Dexter. "C'mon!"

"All right, how about the fact that several people have been known to subsist solely on Holy Communion for dozens of years without eating any other food?"

"Pssshh! Once again, pious fairy tales! I bet every time the village historian wasn't looking, the guy stole out back to the pantry and snacked on Doritos and Coke."

"Look," said Father Rankin, "there's a girl right now in Worcester, Massachusetts who is the subject of several miracles. Her name is Audrey Santos. She's a disabled teenage girl. There have been reports of religious statues weeping oil and Communion Hosts have bled during a Mass said there. The scent of roses from an unknown source often fills Audrey's room."

"Miracles, schmiracles," said Dexter with a dismissive wave of his hand. "I thought only peasants believed in them."

"Look, I just read something in the 'New Oxford Review.' This happened just a few months ago to some guy here in the US. His wife accidentally slammed the car door on his hand when they were getting ready to go to Sunday Mass. His hand was all smashed up and bloody, but instead of going right to the hospital, he drove to Mass. After he came back from Holy Communion, his hand was completely healed and all the blood was gone! This really happened, I mean just recently. I can let you read the article if you want."

Dexter wasn't convinced. "What physical proof does the guy have? Pictures? Doctors' statements?"

"My dear Dexter, you fulfill the maxim to the letter."

"What maxim?"

"I've often heard it said about miracles: for those who don't want to believe, no explanation is possible; for those who want to believe, no explanation is necessary."

"I want to be--well, do I want to believe?" asked Dexter. "That's a good one. I'm not too sure *what* I want to believe. I really just want to go back to the days when I didn't think about all these deep things. Hell! It used to be just me, Daphne, and robots, and I was happy! Now, it's Heaven and Hell and all this philosophical rubbish. I've lost Daphne and now I'll probably lose the robots too, if this Chastisement thing that Thad just told me about is true. Why did I have to be born at the time of all this Warning, and Miracle stuff? Used to be a guy could enjoy life, drink beer, and have some fun!"

"But, Dexter," Father Rankin said in a soothing voice, "good times *are* coming. Has Thad told you about the period of peace after the Chastisement? In a few years you'll either be living in a wonderland on earth, or in complete bliss in Heaven if you die--if you die with no unrepentant sin on your soul, after maybe a short stay in

Purgatory."

"Thad *hasn't* told me much about the period of peace," said Dexter. "Is that the same as the Millennium or whatever it's called?"

"Well," said Father Rankin, nodding his head up and down, "as always when dealing with the end times, no one knows the details *for sure*, but there is evidence from certain mystics in the Church that after the Chastisement there will be a period of peace on earth, before the end of the world."

"All right, say I believe in all this," Dexter said, turning both palms of his hands up and dipping his head, "how long is this 'period of peace' supposed to last?"

"No one knows exactly. Our Lady said an 'era' of peace. My personal opinion is about a generation, say thirty to forty years. But I've also read that some mystics report that the Blessed Mother says it will last for a thousand years. Of course the Church has always condemned that—what's known as millenarianism. Anyway, from what I've read about the final days of the end of the world, it would be better to die *before* that happens."

"Huh!" scoffed Dexter. "Then why not die now, before all this Chastisement stuff happens?!"

"You have a point there," said Father Rankin, "but remember the more we suffer, the greater our reward in Heaven."

"Well, then 'Yay, team!'" said Dexter. "Let's live through the Chastisement *and* the end of the world, and get a *really* big reward!"

"Be my guest, big guy," laughed Father Rankin. "Why don't you become a Catholic to start with?"

"Who says I'm going to become a Catholic?"

"Heck, you've been coming to see me for four months now. When are you going to make up your mind?"

"I thought you said you don't have to become a Catholic to go to Heaven?" asked Dexter, wrinkling his brow. "Why bother?"

"Mr. Griffith, there are three ways to get from Ohio to Los Angeles: you can drive in a Lexus, you can ride a bike, or you can walk. It's the same way with getting to Heaven. Catholics ride in a Lexus, Protestants ride a bike, and pagans walk. The Lexus is almost certain to get you there, the bike is possible, and the walk is questionable. Why not ride with the best? What if the bike gets a flat in the middle of Death Valley? Who you gonna call? If the Lexus breaks down, you use the car phone to call for a tow truck. If the bike-"

"The guy on the bike could have a cell phone, he could call for a cab," interjected Dexter.

"All right," said Father Rankin, holding up a hand, "we all know that analogies go only so far--you get the point. Catholicism is the surest way of reaching Heaven that man has. So whaddya say?"

"What do you mean, 'Whaddya say'?"

"How 'bout it?"

"What--*me* become a Catholic? Do I fill out an application? Is there an entrance fee?"

"It's best to batten down the hatches *before* the ship hits the storm," said Father Rankin.

"Storm?"

"The Chastisement is going to be a whopper of a storm."

"You know, Father, I think I'm in an endless loop. I think about the Miracle and the Chastisement, I tell myself I have to change my life, I wonder if any of these predictions will come true, I question what really happened in the Warning, I think it's all a bunch of superstition, I helplessly throw up my hands, and then I go back to step one."

"Have you compiled recently?"

"Compiled?"

"It's an old computer programming term. We used to have to compile our programs after we finished writing them. It's sort of like baking a cake after you've mixed all the ingredients together. You need to 'compile' all your thoughts about the Miracle and the Chastisement."

"Now how do I go about 'compiling' my thoughts?"

"Spend time in front of the Blessed Sacrament. Talk to Jesus about it."

"Cheeeeshh!" said Dexter. "Endless loop mentality! I need to get *away* from all this religion brainwashing so I can look back *inward*."

"Fine, fine," said Father Rankin. "I understand. Then why don't you just spend some quiet time by yourself thinking all this over. And I mean *truly* quiet time, not just sitting in front of the TV, or in the car with the radio on. Find a park or somewhere and just *think* all this through. You'll be amazed at the insights you can gain. I heard that Coach Panaski down at Ohio State encourages his football players to meditate. My Dad always used to lament the lack of quiet time in the world of today. People seem to fear being alone with their consciences. Joggers wear headphones; people leave the TV on at home, even when they're not watching it. Dad used to say that people were blocking out the Holy Spirit."

"All right, a deal's a deal," said Dexter. "I'll schedule some thinking time."

"Golden!" said Father Rankin.

"Golden?"

"Do they still say that? I remember everyone saying it when I was in college."

"I get the point, Padre. I'll see you later." Dexter walked out of the office.

"Bye Dex."

****

Kevin didn't really want to go to the lecture, but Chad had dragged him to it. A Professor Neubauer from the Psychology Department was giving a talk in Mershon Auditorium on the Ohio State campus entitled: "The Disturbance and Mass Hypnosis." Apparently some people had a different take on what happened on February twenty-fourth than what Sparrow and the boys at Elyria thought. Judging from the steady stream of students flowing into the auditorium, Kevin and Chad weren't the only ones who wanted to hear this professor's views on the events of the past few weeks.

"What's so great about this guy, anyway, Chad?" asked Kevin as they sat in one of the front row seats.

"I heard about it from this guy I know in my Stats class. He took a class from this prof and apparently he's pretty sharp."

"Probably pretty pagan, too."

"You really believe all that stuff those nerds told you when your car broke down? What--the 'Warning?'"

"I'm telling you, I saw the image of Mary up there in Cleveland, Chad--it was like thirty feet high!"

"Dude! You need this talk more than ever! That's exactly what this guy's going to talk about--mass hypnosis!"

"Chad, you're just accepting the B.S. that everyone is dishing out. If you're not--"

Kevin was interrupted by a man speaking into the microphone

up on the stage. "If I could have your attention, ladies and gentlemen."
He waited for the hubbub to die down, then continued. "As you know,
there have been reports of a psychological phenomena on a global
scale in the past few weeks. There has been considerable discussion
recently as to the origins of these events. As chairman of the
Psychology Department here at Ohio State, I am pleased to be able to
introduce someone with a world-class reputation in his field who will
help to shed some light on the situation. Professor Neubauer has
published extensively on the subject of mass psychological events and
has appeared on various national news networks as an expert in this
area. I present Dr Neubauer..."

There was a small smattering of applause as a bespectacled
man of average height with salt-and-pepper hair walked to the podium.
He cleared his throat and arranged several papers in front of him.

"I would like to thank Dr Whitcomb for that introduction and I
welcome you all here to this talk tonight. I will begin by saying that I
know the past few weeks have been difficult for all of us, but I come
with a message of hope, hope in the future of humankind, and hope for
a hurting world. Now I know the news media has been quick to pick up
on the supposed religious angle of this whole thing. I'm sure you've
heard of how the Blessed Virgin Mary is going to turn water into wine
over in Spain..." He paused for a few seconds as a twitter swept over
the audience. "But let me assure you: the Disturbance is most
probably something that has happened to our world before, and may
even occur again--not anytime soon, but, nonetheless, it could. Mass
hypnosis has occurred throughout history to one degree or another
and it all can be scientifically explained, without the need of extreme
religious fanaticism. Some psychologists have speculated that Hitler,
in Nazi Germany, made use of an emotional variant of mass hypnosis
in some of his mesmerizing speeches before the great crowds of
German people. There is even reason to believe that the so-called
'Great Awakening' that occurred in Colonial times here in America
could have had its roots in another variant of mass hypnosis. Maybe
some of you here are too young to remember the Reverend Jim Jones.
This was another case of mass hypnosis. In 1978, Jim Jones and 913
of his followers committed mass suicide down in Guyana, in South
America by drinking a poisonous punch potion. The Reverend Jim
Jones had somehow convinced his clueless disciples that this would
be good for them to do. And possibly one of the best examples of

mass hypnosis comes to us from the Catholic Church itself.   On October 13, 1917, in a small town in Portugal, a crowd of about 60,000 people actually believed they saw the sun crash down upon them. The crowd had gathered because the Blessed Virgin Mary had supposedly predicted that a miracle would occur that day.   The Catholic Church gave its full approval to this event. I ask you: isn't it a little strange that the same Church which asks us to believe that the sun came plunging to earth back in 1917 now asks us to believe that the mass hypnosis which occurred a few weeks ago was some kind of miracle? They even have a word for it: 'the Warning.' What is totally lacking in this whole propaganda effort--and let me emphasize that it truly is a 'propaganda' effort--is a calm, scientific analysis.   There is even reason to believe that the Catholic Church is trying to regain some of the credibility it lost in the priestly pedophilia scandal a few years ago by proclaiming that it knows the cause of, and reason for, the Disturbance.

"In the first place, there is nothing so incredible about what happened to us last February twenty-fourth. It is common knowledge in my field that mass therapy indoctrination often uses repetitive inductions of trance-like states of consciousness. These episodes of hypnosis can be brought about by environmental control and social manipulation. Furthermore, if one analyzes each of the examples I just gave of mass hypnosis, one will see how similar they all are. What we must keep in mind is that..."

Kevin nudged Chad and said in a low voice, "Do you understand what he's talking about?"

"A little--I took a Psych class freshman year. Be patient, he may clarify himself later."

The talk lasted about forty-five minutes after which Professor Neubauer opened the floor up to questions and answers.   Kevin immediately shot his hand up, and since he was in the front row, the speaker pointed to him.

"Professor Neubauer, I just wanted to ask a question about something you said in the first part of your talk. I'm a History major and--"

"We won't hold that against you," said Professor Neubauer, drawing a few snickers from the crowd.

"Yeah, anyway, I've studied a little about that Fatima miracle-- or, that 'event' at Fatima, the town in Portugal you mentioned, and the thing is, uh, well, the stuff I've read said that the people reported that their clothes all dried up, and the ground and everything. It had been raining steadily all day, but after the sun spun in the sky, everything was perfectly dry. How could it have been simply mass hypnosis if everything actually dried up?"

"Uh, ladies and gentlemen," Professor Neubauer said in a low voice, "I think our friend Kevin Conaway may have taken a few too many hits last football season." He chuckled, but only a few of the students joined him. Most wanted to hear his answer.

"Well, I think the thing to remember there is that mass hypnosis can change many things. It may well have been raining that day in Portugal, and everything may have seemed dry later, but dry *to the people there at that time.* See, people are capable of imagining anything: sun dropping out of the sky, rain, dry clothes, dry ground--it's all in the mix."

"But, sir, I really think--" began Kevin.

"Uh, sorry--" interrupted Professor Neubauer, "but we really should answer some other questions, Kevin. Maybe later."

A girl in the last row stood up and loudly called for the professor's attention.

"Yes, the beautiful girl in the last row," he said with a smile. "Go ahead--what's your question?"

"Well, uh, first of all, thank you very much for this talk, Professor Neubauer. I suppose I shouldn't have been, but I've been really worried for the past several days and you've really calmed a lot of my fears. Anyway, what about the Rapture? I've heard a few crazy Fundamentalists yelling on certain radio stations that we all have to get ready for the Rapture. Can you address that issue?"

"Yes, yes, certainly," said Professor Neubauer, "I'm glad you brought that up. What really is in question here is the future of humankind. I, too, have heard rumors about 'the Rapture' and all that stuff, but it's time to look at the big picture. I don't want to touch too much here on religion, but suffice it to say that we're at a turning point in world history and there are certain people of various religions who don't want to face up to the fact that their 'belief systems' are outmoded. We needed structured religions for some of our history, but it's time to move on. This global phenomenon--the Disturbance--is just a sign that the world is changing paradigms. It's hard for people to let go of some of their beliefs, but, as I said earlier, we're at a turning point in world history. I plan to give another talk about this topic next month. Stay tuned for details."

The professor answered a few more questions, skillfully avoiding any that lent any sort of religious slant to his theories. As soon as the speaker walked off the stage, Kevin bolted out of his seat.

"C'mon, Chad, let's go, that was a bunch of hoo-ey!"

"What was so bad, dude? He had some good things to say."

"Yeah, so did Stalin." Kevin walked quickly out the door with Chad on his heels.

"Really, Kevin, what was so bad about his talk?" Chad had to quicken his pace to keep up with his friend.

"He didn't answer my question about Fatima, Chad--for starters. And he just used a bunch of high-sounding names to camouflage his unbelief." They turned onto High Street and continued walking north.

"Unbelief! Ha! Kevin, what's the big deal? Why are you flipping out? First you dump Anne--"

"*I* didn't dump her--she hung up on *me*!"

"Well, you dated her for what--three years? You expect her to hang around forever? Anyway, you've got problems with Anne, then you get mixed up with that Moonie girl, and now you're getting all flustered over some Psych professor's theories."

After walking along High Street for several blocks, they turned onto Lane Avenue and crossed the street after a bus passed.

"Chad, we're not living in the good ol' days anymore. Wake up and smell the java! Do you really believe the Warning was just a little 'anomaly' that NASA hasn't figured out yet? We're occupied by the Chinese Army and the future doesn't look too bright. Do you really think we're going to have a normal, 'business as usual' football season this fall?"

"I don't know, Kevin." They stopped at the corner of Lane and Indianola, where their paths home diverged. "All I know is we had a weird event in February and now you're saying the world's coming to an end."

"Chad, are you seriously trying to tell me that you weren't affected by the Warning--or, all right, 'the Disturbance'?"

Chad looked down, kicked an empty soda can into the street and shuffled his feet. "Sheeet, I don't know, Kevin--yeah, I saw a lot of stuff on that day that I'd rather not talk about. Actually, I'd like to forget the whole thing."

"That's just it--you *can't* forget the whole thing," said Kevin exasperatedly. "The whole point of the Warning is to get you ready for the Miracle, and then, the Chastisement--if it occurs."

"I think I saw something about that in the paper. The miracle's supposed to happen in Spain, right? What's this *chastisement* thing you're talking about?"

"The 'chastisement' is what will happen if we don't shape up after the Miracle."

"By 'we' you mean the world, right?"

"Right."

They stood there silently as several people walked by.

"Kevin, since when are you Mr. Holy-Joe anyway?"

"It's sort of hard not to be, with all that's going on. And then there's that trip I took to Elyria."

"Yeah, what was *that* all about? I remember you saying something about that."

"I went to a site where the Blessed Virgin has been appearing. I just can't seem to get something out of my head."

"What's that?"

"The Blessed Mother gave a message that night. She said to be aware that maybe God is asking 'something more' from you." Kevin stared at his feet.

"And..." said Chad.

"It's just that phrase 'something more.' A day doesn't go by that I don't remember that."

"What do you think it means?"

"I'm not sure, it's just that I sometimes think about a career in the NFL and I wonder if that's what I should really be doing."

"You're looking for something a little more lucrative, maybe?" said Chad with a chuckle.

"No, really, Chad, it's not money, it's--well--I have no idea! The world is so messed up now that I couldn't tell you what I should do. Peace Corps? Can I really think about raising a family with the way everything is now? What's going to happen with this Chinese thing? How much worse will it get? So far, they've let us pretty much do what we want, but how long will that last?"

"Why not worry about that when the time comes, Kevin? Things are okay for now. Heck, if it really bothers you that much, you can give your signing bonus to some church group or something. Didn't you tell me that the Bills were thinking of giving you an extra two million if they got to pick you?"

"I never thought of it that way," Kevin said thoughtfully. "Hmm, I could do a lot of good with the money I'm going to be making."

"There ya go, bro," said Chad, slapping him on the back. "Now you're talking. Hey, I gotta go--we still have tests to take, remember."

"Later, Chad. Keep the Warning in mind."

"Whatever...see ya."

Kevin walked down Northwood Avenue and when he opened the door to his apartment, a small brown package came flying at him.

"Yo! Kevin!" said Kevin's roommate, Steve, who was sitting at the dining room table. "Who's 'Kultida'? From Cincinnati. She sent that there package. You better not let Anne hear about this, dude!" he said with a laugh.

"'Kultida'?" asked Kevin, searching his memory. "The name sounds familiar, but Cincinnati? I don't really know anyone from Cincinnati."

"Whoa! The big multimillionaire NFL player can't keep track of all his girlfriends I guess!" His roommate bounced a sofa cushion off Kevin's head.

"Gimme a break, freak," said Kevin with a grin. "Just because you're not of the Master Race like me..."

"He hasn't even won the Super Bowl yet and listen to him talk!" Steve reached down to pick up the cushion. "So who is she, stud?"

"Ohh, yeah, Kultida!" said Kevin finally. "She's this girl with the Moonies I met in Indianapolis."

"Look, seriously, Kevin--surely you can do better than *that*! The Moonies? Come onnn!"

"Huh," said Kevin after he ripped open the package. "Would you look at that. She sent me a Rosary!"

"Now the Moonies pray the Rosary?" asked Steve incredulously. "They must have really been affected by the Disturbance."

"It's called the 'Warning,' Steve--and she's not really a Moonie. She's a Catholic--or she was a Catholic--or she still is a Catholic--whatever, she just sent me a Rosary."

"That I can see. Who is this babe, Kevin?"

"She's from Sweden and she's hot! She's blond, Nordic good-looks..."

"Kevin, not to rain on your parade, but what about Anne? Remember her? You've only been dating her for what--three years?"

"Things aren't going so great with her, actually, Steve."

"Why is this girl, uh, what is it--Kultida? Why is 'Kultida' sending you a Rosary?"

"She said she wasn't allowed to talk about the Warning with any of the Mooney people. I gave her my name and phone number...she must have gotten my address off the Internet. This must be her way of telling me she wants to start practicing the Faith again."

"Or maybe she wants to grab a share of the bills you'll be pulling down when you sign your contract."

"Steve who really knows if we're even going to have a football season? Have you heard about the Miracle?"

"Oh, you believe those fairy tales? Yeah, the Mother of Jesus is going to pull bunny rabbits out of a hat, right?"

"Maybe there's some truth to all that stuff. You've just been influenced by the liberal media--sure, they've been pooh-poohing it since day one."

"Ha!" laughed Steve. "And you've been influenced by a bunch of extreme fundamentalists. Look, if you must know, I've decided to adopt a 'wait-and-see-attitude' about this whole thing."

"Well, it looks like you won't have to wait too long. The Miracle is supposed to happen in April or May."

"Fine. I'll buy front row tickets from whatever website you tell me to."

"Seriously, Steve. I'm thinking of going to Garabandal for real. You can still buy plane tickets to Spain."

"Pshaw!" said Steve. "Not that I believe all this infantile theology, but if I'm not mistaken, the, uh, 'Miracle,' as you like to call it, is going to be televised worldwide, right? So, I don't even need to go."

"That's true, but from what I hear, if you're there in person, you'll be healed of all your physical and spiritual ills."

"What 'physical and spiritual ills'? I feel just fine, thank you very much."

"If you died right now, would you go to Hell?" asked Kevin.

"Who really cares? I don't plan on dying for another sixty years, thank you very much a second time."

"What about the Chastisement? You could die in the

Chastisement."

"You really believe all that stuff, don't you?" scoffed Steve.

"It's been all over the media for the past few weeks, you know," said Kevin. "I'm not the only one who's been taking this stuff seriously."

"Whatever! So what about Kultida? You gonna meet up with this Swedish swan--girl--Moonie?"

"That's just it--how *do* I contact her? The return address just says plain 'Cincinnati.'"

"You said she has your phone number--you can just wait for her to call you," said Steve.

"That's true...hmm...I wonder if she's having trouble making a phone call...she said they might have people trailing her..."

"Hey, Einstein, she sent you a package; she obviously was able to get away at some point to mail you that Rosary."

"Wait a minute!" Kevin said, spinning around to face Steve. "The motor home! They're traveling in a motor home! It's probably just like in Indianapolis--they're sitting on some street in downtown Cincinnati doing their missionary thing. All I have to do is go there and look for a motor home in downtown Cincinnati."

"Begging your pardon again, Doctor Einstein, but how do you know they're still in Cincinnati? The operative word in 'motor home' is 'motor.' They've probably 'motored' on to another city."

Kevin sat down on a chair across from Steve, a puzzled look in his eyes. "Uhh, yeah, let's see, did she say anything about how long they normally stay in one city? I can't remember."

"They could be square dancing in Kansas City by now, bub," said Steve.

"Yeah, it might be a wasted trip if I did drive all the way to Cincinnati and she wasn't there."

"Ah, rationality rules at last," smiled Steve. "Just wait for her to call."

"You might have a point there."

Chapter 12

As he approached the outer belt, Thad could see the landmark tower of the Josephinum, whose Byzantine architectural style always reminded him of the trip he had taken to Europe in his senior year at Notre Dame. It hadn't been until his brother attended the seminary at the Josephinum that Thad had seen the interior of the Pontifical Institute. *The only pontifical seminary in the United States*, he reminded himself. *Why was that anyway? Who picked lowly Columbus, Ohio to be the site of a learning institution sponsored by the Vatican? Why not some more culturally Catholic town like Boston--or even Cincinnati, for that matter?* Thad turned onto the cloverleaf to head north on Route 23. *Beats me! Maybe it was another instance of what my old priest-brother Matt liked to say: "Thatsa your Churcha politics!" Well, whatever the reason, I'm glad it's nearby.*

Thad turned into the driveway and parked in the rear lot, checking again the name he had written down in his appointment book. His brother had suggested he talk to a "Father Sioux," the dean of students at the Josephinum. Thad's brother, Father Rankin, during his first attempt at the priesthood, had attended the seminary with Father Sioux back in the late 70s up in Boston. By a curious twist of providence, Father Sioux ended up at the Josephinum and had become fast friends with Thad's brother. Thad walked through the rear entrance, walked around some corners, through some hallways--and immediately was lost.

"It happens to the best of us!" said a priest who was passing by and noticed Thad's bewilderment. "Hi! Father Chesrown--welcome to the Josephinum," he said, extending his hand.

"Oh, hey," replied Thad, pumping the priest's hand. "I'm looking for Father Sioux; would you know where he is?"

"Oh, the master of ceremonies himself!" said Father Chesrown with a smile. "Sure, I can direct you to his office--matter of fact, I'm headed that way. I might as well show you myself--wouldn't want you to get lost again."

"Thanks."

A few twists and turns of the hallways later and Thad found himself in the dean's office.

"Just delivering a lost soul, Padre," said Father Chesrown as he walked into the office.

"Oh, good. I've been expecting you, Thad! Thank you, Father."

"At your service, sir," said Father Chesrown with a slight bow. "Nice meeting you," he said to Thad. "I hope we'll be seeing more of you."

"Okay, thanks."

Father Chesrown waved goodbye and walked off down the hall.

"So, looks like you got lost, eh?" asked Father Sioux, closing the office door. He motioned Thad to a chair, then sat down opposite him.

"Yeah! All those hallways look the same."

"Well, I was talking with your brother yesterday. He tells me you're considering the priesthood?"

"Huh, that's Father Matt Rankin for you, always planning out my life before I even know what's happening."

"Big brother blues, eh?"

"You might say that," said Thad with a wave of his hand. "I guess I can't blame him, though. I'm thirty-eight years old, I've got an engineering degree, and I'm driving a cab."

"Where did you go to school?"

"Notre Dame. I won the Joyce." The Joyce was a full-scholarship to Notre Dame, offered to residents of Central Ohio.

"Impressive," said Father Sioux, nodding his head slightly. "What's the story with the taxi driving? Father Matt's told me a little, but I'd like to hear it from you."

"Oh, boy," sighed Thad. "I sure do get tired of this process. Just once I would like to say, 'Oh, yeah, I work as a research engineer at Battelle down on King Avenue. That's all.'" Thad looked out the window and crossed his legs. "All right the nine-words-or-less-version is that I had a nervous breakdown ten years ago and have been unable to hold a stressful full-time job ever since."

"Okay, okay, I can accept that. Sounds simple enough. That would explain the cabbie job."

"Of course, the obvious question is what caused the nervous breakdown in the first place. Basically, I got kicked out of a religious organization and I took it pretty hard."

"Yes, I seem to remember Matt telling me you once were in the Crusaders of Christ."

"Exactly. What happened is that I wanted to be what you might call a 'commissioned officer' and they told me no. Therefore I left the group and eight months later: bingo! Nervous breakdown."

"You must have taken it pretty hard," said Father Sioux.

"Right, I really did--you see the Crusaders were my whole life. I ate, drank, and slept the Crusader life, and when I left it really unbalanced me."

"What exactly do the Crusaders do?"

"Essentially, they try to convert the world to Catholicism through prayer, example, and apostolate. They tend to set up companies and inculcate the corporate culture with Christian principles."

"Interesting...I've read a little about them. I hear they have chapels in all their office buildings?"

"That's true. The ACLU howled about it for awhile, but to no avail. It's really great! You can go to the chapel anytime during working hours, within reason. In most places, the Blessed Sacrament is reserved there as well. And it's not just office buildings, but factories, warehouses too."

"What happened after the nervous breakdown?" asked Father Sioux.

"I've been working part-time, menial jobs ever since--ha!" Thad burst out laughing. "It's really sort of funny! I've worked in a warehouse, as a courier, in a nursery, at a gas station--I even spent a month in a funeral home!"

"Really?"

"No kidding!" said Thad smiling. "But, like I say, it was only for a month. I couldn't take it after that."

"What did you do, exactly?"

"Push dead people around--lift them on and off the embalming table--that sort of thing. I quit after I had to deal with this kid who died of a gunshot wound."

"Sounds macabre."

"Definitely. But I also worked as a telemarketer, projectionist at a movie theater, factory worker, retail."

"You ought to write a book about it."

"That's what this friend of mine is always saying. Now, I'm driving a taxi, and I do have to say that cab driving is the best *menial* job you can have."

"That good, huh?"

"Yeah, there are a lot of pluses to it. You can set your own hours, go where you want, basically do your own thing. The best thing is the freedom you enjoy."

"I never knew it was that satisfying."

"If it paid a little more, more people would do it."

"That leads us to why you're here, then," said Father Sioux. "Matt tells me you've recently considered the priesthood."

"Well, the first thing I want to point out is that I think I may be pretty much completely recovered from my troubles. You see, I've been working the taxi job for over a year now, and I've been working full-time too. It remains to be seen whether I could handle a full-time job that involved some stress."

"Taxi driving isn't stressful?"

"Well, true, it is stressful," said Thad, tossing his head to one side, "but it's a certain kind of stress. The stress lasts from the time you get a call to the time you pick up the fare--well, of course, there's stress from traffic and all that."

"I see." Father Sioux cleared his throat and crossed his arms over his chest. "Thad, you must understand that we would have to look very carefully at your physical health history. We generally don't accept anyone with mental health problems."

"Yes, yes!" said Thad quickly. "I just want to point out that my main symptom has been insomnia--I really haven't had too many, you know--" he pointed to his head, "--psycho problems."

"Did you spend any time in the hospital?"

"Wha--huh. Uh, yeah--five weeks in Harding--you remember Harding? Or at least that's what it used to be called. It's that mental hospital up on Route one-sixty-one; I think it's run by OSU now."

"Five weeks sounds like it was pretty serious."

Thad gritted his teeth and spread his lips apart. "Well, I guess I'd have to say it was pretty serious, umm…"

"Like I say, I'd have to know more about that before we could ever consider letting you look into the seminary."

"I see," said Thad with a crestfallen look.

"Now, don't jump to conclusions yet, Thad. It's just that we have to be very careful these days about admissions to the seminary. I'm sure you can understand, with all the scandals in years past."

"Yeah, I see your point," Thad said in a soft voice, dropping his head slightly. "Maybe I'm just upset with Cheryl."

"Cheryl?"

"Yeah…female problems. I thought I'd found the perfect wife and then she dumps me."

"Now, Thad, I don't want to judge your intentions here, but surely you realize the sacrifice that celibacy requires."

"I know. Actually, Father, I was living a celibate life in the Crusaders of Christ."

"Oh?" Father Sioux brightened at this and sat up straight. "I never considered that aspect. How long were you in that state?"

"Six years--but I had planned to be in it for life."

"So your leaving the Crusaders had nothing to do with the celibacy thing then?"

"Not at all, but now I'm not so sure it's for me."

"Have you been dating since you left the group?"

"Only recently. I didn't think I should unless I could support a family."

"Can you support a family with your taxi business?"

"Just barely, I suppose. That's why I would really like to get back into engineering."

"And you think you can, now?" asked Father Sioux.

"That's the big question I guess you'd have to say."

"What brought you here today?"

"Well, it was the Warning more than anything."

"Oh, yes, *that.*" Father Sioux fell silent for a few seconds as he himself had a moment of introspection. "That really shook everyone up, I guess."

"Are you going to the Miracle?" asked Thad enthusiastically.

"I've had a ticket reserved for the past ten years! I can't wait to get there!"

"Uhh," stammered Father Sioux, "I'm a little hesitant to--I mean, what is the official Church position on that?"

"Different bishops are saying different things. Our bishop has tacitly approved of people going there, but he hasn't really come out publicly for or against it."

"I guess I knew that, but I don't want to...umm, well, you asked me if I'm going...I don't have any plans...are there tickets available?"

"They're starting to pop up all over the internet," said Thad. "I wonder how everyone is going to fit in the valley over there at Garabandal. Do you know that Our Lady said that whoever goes to the Miracle will be cured of all their illnesses, both bodily and spiritual?"

"Boy, that's uhh, really...something Thad. I might have seen that in the paper last week. You sound pretty knowledgeable about all this."

"Oh, Father, I've been following this whole Garabandal thing for years. I'm actually very happy that the Warning occurred last month."

"Now, Thad, have you heard that some people are referring to it as 'The Disturbance'?"

"Yeah, I've seen that stuff in the media. The Blessed Mother even predicted that this would happen--that people would try to pass the Warning off as something natural, not coming from God."

"I guess it *was* from God..."

"Oh, c'mon, Father!" said Thad irritably. "I mean--" He stopped and held up a hand. "Sorry, not to be disrespectful, but what I mean is that how could that have possibly been anything *but* supernatural? You're a priest--I'm sure you experienced something that shook you to the very core of your being, right?"

Father Sioux grew pensive again and looked down at his hands. "Yes, I did," he said quietly. "I saw some things about myself that were really frightening."

"But you went to Confession, right? You've been since the Warning, right?"

"I--I have been--well, I have definitely *heard* a lot of Confessions since the Warning, yes."

"Well, I highly recommend your going to see the Miracle, Father. I promise you won't be disappointed."

"I'll take that into consideration, Thad. Well," he said, beginning to smile, "you came looking *for* spiritual direction and here you are *giving* it."

"True!" said Thad cheerfully.   "Where were we?   We were talking about Cheryl, right?"

"Right.   You mentioned 'woman problems.'"

"Yeah--oh, I don't know, Father--about the priesthood, I mean. I guess if we can set aside the whole issue of whether I would be *allowed* to be a priest, I would just like to discuss my purpose in life."

"Maybe once you're back into your profession, you'll see things a little more clearly."

"I can see that, but--"   Thad stopped and bit his lower lip, nodding his head, "that's sort of part of it: do I want to go headlong into an engineering career, or should I put all my energies into the search for the priesthood?"

"You can do a lot of good in the working world, you know," said Father Sioux.   "Saint Joseph was a carpenter and look where he ended up.   Most theologians agree that, among creatures, he is second only to Mary in blessedness in Heaven."

"I suppose that goes back to one of my patented 'Thad Theories,'" he said with a smirk.   "I've always proclaimed that the purpose of life is to get the highest place in Heaven with the least amount of work!"

Father Sioux chuckled at this.   "Sort of a 'Sanctity Efficiency Coefficient,' huh? Work Output divided by Work Input?"

"Yeah," said Thad.   "I never really thought about it like that. You study engineering or something?"

"Oh, perish the thought," laughed Father Sioux.   "I just remember that from high school physics."

"I'll have to remember that."

"All right, where does that leave us?" Father Sioux looked at his watch, then over at Thad.   "I don't have too much more time."

"I guess I'll go to Garabandal and think about it more after that. With all that's going on in the world right now, I can't be too sure what's going to happen to me, no matter how hard I plan."

"That sounds sensible to me, but, uhh, when is this "miracle" supposed to occur?"

"Ahh," said Thad, rubbing his hands together, "this is where it gets interesting.   It's supposed to happen on a Thursday in March, April, or May at 8:30 in the evening, Garabandal time. It's supposed to happen between the 8th and the 16th of the month, on a feast of a martyr of the Eucharist."

"That really narrows it down."

"Exactly. It looks like it will be on April 12th. See, Conchita will announce the date eight days before it occurs--or rather, after she learns of the date from the Blessed Mother, she will tell her spiritual director, a priest, and *he* will announce it to the world."

"Yeah, I seem to recall reading something like that in the paper the other day."

"So, can I sign you up for a plane ticket?" asked Thad.

"Wuh, uh, whoa," said Father Sioux, raising one of his hands. "Give me some time to think about it."

"Well, it's March 16th now; you don't have too much more time left--and, you know, there's not going to be that much room in the valley over there anyway."

"'The valley'?"

"The valley that Garabandal sits in--it basically makes a natural amphitheater, but some people have estimated that it can only hold about four million people."

"'Only'?"

"Well," said Thad smilingly, "considering that people from all over the world will be coming, four million is not that many."

"You gotta point there...you know, Thad, you sort of have your own little vocation promoting this whole Garabandal thing...do you really think you need to become a priest?"

"I see what you're saying, but I'll be out of a job after the Miracle...Garabandal will have served its purpose."

"Why don't you wait till after you come back from Spain and see what you're thinking at that time."

"Okay, okay. 'Heaven can wait,' as the expression goes." Thad looked up at the clock on the wall. "I better get going now, Father."

"It was good talking with you, Thad. Maybe we can get together when you return."

"I'd like that--yeah, that's a good idea."

They shook hands and Thad walked to the office door. "Let me know if you want a plane ticket to Garabandal, Father."

"I'll think about it. See you later."

"Bye."

****

Kevin always liked the occasional trips he had to take to downtown Columbus, which more often than not were to the main library on Grant Avenue. It was a tidy downtown, clean and pleasant, with plenty of wide sidewalks for a casual stroll. Today he was heading to a small curiosity shop he had seen on High Street to look for a birthday present for his sister. He was driving down Third Street and had just crossed Broad Street when he couldn't believe his eyes! Parked off to the side of the road was a motor home--he instantly recognized it to be the Moonie-mobile by its Illinois license plates! He was about to pull over and park when something told him not to. *Remember what happened in Indianapolis, how Kultida had warned that she might be being watched. Maybe I better try the stealth approach.* Kevin continued driving down Third, turned onto Rich Street and parked his car in the City Center parking garage. Instead of going up Third Street, he decided it best to take a less direct route by walking up High Street till he reached the Statehouse Grounds. He strolled across the elegant landscape that surrounded Ohio's Legislature, stopping now and then and pretending to read the inscriptions on various monuments. When he came to the east side of the Statehouse he selected an appropriate park bench and sat down facing the motor home. Several nondescript people came and left the vehicle, but then his heart skipped a beat--it was *her*! Kultida gingerly stepped off the motor home onto the sidewalk. A line from the Beach Boys' song, "Good Vibrations" wafted through Kevin's head: "...I love the colorful clothes she wears and the way the sunlight plays upon her hair..." Kultida's bright red outfit was only outdone by her shimmering shoulder-length golden-glowing hair. Kevin was about to spring from the bench when he restrained himself. *Stealth is a virtue...take it easy...they're probably watching her every move.* Kevin watched as she turned and walked north on Third. *Ha!* Kevin thought. *I bet she's headed for the Cathedral. Out to snatch some unsuspecting Catholic coming out of the 12:05 Mass!*

It was all he could do to keep from running after her, but Kevin knew he had to be a tad devious if he was ever to talk with her.

Instead of following her up Third Avenue, he turned around and retraced his steps, taking the long way around the Statehouse. Just as he turned east onto Broad Street he looked toward the Cathedral and saw a red figure go up the stairs of the Church. *Oh, Lord, I hope that's her!* He quickened his pace, crossed Broad Street at the next intersection and five minutes later opened the massive door to St Joseph's. He dipped his hand into the huge holy water fount and let his eyes adjust to the diminished interior light of the majestic edifice. Kevin walked through the inner door, into the Church proper when his heart began pounding again in his throat--she was kneeling there in the back of the Church, praying the Rosary! *This is too good to be true*--now *what do I do?* Just then something caught in his throat and he involuntarily coughed twice. Kultida turned around, recognized him, and jumped out of the pew.

"Kevin!" she said in a loud whisper, since Mass was going on up in the front of the Church. She ran into his arms and gave him a hug. "I plan call you--we arrive today--this morning!" She released her hold on him and looked him up and down. "You look good! You feel good? You okay?" she asked, smiling broadly.

"Yes, yes!" said Kevin in a hoarse whisper. He motioned to the vestibule. "Hey, let's go to the lobby--we don't want to disturb the Mass up front."

"Of course, yes, yes, of course!" Kultida practically danced her way over to the door and held it open for Kevin.

After the door had closed behind them, Kevin couldn't wait to question this bundle of energy. "Kultida, what happened? Are you still with the Moonies? I saw you get off the motor home just now."

"What?" she asked, a puzzled look on her face. "How know you I on bus, er, motor home?"

"I saw it parked along the side of the street. I thought maybe I better not let that Doctor guy see me talking to you--do they know you've been praying the Rosary?"

"How long you see motor home--you wait long?"

"No, just a few minutes, actually," explained Kevin. "Oh, yeah, thanks for the Rosary you sent me. Here--just a second!" He slipped his hand into his pocket and produced the beads. "See?"

"Oh, good, Kevin! I so glad you like!"

"So, tell me, Kultida, are you coming back to the Church? What about the Moonies?"

"Oh, I don't know," she said, a shadow passing over her face. "I not know what do." She stared at the floor, the smile gone from her face.

"Does the Doctor and your friends know what's happening?"

"I think they maybe have little guess...I not bring anybody back to bus for week. I supposed come to church here and talk to people, bring them back to bus--you know, like what I do you. But, now I just come to Catholic Church to pray Rosary. I go back to them and they no understand. Maybe they guess."

"What caused you to start saying the Rosary?" asked Kevin.

"You know, the--" Kultida waved her arms around her head. "The big thing last month. How you say, the..."

"The Warning, you mean?"

"Right!" She smiled briefly, then looked down again at the floor. "I see my sins, I see many bad things."

"But, the Warning occurred *before* I met you in Indianapolis--weren't you affected by all this when I saw you two weeks ago?"

"Oh, I, I--how you say--I--no see--I *blind* myself! I not want know truth."

"I see," said Kevin softly, nodding his head. "I understand."

"One day when I standing in front Church in Cin-nnati, something say 'Go into church!' Many, many time: 'Go into Church! Go into Church!' So I go into Church and I sit down--then I cry. Many, many cry! A holy lady sit next to me. How you say?" Kultida made a motion over her head and hair.

"A nun?"

"Yes, yes--a nun sit next me in church in Cin-nnati. She hold my hand and talk me. She good, she...kind. She give me Rosary--I ask her mail you Rosary--I got you post address from library, from Internet."

"That's great, Kultida--have you been to Mass too?"

Again a shadow passed over her face and Kultida replied: "I bad, Rosary good now. I love Mary, she my Mother. But, Doctor Klein no like this, I sure. I no tell him. I yes must go Mass, but no time, Doctor Klein will find out. I need see priest, you know..."

"Confession?"

"Yes, yes, Confession...I bad. Rosary okay now."

They both stopped talking as people leaving the noon Mass began to walk through the vestibule. Kevin deliberated about what to do next, but by the time the lobby was empty again, he had made up his mind.

"Kultida, you can't go back!"

"What?" said Kultida loudly, drawing away from him.

"They'll find out one of these days that you're coming back to the Faith, and they won't like it."

"But they my friend, Kevin! I like them! They my life!"

"Kultida, come to the Miracle with me," Kevin said with a determined look, grabbing her by both shoulders.

"Whaaa? Doctor Klein say TV bad--I only hear little about, what you say--'Miracle'? Spain, right? Sometime I see headline on newspaper."

"Kultida, the Blessed Mother said whoever goes to the Miracle will be healed of all his spiritual and physical ills."

"I no have ills, I fine."

"What about spiritual ills, Kultida? Maybe the Moonies damaged your Faith. If you go to Spain, your soul will be healthy again."

"Ohh…Kevin…I…me sit down." Kultida walked to one of the steps leading up to the interior church doors and sat down. "I need think. I feel crazy."

Kevin sat down next to her and said gently, "Sorry to come on so strong, Kultida. I know this must be hard for you. Something just told me to tell you that…maybe it's the Blessed Mother, I don't know. Could it be the Holy Spirit?"

"I know, I know, you want good for me. We be quiet for minute--I pray. I think."

The two sat silently for a few minutes, after which Kultida stood up and faced Kevin. "Okay, Kevin, I go with you, but--"

"Good deal!" he said, jumping to his feet. "You won't be disappointed, Kultida!"

"Wait, wait, escuse me," she said, holding up a hand. "I say something. I go with you, but I go back and tell Doctor Klein I go." She stared intently into Kevin's eyes.

Kevin tilted his head back and let out a long sigh. He paused a moment before replying. "Kultida, look. I don't know a whole lot about the Moonies, but I don't think they'll take too kindly to your telling them you want to leave."

"But, Kevin." Kultida began to sniffle and choked back tears. "I been friend since last summer. I like...I *love* my people friends."

"Ahh, Kultida," said Kevin, taking one of her hands in his. "I know you like them, but what happens if you go back there and they don't let you go with me? It could get really nasty, I mean, they could *physically* stop you from getting off the motor home once you're aboard."

Kultida looked away, brushing tears from her eyes.

Suddenly, Kevin brightened. "Hey, I have an idea! We'll go to lunch, then I'll show you around Ohio State--I can get into the stadium--I'll show you exactly where I threw the touchdown pass when we beat Michigan!"

Kultida giggled softly, and looked at Kevin whimsically. "You fute-ball! Crazy American sport." She pulled her hand away from his grasp. "Well..."

Kevin looked at her hopefully, noticing for the first time the earrings she was wearing.

"Okay--but I no decide till six clock, okay? I have be back by six?"

"Okay, babe! I heard that."

Staying well away from the Statehouse and the Moonies' motor home, the couple wended its way to Kevin's car, from whence they drove to the OSU campus. Kevin parked behind his apartment on Northwood and they walked from there to the campus. They stopped at Jimmy Guoco's for lunch and then proceeded across High Street to the campus proper.

"This is the Oval," explained Kevin as they walked across the wide expanse that marked the focal point of the University. "So named because of its shape. And right down there--" he pointed to the west end of the Oval--"is the main library. To the right is the Administration Building, which is modeled after Independence Hall in Philadelphia."

"Pennvana, right?" asked Kultida.

"Pennsylvania, right." It was a bright, sunny day with just the right amount of puffy white clouds in the sky and Kevin was glad to have the chance to take a walk on such a sparkling afternoon. They walked to Mirror Lake and Kevin explained about the tradition of young men proposing to their girlfriends there.

After showing her Dulles Hall, where Kevin took some of his History classes, he walked Kultida by the impressive OSU medical complex and finally arrived at the "piece de resistance," the beloved

Ohio Stadium. One of the gates was open so they walked under the stands and out onto the playing field.

"This is it, Kultida," he said reverently. "Some of the happiest memories of my life occurred right here."

"It so, um, big, er, so, what word is--hue, hue..."

"Huge?"

"Yes, yes, 'huge'!" said Kultida. "We have nothing this big in Sweden." She ran out onto the grass and spun around. "Let play 'fute-ball,' Kevin!"

"Huh! You need to gain about a hundred pounds, babe!"

"What is this 'babe' you say?" asked Kultida. "You say that in church. What that mean?"

"Ha!" Kevin laughed. "It's short for 'baby.' It's just an expression. Don't take it literally."

"So you say you beat Mitch-ee-gun?"

"Yeah, good memory, Kultida. Yeah, we beat Michigan last year."

"We go to Mitch-ee-gun last year...how you say--Dee--troy?"

"Detroit?"

"Right, Detroit. So I hear about Mitch-ee-gun then."

"Good deal," said Kevin, staring at Kultida as she danced around. He shook his head and ran up to the twenty yard line. "Here, you stand here." He pointed to a spot near the center of the field. "Now when I say 'Hike!' you run to the end zone."

"End zone?"

"Oh, right, you're from Sweden, I forgot. That big area there, where that big pole is," Kevin said, pointing to the goalposts. "It was the Michigan game two years ago. Michigan was ahead, thirty-five to thirty. There were only four seconds left in the game. I got to play because the starting quarterback got a concussion with one minute left in the game. You are standing right where Garrity was standing. HIKE!"

Kultida jumped a little and looked at Kevin. "What?"

"You run to that big pole."

"Oh, okay!" Kultida skipped across the grass and stopped in front of the goalpost. She turned to face Kevin, who had "faded back" for a pass.

"Okay, Garrity was right where you were, there was no time left on the clock and I threw it just like this." Kevin motioned with his arm.

"Now all you have to do is catch it!"

Kultida jumped up and pretended to catch the game-winning touchdown.

"You did it" shouted Kevin, running up to Kultida. "Now give me a high-five!"

Kultida stood there smiling. "What you mean, you crazy American...'high-five'?"

"Like this," said Kevin, raising her arm and slapping her hand with his.

"And you win game?" asked Kultida.

"You bet 'we win game'!" said Kevin. "You'll have to come to a pro game this fall," he said excitedly.

"Oh, you play big league now, yes?"

"'Big league' is right."

Kultida twirled around and looked again at the towering stands that held one-hundred and five thousand on Saturday afternoons in the fall. "Kevin, everyone in America happy like you?"

"Not everyone, but a lot of us are," he said. "Not everyone is as lucky as I've been. Heck, when I was a kid growing up in Rocky River-_"

"What is 'Rocky River'?"

"It's a suburb of Cleveland--up north."

"Oh."

"When I was growing up in Rocky River, I was satisfied when I made starting quarterback in high school. It was beyond my wildest dreams to play for the pros. Heck, I couldn't believe it when Ohio State signed me up. I've been really, really lucky, Kultida. I could've been injured in high school or here at OSU. So far, everything's gone my way."

"I played fute-ball in Sweden--or, I mean," Kultida chuckled, "I mean, how you say--'soccer'--in school."

"Oh, how'd you like it?"

"Ahh, I not too good." She tilted her head from side to side.

"Well, you were good enough to catch that touchdown pass just now," Kevin said with a smile.

"You crazy American," Kultida said, jabbing her finger into his shoulder. "You like Steve Martin."

"Whoa! You're really up on your Hollywood stars, girl."

"All road lead to America, right?"

"Mighty impressive, Miss Kultida. We'll make an American out of you yet."

The smile fell from her face and a worried look came into her eyes. "That reminds me...I maybe not be in America."

"What do you mean?"

"Well, you say I not go back Moonies? Where I go?"

"You could stay with my sister. She lives right here in town. She'll take care of you."

"How you be sure? You no talk to her, no?"

"That's true, I haven't talked to her about it yet, but she has a big heart--she'll put you up."

"But how long? My visa not forever."

"Kultida, first things first. Let's wait till after the Miracle, then we'll see what happens."

"Maybe I no want to go to Miracle."

"That's fine," said Kevin. "You don't have to go. I just want to make sure you get away from those Moonies. I want to see you come back to the Church."

"That true."

They stood there for a minute, Kevin looking at Kultida, and Kultida staring at the ground. Abruptly, Kultida turned to Kevin and said, "Okay, Kevin, I no wait till six clock, I know now. I stay your sister, yes?"

"Way to go, girl!" Kevin said, taking her hand and shaking it vigorously. "You made the right decision! You're going to love Ohio-- or rather, you're going to love living *free* now in Ohio."

"But I no promise Spain travel," she said, looking expectantly at him.

"I understand, I understand," Kevin said, holding up a hand in surrender. "I'm just glad to see you saying the Rosary and living free again."

After dinner, Kevin called up his sister, who gladly agreed to host Kultida for a week or two. Kevin drove Kultida to a drugstore in Upper Arlington, where she purchased some toiletries. A few minutes before nine, Kevin parked in front of his sister's condo at Hidden Lake. He made the usual introductions to his sister and explained that they were a little unsure how long Kultida would be staying.

"I understand, let me know when you know more," said Cathy, his sister.

"Will do. See you tomorrow, Kultida, and don't eat her out of house and home."

"You no worry, Kevin. I do dishes and sweep rug. I no free live."

"Just kidding! I'll call you tomorrow, okay?"

"That fine. Bye."

"Bye."

****

Dexter hadn't been to Byrne's Pub in a while. A cozy little bar at the corner of Northwest Boulevard and Third Avenue, it was a watering hole for the twenty-and-up-somethings of near-Northwest Columbus. Many were the nights Dexter had driven there to wind up a day's work at Grobotics. It was there that he'd first met Daphne, some three years ago. Too often he had to take a cab home, rather than risk smashing up his beloved Charger in a drunken stupor. But some habits are hard to break, and Dexter found his way back to Byrne's on a frigid Saturday night in March. He slipped in the side door, half-hoping that no one would recognize him, save for the bartender, maybe. Tony had always been a good pal, looking out for his young patron, especially when he had imbibed one too many. But Tony was out-of-town that night, and Dexter furtively glanced around to look for any old drinking buddies that might have shown up.

Dexter ordered a Molson Ice, his favorite, and settled into a seat in the corner. *Maybe it'll all go away*, he thought. *Maybe all this religion and priests and "Miracle" talk will just fade out--like the setting sun. Maybe the Warning--the Disturbance--was all just what so many others asserted--mass hysteria. Hadn't it happened before in history? Was it a leftover from the Y2K scare? And, even more*, reasoned Dexter, *why did it have to be religious? Why couldn't it have been just a natural phenomenon? After all, it did have a good effect, didn't it? People were treating each other better, crime rates were lower. Who did Father Rankin think he was? And Thad? It was like they appropriated the whole thing for their own use! Garabandal...riiight...*

"What's a sailor like you doin' all by himself?" The woman's question jarred Dexter out of his thoughts.

"Huh? Oh, me? Yeah, uh, hi! I was just going over some things in my head."

"You say some things are going right over your head?" The shapely brunette smiled at Dexter.

"Not over my head--uhh, hey, why don't you have a seat? The name's Dexter." He stood up and offered his hand.

"Stephanie," she said, shaking his hand. "Don't mind if I do, Dexter." She sat down and took a drink of the marguerita in her hand.

"So, you new around here?" asked Dexter. "I used to hang around here a lot a while back, but I don't recognize you."

"I just moved here from San Diego, actually. Only been here a few weeks."

"How 'bout that! A real 'foreigner,' huh?" Dexter leaned back in his chair and glanced around the room. "You here all by your self, Stephanie?"

"Just me, myself, and I," she said giggling.

"Well, I'll be a monkey's uncle!"

"How about a bear's nephew?"

"A woman with a sense of silliness!" said Dexter. "I like it!"

"What else do you like, sailor?"

"Now that's a loaded question, isn't it?"

"Not as loaded as you're going to be if you keep downing those beers," said Stephanie with another burst of giggling.

"How 'bout we go for a little walk, Stephanie?"

A little red flag went up in Dexter's mind. He could easily hear the small voice in his head despite the loud bar music. *"Just what do you think you're doing, Dexter!"*

He ignored Albert, the so-named little voice in his head, and smiled at Stephanie.

"Any particular destination, Dexter?"

"We could just follow the stars...I think it's clear out tonight."

The duo got up and walked out onto Third Avenue.

"You're right, sailor boy, it *is* clear out here!"

"See, what did I tell you? What's your favorite constellation?"

"The only thing I know about is the Big Dipper...what's your favorite?" asked Stephanie. They started walking toward Grandview Avenue.

"It would have to be Ursa Minor, my little chickadee."

"That's what I like, a man with a well-honed mind."

"What else do you like, Stephanie?"

"That's *my* question, if I'm not mistaken."

"Yes, what *do* I like, I wonder." Dexter put his arm around Stephanie's shoulder. "I'll have to think about it."

"Mmmm, that you should do," replied Stephanie, slipping her hand around his waist. "Do we have a destination yet, big guy?"

Albert shouted inside Dexter's head: *"You Asshole! Dump this chick! Just like a dog returning to its vomit! Father Rankin will have your head!"*

To Stephanie: "I thought I might show you my domicile, little girl." To Albert: "Go play in traffic! Can't a guy have a little fun now and-then?"

"What's your favorite room in your mansion?"

"Oh, now that's the big surprise!"

The vomit tasted surprisingly good to Dexter that night. She was gone before he woke up.

****

When the phone rang the next morning at Grobotics, Dexter answered it himself since Mrs. Downing was out for the day.

"Grobotics," he said.

"Hey, Dexter, this is Thad!"

"Yeah, Thad, what's up? You sound excited."

"Dexter, they've taken him!"

"Who's taken who?"

"The Chinese! They've taken my brother!"

"Whaa?" said Dexter, bolting upright in his chair. "What did he do?"

"The secretary at Saint Michael's said they took him to the fairgrounds. I've been hearing rumors that they've made it into a temporary holding pen for political dissidents."

"Your brother is a 'political dissident'?"

"He didn't do what they've been trying to get every other priest to do: change the Mass--the words of Consecration specifically."

"How long are they going to hold him?"

"I have no idea, but, look--Dexter--you have to go see him. I can't! They would probably get me too!"

"You sure you're not being a little too paranoid?"

"Dexter, just last month they murdered everyone at the Mass I normally attend everyday, and now they've got my brother in a concentration camp--I think I have a little reason to stay out of sight!"

"You've got a point. All right, I'll go see Father Matt today."

"The sooner the better. Dexter, I've heard they've got guillotines down there."

"Come on, Thad! Isn't that a little extreme? They might want to lock up your brother, but is there any reason to *kill* him?"

"Please just go see him right away…please!?"

"Fine, fine. I'll go right now, okay?"

"I appreciate it, Dexter."

"Later."

"Bye."

After Dexter told Jerry that he would be out for a little while he got into his car and drove to the fairgrounds. He parked behind the Rhodes center and walked inside the red brick structure. A Chinese guard asked him for his driver's license and then ran the card past a scanner.

"Why you here?" asked the guard.

"I'm looking for a Father Matthew Rankin. I was told he was taken here recently. I'd like to visit him."

"Wait," the guard said tersely. He walked through a door toward the rear of the lobby and came back a few minutes later, followed by another guard carrying an AK-47.

"Follow I," said the gun-toting soldier.

Dexter was led through a series of hallways, occasionally hearing a blood-curdling scream coming through the door of one of the rooms off to the side. Two minutes later, the guard opened the door to what at one time had been an office.

"You stay five minute!" said the guard in a loud voice. "No more!"

Dexter walked into the "cell" and the guard closed the door behind him.

"Dexter!" said Father Rankin, who rose to his feet and embraced Dexter. "Oh, I'm so glad to see you! How did you know I was here?"

"Your brother told me. Are you all right?"

"Better than you know, Dexter." Father Rankin let go of the bear hug he had given Dexter and took his hand in both of his. "How about you?"

Dexter thought back to the night he had spent with the girl from the bar and looked away. "Pretty good, Father, but I, uh…"

"Here, sit down." Father Rankin motioned to the chair in the middle of the room.

"Father Rankin…" Dexter averted his eyes and hung his head. "Father, I…completely blew it last night. I didn't know you were in trouble! I'm not good…I…"

"A woman, I suppose," said Father Rankin knowingly.

"Yeah, I need to shape up, I guess."

"Dexter, it's never too late to put yourself right with the Lord."

"I'm sorry, Father. Last night, I just thought I'd go out for a drink, and…"

"Well, you'll have a lot to tell in your first Confession."

"I know, I know." Dexter slowly raised his head and finally looked the priest in the eye. "What about you, Father? Here you are consoling me--I should be helping you."

"Oh, all this is nothing compared to the mansion I'll soon be in."

Dexter hesitated a second and gave the priest a quizzical look. "Mansion?"

Father Rankin sat down on the edge of the bed and looked into Dexter's eyes. "Dexter…you will be the first one to know."

"What are you talking about, Father Rankin?"

"It's the same old story that's been repeated for two thousand years, my friend."

"What are you trying to tell me?"

"The game's just about up, and the victory party is about to begin," said Father Rankin in a soft voice. "Dexter, by this time tomorrow, I'll be in eternity."

"Father, don't be ridiculous! You don't have to--" He was interrupted by a bone-chilling scream from the "office" across the hall. Just then the door opened and the guard thrust his head in. "You one minute! Then you go!"

"Dexter, I want you to tell my family that I'm dying for Christ and that--"

"Father Rankin, stop this! Look, I--" He lowered his voice to a whisper. "Father Rankin, look. I've got plenty of gold bullion hidden

John Klee

away. We can bribe these guards into letting you go--heck, we can bribe the camp commander to let you go! How much do you think it'll take?"

"Dexter, Dexter," said Father Rankin calmly, reaching out to take Dexter's hand, "please don't worry. I'm ready to die. I've been preparing for this day for the past ten years. I knew it would happen one day."

"Father Rankin, don't be a fool! You should try to save your life if you have the chance! Think how much good you could do on the outside!"

"Dexter, in the first century of the Church, the same thing happened to Ignatius of Antioch. He was condemned to death for being a Christian and some people were trying to arrange for his release. He told them not to take away his chance to be a martyr for the Lord. It's the same thing here."

The guard opened the door and waved his rifle. "You go now! Stop talking!"

Dexter rose from the chair but stood in place. "No, Father Rankin!" His voice faltered as he began to cry. Father Rankin stood up and embraced Dexter.

"You'll be fine, Dexter," Father Rankin said, patting him on the back.

"But...Father..." Dexter said between sobs, "who...who will I talk to from now on?"

The guard pulled Dexter away from Father Rankin. "No more talk! You go!"

"Ask Thad--he'll know what to do."

The guard prodded Dexter with the muzzle of his rifle and forced him out into the hallway.

As the guard was closing the door, Dexter could hear Father Rankin: "...bless you, in the Name of the Father, and the Son, and the Holy Spirit. Amen."

Dexter dried his tears, climbed into the Charger, and drove back to Grobotics.

****

Curt and Sparrow had called Kevin a few days earlier to setup a lunch date and now they were sitting in the Wendy's on High Street across from campus.

"Glad you could make it on such short notice, Kevin," said Curt. "I know you must be busy with all your football tryouts and stuff."

"No problem, guys. Believe it or not, there are more important things in life than football. Hey, you guys were right about the Warning--it happened just like you said--the day after I met you, when we went to that Elyria place."

"The question is," said Sparrow, "are you going to the Miracle?"

"Yeah," said Curt, "the Warning was important, but you've *got* to go to the Miracle!"

"Aw, I don't know, you guys..." Kevin squirmed in his seat. "I was just trying to convince this girl to go, but now I'm a little hesitant. I went to a talk a week or two ago by this professor over at OSU and--well, I guess I believe all this stuff...I'm still a little confused..."

"C'mon, man!" said Sparrow, "what's there to be confused about? Didn't we tell you all this was going to happen? It's been predicted for decades."

"I know," said Kevin, biting his lower lip, "but why go to the Miracle? We will be able to see it on TV, right?"

"C'mon!" said Sparrow, "you know that! It's been in all the papers!"

"Yeah, I *do* know," said Kevin sheepishly. "I'm just a little scared to go to the Miracle, I guess."

"What's there to be scared about?" asked Sparrow. "Heck, you say you're confused--here's the chance to clear everything up. I'm sure Mary will help you if you ask her."

"I really think Sparrow has a point, Kevin," said Curt. "I think there will be great graces to be had for anyone who goes to the Miracle."

"Well, what about plane tickets?" asked Kevin defensively. "I probably won't be able to get tickets--I hear they're really scarce."

"Problem solved, hombre," said Sparrow. "We've got an extra ticket on Sunny Airlines and it's got your name written all over it."

"Seriously?"

"As serious as sudden death overtime," said Sparrow.

"What about Kultida?" asked Kevin.

"Who's Kultida?" asked Curt.

"Didn't I tell you about her?" asked Kevin. "Well, I guess I met her after the Elyria thing. She's the girl who I just said I was trying to convince to go to the Miracle."

"No, you didn't tell us," said Sparrow. "Kultida...sounds foreign."

"Righto, Sparrow," said Kevin. "She's a hot woman from Sweden--I first met her in Indianapolis a few weeks ago."

"You were in Indy for the combine?" asked Sparrow.

"Right. This chick was in the Moonies."

"Whoa!" said Curt. "You're dating some girl who's in the Moonies?"

"Hold the phone!" said Kevin with a laugh, holding up one of his hands. "All is not lost! I convinced her to *leave* the Moonies."

"Oh...that's different," said Curt. "You want to take this girl to the Miracle?"

"I sort of asked her, but, yeah, I think she should go."

"You've known her for *how long*?" asked Sparrow.

"Only about three weeks."

"Is she Catholic?"

"Yeah...she's Catholic--she's just getting back into the Faith. She says the Rosary, she needs to hit the Confessional box and all that, but she knows that."

"Huh! Whaddya say, Curt?" asked Sparrow, casting his eyes on his friend.

"Whadda *you* say, Sparrow?" rejoined Curt.

"Thumbs up here," said Sparrow.

"Thumbs up here, too," said Curt. "All right, Kevin, it's a deal. We've got tickets for both you and your Swedish dream girl."

"Really? I thought you said you had just *one* ticket."

"Let's just say we got our priorities straight, bub," said Sparrow. "We were thinking of giving it to someone else, but we consider you a good investment."

"Good deal!" said Kevin. "Now all I have to do is convince Kultida to go. What are the exact dates anyway? I've read in the paper something about it being either in April or May."

"Correct," said Curt. "It looks like it might be on April 12th. It will be announced eight days ahead of time. The Blessed Virgin told the visionaries that the Miracle will happen within one year of the Warning, and that it will happen in March, April, or May, on a

Thursday, between the eighth and the sixteenth of the month. So--
elementary calculus gives us April 12th--of this year."

"Pretty detailed instructions, huh?" said Kevin.

"Hey, Noah got pretty detailed instructions on how to build the
Ark, too," said Sparrow.

"I'd have to admit that," said Kevin, scratching his chin. "I bet
there's going to be a boatload of jumbo jets heading toward Spain in a
few weeks."

"Actually, it's happening now," said Curt. "There are some
pioneering types who are already there. Among other things, they're
helping setup the thousands of tents that will be needed when the
stampede begins."

"And porta potties," said Sparrow.

"Thank you for reminding us," said Curt with a smile.

"It's going to be like a giant Scouting Jamboree," said Sparrow.
"I wonder if I can get a merit badge for this."

"Yeah, you can wear your neckerchief everyday," said Curt.
"Just be careful you don't start any forest fires when you're having a
campfire."

"Seriously," said Kevin, "it is going to be quite a logistical feat.
How many do you think are going to be there?"

"I've heard estimates of four million," said Curt.

"And the population of the town of Garabandal is?" asked
Kevin.

"Three hundred and twelve souls," replied Sparrow.

"What are you a walking tour guide of Spain or something?"
Kevin asked Sparrow.

"When you've followed this apparition for as long as I have, you
tend to know these things," said Sparrow. "Garabandal lies in the
Cantabrian Mountains in the northeast corner of Spain."

"Fine. I know where to go when I need tourist info," said Kevin.

"So, it's settled," concluded Curt. "You and your girlfriend--"

"--She's not my 'girlfriend,'" Kevin said quickly.

"No?"

"I'm confused about her. She's only been away from the
Moonies for a short time."

"Well, yeah, guy," said Sparrow, "you said you've only known
her for what--three weeks?"

"It's not just that--did I tell you I broke up with this girl that I had dated for three years?"

"Yeah," said Sparrow, "that was pretty recent, wasn't it?"

"Right, just last month."

"So you're having woman problems," said Sparrow.

"I can't quite figure the whole thing out," said Kevin. "Yeah, you could say I'm having 'woman problems.'"

"Well, anyway," Curt said, glancing at his watch, "I have to get going. Like I was saying then, it's settled, right? You and this Swedish girl will be flying over with Sparrow and me, right?"

"Yeah, I guess," said Kevin, brushing his hair with his hand. "I mean, I have to convince her to go, but I think she'll say yes."

"All right, we'll keep in touch."

The trio emptied their trash into the wastebaskets and left the restaurant.

****

They had let him keep his Scapular and medals, which surprised Father Rankin. He expected those would be the first things he would lose to the Chinese when they threw him into "prison," as the Rhodes Center on the Ohio State Fairgrounds had become. What surprised him even more was the fact that he was even allowed to keep his Breviary as well. Father Rankin had spent the three days since he had been "captured" praying and meditating, especially on the Passion of Christ. *How grateful I am to Mel Gibson for that movie he made on the Passion of Christ!* thought Father Rankin as he lay on his cot, watching the sun rise through the slit in the boarded up window of his "cell." He had read the writings of Anne Catherine Emmerich, on which the Passion movie was based, but how powerful those scenes were in that movie! *I won't even have to suffer at all like Christ.* Father Rankin knew what was coming. He had heard the rumors for the past few years about believers losing their heads in the end times. He had read on the internet that the modern guillotines were vastly improved over those used in the French Revolution. Gone were the days of the slow, gravity-powered contraptions that claimed the lives of King Louis XVI and Marie Antoinette. Nowadays, guillotines were spring-loaded and mass produced. When the blades fell this time, heads would roll much more quickly.

"Father of providence, look with love on Benedict, our Pope, your appointed successor to St Peter on whom you built your Church. May he be the visible center and foundation of our unity in faith and love. Grant this through Christ Our Lord. Amen." Father Rankin recited this prayer quietly to himself, reading it from a slip of paper he had kept in his Breviary. The guards permitted condemned prisoners to talk during the night before their execution, so Father Rankin had been singing hymns occasionally for the past few hours, since he couldn't sleep. His favorite was a song he had often heard his parents sing, "Bring Flowers of the Fairest." It was a joyful tune about honoring the Blessed Mother with bouquets of flowers. It always reminded Father Rankin of the many May Crownings he had been to over the years when it was springtime and the balmy air was full of promise. *But the air is full of promise now, right?* he asked himself. *In a few hours, I'll be in Heaven, right? I'm dying for Christ and His Church, and the Church has always taught that martyrs go straight to Heaven without having to be purified in Purgatory.* A mixture of joy and fear coursed through his veins. On one hand he remembered what his uncle had often repeated about a priest who was asked how he felt as he lay on his deathbed. The elderly priest had replied: "Like a schoolboy going home for the Holidays!" On the other hand, Father Rankin recalled the words of a martyr of the Coliseum. As he was led to his execution, he had prayed to God that the beasts "finish me off quickly; be quick about what they do." *Of course, I'll be dying in the same manner as Saint Thomas More died, and he made jokes as he was led onto the scaffold. Why shouldn't I have the same attitude?* A smile spread across Father Rankin's face as he remembered what that saintly Dominican priest at Saint Pat's had said back in the 90s: we should have a "devil-may-care" attitude about the whole process. *He's right,* concluded Father Rankin. *Like my Dad used to say, quoting Saint Paul, as he walked around the house when I was a kid: "Oh, Death? Where is thy sting?"*

Father Rankin rolled out of bed and said his morning prayers on his knees. *That settles it!* he decided. *If Thomas More can be joyful, so can I!* He walked over to the door and knocked from the inside.

"Guard, sir?"

"What you want?" asked the guard from the other side of the

closed door.

"I was just wondering if I could read the morning paper."

"What you want? You die today, priest! You no get paper."

"Please, I just want to see what's happening out there."

"Wait…I ask."

Five minutes later the guard opened the door a crack and tossed in the paper.

"Here paper. You not have much time. We leave soon."

"Thank you, sir," Father Rankin said cheerfully. He scooped up the *Columbus Dispatch* and sat on the chair. *Might as well catch up on the latest news if I run into some Buckeyes Up There later today.* He breezed through the hard-news section, mainly talking about the latest directives announced by the Global Federation. In the Sports section, he saw that the OSU football team had cancelled their spring practice. *Ha! So something is finally able to bring Buckeye football to a halt! I bet there are some truly diehard Buckeye fans who are complaining about that.* Father Rankin turned last of all to the comics and was particularly pleased to see a cartoon poking fun at the ostriches who *still* had their heads in the sand. Below a picture of two men watching a Chinese soldier cross their street was the caption: "Oh, c'mon! There's nothing to be alarmed about; we've *always* had Chinese soldiers patrolling our streets!"

The door abruptly opened and two heavy-set soldiers walked into Father Rankin's cell. "You die now, priest!" said the slightly balding guard. "You ready go?"

"No problem, boys," said Father Rankin calmly. "May I take my Breviary with me?" He held it up with his right hand.

The balding guard hesitated, then said, "Just one book, yes."

"Thank you," said Father Rankin. He smoothed out the blanket on his cot, stood up and walked out the door, followed by the two soldiers.

"Nice weather, huh?" asked Father Rankin as they passed a window in the hallway in which they walked. "Looks like it'll be sunny today."

"No talk, priest!" said one of the guards, giving Father Rankin a shove. "You not worry you die?"

"Why should I worry about meeting Jesus Christ? I've been preparing for this my whole life."

They came to a set of double doors which opened into a large room, what looked to be a former dining area. At first Father Rankin was shocked by what he saw, but soon the soothing rays of grace calmed him down. Arranged all in a row were about a dozen guillotines, with a line of men standing in front of each one. Some of the men were crying, others looked horribly depressed. Two Chinese guards stood by each prisoner, holding him in line. Father Rankin was directed to the closest killing machine and watched as the blades did their macabre work. The guillotines were designed for high-volume operation, and their performance didn't disappoint their designers. These guillotines were spring-loaded and could chop off a head every fifteen seconds. A conveyor belt moved past each machine, taking the heads and bodies out to the back of the building where they were quickly dumped into waiting trucks. Father Rankin cringed each time he heard the loud Ching! of the blades, decapitating another "resister," as the news media had dubbed these hapless men, men who had done nothing more than object to the Chinese invaders and their plans for world domination.

Father Rankin opened his Breviary to another slip of paper he kept in it, the prayer for the Anointing of the Sick. *There's no priest around to say it for me...I might as well say it for myself: "Through this holy anointing, may the Lord in His love and mercy help you with the grace of the Holy Spirit. Amen. May the Lord Who frees you from sin save you and raise you up. Amen."* Father Rankin made the sign of the cross on his forehead and the palms of his hands. *God has provided the oil,* he reasoned. He closed the book and said a silent Act of Contrition, then made an Act of Perfect Contrition, telling God that he was sorry for all his sins, solely because they offended Him and for no other reason. He then quietly spoke the words of general absolution for all those dying around him. Father Rankin took a deep breath and handed his Breviary to the guard on his right.

"This is for you."

"What you say?"

"This book...here, you keep it." Father Rankin held the book out.

"I no permission to take!"

"Here," whispered Father Rankin, "put it inside your coat."

The guard furtively looked around him, then wordlessly grabbed the Breviary and zipped it up inside his coat.

Father Rankin's heart hammered in his ears as the prisoner in front of him lay down on the guillotine. Just then a Chinese general burst through the double doors behind them and rushed up to the priest.

"You Rankin, right?" he said harshly.

Father Rankin could only stare at him blankly.

"Here," he said, holding out a clipboard and pen to Father Rankin, "you sign here--you no die. Here, take!"

Father Rankin took the proffered paper and read it. About halfway down the page he saw what he expected:

I agree to use the revised formula for the Eucharistic Prayer at all my Masses:

"....*This is a symbol of my Body...This is a symbol of my Blood.*"

Father Rankin looked up at the Chinese general, then over at the two guards beside him.

Ching! The blade came down on the neck of the man just ten feet from him.

"Sign it!" screamed a voice in his head. *"Don't be so proud! You're just doing this so you can be a hard ass! Come off your high horse!"*

"You sign now or you die!" said the general loudly. "Sign!"

Am I doing this for the right reasons? he asked himself. *I can find a way around these silly words of Consecration...I don't have to die! All my parishioners need me!*

Father Rankin said a Hail Mary, then handed the clipboard and pen back to the Chinese general. "Thank you for trying to help me, sir, but I cannot deny Christ. God bless you."

The general stood motionless for a few seconds, his eyes blazing, boring into Father Rankin. "You crazy, priest! I try help! Okay," he said with a dismissive wave of his hand, "you die now."

The guards shoved him toward the guillotine and the executioner roughly threw him onto the bench. He strapped the priest's torso and head down and stepped back.

Father Rankin raised his right hand as far as he could and said in a low voice, "I bless you in the name of the Father, and the Son, and the Holy Spirit. Amen."

The executioner pressed the release button and the spring-loaded steel blade plummeted down with seven-hundred pounds of force at a speed of sixty feet per second. And thus it was that this man of God paid the ultimate price for his belief in the humble carpenter of Nazareth.   A blood-spattered Chinese soldier man-handled Father Rankin's body onto the conveyor belt, where it followed his head on its way to the city dump.

Chapter 13

Thad pressed the numbers for Dexter's workplace and waited while Mrs. Downing transferred his call. He moved the cell phone to his left hand, using his right hand to put another log on the fire he had started in the fireplace of the shack.

"Yeah, Thad, this is Dexter."

"Hey, Dexter, did you hear about Father Matt?" Thad asked, on the verge of tears.

"I went down…to see him…just yesterday." Dexter also found it hard to talk without his voice breaking.

"I just want to--to tell you that he's--gone." Thad's shoulders shook as he tried to hold back a deep wail coming out his throat.

Neither man spoke for a few seconds as they wiped their eyes.

Eventually, Thad spoke up: "I just called Saint Michael's--they said they killed him…early this morning."

"Thanks for letting me know," Dexter said in a gravelly voice.

"I'll be in touch, Dexter. Just to let you know, I'm still out at 'the' place and I'm doing okay…I just wish it would warm up a little."

"Okay, Thad, see you later."

"Bye."

Thad spent the rest of the day cutting up some dead trees he found in the woods behind the barn. Several times he couldn't hold back his emotions and drenched his cheeks in a stream of tears for his fallen brother, his comrade-in-arms in this fight for the Light of the World. It turned out to be a long day for Thad. On top of the news of Father Matt's death was the fact that he hadn't been able to sleep too well the previous night because of the cold. Although it was beginning to warm up a little, the shack on Dexter's farm had little insulation and Thad often felt every strong wind that blew through the nearby fields. He was now reading the code-book novel, <u>Dreaming of Montana</u>, by the light of the fire he had started in the shack's fireplace. Dinner had consisted of one can of chunky soup, grape juice and a small chocolate bar he had been able to finagle from the grocer in Mechanicsburg. He found it best not to frequent any store or town regularly, lest the Chinese discover his buying habits. In the big cities one needed an official ID card to buy food, but Thad found he could purchase a modicum of supplies in the smaller towns with his supply of gold coins. A black market had grown up in the past few months, used mainly by those unwilling to submit to the newly established Global Federation and its ironclad rules prohibiting any commerce not transacted using its SMARTCARD. For now, all citizens of this emerging worldwide government were required to use the SMARTCARD for all business transactions and there were rumors that soon the electronic information contained on the SMARTCARD would be implanted in the right hand, ostensibly to make it more convenient, eliminating the worry of losing or forgetting the SMARTCARD.

Thad's cell phone rang and he put a twig in the book to keep his place as he reached in his pocket for the phone. When he looked at the caller ID, he didn't recognize the number. *It could be a trap,* he thought. *Only Dexter knows I'm here, right? Yeah, but, he's not the only one who knows my cell number.* Thad deliberated for a few more seconds until something told him to answer. *I haven't talked to anyone all day! I'll hang up if it sounds fishy.* He pressed the "Send" button and brought it up to his ear. "Hello?"

"Thad, this is Cheryl!"

"Oh," said Thad with a sigh of relief. "Good to hear from you, Cheryl--a lot's happened since I saw you last."

"Right, it's been about 6 weeks."

"Yeah, I sort of lost track with the, uhh, with all that's been going on."

"The Warning, you mean," said Cheryl.

"That's right, I'm glad you're calling it by its proper name."

"Oh, I know, I don't believe all that 'Disturbance' stuff--it's the Warning."

"Are you going to the Miracle?" asked Thad.

"I'm pretty sure, I'm still trying to get a ticket…are you?"

"Definitely! I've had my ticket purchased for over ten years."

"So what have you been doing since we talked last? Are you still driving a taxi?"

Thad nervously glanced around the shack, as if spies were sitting in the same room with him. "Actually, what happened was--" *Should I tell her anything? What if someone's listening?…But, this is* Cheryl *for goodness sake!*

"Don't be a fool! Don't tell her a thing!" warned his conscience.

"Cheryl, I really had a bad time during the Warning, and I--"

"Oh, be serious, Thad!" she said jokingly. "You're Mister Catholic himself! You should hear what *I* went through."

"How was it for you?"

"Well, suffice it to say that I no longer think religion is just a *hobby* anymore. I would hate to think how it would have been if I *hadn't* at least heard about it before."

"Oh, so you 'saw the light,' as the expression goes?"

"Did I ever!" said Cheryl. "What about you, Thad? You said you had a bad time of it?"

"Well, I thought I would be prepared for it, considering I'd known about the Warning for years, but it still was pretty scary. I guess when you encounter a light as bright as the Holy Spirit, you tend to find some imperfections in your painting no matter how good an artist you think you are."

"I know exactly what you're saying…"

There was a pause for a few seconds as both Thad and Cheryl each thought about their personal experience during the Warning.

"So, anyway, you keeping busy?" asked Thad. "How's things at Battelle?"

"Things get a little crazy now and then--people sometimes show up for work and sometimes they don't. With the Chinese looking over our shoulders all the time, it's tough to get stuff done. And, of course, ever since the Warning, people are sort of schizophrenic. I'll talk with someone one day and they're completely normal, then the next day, they look like they haven't slept in three weeks."

"I see." There was another pause as each waited for the other to speak.

"Thad," Cheryl finally said, "I just wanted to say I'm sorry for the way I talked to you last time we went out--I've really done a lot of soul-searching since the Warning...and if you're willing I'd like to go out again."

"Have you been to Confession?"

"Oh, yes! Three times as a matter of fact! I had so many things to confess that I had forgotten about---the Warning sure improved my memory."

"That's good to hear...uh, Cheryl, as far as going out...um, well, during the Warning I sort of thought about...the priesthood."

"Ohh..."

"Now I'm not certain about anything, but last week I visited the Josephinum and talked with a priest up there."

"You visited the *Josephinum*?" Cheryl asked trepidatiously.

"I haven't signed up yet--well, actually, the priest seemed to think I might have a problem getting into the seminary with my history of mental problems."

"That's right," said Cheryl, "maybe they wouldn't take you."

"He said I should wait till after the Miracle--after I get back from Spain, before I make any decisions."

"Oh, yeah, Thad," Cheryl said, with obvious relief in her voice, "I think he's right. You'll probably be given a lot of grace while you're there."

"Let's hope so."

"So, are you getting enough to eat? With all the food shortages, it's getting harder and harder to buy groceries."

"Yeah, out here I've been using--" Thad stopped abruptly. *Better not tell her about the gold right now. And better not tell her where I am.* "I mean, you're right, it is hard to find any decent food anymore. I haven't had a piece of lettuce in over a month."

"What do you mean 'out here'? Where are you?"

"Oh, I just mean, here in Columbus...maybe in other parts of the country it's a little better."

"Maybe you're right."

Thad threw another log on the fire and switched the cell phone to his other ear. "Well, I'd like to talk more, but I don't want to wear down my cell phone battery too much."

"Okay, Thad...let's keep in touch, okay? Let me know how everything goes at Garabandal."

"Sounds good, Cheryl."

"See you later."
"Bye."
"Goodbye."

****

"Ya, that good," said Kultida as Kevin drove out of his sister's parking lot after picking up Kultida. "I like Italian food. What that name--Florence?"

"Florentine," said Kevin. "They have really good food. It's not a chain, it's locally owned and operated. I really like their menu."

"I take you sometime to Swedish restaurant, yes?"

"Ha! That'll be the day that Columbus gets a 'Swedish Restaurant.' I'm afraid the closest we can get to that is Schmidt's--it's a German restaurant in German village."

"German Village?" asked Kultida.

"Oh, yeah. German Village is a section of Columbus just south of downtown--it was originally settled by German immigrants, but now it's the favorite roosting place of young professionals, you know, lawyers and such."

"My father lawyer," said Kultida.

"I guess I better not tell any lawyer jokes then, right?"

"I hear many. Anyway, I not understand English too good, you know?"

"I heard that."

Five minutes later, they walked into Florentine and only had to wait ten minutes before being seated in the well-appointed rear of the restaurant.

"I hope you don't smoke, Kultida."

"No, no--you?"

"Hey, I played football for Ohio State! C'mon! You think I smoke?"

"I see. No, no, you no smoke."

Kevin waited till after the entrée was served before he broached the subject of the Miracle.

"So, look, Kultida, have you thought anymore about the Miracle?"

"Oh, I must say to you," replied Kultida excitedly. "I go to Confession yesterday! Your sister take me to, uh, Saint, uh, Saint--uhmm--"

"Saint Patrick's?"

"Yes, Saint Patrick's. It was four year since I go. Now I happy," she said smilingly.

"I'm surprised the Chinese allow confessions there. I've heard that they've completely closed some other churches," said Kevin.

"I think the--the--Warning change them even, no?" asked Kultida, making a motion with her hand around the top of her head. "They get, uhh, how say...?"

"It affected their conscience, too, you mean?"

"Right, right! I'm just glad I get to tell my sin."

"Glad to hear it, Kultida. What about the Miracle...you think you want to go?"

"Maybe, maybe...that strange...priest in confession also suggest I go."

"Strange!? It's the event of the Millennium--of course he's going to suggest it too. Well, there you have it!" Kevin lightly slapped the tabletop. "What more do you need?"

"I don't know, Kevin. I like Mary and Rosary and Confession, but this 'Miracle'--I, I no see, I don't know..."

"What did you see in the Warning, Kultida? You believe in that, don't you? I mean, don't you think that was from God? You don't really think it was some mass hypnosis like the newspapers are saying, do you?"

"I tell all in confession," said Kultida. "In Warning I see all my bad things. But I am peace now...I tell priest everything."

"That's good, but don't you see that the Miracle would be good for you? Don't you think that Mary wants you to go?"

"Do I must go? Why I need go?" asked Kultida. "I start go Mass here...I pray...I pray Rosary."

"But the Blessed Mother said everyone who goes will be cured of all their physical and spiritual ills."

"I no have ills, Kevin...I feel good, fine."

"But just think about all the graces you would receive."

"What exactly that mean, 'grace'?"

"The best way to describe grace is that it is a sharing in the life of God Himself."

"I share in God life here--in Ohio. I still no understand go to Spain."

"It'll be a great atmosphere over there. There'll be all kinds of holy people you can meet. Look, Kultida, I mean--it's the *Miracle*, for crying out loud! This is *the* event of the End Times. You'll see the Miracle itself right in front of your eyes! Sure, you can pray here in Columbus, and you'll be able to see the Miracle on TV, but if you're there, everything will be so much more *real*! Why do you think people go to football games when they can just as soon watch it on TV?"

"But, Kevin, I no get plane ticket--I no go if no ticket."

"I'm light-years ahead of you, girl," he said with a laugh, extracting a paper from his pocket and showing it to Kultida. "There you have it, Flight 305 on Sunny Airlines. Now you don't have any excuses."

Kultida wordlessly looked at the paper and leaned back in her chair, then looked up at Kevin. "I no have more excuse," she said, breaking into a smile. "All right, Mister fute-ball man, I go. You win." She reached over and squeezed his hand. "It be fun. I like travel. It be just like Moonies, but now it Catholic!"

"Good deal, Kultida," said Kevin, picking up her hand and shaking it. "I knew you'd see the light sooner or later."

"How we know when to go?" asked Kultida.

"Oh, don't worry about that. Conchita--one of the visionaries--will announce the date of the Miracle eight days before it happens. It'll be all over the media. The airline will then fly us over three days after the announcement is made, which will be five days before the Miracle. That'll give us plenty of time to move into our lodgings and get a front row seat for the Miracle."

"I have no money, but, though."

"Don't you worry, my little Moonie runaway. I've gotcha covered."

"You good boy, er--good *man*," smiled Kultida. "I happy I leave Moonies."

"You just hold up your end of the bargain, lady," Kevin said, a warning in his voice. "Perseverance is a virtue."

"What mean 'perseverance'?"

"It means to keep on doing what you're doing even if it gets tough to do it."

"Oh, I see," said Kultida, nodding her head. "I understand."

A half-hour later, Kevin paid the bill and drove Kultida back to his sister's condo.

"I call you next day," she said as she climbed out of the car.

"Sounds great!" said Kevin. "Tell my sister I said hello!"

Chapter 14

The best way, Dexter discovered, to keep his sanity after learning of Father Rankin's death was to immerse himself in work. He and Jerry did their best work in the evening. It really wasn't until after about nine that the creative juices really started flowing. The fruit juices started flowing as well, since Dexter's drink of choice was grape juice and Jerry's was apple juice. They had long ago forsaken caffeine-drenched drinks except for real emergencies, and then only in the wee hours of the night. They were in the Grobotics lab, the only two employees left in the building. Dexter wanted to get Bobby Five's eyes just a little more sharp than they had been for the previous demo. Granted the pepper spray was only about two inches off target, but in a restricted urban setting, that could mean that Bobby Five might accidentally spray some innocent bystander, rather than the more deserving criminal.

"Did you load that latest vision upgrade?" Dexter asked Jerry as he sat down at the computer next to the motionless Bobby Five.

"Finished it just two minutes before you walked back here."

"No glitches this time, then?"

"Hey, glitches are robots' middle names," said Jerry with a laugh. "I can tell you right now this thing won't work till the fourth try this evening." He tossed an empty juice container at Bobby Five.

"You do that to Bobby Five too much and he might just turn on you, pal," said Dexter.

"Oh, yeah, 'Terminator!' 'I'll be back!'" mimicked Jerry. "By the way, where's that security guard you hired? I thought he was supposed to be here every night."

"The agency called me a couple of hours ago. The guy is having car trouble and they said they'll send out a replacement if he can't make it. Now why don't you explain this subroutine to me, Jerry," said Dexter, pointing to the computer monitor.

"What?--'saccade'?"

"Yeah, what the 'h' is 'saccade'?"

"I got it from that MIT professor. It just means to scan with your eyes."

"Oh, I see--well, let's fire it up," said Dexter. "And disable the password protection. Just let it work with the 'Enter' key."

"'It'? I'm not allowed to throw a plastic bottle at dear old Bobby Five, but you're allowed to call him 'it'? Okay, *he* is ready. I disabled the password control."

"Prairie-dung! Cry havoc and loose the dogs of robotics!" yelled Dexter.

Jerry hit the 'Enter' key on his computer and--nothing happened.

"Hit it!" said Dexter.

"I did! I told you it wouldn't work until the fourth try."

"Crap-crap, Jerry! I thought you worked all day on this."

"Restrain your ponies, bro. Let me take a look at this." Jerry sat back down in front of his monitor and started tapping the keys. "All right, that should do it now."

"Fine," said Dexter. "You have two more tries, but I'm warning you if---"

A loud thwack! Cut Dexter off in mid-sentence. Two heavyset men, all dressed in black, burst through the door next to the loading dock.

Dexter reached for his cell phone clipped to his belt.

Phhwwwt--clang! A bullet from a silenced gun bounced off the table next to Dexter.

"I wouldn't be reaching for any electronic devices right now," said the taller of the two intruders as he walked over to Dexter and Jerry. "I wouldn't want to have to reach out and touch someone this early in the evening."

The other masked man stood guard by the door, keeping his pistol trained on the two Grobotics engineers.

"How did you get in here?" demanded Dexter. He turned to

Jerry. "You locked all the doors and turned on the alarm, as usual, didn't you?"

"I'll be asking most of the questions from now on, Dexter," said the gunman casually.

"How!--How did you know my name? Who are you?"

"Oh, we know a lot about you--and about Jerry, here," he said with a faint smile. "The Internet is just an amazing tool when you think about it. Besides, I thought you would recognize my voice--don't you remember all those crank calls I made to you on your cell phone?"

"That was *you?*" asked Dexter. "What do you want?! There's no way in hell you're taking this robot!"

The gunman chuckled. "Relax, chump! We won't be taking your beloved robot with us."

"Then, what? Money? All the banks are closed! I suppose you want to go to an ATM or something?"

No one noticed as Jerry slowly started to move his hand in the direction of the "enter" key.

"All that we want is *you*, dear Dexter," said the gunman, his eyes boring into Dexter's.

"What is *that* supposed to mean?"

"The big 'R', my friend. Ransom is as old as civilization itself. We just happened to pay a little midnight visit to the numismatic dealer from whom you've been buying your gold. We learned that you've purchased quite a bit of gold bullion over the past several years. Now with your cooperation, we're going to load up our truck with your precious metals. We aren't quite sure where it's located, but I'm sure we can convince you to tell us, right? And if you decide not to tell us right now, we have arranged for some nice accommodations to hold you and your friend until you can arrange for someone else to pay us. Like I say, the art of ransom is fascinating when you really take the time to study it."

"Forget that, jerk! I'm not giving you a red nickel!" Dexter started to turn toward the door to the office.

Phhwwwt-clang! Another bullet ricocheted off the table next to Dexter. He stopped in his tracks and stood motionless.

"If you have to go to the bathroom, all you have to do is ask," said the intruder. "Now, why don't you and your friend here try these on for size." He walked closer to Dexter and Jerry and tossed two sets of handcuffs on the table.

Dexter picked up one of the sets and began to put them around his wrists.

"Not so fast," said the gunman. "*Behind* your back." He walked toward Dexter until he was standing in front of Bobby Five. Waving the pistol in Jerry's direction, he said, "Jerry, you put them on your friend first."

Dexter exchanged looks with Jerry, then walked over to where Jerry sat by the computer.

"I hope you have the keys for these things," said Jerry, taking the cuffs from Dexter.

"As a matter of fact, the keys are on sale," said the gunman. "For five million dollars, you can have them."

Dexter turned his back to Jerry, who started to place the restraints on him. Jerry fumbled with the handcuffs and "accidentally" dropped them onto the cement factory floor. In one continuous motion, he bent down, hit the enter key and said: "Fire!"

The robot sprang to life and immediately spit out a four second burst of eye-stinging pepper spray, right into the face of the unprepared gunman! He dropped his pistol, emitted a string of obscenities, staggered backward, and began rubbing his eyes.

"Fernando!" he yelled to his partner, "Get them! I can't see!"

Dexter and Jerry bolted for the door to the office area, but quickly dove for the floor as a hail of bullets from Fernando made mincemeat of the wooden door in front of them.

"Sorry, not this time!" yelled Fernando, as he ran over to the two men cowering on the floor. "On your stomachs--now! Put your hands behind your backs!" The two complied with his commands, seeing as they had no other choice. Fernando put his shoe on Dexter's neck and held the end of his pistol against Dexter's head.

"I oughta just take you out right now," said Fernando. "You're not worth five million. We can find your gold without your help."

I'll go to Garabandal! Dexter screamed silently to himself. *I promise you Mary, if you get me out of this, I'll go!*

"Don't be an idiot," said Lance, the other gunman, still unable to see, but knowing what was going through his partner's head. "Cuff them and let's get out of here. This pepper spray should be wearing off in a few minutes."

Fernando walked over to retrieve the handcuffs that were still lying on the floor. Jerry, his head turned so he could follow him, couldn't believe his eyes! The idiot walked right in front of Bobby Five!

"Fire!" yelled Jerry.

Bobby Five sent out a three second stream of pepper spray, right into Fernando's eyes.

"Aaaaagghhh!" Fernando dropped his pistol and crumpled to the floor, burying his fists into his eye sockets.

"Grab his pistol!" shouted Dexter. "I'll get the other one!"

Jerry scrambled to his feet and picked up the pistol, which he quickly trained on the quivering Fernando. Dexter put the handcuffs on Lance, who complained loudly that he couldn't rub his eyes with his hands cuffed behind his back.

"You shoulda thought of that *before* entering *my* factory," shot back Dexter. He next restrained Fernando with the manacles. After he was finished, he stood up and pointed to the robot. "Hey, we forgot all about the *real* hero! Bobby Five--job well done!"

"Acknowledged, mission completed," replied Bobby Five in a surprisingly real voice. "Should I remain on high alert?"

"No, Bobby Five," said Jerry, "stand down to alert mode one."

"Acknowledged."

The police came and asked all the usual questions, surprised at the timely intervention of the robot. A reporter from the "Columbus Dispatch," expecting another boring crime story, was elated to hear of the exploits of Bobby Five and asked to come back the next day to do an exclusive on the metal man. The hubbub finally died down about midnight and Dexter was left alone in the building to clean up the mess. *Best to put things back in order before the employees show up in the morning,* he thought. It wasn't until he sat down at his desk, exhausted, that he remembered the promise he had made to Mary. He could still remember it verbatim: *I promise you Mary, if you get me out of this, I'll go. Man,* he thought, *now I'm stuck! I have to go to some peanut-sized town in the wastelands of Spain. Who even knows if anything's going to happen? All this is predicated on that one thing in the plane, the Disturbance--all right, the 'Warning'-- if I don't want to be politically correct. Maybe this whole thing is a hoax; maybe I'll go over there and nothing will happen. Or maybe a cloud will drift in front of the sun and they'll call that a miracle.*

"A promise is a promise," said Albert.

"Give me one good reason I should hold up my end of the bargain, Albert," Dexter silently replied.

"Are you a cat or a man? How many lives do you think you have, bubba?"

"You got a point there, I suppose." Dexter thought back over the last eight months: *first there was the near-drop from the Lincoln-Leveque Tower; then came the airplane crash; and now I nearly had a bullet in my brain tonight.* Dexter shook his head back and forth as he stared off into space. *I don't think I'd make it through another brush with death.*

"So it's decided," concluded Albert. *"You're going to Garabandal to see The Miracle."*

Dexter ignored the voice and sank deeper into thought. *I wonder...why don't I just walk away from this whole thing? I've got a taxicab driver pulling me one way and the rest of my life pulling me the other. What does Thad really have going for him anyway? He's a taxi driver, for Pete's sake! I've based the whole last few months of my life on the advice of a cabbie!*

"And Father Rankin?" asked Albert quietly.

Well, yeah, I forgot about him...he did die for his beliefs...but what did he know about the business world? He was just a priest--a cleric. I'm sure he had faults himself. What did he know about the real world? I'm running a company here, I'm rich--hell, I've got people trying to kidnap me for ransom!

"Father Rankin was an engineer, too, remember?" Albert reminded him. *"He knew what it's like to be out in the world. You think he was completely clueless?"*

"Well, who says I need to go to Garabandal? I have a pretty nice life right here. Why upset the applecart?"

"Noah had a pretty nice life too."

"I knew you'd bring that up," thought Dexter.

"Well," reasoned Albert, *"do you want a nice life here or in the hereafter?"*

"How 'bout both?"

"How 'bout you keep your promise?"

"All right, I'll go--but this is the deal: if there's no Miracle, it's over. I've been toeing the line on this whole business since last year, and I'm getting tired of it. The Warning, the Miracle, the Chastisement-

-the world's too nice a place for all that doom and gloom. For all we know the psychologists may be right. Maybe the Warning was just what they say: mass hysteria. Nothing's happened since then. I'll go, but it had better be a good show."

"You just hold up your end of the bargain, my friend," said Albert.

"Count on it. Now I just have to find a plane ticket."

****

Thad had gone back to his apartment just once to gather a few supplies. Besides some canned goods and clothing, the one thing he made sure he brought back to Dexter's farm was his trusty shortwave radio, which was capable of picking up stations from thousands of miles away. Thad had found it an invaluable tool in the past few years. Fortunately, he had had the foresight to buy a long-duration battery pack, so he was able to listen to the set even now, two months after he had last charged it. He was sitting in a lawn chair he had brought along and was flipping through the usual stations when a familiar phrase spoken by one of the broadcasters perked up his ears: "…was announced at noon today from the small Spanish village of Garabandal." *This is it!* thought Thad. *I've been waiting ten years for this!* The announcer continued: "I repeat, Father Enrico Carballo stated that Conchita Gonzalez Keena received a message from the Blessed Mother that the Miracle of Garabandal will occur a week from tomorrow, April 12th at 8:30 pm Garabandal time. Conchita reiterated that all people of the world are invited to come to Garabandal to witness this incredible event. She stated further that the Blessed Mother promised that whoever comes to the Miracle will be healed of all illness, whether physical, mental, or spiritual. It should be noted that the Miracle will be able to be televised all over the world, so it is not necessary to be physically present to see it. Stay tuned to this station for further updates." The announcer continued to talk about news of the day, but Thad was lost in reverie. *I can't believe it! It is actually going to occur! I've been expecting this since…since…what? 1992?*

"Son a bitch!" Thad yelled out loud inside the shack.   He

jumped up and did a little jig in front of the picture of the Blessed Mother he had hung on the wall. "Yesss! Thank you, Mary! Glory be to the Father, and the Son, and the Holy Spirit!" He popped a tape into the boom box from his apartment and danced around to the sound of the Boogie Woogie music he had inherited from his grandfather. *Finally, finally, finally!*

****

Kevin inserted the key to his apartment and opened the door only to find Steve, his roommate, kneeling on the floor, doing the classic "Wayne's World" worship routine, i.e., bowing down to the floor, worshipping Kevin.

"All praise to Kevin, the football god!" chanted Steve.

"Up, you knave!" shouted Kevin. "What brought this about, other than my natural good looks?"

Steve said nothing, only pointed to the answering machine while continuing his bowing.

"Whaaa?" asked Kevin as he walked over to the answering device. He pushed the 'play' button and listened as an excited voice said: "This is a message for Kevin Conaway. Hey, look, Kevin, this is Dan Jenkins with the Buffalo Bills, and we'd like you to come up next week and spend a few days with us. We think we might have a spot for you on our team. Call me back at seven-one-six, five-five-five, two-one-two-seven. We look forward to hearing from you."

"Oh, great one," chanted Steve. "Possessor of magnificent gold."

"You can stop the worship service now," said Kevin. "I might not be going."

"What?" gasped Steve as he got to his feet. "What do you mean, you 'might not be going'? This is the *NFL* we're talking about here, bud. You should be asking 'how high?', now that they've told you to jump."

"Steve, didn't you hear about the Miracle? It was just announced today. The Miracle will happen a week from tomorrow."

"Oh, puuleasse!" sneered Steve. "Not that rabbit trick thing that the Virgin Mary's going to do."

"That's exactly what I'm talking about. And I'd prefer it if you wouldn't refer to it as 'rabbit tricks.' It's going to be a lot more fantastic than pulling rabbits out of a hat."

"Hey, I heard this, this--whatever you want to call it--is going to be televised, so you can watch it right here." Steve gestured toward the TV set. "You don't need to be winging it three thousand miles, just so you can say you were there in person."

"Hmm," said Kevin as he plopped down on the couch and scratched his head. "This sounds just like the conversation I had with Kultida a week or two ago."

"What, she was trying to convince you not to go, too?"

"More like I was trying to convince *her* to *go* -- but I don't know now," said Kevin in a low voice, "maybe I should go to the workout with the Bills...I could watch the Miracle on TV..."

"*Now* you're talking sense, Mister Moneybags," said Steve, rubbing his hands together. "Hey, I've got nothing against the Virgin Mary and her stuff, but we're talking *pro football*, Kevin ol' pal. We're talking seven-figure income."

"That *is* true," replied Kevin, biting his lower lip and staring out the front window of the living room. "Of course, who's to say if we're even going to *have* a football season this fall. With the Chinese taking over..."

"Hell!" said Steve. "The Chinese love it too. They're probably going to skim off the profits for themselves anyway. They want to keep our society running as smoothly as they can, so I bet they'll keep football going."

"Maybe I could reschedule the meeting with the Bills," suggested Kevin. "Maybe I could do both things."

"You don't tell the Buffalo Bills to *reschedule* a workout session, Kevin. Like I said before: they've asked you to jump. All you should do now is ask: how high?"

"Yeah, you've got a point," said Kevin. "I'll have to think about this."

Just then the phone rang and Steve snatched it out of its cradle. "Yo!" he said into the receiver. "Kevin? Sure, he's here. Just a second."

Kevin gave him a questioning look. Steve covered the mouthpiece with his hand and whispered: "It's Kultida."

Kevin walked over to Steve and took the phone from him.

"Hey, Kultida!"

"Kevin, you hear news? About Miracle?"

"Yes, I heard," Kevin said, grimacing at Steve.

"That good, no? We go, yes?"

"Yes, that's good news, Kultida. Looks like it'll be in April after all."

"I excited! You excited?"

"Yeah, I guess I'm excited," said Kevin unenthusiastically.

"Kevin, what wrong? What happen?"

"I was just invited up to Buffalo to sort of interview with a pro team next week."

"But, no! We leave to Spain in three day, right? You no go to Buf-lo, you go Spain!"

"Right...yeah" said Kevin in a low voice.

Kevin looked over at Steve, who was shaking his head from side to side.

"Kevin," she said. "Now it *me* time tell *you*: you *must* go to Miracle! Just like you say: TV not good, you see Miracle in person."

"Right, right."

"Kevin, I listen on radio...much grace to people go to Spain-- much grace."

"All right, you're right," said Kevin, making up his mind.

"You sure you go?" asked Kultida.

Kevin looked over at Steve, who wore a look of disbelief. Kevin turned around and looked away from his roommate. "Yes, I'm sure, Kultida. Yes."

"Good!" said Kultida with relief. "I see you on Saturday. You sister drive me to airport Saturday morning."

"Okay, I'll see you Saturday. Right...talk to you later."

"Bye, Mister fute-ball guy."

"Bye, Kultida."

As soon as Kevin put the phone down, Steve said, "Uh, excuse me, but what was that all about? That was just to get her off the phone, right? I mean, you're not really going to blow off the *Buffalo Bills* to see it rain mainly on the plain in Spain...right?"

Kevin took a deep breath and let out a long sigh. "Steve, I appreciate your concern, but I've got to go to this thing."

"You're just letting your woman push you around."

"Steve, this is ridiculous! Just a few days ago, I was trying to convince Kultida that *she* should go with *me*, and now here she has to convince *me* that I should go with *her!*"

"Why don't *I* convince both of *you* not to go at all? Sheeesh!" Steve threw up his hands in exasperation.

"Steve, the Buffalo Bills will still be here when I get back. Come on! I can't miss the *Miracle*! This is a once-in-a-lifetime-opportunity! Hey!" Kevin turned to face Steve, who had walked into the kitchen. "Why don't *you* go too?"

"Ha! Double Ha!" said Steve. "I'll be lucky if I just watch the thing on TV!"

"Well, as you wish." Kevin took his jacket off and headed to the stairway. "I better do some laundry if I'm going to be leaving Saturday."

****

"It's a little too early to be planting those, you know."

Thad jerked his head around and saw that it was only Blake Townsend. "Oh! Hey!" said Thad, nodding his head. He was down on all fours planting some corn in a plot of ground he had prepared next to the shack. "You had me scared there for a second...I thought it was some Chinese soldiers checking up on me."

"Now, do I sound like your average Chinaman, Thad?" asked Blake.

Thad pushed himself up to a standing position and turned to face his neighbor. "Well, now that I'm thinking logically, I guess I'd have to say no," Thad said with a smile.

"That's good to hear...so you're doin' a little farming, eh? Or should I say 'gardening'?" Blake said as he pointed to the plot of ground on which Thad had been working. "Don't you think the fifth of April is a bit early to be planting corn in these parts?"

"Something to keep busy, I guess, uhh...sorry, I seem to have forgotten your name, I'm sorry." Thad took off his work glove and held his hand out to Blake.

"Blake. Blake Townsend," he said, pumping Thad's hand. "And you're Jeff Mason, right?"

"Uh, yeah, uh, good memory, Blake."

"Yeah, my wife can't stand it sometimes. She says I have a photographic memory--she might be right."

"So I'm a little early planting the corn, you think?"

"Yeah, just a bit…you might do okay, but you never know when a frost is going to come along. It's still the beginning of April and this is Ohio."

"Yeah, I'm just a city slicker actually…I don't know much about farming. I just found some corn kernels in the shack here and thought I'd put 'em in the ground and see what happens."

"My wife and I were sort of wondering about that, actually, Jeff. We've been seeing your car out here for the past few weeks and wondered if you've decided to move out here."

How much should I tell this guy? wondered Thad. *Maybe he'll turn me in…but I'm not ready to die like my brother!* "It's just a temporary arrangement…I'm a friend of Dexter--and he is letting me stay here a little while."

"Oh, yeah, Dexter's quite a guy--he's doin' robots or something, right?"

"Right, I met him a few months ago."

"Do you work for him?" asked Blake. "You a robot guy also?"

"No, actually I drive a taxi for Orange Cab in Columbus."

"I see." Blake slowly scratched his chin and gazed intently at Thad. "Did you hear the news?"

"The news?" *Does this guy know all about it?* thought Thad excitedly.

"You know--about Spain?" asked Blake.

"About Conchita Gonzales?" Thad thought it best to be cautious about using the name of Garabandal.

"So you know about the Miracle? About Garabandal?" asked Blake.

"Heck, yes!" said Thad, nodding his head. "Are you a believer?"

Blake broke into a wide grin. "Only since 1972!"

"Totally awesome!" Thad pumped his fist up and down. "I've been following this since the early 90s!"

"So, are you going?"

"I've had a plane ticket for awhile. How about you?"

"Yeah, I'm going," said Blake. "Wouldn't miss it for the world!"

"Look," said Thad, "first things first. I have to level with you--my name's not Jeff Mason, it's Thad Rankin."

Blake reached out and patted Thad on the shoulder. "No problem, Thad. I suspected something like that. I figured something was going on, with your living out here in this shack all by yourself. You in trouble with the Global Federation?"

"Let's just say I didn't give them a chance to *get* me into trouble--I left town when they killed all the people at the daily Mass I used to attend."

"So, it's true? That was at Saint Margaret of Cortona, right?"

"Yeah, was it on the news?"

"Not by a long shot," said Blake. "My wife and I have been hearing rumors about this type of stuff but it wasn't confirmed until you just told me that. No, the news continues to whitewash everything. All's lovely in the New World Order."

"Have you been to Mass since the invasion?"

"Oh, yeah, *Mass*," said Blake, derisively. "That's a joke, if I ever heard one. They've changed the words of consecration so that the Real Presence of Christ is no longer there. But, to answer your question, no, we haven't been back for about a month now. Why go to an invalid Mass?"

"Yeah, my brother wouldn't say the new form of the Consecration."

"Oh!" exclaimed Blake. "So your brother is a priest?"

"Well," Thad said sadly, bowing his head, "'was' a priest."

"Oh, no--*that's* true, too? At the fairgrounds?"

"Yeah. I'm sorry to have to say it, but they're taking out all the *real* priests as fast as they can find them."

"Oh, my God!" said Blake, bringing his hand up to his head. "Sorry, I really mean that as a prayer--I just can't believe all this is really happening! Up to now, this has all been just rumors for Betsy-- my wife--and me. Now you've confirmed all our worst fears."

"I just hope the Miracle will have an effect on people," said Thad.

"Yeah, me too--say, is Dexter a believer? Is he going to Garabandal?"

"That's a tossup, right now," said Thad, scrunching up his face. "I've been talking to him about it since last fall. Your prayers would be appreciated on that."

"Count me in," said Blake. "I'll keep him in mind."

"Of course, there would be the small problem of finding a plane ticket for him. I imagine it's a nightmare trying to find a seat by now."

"Hmm," said Blake, nodding his head slightly while studying Thad. "So he needs a ticket, eh?"

"Well, he has yet to ask me, but it wouldn't hurt to line up one for him, as far as I can tell."

"I'll tell you what, Thad," said Blake, having made a decision. "I wasn't sure when we first met, but now I am: you and Dexter have a reservation on Romalov Airlines."

"Huh? 'Romalov Airlines.' Never heard of it."

"I'm partially jesting, but this is your lucky day! I have a friend who will be picking me up three days before the Miracle in his business jet, and he told me he has a few seats empty right now. You're going to go to Garabandal first class, my friend!"

"You're serious?" asked Thad timidly. "You mean a Learjet-type of thing?"

"I mean a Gulfstream 550-type of thing, to be exact."

"Far out! I don't know if I told you, but I'm an aerospace engineer by training, and I know a thing or two about planes. The Gulfstream 550, if I'm not mistaken, needs only about two-thousand feet to land--this is awesome--we can land at some small airport really close to Garabandal!"

"That's the idea," said Blake, nodding his head. "At maximum weight, this baby only needs twenty-seven hundred feet to land, but we'll be well under that by the time we will have burnt all that fuel. We're going to be able to bypass the hoi-polloi arriving by the thousands in Madrid. Of course we need about six-thousand feet to takeoff, but with a minimum fuel load we can reduce that. We can fly to a longer runway somewhere and fill the tanks there for the trip back to the US."

"This is going to be one of the most suffering-free pilgrimages I've ever been on," smiled Thad.

"Who said religion has to be painful?" asked Blake with a laugh. "What are you, a Montanist?"

"Have you got that book, too, <u>Dreaming of Montana</u>?"

"What?"

"Are you referring to the book Dexter gave me?"

"No, uh, Montanism was a sect back in the early church known for its harshness."

"Wow, you sure are up on your Church history!"

"Actually, I just came across it yesterday in a book I was reading."

"Oh, I see."

"All right," said Blake, clapping his hands together, "we'll be taking-off from Delaware Airport on this Monday, April 9th, probably about ten in the morning. I can give you a ride up there--I'll pick you up at nine."

"Great, I'll try to convince Dexter to go. Do you think you can try to sell my airline ticket to someone, Blake? I try not to show my face too much around Columbus these days...maybe you could post it on the internet or something."

"Sure, I can do that, Thad--and, hey, why don't you stay in our house from now on? I'm sure Betsy wouldn't mind if you use our spare bedroom."

"Welll, uh..." Thad looked over at the run-down shack off to his left. "Uh, thanks for asking, but I sort of think I'd better continue to lie low for the time being. I wouldn't want someone who visited your house to pass it on that I was there. And I would appreciate it if you don't tell many people I'm here."

"You sure you're not being a little too paranoid, Thad?"

"I would rather err on the safe side. The Federation has already murdered my brother, and killed all the people at the daily Mass I usually attend. I think I've written too many letters to the editor to go unnoticed."

"Okay...all right...you might have a point there. By the way, let's exchange phone numbers for future reference."

"Good idea," agreed Thad. He pulled a piece of scrap paper from his pocket when his cell phone rang. He looked at the incoming phone number, and gave Blake a thumbs up. "Say a prayer--it's Dexter! Maybe I can talk him into going." He pressed the "Send" key and brought the phone to his ear. "Dexter--good to hear from you, did you hear about the announcement of the Miracle?"

Dexter wasted no time with pleasantries. "Thad, I want to go to the Miracle--can you get me a ticket?"

"Whoa! Said Thad, smiling at Blake. "What brought about this sea-change, my friend?"

"It happened again, day before yesterday."

"What's that?"

"Another near-death experience," said Dexter sheepishly. "They're starting to be second nature with me."

"Well, you called the right, guy, Dex, because I have you reserved on--" Thad hesitated, then continued, "Uh, whoa! Time to get out the old code-book. Wait one while I get it out of the building." Thad briefly explained the procedure to Blake, ran into the shack, retrieved <u>Dreaming of Montana</u>, and came outside again. Using their agreed-upon procedure, by looking up words in their mutually shared books, Thad was able to tell Dexter to meet them at the Delaware County airport next Monday morning.

"You're totally awesome, Thad!" said Dexter.

"If I've said it once, I've said it a thousand times, if aerospace engineers ruled the world, it would be a paradise."

"Let's not go too far, bud…where would we be without electrical engineers?"

"All right, I'll just say engineers in general. I'll see you next week, then, Dexter."

"Right--and thanks for everything."

"Bye."

"Bye."

"That solves *that* problem," said Blake as Thad put his cell phone away.

"I heard *that*! Dex couldn't have called at a better time. Incidentally, Blake, how much luggage can we bring?"

"Oh, so Mister Aerospace Engineer isn't up on his Gulfstream specs, huh?" teased Blake.

"Hey, I may have a mind like a steel trap, but I still have only two gigabytes of RAM!"

"Computer geek."

"I would prefer to be known as a 'technocrat.'"

"A politically correct computer geek!" laughed Blake.

"How 'bout a 'euphemistic technocrat'?"

"You got a deal."

"Anyway," said Thad, "what--ten pounds of luggage? Twenty?"

"You probably don't even have a suitcase with you anyway, right?"

"Actually, no--I could use one of yours?"

"Definitely! To answer your question, I think if everyone brings just one suitcase, we should be fine."

"Sounds good. Oh, yeah, here--let me give you my phone number." Thad and Blake wrote down their numbers, gave them to each other, and parted.

****

Monday dawned bright and clear and Thad was awakened by the melodious chirping of the birds around seven-thirty a.m. He washed himself in the makeshift shower he had setup, glad that Dexter had thought to install a manual pump next to the shack. After fifteen minutes of meditation and a quick breakfast of canned peaches and grape juice, he took his suitcase outside and sat on his chair in front of the shack. Ten minutes later, Blake and Betsy pulled up in their SUV and helped Thad put his luggage in the rear of the vehicle. Blake gave Thad a padlock which he used to secure the door of the shack, and then they headed north on Route 42. By nine-forty-five the trio was in the parking lot of the small Delaware airport.

"There she is!" said Blake, pointing to a gleaming red and yellow airplane sitting on the airport apron. "Isn't that a beaut, Thad?"

"Bee--u--tiful," said Thad.   "It looks even better than I expected!" He searched the cars in the parking lot and his eyes fell upon a Dodge Charger. "And, look! Dexter's already here!"

"Oh, yeah," said Blake, "so I see he's driving that Charger...I wonder where Bob is."

"Bob?"

"Bob Romalov--he's the owner of the Gulfstream, maybe he's getting gas--oh," Blake pointed toward the gas pump, "there he is."

"Oh, great," said Thad sarcastically, "look at *that*." Bob was speaking with a Chinese soldier, who was standing with arms akimbo, shaking his head back and forth.

Thad and Blake walked over to the gas pump and waved to Bob.

"Bob, how are you? Is there a problem?" asked Blake.

"Blake! Good to see you! No--no problem, only this *short* little gentleman won't accept my credit card to pay for the fuel I just took."

"He no have Smahtcahd!" said the Chinese soldier insistently. "He no have Smahtcahd! We no take credit cahd!"

"Calm down," said Blake, gesturing to the Chinaman with his arms, "I'm sure we can work something out. Now how much money are we talking about here?"

Thad saw Dexter walk out of the small airport "terminal" and called over to him. "Dexter! Yo!"

"Thad, ol' buddy!" Dexter walked over and shook Thad's hand vigorously. "Long time, no see, pal!"

"Happy April, Mr. Griffith," Thad said with a smile. "You don't look the worse for wear!"

"I don't know if I can say the same for you, Thad! You ever thought about getting a haircut?"

"I know, I know," said Thad. "I haven't felt too comfortable about stopping at a barbershop recently. You know how barbers are...sort of like a sorting department for all the latest news. I didn't want any good ol' boys asking too many questions about where I've been since the invasion."

"Fine. You can get a haircut from a Spanish barber." Dexter pointed toward the red and yellow jet. "So this is our ride, I guess?"

"That it is! Isn't it a beauty?"

"I hope it flies as good as it looks. So, is this our host?" Dexter asked, motioning to the three men standing around the gas pump.

"Yeah, that's your neighbor Blake, and the tall guy is Bob Romalov; he owns the jet."

"They seem to be having a little problem with the Chinaman."

"Yeah, the powers-that-be won't take Mr. Romalov's credit card."

"I suppose they're insisting that he use the SMARTCARD, right?"

"Exactly," said Thad. "And I imagine Bob doesn't have one. Of course, I've been surviving without it, thanks to your--hey!" Thad jerked his head around and looked at the parking lot, but then his face fell. "Oh...no..."

"What?" asked Dexter.

"I thought there for a second that I had driven *my* car here. We could have paid this fine young Chinaman with the, uh, 'stuff,' I have in my trunk."

"'Stuff'?"

"You know," said Thad, grabbing an imaginary coin with his fingers. "Cha-ching!"

"Ohh, that--wait a minute!" Dexter's face brightened immediately. "I almost forgot!" he half-whispered. "Problem solved! I made a little trip to the bank the other day."

Thad and Dexter walked over to Bob, Blake, and the Chinese soldier. "Ahem," said Dexter, "I think we may have a solution to the problem."

"What you mean?" asked the Chinaman gruffly. "You have 'Smahtcahd'?"

"I want to show you something...here, walk this way." Dexter gestured toward his car. Bob gave Blake a questioning look, then followed the group over to the Charger. Dexter opened the trunk and surreptitiously pulled back a tarp to reveal eight gold bars lying there. "Here's all the gold I have in the car." Dexter pulled the tarp back farther to show the Chinaman.

The Chinese soldier's eyes widened and he casually looked around to see if anyone was watching them. He seemed to deliberate for a few seconds then whispered to Dexter: "Carry them my truck...over *there*...and keep covered up." The soldier turned to Bob. "You paid, now go! Quickly! My leader not know--go!"

"Righto, sir," said Bob. "Blake, put your stuff in the jet--let's get outa here fast!"

"Gotcha!" said Blake. He turned to Thad: "Tell Betsy to get on board, then help me with the luggage."

"Thad jogged over to the SUV and informed Blake's wife of the situation. Four minutes later, all were on board the Gulfstream jet and they were rolling down the taxiway preparing for takeoff.

"Everyone needs to have a seat and strap in," said Bob over the plane's PA system. He and his copilot went through their preflight checklist.

"Flaps ten," said Bob.

"Check," said the copilot.

"Transponder on."

"Check."

"Anti-collision lights on."

"Check."

"Pitot heat on."

"Check."

"Panel clear."

"Check."

"Cleared for take-off."

Blake turned onto the runway and applied full power.

"...Airspeeds alive...Eighty knots..." The copilot read off the airspeed as the plane accelerated.

"Holy hell!" exclaimed Thad from back in the passenger cabin. "Here comes a truck!"

Bob shot a glance out the right side of the cockpit and saw a military truck heading for a spot on the runway just a few hundred yards in front of the speeding airplane!

"We'll never make it!" shouted the copilot. "We've got to abort!"

"I don't plan on going to prison just yet," said Bob. "We only need about ten more knots of airspeed..."

Bob pulled back on the yoke and the jet clawed its way into the sky, its landing gear missing the top of the truck by a mere five feet. He pushed the nose down and the plane plopped back onto the runway. As soon as they reached sufficient airspeed, Bob lifted the nose and the Gulfstream started climbing on an easterly heading.

"St Jude, thank you!" yelled Thad from the rear.

"Aaa--men," said Blake, flashing a smile at Thad. "That sure was a hopeless case."

"They must have found about my not having a SMARTCARD, I guess," said Bob.

"And the gold, probably. Let's just hope they leave well enough alone," said Thad loudly. He unbuckled his seat belt and walked up to the cockpit. "That was some good piloting back there," he said to Bob. "How long you been flying?"

"About ten years, but, hey--hats off to this airplane. It's a wonder-bird in every sense of the word."

"What's she cruise at?"

"For this trip, since it's long range, we'll be keeping her at about Mach point-eight-zero, which would be about --"

"Five hundred and thirty miles per hour," interjected Thad.

"Very good, uh...I'm sorry, I've forgotten your name."

"Thad, Thad Rankin...and you're Bob Romalov, right?"

"Right, and this is my copilot, Drew Goddard." Bob motioned to the right seat.

"Glad to meet you," said Thad as he shook Drew's hand. "Any relation to Robert Goddard?"

"Robert Goddard?" asked Drew.

"You know, the rocket pioneer?"

"Oh...no, not that I know of."

"So, Thad," said Bob, "you're pretty knowledgeable about aviation; you an airplane buff or something?"

"Actually, I'm an aerospace engineer, by training."

"Good! So if we have any problems while we're flying along, I'm sure you can solve them, right?" asked Bob.

"Not a chance!" Thad said with a laugh. "Typical attitude of most non-engineers...they think that engineers should be capable of solving any physical problem, no matter how intricate or arcane."

"All right, we'll take it easy on you," said Bob with a smile.

"What altitude will we be cruising at, by the way?"

"Forty-one thousand, unless we're directed otherwise," said Drew.

"One other thing--how were you able to get off on such a short runway?" asked Thad. "I mean with all the gas you pumped in this thing, and the number of passengers..."

"Hah!" said Bob. "I did my homework on that. Luckily Delaware airport lengthened their runway to six thousand feet just last year. Would've been a lot harder when it was just five thousand."

"Well, keep the shiny side up!" Thad said, then walked back to the cabin.

Ten minutes later he was sipping a Coke he had found in the refrigerator and gazing out the window, admiring the patchwork of farms down below in Pennsylvania when he visibly jumped in his seat--there was a Chinese J-11 fighter jet positioning itself on their right wing!

"We've got a problem!" he shouted. "There's a Chinese fighter out there!" He ran up to the cockpit.

"There's one over there, too!" gasped Bob, pointing out the left side of the cockpit. "Drew, turn to 123.45; see if they're talking to us."

Drew fumbled with the scroll knob and listened.

"Gulfstream NJ 1755," said the accented voice in the pilots' headsets, "follow us to Pitt-burgh airport...you order land imme-dately!"

"Don't do it!" said Thad. "The Federation has relaxed its rules about flights to Garabandal...they're just bluffing."

"I don't think those Alamo missiles are bluffing," said Drew, pointing to the missiles hanging on the wings of the J-11 off to the right.

"Someone must have found out about that gold we gave them and figured out we don't have SMARTCARDs," said Bob.

"Just keep going," urged Thad. "There're thousands of planes all around the world heading to Spain this week. The Chinese aren't stupid! They're not going to shoot down a civilian jet!"

"American jet! This your last warning!" said the Chinese pilot into Bob's headphones.

"All right, everyone pray the 'Saint Michael the Archangel' prayer with me!" said Thad loudly. "Saint Michael the Archangel, defend us in this day of battle, be our safeguard against the wickedness and snares of the Enemy. May God rebuke him we humbly pray, and do thou, Prince of the Heavenly Host, cast into Hell, Satan, and all the evil spirits who prowl through the world seeking the ruin of souls. Amen."

"They're still there," said Dexter from the rear of the aircraft. "I don't know if that prayer did much good."

Everyone was hunched over the windows, silently staring at the two fighter jets.

"No, look!" said Betsy triumphantly, "they're breaking off!"

"I don't believe it!" said Blake.

"Unless, of course, they're lining up for a missile launch from the rear," said Dexter.

"I don't think so," said Thad. "See! They're turning away and descending! They're pairing up...looks like they're probably heading back to Pittsburgh or somewhere in that area."

"A Hail Mary in Thanksgiving!" said Betsy loudly. "Let's not be like the nine ungrateful lepers."

"Huh?" asked Dexter.

"It's a story in the Bible," explained Thad.

Betsy led them in the prayer, then walked up to the galley area. "How about a little lunch, gentlemen?" she asked.

"Sounds great!" said Blake.

She passed out the sandwiches and soft drinks and all had their fill.

Chapter 15

As the bus topped the hill and the small town of Garabandal came into view, Kevin's first thought was that of the Middle Ages. This small village near the north coast of Spain seemed stuck in a time warp. The red-tiled roofs and adobe houses seemed ready to host the filming of "Don Quixote" or some such medieval tale. The thought struck Kevin that there was probably not a single ATM machine in the area. But there was no mistaking the importance of what was going on now. In every direction he looked, Kevin could see tents covering the green hillsides, except around the area of The Pines, where many of the apparitions had originally occurred back in the 1960s. A fence had been erected around the hummock containing The Pines, and Kevin could see a number of Spanish policeman strolling along the fence, just to make sure no over-enthusiastic pilgrim tried to jump the barricade and make a break for the sacred site.

"Usted tiene que andar de aquí!" said the bus driver as the bus ground to a stop.

"What's he saying?" asked Kevin.

"He tell us we need get out and walk now," explained Kultida. "Traffic is backed up."

"How many languages do you know, anyway?"

"Oh, say it is nothing," smiled Kultida. "In Europe, some person know two or three language. It common thing."

The bus driver continued to speak and Kultida explained he was giving information on where to find tents for sleeping. A few minutes later, Kevin and Kultida descended the bus stairs, collected their luggage, and started to walk toward the center of town, following the general flow of pedestrians. Curt, Sparrow, and Ryan had to get their baggage from another bus and agreed to meet up with Kevin later. Following the multilingual signs, they soon found the appropriate areas for tents. Since the valley had been divided into separate areas for single men, single women, and families, they agreed they would meet back at the center of town in one hour. Kevin turned north and followed a well-worn shepherd's trail that led up the side of one of the many hills in the area. He came to a fork in the trail and, seeing that the sign there was written only in Spanish, he stopped and scratched his head.

"Having a little problem with the local language?" asked a voice behind him.

"Well, yeah, I, uh…" Kevin turned around to see a large priest grinning at him.

"Oh, hello, Father…yes, my Spanish is a little rusty, do you know where we're supposed to go?"

"Well, I assume you're going to the single men's tent area, right?"

"Right…why don't you lead the way?"

"Will do. By the way," the priest said, holding out his hand, "I'm Father Chapman."

"Kevin Conaway," he said, shaking his hand. "Where you from?"

"Nebraska, of all places, if you can believe it."

"Oh, a Cornhusker! Are you a fan of football out there?"

"A fan!" said Father Chapman, "I only played for Nebraska for four glorious years!"

"Far out!" said Kevin. "I play for--or I should say I *played* for Ohio State. I graduate this year."

"Oh, you're *that* Kevin Conaway. I thought I had heard that name before. Congrats on winning the championship!"

"Oh, so you're of the party that says we actually won, huh? Since the game was so rudely interrupted by our Chinese friends, some people aren't so willing to give us the title."

"Hey, the ball dropped down on the far side of the goalposts, as far as I'm concerned. It was a field goal! Besides, it would have sailed on through anyway, if it hadn't been shot out of the air."

"Well, I'm glad we have a friend in Nebraska at least. So what position did you play for the Huskers, Father?"

"Tight end, if you can believe it."

Kevin looked the priest up and down. "Judging from the size of you, yeah, I can believe it."

"Did you travel alone?" asked Father Chapman. "I would think that you might have some fellow college buds with you."

"Actually, yes, I do have some friends here...they are the ones who convinced me to come. They got delayed with some lost luggage, so I'll have to hook up with them later. Oh, and there's also a girl...she went to the single women's tent section."

"I see...so are you going to be playing on Sundays, Kevin? That is, if there's even going to be a football season this fall."

"Well, the Bills and the Seattle Seahawks definitely say they will pick me in the first round, if they get the chance, so, we'll see."

"Oh, excuse me," said Father Chapman as he moved to the side of the trail to let a group of men go by. "Well, Kevin, we had best get moving if there's going to be any tents left for us."

"Good deal. You might as well lead the way, since you know Spanish." Kevin let the priest go ahead and followed in his footsteps. After five more minutes of hiking they arrived at a collection of tents marked off with a sign saying, "English-speaking single men."

"This looks like us, Kevin. Let's try to find some tents that don't leak."

"You think it'll rain, Father?"

"Well, I did look up the weather statistics for Spain before I left. It said that Spain overall gets two to three inches of rain in April, so we might be using our umbrellas before this is all over."

They walked through a large area of tents and selected two that were next to each other.

"I hope you don't snore, Father."

"Ha! That's one of the reasons I didn't get married, Kevin. My snoring would drive any normal women insane."

"Seriously?"

"*Just* kidding! Not to worry, you should sleep just fine."

****

Just over the hill from Kevin, Dexter and Thad had finally found an empty tent and were stowing their gear inside it. They had arrived the night before and spent the night in the airport terminal in San Sebastian.

"For a minute there, I thought we might be sleeping under the stars," said Dexter.

"Might not be too bad a situation," said Thad, looking up at the sky. "Doesn't look like it's going to rain anytime soon."

"Well, one miracle at a time is enough for me; I don't want to ask God to stop the rain as well as perform the *big* miracle."

"Fine," sighed Thad as he stooped down to look into the tent. "Should we sleep with our heads by the door, or our feet by the door?"

"I definitely think the appropriate setup would be to put our heads at the far end of the tent, and stick our feet by the door," said Dexter.

"Huh," said Thad, fingering the door of the tent. "Talk about living in luxury: these tents have screened doors and windows, and a sewn-in floor. That's a far cry from the canvas jobs we used in Boy Scouts."

"You were in the Scouts?" asked Dexter. "Were you an Eagle Scout?"

"I *am* an Eagle Scout," said Thad proudly.

"*Am?*"

"That's right: 'am.' That's the proper protocol. You don't say 'I *was* an Eagle Scout.' You say 'I *am* an Eagle Scout.'"

"'Semper Fi,' huh?"

"More like 'Sum Preparatus,' 'Be Prepared.'"

"You sure about that Latin?" asked Dexter.

"Not really. Call it pig Latin, if you want."

After a few minutes they had unpacked their bags and sat down in front of the tent, each drinking from a bottle of water.

"What do you think it's going to be, Thad?"

"The Miracle? I don't know...some image of Mary in the heavens, or a circular triangle..."

"A circular triangle? What's in that bottle--Vodka or something? Are you hallucinating?" asked Dexter, squinting in the sun to look over at Thad's face.

"I just mean, maybe it'll be a logical contradiction. Something that explains the Trinity or something. A giant waterfall and we can taste the water--yeah! And everyone that tastes the water is instantly cured!"

"Nah...too Hollywood."

"Well, what do you think, Dexter? What do you think it will be?"

"I'm only half-convinced it'll be anything, if you want to know the truth."

"You came all this way and you think it'll be a dud?" asked Thad with a pained expression.

"Not a *dud*," said Dexter. "Maybe just not as spectacular as everyone thinks."

"Well, we don't have much longer to wait. Today's, what-- Tuesday? The Miracle will be Thursday evening. So, Dex my friend inside of two and half days, your curiosity will be satiated."

"Yeah, me and the other seven billion people on this planet."

"You think everyone is going to watch it on TV?" asked Thad.

"Heck, didn't everyone watch the first moon landing on TV?"

"You asked the right guy. It's estimated that six-hundred million watched it, which would be about twenty percent of the earth's population at that time."

"I betcha this thing is going to have about three billion viewers."

"Let's hope so."

Dexter and Thad spent the rest of the day meeting and greeting their neighbors in their "tent city."

****

After they had put their personal belongings into their tents and squared everything away, Father Chapman and Kevin sat down on the side of a hill, where they could see the expanse of the valley of Garabandal spread out before them. Almost as far as they could see white and green tents covered the hillsides.

"It really is beautiful, isn't it, Kevin?"

"Sure is. Reminds me of the descriptions of Civil War encampments I've read about."

"You a Civil War buff?"

"Actually, I'm a History major, but, yeah, you might say I'm a Civil War buff."

"There definitely is something intriguing about that war, I have to admit," said Father Chapman. "You know, your own Woody Hayes was writing a book on the relation between war and football at the time of his death."

"I had heard something along those lines."

The duo fell silent as they warmed themselves in the afternoon sun, taking in the vista before them.

"What was your major, Father--at Nebraska?"

"English Lit, of all things, if you can believe it."

"What did you plan to do with that?"

"Play football," chuckled the priest. "No...oh, I don't know...I guess I was going to teach high school or something...I suppose I had at one time entertained dreams of being a novelist."

"A 'Paperback writer,' as the Beatles say?"

"Yeah, a paperback writer," said Father Chapman, nodding his head. "That was before Medjugorje."

"What's 'Medjugorje'?" asked Kevin.

"*That* is the 'Garabandal' of the 1980s."

"I've never heard of it. Did you go there? Where is it?"

"It's in former Yugoslavia, and, yes, I did go there--four times, as a matter of fact."

"Whoa! *Four* times?"

"It would've been five times, if my spiritual director at the time hadn't dissuaded me from going right before I entered the seminary."

"When was that?"

"Nineteen-eighty-eight. September the fourth, to be exact."

"Good memory!"

"We all tend to remember the important dates, you know."

"So the Blessed Virgin appeared there too?"

"Oh, yeah, big time. Millions of people went there over the years."

"What made you decide to become a priest? What about football?"

"I enjoyed college football, but somehow it didn't seem like I was cut out for pro football, if you know what I mean."

"Yeah! I do know what you mean!" said Kevin. "Sometimes I feel the same way now. Although this friend of mine says I can give the millions of dollars to charity."

"Doesn't seem to cut it, does it, Kevin?"

"Yeah, I don't know, maybe I can join the Peace Corps, or--I don't know, be a doctor, or whatever! Something altruistic."

"I know exactly what you're feeling."

Kevin looked away from Father Chapman at the throng in the valley below and marveled at the immensity of it all. "Isn't it unbelievable, Father? I mean, considering the circumstances, everything seems to be going pretty smoothly, don't you think?"

"I really think it's nothing short of miraculous. I suppose the Blessed Mother is performing a myriad of minor miracles without our even noticing."

"Speaking of miracles, I was wondering, Father: how did you escape martyrdom in the past few months? I mean, I had heard rumors here and there that priests were quietly being executed if they didn't toe the party line of the Global Federation and the Chinese and all that. You don't seem like the type to deny the Faith."

"I basically went underground and only came out for this trip. You're right, there have been quite a number of executions of priests-- some of my best friends, at that. And who knows what will happen after the Miracle? I'm wearing the Roman collar now, but I might have to 'disappear' again when I get back. I guess it all depends on how the world responds to the events here at Garabandal."

"I have noticed some slight changes at Masses I've attended. It seems like they've changed the words the priest says when he consecrates--or *attempts* to consecrate--the Host."

"That's exactly what they've done. Sorry to say it, but those Masses you've gone to are invalid--they're basically not Masses at all. They've been eviscerated."

"But, anyway, Father, back to my question: what made you decide to become a priest? It doesn't sound like it's something you've wanted to do your whole life."

"Well, when I started going to Medjugorje, it just seemed like Mary was talking directly to me in some of her messages."

"Right!" said Kevin. "The same thing happened to me at Elyria--you've heard of 'Elyria'?"

"Yes, Cleveland, right? Holy Love?"

"Right. When I went up there back in February she said something I just can't seem to get out of my mind. She said we should all be ready if God were to ask something 'more' of us. It was that word 'more' that keeps bouncing around in my brain. What does that mean?"

"That's something you'll have to decide, Kevin...any ideas?"

"Oh, uh, I just sort of 'rescued' this girl from the Moonies back in Columbus. I'm sort of proud of that. Maybe I could do that type of thing--go around leading people back into the Church."

"And how will you pay the bills? What about football?" asked Father Chapman.

"That's just it--do I really want to play pro ball? And what about all this Chastisement stuff? Are we even going to have a football season this fall?"

"Well, Kevin, as you know, the Chastisement all depends on how humanity responds to this Miracle we're here to see. We'll just have to wait and see what happens."

"Yeah," began Kevin, clenching his teeth together, "I know that, but--I'm just so confused!"

"I would just start living day by day, one day at a time. God will make it very clear to you what He wants of you."

"One more thing, Father." Kevin brushed the hair out of his eyes. "I met this Swedish girl--that's the girl I just told you about--I got her to leave the Moonies. Well, you see, I just broke up with this girl I had been dating for about three years a month or two ago, and now there's this Swedish girl."

"Is she Catholic?"

"Oh, yes, very definitely. But I don't know about her. I mean-- she's from Sweden and all that. I mean she's really beautiful, don't get me wrong, but I sort of think about her and then I think about what Mary said about God wanting 'more' from us, and--I get so confused!"

"That very confusion is a signal from God to slow down and keep your eyes and ears open for the Will of God," said Father Chapman. "When God calls, he makes it very clear and evident. My advice is to pray and wait for things to clear up."

"Yeah, I see your point; it's just hard to wait sometimes." Kevin glanced at his watch. "Actually, I better get going now. I told that girl, the Swedish one, that I would meet her down in the village in about ten minutes."

"Oh, so she came with you?"

"Yeah, I told her about Mary's promise to heal her spiritual ills if she came."

"Excellent! Well, I'll be seeing you around."

"All right, see ya, Father."

****

The weather on Thursday, April 12th was, by anyone's standards, idyllic. The morning dawned bright and clear and the temperature stayed in the sixties most of the day. By eight o'clock that night, it was balmy and still in the environs of Garabandal. Upwards of four million people now were sitting in the valley facing the Pines, and all eyes were on the four visionaries, Conchita, Mariecruz, Jacinta, and Mary Loli, as they knelt next to the pine trees, taking turns leading the Rosary.

Dexter was standing and talking with Thad when his senses were totally overwhelmed by the sight in front of him. Along with the other pilgrims around him, he dropped to his knees, not even thinking about the action his body had taken. It was as if the very cells of his body had commanded his muscles to kneel. Even the smallest molecule in his being seemed to recognize the sacredness of what was happening in this valley. The entire countryside was silent, not even the birds or crickets were chirping, nor the wind sighing. Dexter never knew how majestic silence could be. But then he looked up and saw a sight more beautiful than he had ever imagined possible. He finally understood what was meant by the expression that "words were insufficient to explain it." Suspended in mid-air above the Pines was a golden Chalice, perhaps 500 feet in height. Encircling the Chalice were diamonds unsurpassed in beauty. Although the diamonds shone with a light more intense than the sun, no one shielded their eyes. In the center of each diamond were pictures of the faces of some of the more saintly Popes in the history of the Church. All eyes, however, were not on the Chalice, but on what was suspended above it. An immense Host hung there, blazing white against the black night sky, imprinted with the three letters: I H S. Dexter had lost track of time long ago, but it seemed as if time were out of place here, something that had no place in such a sublime setting. After what could have been 3 hours or three seconds--it didn't matter--the Great Miracle began in earnest. Originating from the golden Chalice, small Hosts began to descend and arrived suspended in front of each and every single person in the Valley of Garabandal. Dexter himself found a Host suspended right in front of his mouth. He began to hear, muffled at first, but growing in number, distinct "Amen's" from people around him. After others around him said "Amen", he noticed them extending their tongues and receiving the Host.

The battle started raging in Dexter. At first he thought that this was going to be another frightening experience like he had in the Warning. Dexter began to feel a tug of war in his soul. The Host was speaking to his inner sanctum: "Do you accept Me? Will you repent of your sins? Will you die so I can live in you?" Dexter tried to speak but was unable! He formed the words in his brain, delivered them to his messenger neurons, which relayed them to his jaw muscles, but there the process stopped. He could not speak! He was struck dumb! He was unable to say "Amen" or anything. The Host seemed to dig deeper into his soul until Dexter could see the marrow of the bones of his soul. How Dexter wanted to believe, but the Host showed Dexter what was lacking. Dexter next saw, in an instant, the parable of the Prodigal Son acted out in front of him. The Host seemed to be telling Dexter that he was still off in a foreign land, like the Prodigal Son. How it hurt to see the truth! "Do you see?" asked the Host. Dexter still struggled. "*No!*" his inner voice grunted. "*That's not me--I'm not the Prodigal Son! I'm a decent, rational 21st Century man! My faith is Rational!*" The Host seemed to hesitate for a minute and then, astonishingly it was transformed into a beautiful little white cyclamen and floated gently to the ground.

At this point the spell was broken. Dexter looked around and saw that there were other white cyclamens lying on the ground in front of a few people. What did it mean? Did other people have similar experiences? He had seen some people receiving the Host, why couldn't he receive It? Before he had a chance to ask the burly looking gentleman off to his right, he began to hear what he would later recall as one of the most moving songs that had ever graced his ears. The entire multitude--white, brown, black, Europeans, Americans, Hispanics, Asians, Moslems, and Indians--to name just a few--began singing, with one voice, a song Dexter had never heard before, "Tantum Ergo." Dexter tried to join in, but found he was unable: he was still dumb! He moved his lips, but nothing came out. As he looked around, he saw others in the same predicament. In an instant, he made the connection: those with the white cyclamens in front of them were all struck dumb. So that was it! All those who had not received the Host had been struck dumb! Moreover they all had their Hosts transformed into the white flowers. What was Heaven trying to tell them? How long would they be unable to speak? The funny thing was, Dexter now felt absolutely no anxiety about the whole situation. His earlier rebellious attitude had changed into docility. It was as if God meant things to be this way, so Dexter accepted it. The sound of the singing soothed his mind. Even the singing was miraculous. There were upwards of four million people in this valley, strung out over a four square mile area, yet the song sounded as synchronized as if it were a well-trained choir of 20 people. The entire assemblage finished each stanza at exactly the same time! There was no lag, no group had to wait for another group to finish up before they could start the next verse. Dexter serenely listened to the singing as it was repeated for the third time.

****

Meanwhile Thad, kneeling next to Dexter, was having his own visions. He saw his guardian angel handing him a golden calculator and a silver slide rule. In addition, as his angel waved his hand over Thad's head, Thad felt a deep sleep come over him, although he was still kneeling upright. In the silent language between hearts he asked his guardian angel if this meant he was cured and could get a job in engineering. Thad saw the angel smiling at him, and begin nodding his head up and down. *Thank you, Lord!* Thad shouted in the depths of his soul. *As much as I like the taxi business, now I'm free to get back into engineering!* But then he saw his angel hold up his hand as if to tell him he had something else to give him. The angel held up a white pillow on which there were two golden rings. As Thad watched the vision, one ring lifted from the pillow and placed itself on Thad's left ring finger. The other ring slowly flew onto the image of another person...onto...*Oh, Lord, really?* Thad gasped in exclamation...onto the left ring finger of...Cheryl! *I'm supposed to marry? The priesthood's not for me?* Again Thad saw his angel smiling broadly and nodding his head. *Thank you, Lord! Thank you, thank you, thank you!*

****

Just fifty yards away from Thad Kevin's guardian angel was also giving him a vision of what God wanted of him. Kevin watched as a luminous halo encircled both of his thumbs and index fingers. Then his angel placed a brilliant white Host between Kevin's digits. Kevin was overcome with awe, yet somewhat puzzled at the same time. He gazed up into the face of his angel who then held up the Roman collar of a priest. The angel reached down and placed the collar around Kevin's neck. An unchecked torrent of grace, peace, and joy poured into Kevin's soul. *Me, Lord? You want me to become a priest?* His guardian angel simply gazed into Kevin's eyes. Kevin immediately thought about his yearnings for altruism, the Peace Corps, and service to his fellowman. Then the image of Kultida suddenly appeared in front of him and his face fell. *What about her?* he wordlessly asked his angel. In answer, he saw the picture of Kultida slowly fade away, her head covered by a veil.

****

Eventually, some people began to walk back down the road to the center of the village, first pausing to bow, on both knees, to the immense golden Chalice, which was still suspended in midair above the Pines. Not a sound did these pilgrims make, for they realized they were in the Presence of the Body, Blood, Soul, and Divinity of their Savior in the form of the Host suspended above the great Chalice. The singing continued, now to the strains of "O Salutaris Hostia." Dexter motioned to Thad that he wanted to leave and the two of them started to make their way down the mountainside. As they turned to get on the main road, Thad paused and bowed on both knees to the Host above the Pines. Dexter was about to follow suit, but something held him back. *Not yet?* he asked himself.

"That was sooo beautiful!" exclaimed Thad. "I still think I'm dreaming. Here, pinch me to see if I'm awake!" Thad said jokingly.

"What do you think, Dexter! Are you a believer now?"

Dexter moved his lips and pointed to his mouth, trying to tell Thad of his predicament.

"Cat got your tongue, Dexter?" asked Thad with a laugh.

Dexter shook his head and patted his Adam's apple.

"What?" Thad exclaimed. "Can't you breathe?" He looked around him and shouted "Is there a doctor around? This man can't breathe!"

Kevin and his friends happened to be just behind Dexter in the flow of pilgrims and when Kevin heard Thad shouting, he came to the rescue.

"Hold on, buddy," said Kevin, wrapping his arms around Dexter, "I know just what to do!" Kevin began to perform the Heimlich maneuver on him, at which point Dexter began gasping for breath.

"Don't kill him, dude!" said Sparrow as he ran up next to Dexter and Kevin.

"He's just trying to help," said Curt.

"No! No! He no breathe!" said Kultida, trying to loosen Kevin's grip on Dexter.

"He knows what he's doing!" said Ryan loudly, pulling Kultida away from Kevin.

Dexter was doing his best to free himself of the football player's grasp when luckily one of their fellow pilgrims ran over to tell Thad what was happening.

"El hombre es mudo, así como mi hermano! No, no, Senor!" said the Hispanic man, trying to get Kevin's attention. "El hombre es mudo!"

"What are you trying to tell me, man?" Kevin was frantic now, still squeezing the living daylights out of Dexter, who by this time was practically blue in the face.

A small crowd of pilgrims had gathered around the scene and now a young German man was shouting at Kevin too, trying to loosen his grip. "Der Mann ist stumm, gleich wie einige andere!"

At this point, Dexter fell to the ground, mercifully slipping out of Kevin's grasp.

Luckily an elderly British-looking man grabbed Kevin and shook him. "It's all right, he's okay, he's not choking! Look, he can breathe just fine. He's been struck dumb. That's what these people have been trying to tell you."

Dexter was lying there on the ground, panting heavily. As he looked up at Kevin and Thad, though, he couldn't help but grin at them as he shook his head.

"Oh, sorry!" said Kevin as he leaned down to pat Dexter on his shoulder. Then he said to the people standing around: "Thank you ever so much! Gratias!" Seeing that the German man didn't understand his words, he gestured in the universal language, striking his chest and saying "Mea culpa! Mea culpa!"

The German laughed and smiled, shaking Kevin's hand. Thad helped Dexter to his feet and turned toward Kevin.

"Thanks for trying at least," said Thad, extending his hand. "My name's Thad Rankin."

"Kevin Conaway, nice to meet you," he said, shaking Thad's hand.

"Oh, I thought you looked familiar!" said Thad. "You're the quarterback, right?"

"One and the same. Who might our mute friend here be?" asked Kevin, looking at Dexter.

"This is Dexter Griffith. Dexter: our own Kevin Conaway."

Dexter shook Kevin's hand, while nodding his head.

"So, we're all from Columbus, then," said Thad. "It's a small Ohio, as I like to say."

"Ahem," said Kultida, tapping Kevin on the shoulder.

"Oh, sorry! Yeah, guys, this is Kultida, my friend...she's from Sweden originally, but she's staying in Columbus for now."

"Glad you could come," said Thad, shaking her hand.

"Yes, I happy be here," said Kultida as she shook first Thad's, and then Dexter's hand.

"And these are my friends too; they're also from Columbus," said Kevin. This is Sparrow, Ryan, and Curt."

"The more the merrier!" said Thad as he shook each man's hand.

Just then a burly, well-dressed man came up behind Kevin and held both hands over his eyes. "Guess who?" said the man to Kevin.

"Uhhh," stammered Kevin, "your voice sounds vaguely familiar--uuhhh..."

"It's me, you big lug!" said the man, spinning Kevin around to face him.

After a few seconds, recognition came into Kevin's eyes. "But, you're--you're--"

"That's right! I'm not in a wheelchair, anymore, my friend! It's me--Jake Bricker! The *former* bum of Rocky River!"

"But, you--you--you--" Kevin couldn't believe his eyes. "You *got your leg back?*"

"Be a believer, Kev-man!" said Jake, smiling from ear to ear. "When the Blessed Mother makes a promise, she keeps it!"

"This is incredible!" said Kevin. He turned to Thad and Dexter. "You guys, this is Jake Bricker...I met him up in my hometown over Christmas. He used to have a leg missing--I mean he used to be in a wheelchair, but now--now he's--well! Take a look!"

"Truly amazing," said Thad, shaking his head.

Dexter retrieved a pen and piece of paper from his pocket. 'Priest?' he scribbled and showed it to Thad.

"Huh?" said Thad. "Father who? Who do you want to see?"

'Any priest,' Dexter wrote.

"Ohhh," said Thad, grinning expansively, then quickly turning serious. "Sure, sure. Let's look around, there should be plenty of English speaking priests around here. Thad scanned the crowd and after talking to three priests, found a Polish priest who knew how to speak English. Thad explained the situation to Father Domalik who quickly understood, since he had noticed several others around him in the same predicament as Dexter.

"My son," Father Domalik asked Dexter, "do you wish to talk with me?"

Dexter nodded his head, a look of determination and fear showing in his eyes.

"Fine, follow me to the church." The two of them walked to Saint Sebastian's. Father Domalik found an empty room in the rectory, since the confessionals in the church were quickly being engulfed by other frantic pilgrims streaming in from the hillsides.

Dexter pulled out the piece of paper from his pocket and wrote: "I would like to go to Confession."

"Are you a Catholic?" asked Father Domalik. The priest's sixth sense told him that Dexter was not the usual fallen-away Catholic he had often encountered.

Dexter shook his head and wrote: 'It's an emergency!'

"All right, my son, I understand," he said. "Have you been baptized?"

Again Dexter shook his head up and down and quickly wrote: 'I've been talking to a priest back in Ohio, Father Rankin.'

"Do you want to be baptized, uhh---first of all, what is your name?"

'Dexter Griffith," he wrote.

"Fine, Dexter, do you wish to be baptized?"

Dexter wrote: 'I was baptized as a baby, now I want to become a Catholic--I want to go to Confession.'

"Now?"

Dexter nodded again, more vigorously this time.

Father Domalik sat in the chair and Dexter knelt down beside him. The priest said, "In the name of the Father, and the Son, and the Holy Spirit. Amen. May the Lord be on your lips and help you to confess your sins."

And with those words Dexter regained his voice. Out of his mouth came the accumulated sins of twenty-eight years of his past life. There in a small town in Northern Spain, he experienced the ineffable joy that comes with the breaking of the shackles of sin. Even the noted psychiatrist Sigmund Freud had recommended "lay confession," i.e., the telling of one's misdeeds to a trusted friend, in order to get them off one's chest. Here Dexter not only told his sins to another, but did it in the beautiful Sacrament of Confession. In his infinite wisdom, Christ had instituted this Sacrament of Mercy, knowing of man's need to *know* that he had been forgiven. Dexter needed a half hour to clear his conscience of all the errors from his childhood into adolescence, and into young adulthood. Out came all the sins of the flesh, all the sins of lacks of charity toward family and friends, all the sins of dishonesty in financial matters. Father Domalik, seasoned confessor that he was, gently helped Dexter to clean out all the dirt from the wounds in his soul. Although he had never been fully taught all the rules of the Church, with the graces he gained during the Miracle, Dexter was able to make a complete Confession.

"Can you think of anything else, Dexter?" asked Father Domalik.

"Well, there are some smaller things that I suppose I could mention."

"You can save those for next time...as long as you've told me all the grievous things you can remember, I can give you absolution."

"Yeah, I've told you all the big things."

"Okay," said Father Domalik, "for your penance--"

"What's that?"

"I will just give you a prayer to say in reparation for your sins."

"Okay."

"For your penance, say the Our Father three times, and now make an--well--have you heard of the Act of Contrition?"

"I have a vague idea."

"Let's see," said Father Domalik. "Let me see if I can find it in this Missal." Father Domalik thumbed through the prayer book that he had found earlier in the church. "Ah, here we go, say this." He handed the book to Dexter.

Dexter took the red covered Missal and read aloud: "Oh my God, I am heartily sorry for having offended you, and I detest all my sins because I dread the loss of Heaven and the pains of Hell, but most of all because I have offended You, my God, who art all good and deserving of all my love. I firmly resolve, with the help of your grace, to confess my sins, do penance, and amend my life. Amen."

Father Domalik gave a small penance to Dexter, then raised his right arm, and while making the sign of the cross, said: "May the Lord grant you pardon and peace, and I absolve you from all your sins, in the name of the Father, and the Son, and the Holy Spirit. Amen...Go in peace."

Dexter had never before known the transports of joy that now flooded into his being! He pictured Hoover Dam with all its gates open and millions of gallons of liquid happiness dropping into his soul! Peace and joy!   Peace and joy!   *Now* he understood all those catchphrases that he had once considered gibberish! How light he felt! How utterly carefree!

"Thad!" he yelled, yanking open the door to the room. "This is all your fault, you idiot!" As Thad came through the doorway, Dexter embraced his friend in a smothering bear hug. "Why didn't you tell me about this sooner! Son of a bitch! I feel so light! I could go flying on my own right now! You're awesome, bro! You did it! It's all your fault!"

"Ahem," said Father Domalik.

"Oh, Father, I forgot, thank you! Thank you!" said Dexter, shaking the priest's hand. "I'm so glad you were around today!"

"I just wanted to remind you that Mass starts in five minutes and it's time for your First Communion!"

"Today? Now?" said Dexter in a laughing voice, wiping a tear from his eye.

"Why not now, you *Catholic!*" said Thad.

"I can't take any more joy now!" exclaimed Dexter. "I'm supposed to receive the Body of Christ *right now?*"

"Hey, these aren't normal times we live in, my friend," said Thad. "You know what I've been saying about the Chastisement. It could start anytime now. You need spiritual firepower as fast as you can get it."

"I would have to concur with that," said Father Domalik.

"I can't believe this is happening," said Dexter, shaking his head. "Is it legal to be this happy? There're poor people starving in Africa and look at me!"

"How do you know there's not someone in Africa going through the *same thing* you are right now?" asked Thad.

"All right, all right, you've convinced me," said Dexter. "What did I do to deserve all this?"

"Funny you should ask that, Dexter," said Father Domalik. "I was just reading a book by Saint Alphonsus Liguori. In it, he says that some spiritual writers allege that the reason the good thief was given Paradise by Christ on the cross was that the good thief had done Mary and Joseph a kind service when the Holy Family was fleeing into Egypt."

"It must have been those homeless guys I've helped from time to time," said Dexter. "Whatever it was, I got an incredible return on investment."

Dexter and Thad, after getting Father Domalik's blessing, walked out into the church proper and prepared for Mass. Due to the immense number of people they were forced to stand, which didn't bother Dexter in the slightest, considering the number of the cloud on which he was standing. After Mass, Dexter joined Thad and the rest of the Columbus group outside the Church.

"So what do you say, Miracle Man?" Thad asked Dexter. "Are you on cloud ten or eleven now?"

"Forget the clouds," Dexter said with a laugh, "it's more like which *galaxy* I'm in right now!--say, does this stuff come in six-packs?"

"Sure, the seven Sacraments--seven-packs, if you will."

"That'll work," said Dexter.

"So, look, we're all going to head down to the local cantina for some well-deserved celebrating...whaddya say, Dex?"

"I'll be right behind you, bud. Just gimme a few minutes to take all this in."

"Hey," said Thad, "take all the time you need. See you in a bit." Thad turned to talk with Kevin when he couldn't believe who was standing two feet in front of him! His mouth dropped open and his eyes practically dilated they were so wide.

"Hey, Thaddeus!" said Cheryl affectionately.

"You--you--I can't believe this!" He wrapped his arms around Cheryl, spun her around and set her back on her feet. "Did you have the same vision that I did during the Miracle?"

"I already know what I want inscribed in our rings, hubby," Cheryl said, wiping a tear from her eyes.

"Excuse us," Thad said to Kevin and Kultida, "we have to talk--oh, I forgot." He introduced Cheryl to all in the group, then took a stroll down the dirt road with Cheryl.

"Did you see my cure?" he asked Cheryl. "Did your angel show you that I'm cured of my insomnia?"

"Yes...yes!" said Cheryl expansively. "I even saw--no, you won't believe it!"

"What!? What did you see?"

"I saw--" Cheryl's voice broke and she leaned her head on Thad's shoulder. "I saw our first two children. First a boy, and then a girl!"

"This is crazy! Ohh, man," Thad said, shaking his head from side to side. "But, wait a minute." He stopped walking and turned to face Cheryl. "Cheryl, you know what's next...what about the Chastisement? I didn't see anything about that, did you?"

"Thad, I have such a deep peace in me right now I don't see how anything could take it away," said Cheryl. "I know about the Chastisement and all that, but we'll always have each other...we'll always have the Rosary."

"But what about Father Matt? Did I tell you about my brother? They killed him! They cut off his head!"

"Yes, yes," said Cheryl soothingly. "Actually, I knew about it when I called you up on your cell phone last time. I didn't want to mention it unless you did--Thad, the worst that can happen is we are killed. Then we'll just go on experiencing in heaven what we just experienced here in the Miracle--but it'll last forever!"

Thad took Cheryl's hand and kissed it. "I love you, Cheryl."

Cheryl brushed her hand through Thad's hair and said: "I've loved you ever since---

"Don't say it."

"Say what?"

"You know," said Thad, rubbing Cheryl's shoulder. "What they always say in love scenes."

"I wasn't going to say that--Thad, I--!" She grabbed him by the head and kissed him furiously. "I've loved you ever since I made the first call to get a cab that day."

"You loved me before you ever saw me?"

"Call it intuition, call it my guardian angel, but when I set the phone down that day, I knew it wasn't going to be just any ordinary taxi ride."

"What are their names?" Thad asked.

"Whose names?"

"The names of our first two children!"

"Ohh, Thaaad." She put her arm around his waist, squeezed him and gently giggled.

"I suppose you're right, you know," he said. They both stopped walking when they were a few hundred yards from the Pines and gazed up at the Miraculous Chalice, as the priest at the Mass had just named it. "We really shouldn't worry about the future."

"Mmmm," murmured Cheryl, "reminds me of something my grandfather used to say...I think he got it from some book of quotes: 'To the young, death is just a distant rumor.'"

"I don't know, Cheryl; it sounds sort of pagan-ish."

"Well, I'm sure your Notre Dame mind can Christianize it, no?" said Cheryl, gazing into Thad's eyes.

Thad shrugged and looked away. "Well, what about...to the holy person...uh...death is...uh..."

"...just a long-awaited friend!" finished Cheryl.

"Hmm," said Thad with a smile, "I guess they really did teach you something worthwhile at Brown."

Cheryl reached over and pinched Thad lightly on the cheek. "We're going to have a happy life together, I'm afraid, milord."

Thad hung his head and slowly shook it from side to side. "I'm awfully afraid your prognosis might be right," he said morosely.

"Is there any known cure for this condition, do you think?" she asked with a concerned look in her eyes.

"Absolutely not! All medical research on causes for an unhappy marriage is hereby forbidden!"

"In that case, I think it's time, Thad." She pulled a Rosary out of her purse.

"As you wish, milady," he said, kneeling down and extracting his own Rosary.

Thad held up his Rosary until it was silhouetted against the brightly glowing Miraculous Chalice. "Here's to a horribly awfully happy marriage with too many kids!"

Cheryl raised her Rosary-draped hand until it was next to Thad's. "May our life together be so miserably joyful that the cure is never found!"

Thad took Cheryl's arm in his and began the Rosary: "I believe in one God, the Father Almighty, and in Jesus Christ, his only Son..."

****

After Thad, Cheryl, Dexter, and the three friends from the Elyria trip had walked away, Kevin found himself standing uncomfortably next to Kultida. He brushed his hair back with both hands and turned to face her. "Kultida, I don't know how to say this, but--"

"Kevin, no--" interrupted Kultida, holding up her hand. "I sorry I stop you talk...I have same--same--" She made a waving motion in front of her eyes with her hands.

"Vision?" offered Kevin.

"Right!" said Kultida. "I know, I see your eye now. I have same--vision--that you have."

"You mean you know?"

"You be priest, Kevin--I know. Mary tell me during Miracle."

"Ohh, thank you, Kultida," said Kevin, visibly relieved, dropping his shoulders. "And you--I thought I saw that you were a, you know--a--"

"I be nun," said Kultida, smiling broadly. "God lead me to Moonies--to you--to this!" She pointed in the direction of the Miraculous Chalice. "All life have purpose, right? You play fute-ball, you go to Indy-ap-lis, you meet me." She stopped and looked soberly at him. "Kevin--you happy, yes? You happy be priest? I happy, I think, be nun. I want to be in Moonies--it is--uhh...*under* me...you know..." She looked around, waving her hand back and forth. "How you say--I have need in me...that..."

"I know, I know," said Kevin. "You're trying to say you had it in you all along, right? The Moonies was just your way of trying to live a life of service to God and your fellowman."

"Yes, yes, Kevin!" she said enthusiastically. "You say spot on!"

Kevin stood with his arms akimbo and shook his head from side to side. "The story of my life, Kultida. We're kindred spirits! I had it in me all along, too. I was looking for more in life myself."

"Kevin, I not be rude, but I go now and pray at big golden thing, okay?"

"Sure, Kultida, that's fine. I need to do some praying myself now."

As Kultida walked away, Kevin felt someone push him on the shoulder from behind. "Fifteen-yard penalty!" said a voice behind him. Kevin spun around to find Father Chapman grinning at him.

"Father!" said Kevin laughingly. "Figures a Cornhusker would get called for roughing the passer."

"So, whaddya say, Mister 'K'?" asked the priest, gesturing toward the Miraculous Chalice. "Are you a believer now?"

"A 'believer'!" said Kevin loudly. He lowered his voice to a whisper. "Father, I had this great vision during the Miracle! I'm supposed to be a priest!"

"'Supposed to be'!?" said Father Chapman. "Is there any room for 'want to be' in there?"

"Whoa, uh, yeah--I guess..."

"I'm just joking with you, Kevin. I know it's all new to you, but you'll come to accept it in due time."

"I sort of have a few questions, though, Father, I mean, like, how will I--uhh--"

"You're wondering where will you find a nice cozy seminary when you get back?"

"Whuu, uh...yeah, I mean, you're an underground priest, right? You're going to have to go incognito after tonight, right?" asked Kevin.

"All valid concerns, all valid concerns," said Father Chapman calmly. "You're definitely going to have a unique training to be a priest. The Global Federation isn't going to look too kindly on any guy expressing an interest in becoming a priest these days."

"Give me your e-mail address and phone number, and we'll go from there. I've been known to travel around from time to time, and we'll have you in Moral Theology in no time at all."

"'Moral Theology'?" asked Kevin. "I'm going to start studying *that* right off the bat?"

Father Chapman patted Kevin on the back. "I was sort of kidding a little. You're definitely going to receive an accelerated course in the priesthood, that's for sure."

"You know Father Chapman, it sure was a coincidence my meeting you here--your being a former football player, just like me."

"Kevin, my son, there are no such things as coincidences. It reminds me of what G.K. Chesterton used to say."

"Oh, he's a rather renowned Catholic writer--lived in the first half of the twentieth century...anyway, he liked to say that 'coincidences are spiritual puns.'"

"Heh," chuckled Kevin, "a lot of truth in that. Who is this guy again?"

"G. K. Chesterton," said Father Chapman. "You should look him up when you get back. He wrote a lot of great books--funny guy, too."

"Would he be on the web?"

"Oh, definitely. Lot of good stuff about him on the internet."

"So..." said Kevin, looking out at the Miraculous Chalice, "isn't this awesome?"

"Next best thing to the beatific vision, Kevin."

"That's God, right? The 'beatific vision' means the vision of God?"

"So how long will this chalice be here?" asked Kevin.

"Well, the Blessed Mother said that a permanent, visible, supernatural sign will be left here until the end of time. You'll be able to photograph it and televise it, but not touch it."

"'The end of time,' huh? What does that mean, 'the end of time'?"

"The Blessed Mother has said that we are coming to the end of this *age*, not the end of the *world*," said Father Chapman. I'm not as well versed on the theology of the book of Revelation as I should be. I'll have to look that up when I get back."

The two stood there for a few minutes, staring in awe at the Miracle. Kevin turned to Father Chapman and opened his mouth to speak.

"I don't know, either," said Father Chapman.

"What? Can you read my mind?" asked Kevin.

"I know exactly what you were thinking. You were going to ask me if the Chastisement is really going to happen, or if the world will change its ways and return to God…right?"

"Right!" said Kevin. "You *sure* you can't read my mind?"

"Kevin, millions of forward-thinking people around the world are asking the exact same thing right now--and, no, I cannot read your mind."

"Will I die as a martyr? The life expectancy of a priest can't be too high these days."

"Kevin, I ask myself that question several times every day. The best answer to that question is to live each day as if it's your last. That way, if push ever does come to shove, you have nothing to worry about."

"Hmm," mumbled Kevin, pursing his lips and looking pensively at the ground. "Good advice."

"Enough of this doom and gloom, Kevin my boy!" said Father Chapman jubilantly. "Let's go celebrate! We're living in enchanting times, Kevin!" He patted Kevin on the shoulder and they began to walk toward the center of the village.

****

At the same time, Dexter had wandered away from the crowds and sat down on the ground, gazing up at the Miraculous Chalice. *Here I am,* Dexter thought, *it's a balmy Spring night on the Iberian Peninsula. I just received the Body of Christ for the first time in my life. What was that poem my grandmother read to me once? Something about a dog? I think it was by Milton…the "Hound of"-- what was it? The "Hound of--" Well, Christ has finally tracked me down. I remember that line he wrote as if I heard it my whole life…"Down the beaten path have I tracked your forlorn soul. For many a year you have eluded me, but in the end I finally found you."* It's funny... Dexter scratched his chin and stretched. *I never planned all that has happened to me, nor even dreamt of it. I simply put one block on another until finally the spiritual house that was my soul was completed in full detail. Eight months ago, I had been like any other young American at the dawn of the 21st Century: industrious, generous, and sensitive, but wholly lacking in the things of God. And what am I now? Well, my conscience is clear and my heart is free to fly up to the purity of Heaven. I no longer feel weighed down by the baggage of sin and unbelief. I no longer fear Hell! I can stand before God and look straight into His eyes! Just by confessing my sins and receiving Absolution!* A wide grin spread across Dexter's face and he chuckled when he remembered the scene just a short while ago when people thought he was choking. *Lucky someone figured out what was going on before they broke one of my ribs.* Dexter looked up at the stars and happened to see a shooting star race across the blackness. *Comet? Will we get hit by a comet? Well, do I really care now what might happen if...when...the Chastisement comes? Hunger? Ha! Thirst? Thanks! Pain? Pshaw! I have Christ! Not just a symbol, not just a theory--the real thing! I have Confession! How long was the Chastisement supposed to last? Three years? What was that compared with Eternity! So I might be martyred? Well, I wouldn't be the first, and I won't be the last. Besides, if I were martyred, I would go straight to Heaven without having to go through Purgatory. Where was the downside? As St Paul used to say: "O death! Where is thy sting?"*

Dexter looked out at the multitude of people surrounding the Miraculous Chalice and uttered a prayer from the deepest recesses of his newly-minted soul.

So just what does the future hold? Dexter asked God. *Will we have the Chastisement and all that stuff that Thad talks about? Will I stand firm in the Faith? Will the Chastisement be avoided? Will other people turn back to God as I have done?*

"Look, God," Dexter said in a low voice, "I never hated you...it's just that I never took the time to get to know you...I didn't think it was important."

What about my parents? wondered Dexter. *What about my sister? My aunts and uncles? All my friends? I've got a lot of work to do. I can't just sit around and let my friends and family drift away from*

God. The Miracle may have changed a lot of people...more than I might think. Well, concluded Dexter as he got up and walked back to the church, *upward and onward! Time for some intense apostolate. I've got a world to convert!*

www.ingramcontent.com/pod-product-compliance
Lightning Source LLC
Chambersburg PA
CBHW020257030726
47499CB00001B/227